Praise for *A Familiar Tail*

"Much like *Bewitched*, the feline in this one is a blast, and Annabelle is perfect when it comes to magical thinking and doing in New Hampshire. It will be more than fun to follow her journey for a good, long time to come."

—*Suspense Magazine*

"Anna is so genuinely likable, the dialogue so cleverly written, and the plot so compelling, that readers will enthusiastically follow her adventures and eagerly await their next chance to enter her world. Continual twists guarantee that readers will be as surprised by the truth as Anna, and the wit and confident writing by the author will cement her place on the list of must-read paranormal mystery series."

—*Kings River Life Magazine*

D0959144

Titles by Delia James

A FAMILIAR TAIL
BY FAMILIAR MEANS

By Familiar Means

A Witch's Cat Mystery

DELIA JAMES

BERKLEY PRIME CRIME
New York

BERKLEY PRIME CRIME
Published by Berkley
An imprint of Penguin Random House LLC
375 Hudson Street, New York, New York 10014

ISBN: 9780451476586

First Edition: September 2016

Printed in the United States of America
1 3 5 7 9 10 8 6 4 2

Book design by Kelly Lipovich

🐾 1 🐾

🐾 I WANT TO be really clear about a few things. I do not follow people into abandoned tunnels, even if they are pay- ing me. I do not remove valuable historical documents from private archives, and I do not believe in ghosts.

At least, I didn't used to.

My name is Annabelle Amelia Blessingsound Britton and I am (in order of appearance):

1) A freelance graphic artist

2) A brand-new resident of Portsmouth, New
   Hampshire

3) A witch

The last came as a major surprise. I found out about my magical background only when I arrived in Portsmouth. That visit was supposed to be for only two weeks—just long enough to see my best friend, Martine, and find a little relief from a (relatively) recently broken heart. Instead, I was plunged straight into a murder investigation involving the death of a local witch.

From all this, you may have guessed that my life had gotten a little complicated. This was, however, only the beginning. Now, not only had I invited my grandmother to come visit me; she'd said yes.

And she was early.

"Grandma B.B.!" I shouted as I bolted out the door and down the front walk.

"Hello, Annabelle, dear!" My grandmother climbed out of her massive land yacht of a car and spread her arms.

Grandma B.B. is more formally known as Annabelle Mercy Blessingsound Britton. I was named for her. She's plump and wrinkled and beautiful and tends to dress in the brightest available colors. This time, she'd gone with a distinctly tropical theme: a lemon yellow sweater with a glowing lime green jacket and skirt. Her cat's-eye glasses had rhinestones sparkling at the corners, and coral beads gleamed around her neck and wrists. And, of course, her white hair was covered by a filmy pink scarf, because she was a lady, and she was driving a convertible.

"I can't believe you drove the Galaxie all the way up from Arizona!"

"And why *shouldn't* I drive it? It's mine. Well, all right, it was your grandfather's. But really, for a road trip, why would I want *anything* else?" Grandma spoke in italics. She liked to make sure she was being understood, *exactly.* "You *know* I can't stand these little modern things. They're not cars; they're *roller skates.*"

The car currently blocking my entire driveway was definitely not a roller skate. It was a vintage Ford Galaxie. Picture the ultimate turquoise-and-white 1950s dream machine—one with huge headlights, a retractable hardtop, and chrome everywhere you can think to put it. Naturally, there were tail fins, not to mention a trunk that could hold at least half a dozen bodies. I knew from direct experience that you could take four wriggling kids to the drive-in in that backseat and still have room for stuffed animals, blankets and popcorn. "Besides, it's a gorgeous drive, and I haven't been on the road in *such* a long time."

"That means, what? Three months?"

"Six, if you can believe it!"

We both laughed. Grandma B.B. was never anybody's little stay-at-home-and-bake-pies kind of grandma. When she visited us, every day was an adventure. Within five minutes of her arrival, Grandma always seemed to know her way around any town better than the people who lived there. She could (and would) talk to anybody about anything and find out all the important information, like where to get the best French fries and ice cream and what was the coolest stuff for a bunch of kids to do. She could also park that massive car in spaces you would swear wouldn't fit an Austin Mini Cooper.

"Now, let me look at you." Grandma backed away until she was holding me at arm's length. "Oh, dear!"

"I swear, I've been eating enough." I crossed my heart.

"You look beautiful, Anna." She patted my cheek, because she's a grandma and gets to do that. "Portsmouth agrees with you."

"Well . . . maybe. It's been kind of . . . eventful."

"Yes. I know," she said softly, and we were both suddenly looking around for ways to change the subject. Because what I hadn't known until a couple of months ago was that my wonderful, eccentric grandmother was a witch, like me.

This was something we would definitely be talking about, but later. For now, I just grabbed Grandma B.B.'s suitcase and a small, square train case off the Galaxie's passenger seat. "Is this all you've got?"

"Now, Anna, you know I *much* prefer to travel light."

This is just one of my grandmother's many mysterious talents. She could fit more into a suitcase than Mary Poppins could into a carpetbag. "Well, come on in. Everything's all set."

"I adore the house!" Grandma beamed at my fieldstone cottage as I led her through the gate and up the (very short) front walk. "Oh, Anna, you didn't tell me it was so lovely!"

Technically, the cottage wasn't mine—I was just renting

it—but it really was lovely. Its slate roof was a complex landscape of peaks and gables topped by a weather vane in the shape of a crescent moon shot through with an arrow. The multipaned windows were glinting in the autumn sun and the spray of gold leaves and bright red rose hips that were what was left of the rambler roses added a splash of color across its mottled gray stone walls.

"I would have thought you'd recognize it."

"Oh, no," said Grandma. "I've never been here. When I left town, Dorothy and her family were still living over on Park Street. But I do recognize this beauty!" Grandma exclaimed to the large smoke gray cat pacing back and forth on the porch, blinking his blue eyes as if to say, *What took you so long?* "Hello, Alistair! Who's a *good* kitty?"

Grandma crouched down to scratch Alistair's ears. I wasn't surprised they knew each other. Grandma B.B. and Dorothy Hawthorne, the cottage's previous owner, had been friends back in the day. That day, however, was around fifty years ago, before Grandma decided to pack up and leave Portsmouth for good. Around about that time a very quiet but very intense feud had broken out among certain families in town. Alistair is not the sort to hold a grudge, though, and adopted me fairly readily. He's also ready to accept a good head rub from almost anybody. He began purring immediately, to let Grandma know she was a good human.

He also vanished.

I mean this literally. Like most things connected with the cottage, Alistair is magical. So, one second he was there; then—*blink!*—he was gone and Grandma's hand curled over empty air.

"Erm . . ." I felt myself blushing, which was a weird reaction to having my familiar demonstrate his showiest bit of magical talent, but it was the only one that seemed to be coming to me right then. I felt like I'd been caught sneaking Mallomars out of the back cupboard.

"It's all right, dear." Grandma straightened up and brushed her sleeves down. "It's nothing I haven't seen before."

That talk later was going to be a very, very long one.

I let us into the house. Grandma B.B. followed, exclaiming her approval of everything she saw, from the front parlor with its cushioned window seat to the formal dining room with the stained glass window. Even the narrow stairway that ran from the little foyer up to the second floor was "absolutely lovely."

I had set my studio up in the front bedroom, which over-looked Summer Street, but I'd moved the easel and other paraphernalia into the corner to make more room around the Arts and Crafts–style daybed and small dresser.

"I hope you'll have enough room," I said as I set Grandma's luggage on the bed.

"This will be *just* fine, Anna. I can fit anywhere."

The best thing about Grandma B.B. is that when she says stuff like that, she actually means it. She and my grandfather had traveled around the world at least twice. Together, they'd survived hurricanes, holdups and at least one military coup, and that was just the stuff I knew about.

Alistair leapt up on the bed and started nosing the luggage.

"Oh, such a *good* kitty!" cried Grandma, in, I swear, the same tone she used when I won second prize at my elementary school art fair. Alistair meowed his approval. "Yes, I brought you something, of course I did!"

Uh-oh. "Um, Grandma, you are not about to give my . . . uh . . . that is . . ."

"Familiar, dear. It's all right; you can say it."

I can, but it was going to take a lot to get used to hearing my grandmother say it back. "You are not going to give my familiar catnip, are you?" I'd recently learned the hard way that it's a bad idea to give 'nip to a cat that can vanish and reappear at will. I still wasn't quite recovered.

"*Really*, Anna, I do have *some* common sense."

I looked away, I hoped innocently.

Grandma reached into her purse and pulled out a bag of K.T. Nibbles. Alistair was suddenly purring and rubbing against her hand like he hadn't been fed in a week. There was a reason my cat had that big, soft tummy.

"Well, you've got a friend for life," I told Grandma as she let Alistair snatch a nibble from her fingers. She grinned up at me; she also winked in a manner that could only be described as conspiratorial.

That's my sweet little grandma.

A beeping started up from my back pocket. Grandma frowned at me and I blushed, pulled out my phone to check the reminder and shut it down.

"Sorry, Grandma, I wasn't expecting you until later . . ." It was still only ten in the morning.

"I know," she said as she unzipped her suitcase. "I made the most *amazing* time after I left Hartford this morning. Almost like *magic*." She smiled, and her blue eyes twinkled behind her cat's-eye glasses.

"Ummm . . . you didn't . . ." I began, feeling suddenly and distinctly non-twinkly.

"Oh, don't I wish I could! But no. Traffic magic is not one of my specialties. I just got up very early."

"But there is such a thing as traffic magic?"

Grandma looked at me owlishly over the rims of her glasses, and I had no idea whether or not she was actually joking. She must have seen my uncertain expression because she grew suddenly serious. "Anna, we are going to talk, about everything."

I sucked in a deep breath. "Yes, yes, we are."

"Merowp." Alistair peeked out from under the bed, indicating his relief that the humans were finally making sensible noises.

"But, like I said, I thought you'd be getting in later. I've got some things to do this morning."

"Oh. Now, is this business or . . . is there *somebody* I should know about?"

"It's clients, Grandma," I told her firmly. I had explained to Grandma B.B. that I was done with men, all of them. In fact, I had gone over this several times, clearly, carefully and in great detail. Somehow she never quite seemed to fully grasp the concept. "At least I hope it's clients."

"A new writer?" A fair amount of my freelance graphics work comes from independent authors who need cover art for their books.

"Actually, it's for a coffee shop called Northeast Java. They're moving to a new location and they want murals for the walls."

"How marvelous! Oh! I know! We can drive into town together!"

"You're not tired?" To New Hampshire from Arizona was a long way, even by Grandma's standards.

But apparently she didn't think so, because she just waved that all away. "Not at all. I took things very easy, and you know how refreshing travel is for me. I'd love to come out and see if I can still recognize my old town."

"Well, sure. Why not? Um, maybe you could go see Julia Parris? She's running a bookshop down near the square. Midnight Reads."

"A bookstore? Julia?" An odd look crossed Grandma's face, almost as if she was holding back a laugh, but that quickly faded into something more serious, and a little sadder. "Does she know I'm coming?"

"Yeah, she does." As soon as I'd invited Grandma to come up, I'd let Julia know. I won't say I was actively planning on repairing their friendship, but I figured it wouldn't hurt to try. After all, it was part of our job as witches to help and heal.

"Did she . . . say anything?" asked Grandma softly.

"Yeah, she did. She said it will be good to clear the air."

Julia Parris and Grandma B.B. had grown up together. But in the sixties, they'd both gotten caught in the feud that broke out among the "old families." The term was a euphemism for the families with magic in their bloodlines. Most of them had immigrated to New England back in the seventeenth century to escape the persecution in England, and then ran from Massachusetts to New Hampshire to escape the persecution in Salem. And it wasn't always the families you might think.

When the feud broke out, Julia Parris took her stand and stayed to face the consequences. Grandma B.B., though, had packed up with Grandpa Charlie and left town rather than take sides. Julia never forgave her.

Julia was now the head of the guardian coven of Portsmouth. The guardians were a group of witches who secretly—well, semisecretly—worked their magic for the protection and benefit of the town and its people. I had been accepted as an apprentice member of the coven, and Julia was my mentor. This all made for a few awkward moments. Julia is a good person, and a better witch, but she also has the spine and spirit of a native New Englander, which comes with a long and coldly accurate memory. I had not been at all sure how she'd really feel about welcoming my grandmother back to town.

From her expression, neither was Grandma.

❧ 2 ❧

❧ GRANDMA B.B. FOUND a parking spot right in front of the Midnight Reads bookshop, which made me doubt her protestations about traffic magic. Clearly, there was some kind of enchantment going on here.

As soon as you walk into Midnight Reads, you know you've found someplace special. Naturally, all bookstores are special, but they're even better when they're filled with that warm, dusty smell of paper, ink and wood polish. The front was very modern, full of open shelves and tables with the books laid out for easy access. There were all the latest releases—and a few surprises. A chalk easel listed the meeting times for the mystery club and the cookbook club, the Stitch 'n' Kvetch club and Saturday story time. One corner had been set aside as a kids' area. A Lego table and a collection of beanbag chairs were fenced in by low shelves painted in bright, primary colors.

But farther back, up a short flight of stairs, the shelves were tall and crowded and old-fashioned. In fact, they were salvaged antiques. They invited you to slip into their twilight and explore, and just maybe get lost. But you got the feeling you wouldn't mind so much, because you'd definitely end up someplace interesting.

When Grandma and I walked in, Julia Parris was behind the counter chatting with a couple of women who were buying healthy piles of cozy mysteries and romances. As the doorbell jangled, Julia looked up with a ready smile. She saw Grandma B.B. and that smile froze.

If Mae West had taken to witchcraft, she might have ended up looking like Julia Parris. Julia is a tall woman with a straight back and a mane of pure white hair. She's grandly curved and despite the fact that she uses a walking stick to get around, she does not give off any hint of frailty. Like Grandma B.B., Julia leans toward the dramatic in her personal fashion choices. That day, she was wearing a sparkling ankle-length duster over a black skirt, and a gold tunic with a necklace of stars.

Grandma met her old friend's eyes. "Hello, Julia."

"Hello, Annabelle," replied Julia coolly. "And Anna. I'll be with you in just a minute."

Julia finished ringing up her customers, who were so busy chatting about each other's book hauls, they didn't seem to have noticed that anything unusual had just happened. The same could not be said for the pair of small wiener dogs in the blue doggy bed by the counter.

I'm not the only witch in Portsmouth with a familiar. Julia is the human partner of two miniature dachshunds; Maximilian is a sleek copper-colored wiener, and his brother, Leopold, is a proud little black and tan. Both dogs scrabbled and plopped out of the basket. They came galloping up to us, yapping importantly to each other as they snuffled busily around our ankles.

"Yip!" announced Leo, and he somehow managed to sound both officious and skeptical.

"Yes, all right, all right," I said to them both. "I'm still me, I promise."

"Anna?" called another voice. Valerie McDermott, my

very, very pregnant friend, waddled slowly out of the stacks, turning a little sideways as she did in order to fit through the narrow aisle.

"Val!" I said, trying to sidestep the dachshunds, who were not making it easy. "How are you doing?"

Val and I weren't just friends and coven sisters; we were neighbors. She and her husband, Roger, owned McDermott's Bed & Breakfast. Our gardens back up onto each other, so we regularly gossip over the fence. At least, we would have if either of us had been taller.

"I'm fine, I'm fine." Val puffed as she maneuvered herself carefully down the steps. Val is a petite, strawberry blond woman. She was over the moon about becoming a mom, but navigating the world from behind a belly that she described as roughly the size of a Volkswagen Beetle was testing her patience. "It's Roger you should worry about. He's got a full-blown case of Impending Daddy Syndrome, and I'm not sure we're all going to survive it." She made it down to the main floor with a sigh of relief and held out her hand to my grandmother. "I'm guessing you're Mrs. Britton."

"And you are Valerie McDermott," Grandma said as they shook. "Anna's told me all about you."

"I don't think she's told me half enough about you. I hope we'll have some time to all get together while you're in town."

"Oh, I know we will, dear."

The customers left, and Julia came out from behind the counter. Max and Leo finished their inspection of our ankles and evidently decided we were who we were supposed to be. They scampered back to Julia as she faced my grandmother.

You would have needed a machete to cut the tension.

"It's good to see you, Julia," said Grandma.

"It's good to see you, too, Annabelle."

The pause was at least as pregnant as Valerie. "You're looking well," tried Grandma.

"So are you," replied Julia.

That first pregnant pause seemed to have spawned another.

Grandma tried again. "What a lovely store."

"Thank you." Julia nodded once in acknowledgment.

"I guess the nightclub didn't work out?"

Nightclub?

Just like that, what might have been a third deeply uncomfortable pause was shattered by the unprecedented sight of Julia Parris blushing like a teenager. "*That* is not something we need to bring up."

"Oh, no, I really think it is," said Val. "Did Julia run a nightclub, Ann . . . You know, we're going to have to do something about your names." She gestured at the two of us Annabelles, but Grandma waved that away.

"Call me Grandma B.B., dear. Anna's friends all do."

"Okay, Grandma B.B. it is," agreed Val. "I was pretty sure you two didn't want the solution Young Sean and Old Sean had come up with."

A startled look crossed Grandma's face. "Old Sean? You couldn't possibly mean Sean McNally?"

"That's him, or them, rather." Val was looking at me significantly, and I wished she'd stop that.

"Did you know him?" I asked quickly.

"I did a lot of babysitting when I was in high school. My goodness. Sean McNally has a son? I can't wait to meet him."

"Oh, you'll be meeting him soon, I'm sure," said Val, far too cheerfully.

"Val." I lowered my eyebrows at her in a way I hoped was darkly serious. "We're coven sisters and neighbors, and so you are going to listen when I say you should shut up now."

"Is there something I should know?" The question was exactly as sweet and innocent as you would expect coming from a grandmother. Somebody else's grandmother.

"That depends who you ask," said Val.

"I *see*," said Grandma.

"No, you don't," I told her. "There is nothing to see. At all."

Val just smiled. "Not sure Young Sean would agree with that."

"All right, Valerie," murmured Julia. "I think that's probably enough."

"Probably," agreed Val magnanimously. Fortunately for all of us, a buzz sounded from the vicinity of her hip. Val rolled her eyes and pulled the cell phone out of its quick-draw pouch. "Roger," she muttered. "He gets nervous if he hasn't heard from me every five minutes." The phone buzzed again. Val sighed and ran a hand over her swollen belly. "Daddy loves us, kiddo. We better go check in at home. Wonderful to meet you, Grandma B.B. I'm looking forward to some really nice, long talks."

We said good-bye and all received her assurances that she was *fine*. When the door shut and the brass bells finished jangling, I was left with Grandma and Julia and the dachshunds, all facing one another.

Julia sighed sharply and shook her head. "You haven't changed at all, Annabelle."

"Neither have you."

"I don't suppose you would care for a cup of tea?"

"Well, I suppose I might, if there was one being offered. But I'd hate to take you away from work."

"My assistant, Maria, is in the stock room. She can mind the register."

"Well, if it's no trouble . . ."

"No trouble at all," said Julia quickly. "But perhaps you two have plans?"

"No, no. Anna needs to talk with a new client." Grandma took a deep breath and let it out slowly. "I'm free as a bird."

"Well then," said Julia.

"Well then," agreed Grandma.

It might have been my imagination, but the dachshunds seemed to be looking at me a little desperately. Leo actually whined.

"Wow, gosh." I clapped my hands together. "I would love to stand here chatting, but if you two are okay, I really do need to get to my appointment. So, *are* you two okay?"

The old friends looked at each other. Both dachshunds looked up at their mistress, tails wagging hopefully.

"I really would like that cup of tea, Julia," said Grandma.

"Yes," said Julia. "So would I."

It wasn't exactly a warm embrace, but I had the feeling that would come, and soon. At least, I sure hoped so.

꙰ 3 ꙰

🐾 BEING A FREELANCE artist is not a high-wage job. I was doing very well to be making any kind of living, but my move to Portsmouth had brought some money complications with it. The house, which I'd come to think of as mine, was not really mine. It really belonged to Frank Hawthorne. Frank had let me stay there for the summer mostly rent-free because I had been helping him find out what happened to his aunt, Dorothy. But the lease we'd signed was for only three months, and those three months were up in two weeks. Frank had hinted he wasn't in any hurry to have me gone, but I could not and would not take advantage like that. I had always paid my own way, and I wasn't about to stop now.

That meant there needed to be some kind of money coming in, real soon.

The Northeast Java coffee shop had become a regular haunt of mine since I arrived, but as much as I loved the quirky little place, it was no wonder the owners had decided to make a change. For starters, the shop was really easy to miss, sandwiched between a shadowy vintage store and

Annabelle's (no relation, unfortunately) Ice Cream. There was no visible sign on the chipped wooden door, and just a couple of old wrought-iron tables and chairs out front. Other than that, you had to hear the babble of voices and smell the rich scent of fresh roasted beans wafting through the open window to know you'd just found somewhere special.

Despite the chill of the breeze off the river six feet away, both tables were occupied by people in business suits, checking texts and talking on their phones over cups of the heavenly brew served up by the shop's owners, Jake and Miranda Luce.

A pair of young women were coming out just as I ducked into the crowded, noisy café. A line stretched from the counter to the door. There was next to no space for seating, so everybody was jostling for a spot to stand or make their way through. Four of the shop's staff somehow managed to fit themselves behind the tiny Formica counter, and there wasn't anything like enough room for any of them.

"Anna!" called Miranda Luce over the heads of the crowd. "Thank you so much for coming!"

Thanks to the combination of my tiny little caffeine dependency and the fantastic brew the Luces served up, I'd actually spent a fair amount of time at Northeast Java since I'd come to Portsmouth, and Jake and Miranda and I had quickly become friends. Miranda and Jake had been hippies at the height of the sixties. They met as teenagers when they both decided to hitchhike down to Woodstock (no, I'm not making this up) and had been together ever since.

Miranda Luce was a tiny, thin woman who somehow managed to be both peaceful and intense at the same time. Her jeans and her vests were still brightly embroidered, and her preferred jewelry was wooden beads and colored quartz. She wore her silver-streaked hair in a long braid, which she currently had pinned in a coronet around her head.

"Jake!" Miranda called as I edged my way through the crowd of people who were trying to make way as best they could. "Anna's here!"

"Tell her to come on back!" shouted Jake from . . . somewhere.

Miranda beckoned, and I slipped behind the counter and through the Dutch door.

I'd seen closets bigger than Northeast's kitchen. The space that wasn't taken up by the industrial-grade fridge was filled by the blocky roaster. The smell of coffee in here was strong enough to wake up half of New Hampshire.

"Hey, Anna. Got your latte over there." Jake jerked his chin toward the counter, but his attention was on the crotchety old roaster and its precious beans.

There was no mistaking Jake Luce's vintage. He was a child of the sixties and had the beard, the bandana, round, wire-rimmed glasses and Birkenstocks to prove it. The only reason he didn't look exactly like Jerry Garcia was that he ran ten miles every morning. Like Miranda, Jake was kind and cheerful. They both believed in living and letting live, organic soy milk and better karma through better coffee.

It said so, on the hand-painted sign right above the chalkboard menu.

"Okay, Starbabe, this batch is ready to go out." Jake scooped the beans from the hopper and handed the container to Miranda, who carried it the very short distance out front to be ground and served with varying degrees of foam.

I sipped my own smooth and perfectly foamed brew and heaved a contented sigh. "Thanks, Jake."

He grunted.

"Business is good," I remarked.

"Almost too good." Miranda laughed as she returned from delivering the beans to the front of the house. "It's Chuck's fault, I swear."

"What did Chuck do?" I glanced through the door at the young barista with slicked-back hair, stubbled jaw and a rhinestone stud in his ear.

"Turns out the kid's some kind of software genius, and he's built this program—"

"App, Jake. It's called an app."

"Anyway, somehow it hooks up coffee drinkers and does some kind of rating on their ideal coffee experience and . . ." He waved his hands. "And all of a sudden, we got this." He waved his hand out front and I swear he sounded annoyed. "He didn't even ask us. Said he wanted it to be a surprise. Kids these days!"

"With the clothes and that *hair*!" Miranda laughed. "Lighten up, old man."

Jake made a face and Miranda shrugged. "Chuck, Luis, have you got it covered?" she called toward the guys manning the counter. "We're going over to the new space."

"It's all good," called back the Rhinestone Barista. "Have fun, you crazy kids."

Jake and Miranda grabbed denim jackets and we all headed up Ceres Street, which is not really a street. It's a narrow, cobbled almost alley that runs along the Piscataqua River. You can use it only on foot, and there are concrete stairs at either end. The high brick warehouses on the inland side had originally been built to receive the cargos from the oceangoing ships that sailed up into the harbor. Now those warehouses held offices and condominiums, restaurants (and coffee shops) and stores for the tourists. The docks for Portsmouth's famous red tugboats were here, along with ticketing booths for various harbor sightseeing cruises.

"And here it is!" cried Miranda as we reached the top of the stairs beside the cut-in for the little marina. "Our new home!"

Architecture was not my specialty, but to me the "new home" looked like it dated from the turn of the previous century. A freestanding brick building, three stories tall, it was a classic of its kind, with a rolled copper roof and plate glass windows that were currently covered over in brown paper. Farther up the street, I could see the curving white sides of the Harbor's Rest hotel, a Gilded Age behemoth that was one of Portsmouth's landmarks, so it wasn't too much of a guess that this building was of about the same vintage.

"It looks fabulous," I told them both.

"It used to be a bar back in the 1910s," Miranda was saying

as she fished in her jacket pocket for her keys. "And then it was a drugstore and soda fountain. It was a gallery for a while, but now it's ours." She squeezed Jake's shoulder like she thought she could impart some enthusiasm by osmosis.

Jake muttered something under his breath.

"Jake." Miranda frowned. "You said you were going to be cool about this."

"Yeah, yeah. I'm cool. I am." He gave me a lopsided grin. "Embracing change ain't always what I'm best at. We been on Ceres Street since the beginning. People always found us."

"Moving to a larger place is not the same as selling out to the capitalist establishment," said Miranda patiently, and I got the sense there'd been a whole lot of conversations on this theme I hadn't heard. "In fact, you were the one—"

"I said, I'm cool," Jake cut her off. "It's like you say, if the people are coming, we should be able to welcome them. Show them what we're really about."

"Having the hotel so close should be great for foot traffic," I tried, but Jake just made another face.

"If any of the yacht clubbers can be bothered to get off their assets and walk . . ."

Miranda sighed and turned back to me. "We're going to have space for community meetings and resources for families with kids. We're going to be able to have a real kitchen to serve locally sourced food, and a music venue and—"

"And it's way too late to back out," said Jake. "Yeah, yeah, Starbabe, I'm still in."

Miranda struggled with the lock for a minute and then pushed the door open. An old brass bell hanging from a metal arm rang brightly. Miranda stepped across the threshold and inhaled the smell of plaster and sawdust, her face lit up with excitement. Jake followed, a little more slowly, and definitely not as excited. Me, I hesitated on the threshold.

You see, my whole life, I've had this little problem. Sometimes, when I walk into a place, I'll get hit by a wave of feeling. I call it my Vibe. I will know whether a place is generally a happy or a sad one, whether the people who have lived in it have had good times or bad ones, and all of this will land on me whether I want to know it or not. Sometimes the event I pick up on has happened long in the past. Sometimes it's more recent. Timing doesn't seem to matter. Whatever has left the strongest imprint on a place, it's going to be streamed straight into my brain.

It doesn't happen all the time. Not every place holds on to its vibrations, which is a good thing; otherwise, I'd never be able to walk into a 7-Eleven, let alone an old building like this one. But it happened often enough that the major focus of my magical training so far had been learning how to keep that flood of emotion from drowning me. Julia Parris assured me that as my skills increased, I'd be able to understand the nuances of the impressions I picked up. I might even be able to tune in to specific happenings or sensations. For now, though, I was just happy to be able to shelter myself, psychically speaking. I just needed to be prepared.

I stuck my hand in my purse to assure myself I had remembered to put my wand in there. Yes, I'm not only a witch with a witch's cat; I have a magic wand. It's not quite as magic as those souped-up models the Hogwarts kids carry. Mostly it's a tool for focus, and I was going to need that focus right now.

I took a deep breath and, with an effort, raised my mental shields.

In need I call, in hope I ask, to stand in the protection of the Light. Three times I silently repeated the invocation Julia had taught me. I also pictured myself surrounded by a shimmering curtain of positive energy. In my case, it was all blue and green and gold like the aurora borealis, because I am an artist and everything must have color.

I was safe in here. I was the woman behind the curtain. Any unwanted vibrations this building was putting out would be redirected around me.

So mote it be, I added to close the invocation. I also crossed my mental fingers. Holding tight to my images, my spell, my wand and, most important, my beautiful latte in its to-go cup, I stepped into the new home of Northeast Java.

"What do you think, Anna?" said Miranda to me. "Isn't it marvelous?

What I thought was that it felt like I'd ducked into the current of a summer creek. Vibrations thrummed through the place, buzzing around my head and ears. They were blurry and indistinct because of my mental curtain, but they were most definitely there. Before my training, they would have gone straight through me. Now I gripped my wand and focused on the shields. They shimmered and wavered, but they held and I could focus on what was really happening in the here and now.

"It's going to be perfect," Miranda was saying. "I mean, look at this!" She ran her hands lovingly over the massive antique oak bar, complete with the brass foot railing. "This will be the service counter, of course, and this will all be open seating." She spread her hands to gesture around the whole room. "Upstairs is going to be the meeting and collaboration space, we're going to have a free library and . . ."

I had to admit, now that I had the mental space to take it in, it was a beautiful place. The remaining tables and chairs had been clustered in the middle of the room while the old plaster was being restored. The pressed-tin ceiling looked original. I turned around in a complete circle, imagining trompe l'oeil–style murals wrapping around the walls. It could be a blend of scenes from Portsmouth's history, all suitably detailed with a coffee theme. There could be crates of coffee on the docks being unloaded for men in tricorn hats here; a cluster of chic young things from the 1920s sitting at a café table here; a man in World War II uniform sharing a table with a Rosie the Riveter from the shipyard there . . .

But while I was looking at those blank walls and imagining possibilities, Jake was looking around the space like he expected something or someone to jump out from behind the bar.

A heartbeat later, I understood why.

Footsteps thudded overhead, as if someone was hurrying across the room above. Jake's head snapped up. Without a word, he sprinted up the narrow side stairs.

"Oh . . . nuts," muttered Miranda, and she took off after him.

I set my half-finished latte down on the bar and followed, fast.

The upstairs was a single lovely, sunny room. There was a half wall down the middle, complete with built-in shelves, which divided it into a front and a back. This was probably destined to be that free library Miranda had talked about. A few ancient folding chairs leaned against the wall along with a stepladder, white buckets and a jug of bleach.

It was also completely empty of, well, people. Except for us, and we were all crowded together at the top of the stairs.

"You heard it, right?" said Jake to me. "We all heard it. Footsteps."

A shiver ran down my spine. The currents swirled hard around my shields, which shivered, but held. Mostly.

"I don't know what I heard," announced Miranda. "We're on the main street now, Jake. There's going to be all kinds of noises."

But Jake was picking something up off the half wall. It was a thick, plain white china coffee mug, the kind that Northeast Java used for its stay-in customers.

"It's your cup," said Jake. "The one that went missing when we were here on Monday."

"It's *a* cup," said Miranda. "One of the contractors could have left it."

Then, we heard it again—a quick, steady thudding—only this time it came up from beneath us. It sure sounded like someone in hard-soled shoes walking across the floor downstairs.

My shields shuddered.

"One of the workmen," said Miranda. "Or maybe Chuck, you know, came by. "

"I don't wanna doubt you, Starbabe, but when we get down there, it's gonna be empty and the door's gonna be locked."

Miranda glanced uneasily toward the stairs. A shadow flickered in the corner of my eye, but I couldn't tell if it was real or just my Vibe-primed imagination. Jake shook his head and started down. Miranda followed him reluctantly, and so did I.

When we got there, the main floor certainly looked empty. Jake went over to the front door and rattled it. It did not open. Not that that meant anything, of course. It was probably the kind of door that locked automatically behind you. But there was that bell hanging on the ornamental arm overhead. We definitely had not heard that ring.

I rubbed my arms. Was it just me, or had it suddenly gotten a lot colder in here?

Then I saw my latte cup on the bar. I walked slowly over and picked it up. There were two immediate problems here. One was that I was pretty sure I had left my cup at the *other* end of the bar. The other was that somebody had drunk the last of my perfectly brewed, perfectly sweetened, perfectly foamed latte.

I set the cup down and folded my arms. "All right. Jake, Miranda, what's going on?"

"Nothing," said Miranda immediately. "Well, nothing much. Jake and I are just having a little disagreement about the building. I think it's perfect."

"And I," said Jake, "think it's haunted."

4

🐾 "HAUNTED?" I REPEATED. Not possible. Okay, I believed in magic, with and without cats, and I believed in my Vibe. I believed my grandmother was a witch, that upright, uptight Julia Parris had once run a nightclub, and that the Red Sox were going to win the World Series again this year.

But I did not believe in ghosts. No. Uh-uh. Not now, not ever. Not that I was scared or anything, but it was a bridge too far. A great big spooky covered bridge in autumn with the bare trees rattling and crows sitting on the roof too far. I'd just misremembered where I'd put that take-out cup. And of course I hadn't actually left any latte sitting around. I'd finished it on my own; I just hadn't been paying attention. And those hadn't really been footsteps we heard upstairs. Or downstairs.

Right? Right.

Jake, however, was not getting with the program. "First day we came in here, there was a rumble in the floor—"

"Which just happened to be when a dump truck was going by outside," Miranda said.

"And there have been sudden drops in temperature, and it's got cold spots."

"Because it's fall in New Hampshire, and the insulation is older than we are."

"Tools have been disappearing and reappearing—"

"Say the contractors, but I haven't—"

"We even put in a security camera. It didn't catch anything."

"One camera," said Miranda stubbornly. "For the entire building."

"You agreed, Starbabe," Jake reminded her. "We have been over every square inch and we've still got these . . . phenomena."

Miranda closed her mouth, but she also folded her arms and looked up at him with her chin stuck out.

Jake faced me. "I need to apologize, Anna. I haven't been, like, totally straight with you." A slow sinking feeling formed in the pit of my stomach. "We heard about how you helped find out who killed Dorothy." He paused again. "And we heard you might have had some . . . spiritual help."

"Or do you prefer the term 'paranormal'?" asked Miranda anxiously. "We don't want to speak disrespectfully about your practice."

What I preferred was not to talk about any of this. At all. But I wasn't going to get that option.

When I came to Portsmouth, I'd helped solve a genuine murder mystery involving a local witch named Dorothy Hawthorne, who used to own the house I was currently occupying. I'd used my wits and my new magic and had a healthy dose of help from Alistair and the guardian coven to do it, too. I hadn't realized that word about that had somehow gotten out. I guess I shouldn't have been that surprised. Most of the members of the coven were pretty open about their practice, but I had planned on staying in the broom closet for a while. At least until I was sure that the practice was really right for me.

Okay, the cat and the house and the wand were pretty strong signals, but it was all still new and it was a little scary.

Before I got to Portsmouth, I'd spent a lot of time and effort keeping my Vibe a secret, because when people found out about it they had two reactions:

1) They wanted me to be their psychic friend and tell them all about what they should do with their lives.

2) They just thought Annabelle Britton, the crazy artist girl, was, well, crazy.

Jake cleared his throat. "Anyway, a place that's haunted— I mean, that's just far out, when it's not yours. But we can't bring our customers into a scene where we don't know what's going to happen to them. No way. So I told Miranda we were backing out of this move unless you could . . . clear it."

See what I mean? Reaction Number One, right there.

"There is *nothing* to clear," said Miranda.

"Then she won't find anything."

They were both looking at me anxiously. I took a deep breath and pushed down my irritation. I liked these people. Plus, I was going through one of those times all freelancers dread. My usual sources of income had kind of all gone dormant at once. I needed this mural project.

"Are you sure it couldn't just be a squatter?" I asked. "I mean, the building was standing empty for a while."

Jake glanced at Miranda and shook his head. "We really did have to clean out the whole place top to bottom when we got in. We found a lot of stuff, but no squatters, at least not recent ones." He sighed. "I'm sorry about dropping you in the middle of this, Anna. But, do you think you could . . . you know, have a look with the third eye or whatever it is you got?"

I could say no. In fact, I should say no. I was only an apprentice witch. I'd been formally initiated into the coven with a lovely moonlight ceremony, but before I got my first lessons from Julia, I'd been required to take an oath (on my own wand, no less) that I would not actively practice or cast any magical working without my teacher or another senior witch present. I'd gotten a pass on my shield spell, since that was for personal protection, but other than that, I was not supposed to so much as try to conjure spare change out from under the sofa cushions.

And naturally, I didn't want to pretend to be looking for something that couldn't possibly be there. I knew it couldn't be there, because there was no such thing as ghosts.

Uh-huh. I looked at my empty latte cup again. *You keep telling yourself that, A.B.*

On the other hand, one of the things I was supposed to do even as an apprentice witch was follow the threefold law. That is: Whatever you send out into the world comes back to you threefold. I didn't want to be sending out more fear and uncertainty to create anger and strife between Jake and Miranda.

And I really needed this commission.

"I couldn't promise anything," I told them. "Not every impression I can pick up has a clear meaning or source."

"Of course, we understand, Anna," said Miranda soothingly. "You just do your best."

I admit, there was something in the way she said it that stung a little. When you're carrying around something like my Vibe, you expect disbelief, but not from someone who's on the magic bus herself.

I could, at this point, do one of two things. The smart thing would be to stall Jake and Miranda until I could get Julia and maybe one or two of the others here to provide magical backup and expertise.

I did the other.

"Okay," I said. "Here goes."

I put my back to the door and faced the room. I reminded myself that by soaking in the Vibe I knew was filling this room, I wasn't actually casting a spell or even performing a ceremony. The vibrations were really going on outside me. I was just a receiver station. So, no harm, no foul. Right?

Right.

I let out a long breath and I pictured that shimmering, positive, northern-lights-ish ripple of energy I'd surrounded myself with lifting slowly, like the curtain at the start of a play.

The first thing I felt was warmth. It was relaxing, like settling into a hot bath. The air sparkled with a kind of suppressed excitement, or at least amusement. I felt it whisper against my skin, specifically, the back of my neck. I raised my hand and brushed it back.

I swear upon my life, I heard somebody chuckle behind me.

But I couldn't have. Because Jake and Miranda were both in front of me, over by the bar. And they were waiting. I swallowed, and I tried to focus. I can't say the real, present world went away exactly, but it did seem to retreat. The Vibe that surrounded me was more real, and more important, than anything else.

"This is a good place," I said slowly. "This is the right place. Things are as they should be and will be." My Vibe can mess with my ability to form comprehensible sentences. Maybe I should have warned them about that.

"There!" Miranda said. "I told you, Jake."

"Okay, okay, I give." Jake threw up his hands. "You were right and—"

The Vibe rippled; it swirled and it spread, like rings across the surface of a pond.

"Secrets," I said.

"What?" they both exclaimed.

"Secrets," I repeated. "Secrets locked away, hidden, vanished, gone . . ."

I could feel them. Deep in the swirling "water" I felt around me. The secrets were down beneath. They were up above. They were in the ceiling and behind the walls.

Everywhere.

My stomach lurched and I had to put a hand on the bar to keep from falling. I should have been scared—terrified, in fact—but I wasn't. I wanted to know what was happening. I needed to know. To be known. Finally.

Someone was laughing at me. I needed to know about

that, too. I needed to pick a direction, but how could I when the secrets were everywhere?

There was a doorway below the stairs. I walked over to it and pulled it open. Another set of stairs led down into the dark.

The Vibe was stronger here, bubbling up from the cellar.

Some vague and distant part of my brain was telling me I should stop this. I might have, too, once upon a time. Now, though, my curiosity had a hold of me as firmly as the Vibe did. I liked this sense of accomplishment. I liked the feeling of being able to finally follow my Vibe instead of just being tossed around by it. I wanted to find out if what I was picking up on was real.

In short, I wanted to know if I was right.

If I'd been thinking straight, I'd have realized this was not necessarily any kind of a good sign.

My fingers found the switch and snapped it on. Dim yellow light filled the stairwell. The steps were old and splintered and a little saggy in the middle. I couldn't seem to muster enough worry to let that stop me.

I was heading straight down the basement stairs, with Jake and Miranda trailing behind.

The stairs creaked. My sneakers made hollow, thudding noises on the boards.

"Take it easy, Anna," said Miranda from behind me. "That last one's kind of steep."

It was. I jarred my knee, and the Vibe shuddered.

"Hang on," said Jake behind me. He must have flicked a switch, because a bare hanging bulb came on overhead.

The chilly basement was made up of a pair of rooms with brick walls and floors. The one we stood in was being used as construction storage. Two-by-fours, white rectangles of Sheetrock, five-gallon plastic buckets and sacks of plaster of Paris were stacked against the walls along with toolboxes and coils of braided cable. An old utility sink from the building's previous lives had been left in place and had half a dozen jugs of industrial-strength soaps and solvents stashed underneath it.

"This is going to be the kitchen," said Miranda. "One of the reasons we chose the building is there's the room to install a walk-in fridge and decent-sized prep area." She gestured toward the side room.

Her words washed over me without touching me. If I'd been wading through the Vibe upstairs, I was swimming down here. Secrets. Something hidden was waiting to be found. It wanted to be found.

I turned around slowly, angling for a direction, like when you're trying to tell where that strange sound is coming from. Something thumped overhead. Jake's nose shot into the air. I ignored it. Because every instinct in me was pointing straight down. I should be going down.

Except there was no more down.

Okay, down, I said to my Vibe and the universe at large. *Down where? Down* how?

Someone whistled, high, sharp and insistent. My head jerked around. Miranda had gone white. Jake took hold of her hand.

The open doorway to the second room was on my right. I bit my lip and walked across the threshold. My Vibe swirled, and it shifted and sank, straight through the floor. I felt it running through the bricks at my feet, like water down a drain.

I stared at the floor. The bricks were old, scarred and chipped. Time, grime and a whole lot of foot traffic had turned the mortar black.

It took a lot of effort, but I got my mouth to move. "Is there a subbasement?" It was like trying to talk underwater. My voice sounded wrong and echoey in my ears.

"This close to the river?" said Jake incredulously. "Bad idea. We are as low as we go."

But there was something; I knew there was something. It was right under my shoes. I was sure of it. A secret, waiting to be found.

I crouched down and pressed both palms to the floor. It was cold and a little damp.

"Anna," said Miranda. "It's not that I don't respect your practice. I do. But—"

That was when the brick under my hands shifted. I stared between my fingers, and I noticed that this set of bricks didn't have any mortar between them. They were just set loosely into place. I scrabbled at one and it came up in my hand. So did its neighbor.

"Well, ain't that a kick?" Jake got on his knees beside me, and we started piling up bricks. Miranda stood behind us, her hand pressed against her mouth.

Underneath the loose bricks, there should have been plain dirt, or at least sand. But what we cleared away was a square of old wood. With a rusted metal latch and a bolt and a very old padlock.

It was a trapdoor.

❧ 5 ❧

❖ "OUTTA SIGHT," BREATHED Jake as he stared at the trapdoor. "I mean, like, really."

I sat back on my heels. The Vibe had receded a little, and I was fizzing on the inside with that kind of zingy triumph that comes from being proved right. Miranda, on the other hand, looked positively green around the gills.

"Did you know about this?" she demanded, but I wasn't sure which one of us she was talking to.

I shook my head. "I . . . there was a secret. There is. It's down in here."

"Well, like my pop used to say, no time like the present." Jake climbed to his feet, flipped up the lid on the nearest toolbox and fished out a screwdriver. He set to work on the trapdoor's hinges, which were marginally less rusty than the padlock.

"Jake, maybe this is not a good idea," Miranda murmured.

"Can't back out now, Starbabe," he said. Just like that, the pair of them had switched places. Now that there was something tangible under his hands, Jake was all action and Miranda was the one holding back.

Miranda muttered something under her breath, but she found a second screwdriver in the toolbox and got going on the second set of hinges.

I backed away and let them work, rubbing my hands together. It was cold down here and smelled like earth and damp. But there was something else, too, and I felt it prickling up my arms from my fingertips.

Magic, and not mine. At least, not entirely.

Movement caught my eye. There, behind the two-by-fours and the Sheetrock leaning against the wall, was a flash of blue, like a cat's eyes gleaming in the dark. Specifically, like Alistair's eyes.

Since he's my familiar, Alistair cannot be kept away from me. He can, and has, appeared in a locked room, or down in a basement, or anyplace else I've gotten myself, unless there's a spell deliberately keeping him out. Since he's also entirely a cat, this means he comes and goes as he pleases, or when he's sure I've gotten myself into trouble.

"Got it," said Jake behind me. "Grab the corner there, Miranda."

Alistair blinked at me from the shadows behind the Sheetrock. I made myself turn my back and watch Jake and Miranda lift that splintering trapdoor out of its recess. Underneath was a roughly circular opening that led straight down and bottomed out at a floor of what looked like packed dirt.

"It must be an old cistern or a well, something like that," said Miranda.

"No chance. Look." Jake pointed. Miranda and I leaned closer. A set of big, rusty iron staples had been pressed into the wall.

"Rungs," said Jake. "It's a ladder."

Jake and Miranda locked gazes with each other. There is a kind of telepathy that happens with couples who have been together a long time, and I knew it was zinging between Jake and Miranda now.

"Well, are we doing the smart thing or the dumb thing?" asked Miranda.

Jake pushed his glasses up farther on his nose. "Something still down there, Anna?"

"Oh, yeah." The Vibe fountained up fresh and clear from the open space at our feet. I felt it all the way up to my neck.

"Groovy." Jake fished around in the toolbox again, and this time he came up with a flashlight. He flicked it on and off a couple of times, making sure of the beam. "Let's go see what it is."

I glanced back toward Alistair, but my cat had already vanished.

"Groovy," I muttered.

Jake went first, while Miranda held the flashlight. He climbed carefully down into the hole, stomping on each rung as he went, but they all held firm. He reached the bottom and held up both hands. Miranda dropped the light down and Jake caught it easily.

"What do you see, old man?" she called.

"There's a tunnel." Jake was pointing the light and crouching down. "Goes pretty far back, slopes up. Looks old."

"Any water in it?" I asked. It would be very bad if all this feeling I was getting about sinking and bubbling and swimming was because this place was flooded.

Jake crouched down and touched the dirt floor. "Seems dry. You coming down, Miranda?"

"Why the heck not?" she muttered.

Jake shone the beam up for her and Miranda climbed carefully down to stand beside her husband. I still had the powerful sense of secrets that wanted to be discovered, but reality was—finally—starting to creep in. This tunnel, wherever it went, had probably never known the loving gaze of a building inspector. It was way too close to the river, and it ran under the foundations of a set of buildings that were old when Grandma B.B. was still Baby B.B.

But I didn't feel any danger. Not really. I was swimming through the mystery and I wanted to find out where it was and why it was. Badly.

But why did the answer have to be so far down in the dark?

Miranda noticed my hesitation. "You can wait there, Anna," she called up. "We'll holler if we need help."

"Might not be a bad idea," said Jake. "I can't see how far this thing goes."

It wasn't a bad idea, but I still felt like a coward. I'd gotten them into this, after all. And since I was listening to my Vibe instead of my common sense, I also listened when I told myself I couldn't back out now.

"No, that's okay. I'm coming."

I turned around and began slowly climbing down the ladder. The rungs felt scaly under my hands and I wished I had my boots. And gloves. And a headlamp. And maybe a way to back out gracefully.

I got to the bottom. It was cold down here and goose bumps crawled across my skin.

"It goes this way." Jake shined his beam into the dark.

"This way" was a low, rough tunnel off toward the left, from my perspective. The walls were packed dirt and stone, with what looked like railway ties jammed here and there, along with sheets of corrugated tin, now patched and streaked with rust, to give some semblance of stability.

"Well, if we're doing this, let's do it," said Miranda. "You still getting something, Anna?"

"Yeah," I said. "It's still there."

We all set off into the dark.

The tunnel was so low that both Miranda and I had to walk with our heads ducked down. Jake was practically bent double. We scuffed and crunched across loose dirt and gravel. The air smelled stale and cold. I kept one hand on the wall, and more dirt came loose under my fingers.

My scalp grazed a railroad tie.

"You two feeling okay?" asked Jake. "This thing's been shut up for a long time. The air might not be so good."

"Maybe there's another opening," said Miranda. "I think I'm feeling a draft."

I shivered. I was certainly feeling something. Cold, for starters. Damp. A vibration overhead. The tin sheet under my hand trembled in response. A tiny spill of dirt pattered down.

Miranda sneezed.

"Bless you," I said automatically. "Are we under the street here?"

"Could be," said Jake. "We're headed inland, and up. I think."

The floor underneath us stayed dry, for which I was grateful. I still didn't like the way the walls crumbled so easily as my palm passed over them, or the look of the tin sheets and timber beams jammed into the dirt overhead. Especially the ones with ragged patches where it looked like some kind of wood-noshing bugs had been really busy.

"Why would this even be here?" I asked.

Jake laughed. "Are you kidding? People have been smuggling stuff into Portsmouth as long as there's been a town. Rum, tea, and guns during the Revolution, escapees during slavery, booze during Prohibition." He touched the wall. "You name it, it probably came through here sometime or another."

Which would explain the powerful sense of secrets I was swimming through. If people had been moving contraband through here, they would have been worried about being caught. If they'd been escapees, they would have been worried about a whole lot more than that. It would all add up to a lot of pent-up emotion.

"Wait. Stop," said Miranda. "I think I saw something moving up ahead."

I thought I did, too, just a ripple in the shadows. Then I heard it. A low, distinct and unmistakable sound.

"Meow?"

I closed my eyes briefly.

"Was that a cat?" cried Jake. "Poor guy! How did it get down here?"

"Umm . . . not sure," I mumbled. "Maybe through that other opening where the draft is coming from?"

"Well." Miranda lifted her head, and even with nothing but the flashlight beam, I saw the distinct light of triumph in her eyes. There was a whole lot of relief there as well. "There's your ghost, old man. A stray, hunting rats."

Jake set his jaw and pushed forward. I wished Miranda

hadn't brought up the possibility of rats. Spiders and bugs were bad enough. I looked around the dark nervously.

"Actually . . ." I began.

"What?" asked Jake.

"Nothing." My Vibe might be public knowledge, but I really didn't feel like explaining about Alistair and his personal Cheshire cat–style magic. Besides, I couldn't help wondering what he was doing in here. Had he found something? Or was he just worried about me?

"End of the line, kids," said Jake.

In front of us was a door. This wasn't a trapdoor. It was a proper, person-sized door set into a properly built brick wall. The door had been meant to last, too. It was riveted (and rusted) steel. Actually, it looked like it belonged on an old-fashioned bank vault. The tunnel had widened out around us, and somebody, or several somebodies, had made an attempt to stabilize it. There were bricks pushed into the packed dirt walls, and some extra timbers had been hammered into place overhead. One of them, though, had collapsed and now slanted across a big pile of stones and dirt.

There was something else, too; a very strong smell, and it was not a good one.

"Eww!" I pressed my hand up under my nose. "Sewer?"

"Probably," said Jake. "Maybe one of those rats moved on to his next life."

Could we please stop talking about rats? I shifted uneasily, and Miranda noticed. She squeezed my shoulder reassuringly. It didn't help.

"Any idea where we are?" I asked Jake.

"We must be almost to the Harbor's Rest hotel," he said.

It was hotter now, and the air felt close, but there was definitely a current of air coming from someplace. It curled around my neck and ankles.

I put my hand on the solid metal door and pushed. The door rattled but didn't give.

"Locked," I said. "Or maybe blocked up, on the other side."

"Well, that's kind of it, then," Jake said. He sounded

sorry. I admit, I was feeling a little let down. The Vibe swirling around me had been so strong, I'd expected to find a box of old booze at the very least.

"But what happened to the cat?" Miranda took the flashlight from Jake and started shining it in every direction. "I'm sure I heard one."

"Yeah, about that." I stepped back from the door. At least, I meant to step back. The dirt pile shifted underneath my heel and I toppled sideways instead. I also swore.

The smell got stronger. Miranda and Jake were staring at me. No. At the place I had been.

"Jake, honey, I might owe you an apology," murmured Miranda.

Because when I'd fallen, the dirt had shifted. Now, a pair of clouded white eyes stared at us from out of a human face.

A very dead human face.

❧ 6 ❧

🐾 "AND YOU'RE CERTAIN you didn't recognize the deceased?" Detective Simmons asked Jake.

Jake, Miranda and I huddled together on the sidewalk out in front of the old drugstore. A barrier of police cruisers, sawhorses and yellow tape blocked both the street and the sidewalk. Men and women in blue uniforms filed in and out of the building, talking to one another or into their radios. Naturally, a crowd had gathered on the other side, craning necks and holding up cell phones, trying to get a look at what was going on, or at least take a picture of it.

"I didn't actually get a good look at . . . the body," Jake was saying to Detective Simmons.

"That was my fault," said Miranda. "I kind of freaked out."

"You weren't the only one," I added. It had gotten kind of loud down in that tunnel before the three of us had managed to get hold of ourselves, and the flashlight, so we could get back down the tunnel and up to where my cell phone had reception again and call 911.

Jake put his arm around Miranda, and I had my arms folded tight across my chest.

Kenisha Freeman moved away from the pair of EMTs she had been talking to and touched my arm. Kenisha is an officer on the Portsmouth police force. She's also a member of my coven. The only witch cop in New Hampshire, she says proudly. She has medium brown skin, and a spray of dark freckles decorates her cheeks. Her blue uniform covers a lean, athletic build and she wears her red-and-amber-streaked hair pulled back into a severe bun.

"You okay?" Kenisha asked, and I nodded, even though I was pretty sure I was lying. Finding a dead body tends to have a bad effect on a person. It was a beautiful, sunny day, but the wind off the river seemed to cut straight through my jacket. I could not stop shaking.

Kenisha respected my putting on a brave face, though, and just nodded back. She also jerked her chin toward the nearest police cruiser. I followed her glance and saw a (literally) familiar whiskered face peering out from behind the driver's side tire. Alistair. We blinked at each other for a minute and I let out the breath I hadn't realized I was holding.

"And you had no idea that tunnel was there?" Detective Simmons was asking.

"No." Miranda glanced at me. So did Kenisha, with one raised eyebrow. "We only found it this afternoon, and we were trying to see where it went."

Pete wrote this down, slowly and carefully. Pete Simmons is a short, permanently rumpled fireplug of a man. He was also endlessly patient and quietly, calmly, politely suspicious of absolutely everything. These are traits that make him very good at his job. It also makes watching him take his detailed notes surprisingly nerve-wracking.

Pete scratched behind his ear with the end of his pencil and turned toward me.

"Anna!" shouted another voice.

I spun around to face the street and the crowd. Grandma B.B. was squeezing between the bystanders with their phones, and she had Julia Parris and the dachshunds right behind her. All of them came up to the sawhorses with the crime scene tape wrapped around them and pushed straight on through. Before I knew it, Grandma had hold of me in a very firm hug.

"What on earth happened!"

"What are you doing here?" I demanded, at least as soon as I could, gently, pull free and draw a full breath again.

Max and Leo both started yipping like their doggy lives depended on it and made a beeline, or at least a dog line, straight for the old drugstore's door, noses to the pavement.

"Hey!" shouted Detective Simmons, slashing his pencil through the air. "Miss Parris! We can't have those dogs in the crime scene!"

Julia thumped her walking stick on the pavement. "Max! Leo! Heel!"

The dogs stopped like they'd reached the ends of their leashes and trotted right back to her side.

Under the cruiser, Alistair rubbed a paw rapidly across his ear, in a *you guys are embarrassing* kind of gesture.

"Crime scene!" exclaimed Grandma, as if she'd just noticed all the yellow tape, not to mention the cruisers and the uniforms. "What am *I* doing here? What are you doing here? Julia and I were finishing our tea when we saw the police cars and . . . are you all right?"

"I'm fine. Everything's fine."

Grandma B.B. scrunched her face up at me, an expression indicating serious grandmotherly doubt. I couldn't blame her. The words "crime scene" did not exactly go with "everything's fine."

Pete and Grandma B.B. both opened their mouths at the exact same moment. I braced myself, but a uniformed officer waved over the heads of the crowd. Pete looked at the officer, then looked at us and at his notebook with his list of unanswered questions.

"Wait here, please," he said before he waved back to the other officer and made his way over to her, leaving us on our own for the moment.

"Now, Anna, what's *happened*?" demanded Grandma B.B. "And don't you even *think* about saying 'nothing,' to your grandmother."

"Or to me," added Julia.

Kenisha muttered something under her breath that sounded a lot like "uh-oh." I swallowed. I reminded myself I hadn't done anything wrong. Not really. I looked down to Alistair for some moral support, but my familiar just dodged behind the cruiser's tire. Coward.

But Julia didn't get a chance to ask the questions hovering behind her stern eyes.

"Annie-Bell?" Miranda let go of Jake's hand and made her way over to us or, rather, to Grandma B.B. "Oh, my gosh, is that you?"

My grandmother turned her head to see who was talking and promptly did a double take.

"Miranda?"

In the next second, Miranda and Grandma B.B. were hugging each other and exclaiming, their words tumbling over one another.

"I heard you were back in town but . . . !"

"Had *no* idea you were still . . ."

"Can't believe it's you!"

"*I* can't believe it's *you!*"

I stood back, thinking, *Annie-Bell?* I looked to Julia. She just pressed her mouth into a thin, tight line. She was radiating a kind of high-frequency disapproval, and although she stared at the old drugstore, the police and the crowd, I had the distinct feeling that extra-special tension in the air around my mentor wasn't for any of them.

"Julia . . ." I began, but she just shook her head.

"We cannot have this conversation here." Julia nodded toward Pete, who was standing listening to the uniformed cop but was watching all of us with real interest. "But we will have it."

Suddenly, answering questions for Detective Simmons seemed like it was going to be a walk in the park.

"Come meet my husband!" Miranda grabbed Grandma's hand and pulled her over to Jake. "Jake! This is Annie-Bell Blessingsound! She used to babysit me!"

"Oh, hey." Jake held out his hand. Grandma took both of his and shook them warmly.

"So *wonderful* to meet you, Jake," said Grandma. "Is this your shop? I was so excited to hear that you and Miranda thought of my granddaughter for your decorations!"

Miranda slapped her forehead. "Your granddaughter! Of course, Anna *Britton*. I didn't put the two together. Fate!" she called toward the sky. "It's fate!"

"Yeah, problem is, it ain't the good kind," muttered Jake.

Grandma took both of Miranda's hands. "What's the matter, dear? Why are the police here?"

"Yes," said Julia tartly. "Why *are* the police here, Anna?"

Miranda hesitated, but Grandma shook her hands encouragingly. "Oh, come along, Miranda; you can tell Annie-Bell."

Something was wrong. Something was shifting underneath the surface, and it wasn't just that sweet and innocent Grandma routine, which I never trusted. I felt a distinct prickling on the back of my neck and up my hands, and, yes, in both my thumbs.

Magic.

My little old white-haired grandmother was working a spell on Miranda.

"Gosh, Grandma, you know, I'm really sorry about all this!" I said loudly. "Maybe you can go and wait somewhere until the police say it's okay for us to go! Have you ever been to Joe King's Chowder Shack? It's right around the corner this way . . ."

Unsubtly and unashamedly, I grabbed my grandmother and started pulling her back toward the fence of cars and sawhorses. I didn't make it very far. My grandmother has always been stronger than she looks.

"Annabelle Amelia." She shook me off. "What on earth is this about?"

"That was about you working some kind of spell on Miranda," I whispered harshly. "*Without* her permission!"

"Oh, good heavens, Anna," she murmured. "You are *entirely* overreacting."

"I am not overreacting! We're the good witches! We're not supposed to do that." I looked back toward Julia for confirmation, and what I got in return was a glare that reached right down inside me and turned me from a grown woman to a badly behaved toddler.

"May I remind you, young lady, I've been practicing far longer than you've been alive," said Grandma, softly but very firmly. "*I* know the rules. Perhaps you'd care to tell *me* what you were doing that got poor Alistair so upset he had to come get us?"

I opened my mouth and closed it again.

"We found a dead body," I said.

"Oh, *dear.*" Just like that, the lecture was over and I was being hugged by my grandma. I held on, hard, and for a long time.

"'Scuse me," called Pete Simmons. He'd come back from his other conversation and was waving his pencil to try to attract our attention. "I know this is tough on everybody, but the sooner we're done, the sooner you can get home."

"Sorry, Detective," I muttered and went back over to stand with Jake and Miranda. Naturally, Julia and Grandma followed.

"Now, Mr. and Mrs. Luce." Pete flipped his notebook open. "We were talking about . . ." He turned over another page. "The tunnel. Who found it? Was it the two of you?" Pete sort of waggled his pencil at the pair of them. "Or were all three of you together?" The pencil, and Pete's attention, now pointed at me.

I glanced back at Alistair, looking for a little moral support. He had come out from behind the tire, but he had also hunkered down on the pavement with a calm *you got yourself into this one, human*, air.

"I found the tunnel," I told the detective. "Miranda and Jake were giving me a tour of the space. I'm going to be painting some murals for them—"

"On the basement floor?" asked Pete with perfect calm. He'd probably heard stranger things.

"I tripped over a brick," I lied. "It was loose."

I looked at Pete. Pete looked at me. I was not going to be able to keep this up for long. You cannot win a stare down with a cat—or a cop.

"How long has he . . . the body . . . been there?" I asked, hoping to sort of, kind of change the subject.

Pete shook his head. Kenisha looked grim. They'd both been down to have a look at the corpse. "Rough guess, I'd say it was at least a week."

"Oh." Miranda covered her mouth, and Jake, who had been trying to maintain at least a little calm while the police trooped in and out of the old drugstore, was looking a little green around the gills.

"Are you all right, Mrs. Luce?" asked Pete gently. "Do you need to sit down?"

But Miranda waved him back.

"Jake, that is, we"—Miranda squeezed her husband's arm—"we'd been experiencing some strange phenomenon over the past month, including some thumping we couldn't explain. We thought . . . we'd been thinking, the building might be haunted."

"Haunted?" said Pete.

"It was one explanation," replied Miranda firmly. She might not have believed Jake's claim, but she was not going to talk him down in front of the police. "But, now, I mean, what if . . ."

"What if we were hearing that poor guy pounding on the trapdoor, trying to get out?" Jake reached up under his glasses and rubbed his eyes. "Oh, man."

I couldn't help shuddering. My Vibe had been all about secrets and wanting to be discovered. What if that had been an echo of the man's desire to be rescued? His very desperate and dying desire?

"We can't tell anything yet, Mr. Luce," said Pete. "When did you start hearing these noises?"

"We've really only been in the space for maybe a month," said Miranda. "Regularly, I mean. We've been in and out for longer. Cleaning, and like that. I guess we've been hearing things for maybe two weeks?" She looked at Jake for confirmation. "But the contractors say they've been hearing things almost since they started."

"Well, I'm pretty sure the guy we found could not have been trapped in that tunnel for a whole month," said Pete. I think he meant it to be reassuring, but he in no way succeeded. "And you didn't see any signs that anybody else had been down there recently?"

"No. None," said Miranda before I could even get my mouth open.

"Detective Simmons!" shouted a new voice. A paunchy, pale man wearing a bright red blazer and Clark Kent glasses was striding up the street. The wind from the river blew his black tie over his shoulder as he edged his way between the police cruisers. Kenisha moved to intercept him, but Pete waved her back.

"Mr. Hilde," said Pete coolly. "Sorry to pull you out of your office."

Mr. Hilde was not a big man, or a young one. In fact, he was only a couple of inches taller than me, and if the lines around his face and the sag in his jowls were anything to go by, he was already on the far side of middle age. His hair, though, was an incongruously dark chestnut brown, and he slicked it back nervously with one hand as he came to stand in front of the detective.

"And I'm sorry to bother you," Mr. Hilde said to Pete. "But I've got guests wondering what's going on." Now I could see the hotel crest on the pocket of that bright red blazer. He must be connected with the Harbor's Rest hotel. Then I remembered Jake guessing the door we'd found might open into the hotel.

"I was hoping I could tell our guests there's nothing to worry about." Behind their thick lenses, Hilde's eyes fastened on Jake and Miranda. Jake grinned back at him and flashed the peace sign. A small, satisfied smile tightened Mr. Hilde's sagging mouth. "But maybe I'm wrong. What'd they finally catch you at, Luce?"

Jake shrugged. "Not a darned thing, Dale. Disappointed?"

"No, just surprised." Dale Hilde was still smiling, and it was not a nice expression.

"Jake," murmured Miranda. "Stay cool."

"Oh!" cried Grandma. Very suddenly and very uncharacteristically, she stumbled and toppled over, right into Dale Hilde's arms. He caught her automatically and awkwardly.

"Oh, I am *so* sorry!" Grandma grabbed both his wrists to steady herself, even as I lunged forward to help bring her back upright. "I caught my shoe on the curb." She blinked at him myopically and I felt my fingers prickling. Again. "Why, you must be one of Gretchen's boys!" she said happily to Mr. Hilde. "You look just like her!"

"I . . . uh . . . yes," he mumbled. He also rubbed his palms against his trousers and turned right back to Pete. "Detective Simmons? My guests? I can tell them this is nothing, right? You'll be gone soon?"

"Unfortunately, Mr. Hilde, I can't tell you when we'll be finished here," said Detective Simmons. "In fact, I'm probably going to have to bring some of my people into the hotel."

Dale took at step back. His gaze slid straight back to Jake and Miranda. "What for?"

"Can you tell me anything about an old tunnel, maybe a historic smugglers' tunnel, that leads into the hotel?"

Hilde's eyes skittered this way and that, taking in the crowd, the flashing lights and the uniforms. His smile had vanished. He slicked his dark hair back again. "Well, you know, it's an old building. There were always rumors. But I can't say anybody's ever found anything that I know about. Not that we've ever looked especially hard."

"That's a shame. But I'm afraid it doesn't make a lot of difference," said Pete, his considerable patience finally stretched a little thin. "I hope you'll let my people have a look inside the hotel basement. I can, of course, get a warrant if that will make things easier with the rest of the management . . ."

Mr. Hilde slicked his hair back again. For good measure, he smoothed down his black tie. "Of course Harbor's Rest is always happy to cooperate with the police, but can you tell me what this is about?"

"We've found a body, Mr. Hilde, in a tunnel which appears to end at your hotel."

Mr. Hilde flushed bright red. "I cannot tell that to our guests," he announced, as if the discovery of a corpse was some highly personal inconvenience. Detective Simmons did not even flinch.

"They're going to find out, I'm afraid. So, I'm sure what you want is to help us clear this all up as quickly and quietly as possible."

"Yes, yes, of course. Naturally. I, um, would it be all right if your people used the deliveries entrance?"

"Of course," said Pete blandly. "We certainly don't want to alarm your guests."

"Thank you, Detective. I'll, um, I'll go and tell my brother, and my mother, and our day manager, and . . ."

"Officer Freeman will go with you," said Pete. "To help with the explanations."

"After you, Mr. Hilde." Kenisha stepped back. Mr. Hilde slicked his hair back one more time but let himself be escorted back up toward the grand white hotel that towered over the river's bend.

Pete sighed and glanced through his notebook. "Okay, Mr. and Mrs. Luce, Miss Britton. I think we got what we need for now. There will probably be more questions later, once we know what we're dealing with here. Jake, Miranda, you two try to take it easy, all right? Miss Britton." He nodded at me, and he did not look entirely happy. I couldn't blame him. We'd met over a dead body once before. Probably the detective did not like coincidences. I could completely sympathize.

"Come along, Anna," said Julia.

I did, and so did Grandma B.B., of course. I was pretty sure Alistair was already gone in his own kind of way.

But I also looked back over my shoulder, and I saw Miranda slip her arm through Jake's. I also saw Pete Simmons watching us all leave.

I shivered then, hard.

❖ I KNEW JULIA was upset. I expected I was going to get called onto the carpet as soon as we got to her apartment and closed the door against prying (and police) ears.

Turns out I was wrong. Julia wasn't upset. She was livid.

Julia's apartment is a converted loft above Midnight Reads. The large front room is furnished with a magnificent collection of Victorian furniture and art glass paperweights, most of them spherical. Yes, in fact, Julia Parris, head of the guardian coven of Portsmouth, has a collection of crystal balls. She keeps them on ornate stands spaced among her magnificent collection of dachshund-themed knickknacks, which cover every surface that isn't otherwise occupied, mainly with books.

As soon as we reached the living room, Julia sat in her mahogany and gold velveteen chair by the fireplace with both hands folded on top of her walking stick and both dachshunds at her feet. There was a china cup and saucer on the round table beside her.

Grandma B.B. sat down on one end of the sofa. A matching

cup waited on the oval coffee table. I sat down on the sofa, too, and tried not to be nervous. It didn't work.

"Now, Anna," Julia began.

"Yip!" interrupted Leo. Max was already trotting toward the window.

We all looked, of course. Between the cream-colored lace curtains, we saw Alistair, pacing on the sill outside.

"Merow?" His questioning voice vibrated through the pane. Julia's home was magically warded, so it was one of the few spaces where Alistair couldn't just pop in.

Julia sighed and rolled her eyes toward the ceiling, looking for patience. "Very well. Let him in."

I unlatched the window. As soon as I pushed up the sash and screen, Alistair flowed onto the carpet. Max and Leo, of course, had to sniff around his ankles and belly. Alistair tolerated this for a surprising length of time.

"Sorry, Julia." I sat back down on the sofa. Alistair immediately jumped up onto my lap and hunkered down out of reach of Max and Leo, who yipped a few times in complaint. Alistair yawned and started washing his whiskers at them.

"Now, Anna," repeated Julia firmly, and the words could have been chipped out of ice. "You will explain to me *exactly* what you were doing at Miranda and Jake's."

"You did have us worried, dear," murmured Grandma B.B. "But I'm sure it wasn't your fault."

"Oh, no," said Julia darkly. "None of this is Anna's fault."

"I wasn't doing anything!" I blurted out. "Well, nothing much . . ." There are few things worse than hearing yourself suddenly channeling your inner kindergartener. The fact that I really might have inched closer to my grandmother at that point did not make it any better.

"Nothing much," repeated Julia. "I see. Jake and Miranda just suggested that you all go for a stroll down a lost tunnel and you thought, 'Sure, why not?'"

"Julia," began Grandma. "The sarcasm is not—"

Julia held up her hand to cut Grandma B.B. off. "I'll

thank you to stay out of this, Annabelle." Leo and Max lifted their heads, noses and ears suddenly on the alert.

"She is my granddaughter," replied Grandma B.B. evenly. Alistair climbed up my front and onto the curving back of the sofa so he could come settle down behind my shoulders. I pulled him back down and held on to him. He tolerated this, although both dachshunds watched us suspiciously.

"Yes, Anna is your granddaughter, but she has taken an oath as my apprentice," said Julia flatly. "She has sworn to abide by the rules *I* set."

"And of course there could not possibly be extenuating circumstances," murmured Grandma.

Alistair jumped out of my arms and instead head butted Grandma's elbow, but Grandma B.B. resolutely refused to pay attention. She also didn't seem to notice that both the dachshunds had moved closer to Julia and raised their ears and tails.

"The extenuating circumstances are what we're trying to determine," Julia said with that slow and careful patience that comes when you need to clarify something that ought to be perfectly obvious. "*If* you're finished interrupting."

"I wouldn't have to interrupt if you were ready to listen to *my granddaughter* with an open mind."

"This is not about *your granddaughter*—"

"Okay, okay!" I held up both hands. Clearly, my earlier hopes for a speedy reconciliation between these two were a tad bit premature. "Grandma, it's all right. Julia . . . I really wasn't doing any magic. Jake and Miranda thought their new building might be haunted." I tried to sound nonchalant, but nonchalant is very hard to pull off when you're talking about the possibility of ghosts. "Well, Jake did anyway, and they wanted me to . . . give it the once-over for a Vibe."

"But, Anna, dear!" murmured Grandma. "Opening your mind without proper preparation, you could let in all *kinds* of unwanted influences—"

She didn't get any further. Julia spoke softly, but the words went through me with more force than any shout ever could. "You did this after you swore an oath that you would not use your magic without supervision and permission?"

"I wasn't actually using magic," I muttered, but even Alistair was giving me the fish-eye. "The Vibe was so strong in there, I was having trouble keeping it out."

"What do I have to do to convince you that your ability to receive and interpret vibrations is your strongest magic?" Julia glowered, but not at me. This time her icy disapproval was entirely for Grandma B.B. "It is the magic of your heritage and your spirit. You have only just begun to actively attempt to control it, and you don't know what it will do to you or cause you to do. None of us do. That is why we must proceed carefully."

"But Jake and Miranda needed help," I said, and, yes, I did hear how limp that sounded. "They were arguing about it. I thought I could help if I just sort of took a quick peek, just to reassure them, because ghosts don't exist."

I waited for Julia, or Grandma B.B., to tell me I was right about that. They didn't. Instead, Julia turned a look of absolute shock and disbelief on my grandmother. Leo whined and pawed at Julia's ankles, but Max gave a low growl.

"We will return to that later." Julia picked Max up and laid him across her lap. "Regardless. Anna, you did not just take a quick peek." Julia gave those last three words a particularly tart twist. "You led two innocent people into a genuinely dangerous situation."

"I . . ." I started to say I did not, but I couldn't seem to finish my sentence. I looked to Grandma B.B. for help, but she was busy watching her own hands, which were knotted in her lap. Alistair butted her elbow again. She reached out and scooped him up against her stomach. The sight of my familiar doing his best to comfort my grandmother made something twist under my heart.

Julia thumped her cane once, jerking my attention back to her.

"You didn't think about what you were doing, did you?" she snapped. "You just followed your Vibe. You didn't stop to consider how unstable that tunnel must be. And despite my lessons and your own studies, you didn't think that this 'ghost' that Jake felt might be something dangerous or malevolent? You thought you could just dismiss *all* the warnings about negative energies and influences."

She was absolutely right about that last. I was still wrapping my head around the idea that there might be a real ghost at all. A malevolent ghost was a whole new level of creepy, and I was not ready to go there.

Alistair stopped trying to hold Grandma's attention and settled back onto my lap. He did not, however, take his attention off Max and Leo for even a split second.

"Did you even suggest that the three of you should wait until magical, if not physical, help could be brought in?" I swear Julia's eyes flashed—I mean really flashed, like Alistair's did in the dark.

"No," I admitted. Now that Julia said it out loud, I felt very cold. I was sure I had at least thought about telling Jake and Miranda we should wait and get help, but the truth was, the whole event was turning into one big blur inside me. The only emotion that held steady was that overwhelming sense of wanting to know what was down there. Nothing else had seemed quite as important. Not even when I saw how easily the dirt cascaded down from the walls, or the kind of shape those old support beams were in.

Miranda had been the only one sounding a real note of caution. In fact, she hadn't wanted to go at all. I could have backed her up. I could have put my foot down and said none of us should go at all. But I didn't. I'd wanted to uncover all the secrets.

"Julia, you don't need to be quite that dramatic," said Grandma B.B. "Look at her face. You're scaring her half to death."

"Good!" Julia thumped her cane again and we all jumped, including the dachshunds. "She should be scared. Maybe it will teach her a lesson."

"Julia. This is *not* Anna's fault."

"*This* is," shot back Julia. "Now, as for the rest of it—"

"What do you mean the rest of it?" snapped Grandma, but Julia ignored her.

"I mean all the rest of it. Jake and Miranda could have been killed. Your granddaughter, Annabelle, could have been killed. Not that you've ever evidenced any genuine concern about her well-being when it comes to her magic—"

Grandma shot to her feet. "How *dare* you!"

"How dare *you*!"

The dachshunds had gone very still. Alistair tensed, and I felt the lightest prickling of claws through my jeans.

"Grandma, Julia—" I tried, but that's as far as I got.

"You have no right to say I do not care about my granddaughter, you old prune!" shouted Grandma.

"Don't I?" replied Julia coldly. "You ran away, Annabelle. You broke your promises and abandoned your responsibilities. You did not even test your granddaughter for her abilities. You let her *suffer* for most of her life under the delusion that she had a mental illness!"

Grandma said nothing. Two bright spots of color appeared in her cheeks.

"We would not be having this problem now if you'd taught and trained Anna properly. She is your *family*. Your first duty was to tell her the truth about her heritage and you didn't. But now!" Julia threw up her hand. "Annabelle Blessingsound has changed her mind! Again! After all these years she says she has her granddaughter's best interests at heart, so it's all right and we should just trust her!"

"That's enough, Julia!" I felt Alistair tense to spring, and I grabbed hold of him before he did something we'd all regret.

"No, Anna," whispered Grandma B.B., and her voice shook from the force of everything she was holding in. "She's right. She's just . . . right."

Grandma ran from the room. Before I could get to my feet, the door was slammed shut behind her.

I had no idea she could still move like that.

"Grandma!" Alistair blinked out as I jumped up to hurry after her.

"Not yet, Anna," said Julia.

I stopped with my hand on the doorknob. Alistair reappeared down by my heels, putting himself between me and the dachshunds. The dogs growled. My cat stretched lazily, incidentally displaying the fact that he was longer than either one of them, not to mention more massive than the two of them put together.

"Julia, do not do this," I said, and I was a little surprised at how even my voice stayed. "I know you're hurt and angry about what happened back in the day. Maybe I'm angry, too, but she's my grandmother. Don't make me choose between you. You won't like the way it goes."

"That is up to you," said Julia softly. "But I ask you to consider, Anna, there are very serious reasons an apprentice witch takes her oath. Magic not only affects the people around you, Anna; it affects *you*. It can cloud your judgment and interfere with your ability to reason. Proper preparation is essential before undertaking any magical working. You must be focused and grounded, or you risk being swept away by your own spell." She paused, but she was a long way from finished. "If nothing else, I would have thought you'd show some concern for Alistair."

"Alistair?"

"Merr-oww-oow," muttered my familiar, to the dachshunds and to Julia and just maybe to me.

"Alistair wasn't in danger," I stammered. "He could have, just . . . you know . . . popped out if there was real trouble."

Julia shook her head. "Not if he was hurt, and not if you were still down there and in danger. Familiars have long lives, and a cat may have nine of them, but Alistair is not immortal. He can be trapped, and he can be seriously hurt, even killed."

I should have known that, but I didn't, and I didn't like knowing it now.

Julia correctly interpreted my silence as understanding. "Now," she said. "I expect there are a few things you have to say to Annabelle, and things you need to decide."

"I'm sorry," I breathed.

"I hope we will be able to talk about this again," she told me quietly. "But whatever decision you make, it is yours, and I do understand."

I left then, and quickly. Because I didn't want to think about how I saw the tears standing out in my mentor's bright, hard eyes.

❧ 8 ❧

🐾 WHEN I GOT outside, I found Grandma sitting in the driver's seat of the Galaxie. She had her filmy scarf in both hands, but she wasn't doing anything except staring at it.

I climbed into the passenger seat. Alistair appeared between us.

"Merow?" He head butted Grandma's elbow. It didn't work this time either.

I tried putting my hand on her shoulder. "Are you okay, Grandma?"

"No," she said quietly. "No, Anna, I don't think I am."

"Julia shouldn't have talked to you like that."

"But she should have." Grandma wound the scarf around her hands so tightly that for a minute I thought she was going to tear it in two. "That's the problem. She was right, about everything. I did run away. I didn't follow the first duty of a witch who has children. She *must* tell those children. She has to teach them at least enough that they won't accidently harm themselves or the people around them."

"But you didn't know I'd inherited the magic. I never told you."

"Merow," added Alistair.

"Thank you, Anna. Thank you, Alistair." She patted my hand distractedly. "But I'm afraid that's no excuse. I had plenty of opportunities while you were growing up to find out. I didn't take any of them and I ignored the signs I did see."

My mouth went dry. Alistair climbed into my lap and turned in an uneasy circle. "You . . . you saw signs?"

Grandma nodded and smoothed the scarf across her knee, only to bunch it up between her hands again. "I told myself I was imagining things. Your father was so very determinedly nonmagical, I came to believe none of you could have inherited any talent through him."

"Why didn't you say something?"

"Because Julia was right about something else," she whispered. "I am a coward."

"You are not! Grandma B.B., you are one of the bravest people I know!"

"No, I'm not. I, well, facing highway robbers is one thing, but my own family? That's something else altogether. I couldn't stand up to my mother during the feud, and then, when your father . . ." She swallowed. "When I tried to tell him about . . . things . . . he got so angry he threatened to cut me off from you four completely if I ever brought up witchcraft where you could hear it."

What was I going to say to that?

"It wasn't his fault." Grandma unwound the scarf and wound it back up again. "I waited too long, and I handled it badly. I had nothing ready to show him as proof. He's so hardheaded, so practical . . . And the thought of losing touch with you and your brothers and sister . . . it was too much. So, I told myself that the magic must have ended with me. Or that if any of you really were talented, I would of course see it, or he would change his mind eventually. I told myself so many things I can't remember them all." She wiped her eyes. "But it all came down to the same thing. I would accept any nonsense as long as it would keep me from having to confront my son with what I knew to be the truth. I ran away from it. Just like I ran away from my home rather than confront Mother with her own outdated attitudes toward the true craft.

"But the worst part is knowing now that you suffered for what I did."

My throat tightened up and tears pressed hard against the backs of my eyes. I had no idea what to say or what to feel. My Vibe had given me a lot of bad times. I had thought I was crazy, a lot. I had lost friends when I was a kid. I had grown up scared and I'd spent a lot of time trying to hide or suppress who I was. I had been angry about it. Maybe I still was. But something else was true too.

I took Grandma B.B. by both shoulders and turned her to face me. "Listen to me," I said. "You are the best grandmother I could have asked for. You gave us all fantastic adventures when we were kids. When Mom got sick . . . you were there, Grandma. You helped keep us all together and showed us we could still count on each other, no matter what. You got Hope to come to the hospital and say goodbye when none of us could even get her out of her room." I pulled the scarf out of her hands and laid it down. Alistair, very helpfully, sat himself on top of it. "I don't know if that was witchcraft, and honestly, I don't care. I've always been glad that whoever hands out grandmothers gave you to me, and there's nothing and nobody that's going to change my mind about that. I love you, Grandma B.B."

She looked up at me, her eyes shining. "And I love you, Anna."

We hugged, of course. We hugged for a very long time.

"Do you want to go back upstairs?" I asked when we finally separated. "Maybe we can talk to Julia—"

"Merow," said Alistair. At some point, he'd slipped out from between us to perch on the seat back.

"Yes, I think you're right, Alistair." Grandma rubbed my cat's ears. "We should give her—all of us—a chance to cool off first." She fished her keys out of her bucket of a handbag. "Julia always did have *quite* the temper."

She started the engine and worked the choke, clutch and gearshift.

"So," I said, gathering Alistair onto my lap. "What's the story about the nightclub?"

But Grandma B.B. just smiled mysteriously and eased her land yacht into traffic.

WHEN WE PULLED into the cottage's narrow driveway, it was to find Valerie McDermott standing on the front porch with a big Tupperware container balanced on her hip.

"Kenisha called," Val said by way of explanation as she gave me a one-armed hug. "I'm so sorry, Anna."

"Thanks," I said. "You brought food, didn't you?"

"I always bring food. Roger's apple muffins, made with your apples."

My cottage came with a huge, beautiful garden, and that garden came with two ancient apple trees. The fruit was almost too tart to eat out of hand, but it made the best pastries. Val's husband, Roger, was a terrific cook and had been more than happy to trade baked goods for the lion's share of my fruit harvest. In fact, he'd been setting up a table at the local farmers' market to sell the extras and sock the money into what he called the Baby Fund. Val said he'd started talking about a Web site and delivery.

After a pause so Val could text Roger and assure him that I had come home and everything was still fine, we all trooped through to the kitchen. Except for the stove and the fridge, the cottage's kitchen had never been modernized. It still had the deep, enamel farmhouse sink, the built-in breakfast nook with its window that looked over the garden. Old-school rag rugs covered the scuffed wooden floor. Alistair, who hated car rides, had gotten home on his own. Now he was stretched out on the windowsill in the breakfast nook with the afternoon sun shining on his furry back.

"I expected you back sooner," said Val as she opened one of the glass-fronted cabinets and pulled down a plate for the muffins.

"We should have been." I filled the kettle and put it on

the stove. "We had to stay downtown because Julia wanted to talk."

Val raised her eyebrows at me and Grandma B.B. "Talk?"

"I used my Vibe without permission."

"Uh-oh."

"Yeah," I agreed. "I kind of got read the riot act. The worst part is, I deserved it."

"Don't be too hard on yourself, dear." Grandma started pulling my mismatched collection of mugs from the junk shop . . . er . . . consignment store out of their cupboard. Alistair stretched and got up off the windowsill to stick his face into Grandma B.B.'s purse, probably looking for more nibbles. "I got the same lecture, more or less, when I started practicing formally."

"I just wanted to help," I murmured as I reached for the can where I stored the peppermint tea. I'd started drying some of the herbs from the garden, and the results were surprisingly good. Normally, at a time like this, I would have fired up the coffeemaker, but Val was off caffeine until the baby was born, so it was going to be peppermint tea all around. These are the sacrifices demanded of genuine friendship.

"When you discover the magic is real, it's hard not to use it," Val said. I couldn't help noticing how she'd suddenly gotten very busy arranging muffins on the plate. Alistair turned his attention from Grandma's purse to poke a curious nose toward the baked treats.

"Down, cat." I lifted Alistair and put him on the floor. He looked up at me, deeply affronted. He also climbed back up to the bench, and the windowsill, and the table.

"Oh, Alistair." Grandma sighed and lifted him down onto the floor.

"Merow," he said sulkily, and climbed back onto the bench, and the windowsill, and the table.

"At least you were trying to do some good, Anna," said Val. "Some of us didn't do quite so well."

I paused, both hands full of a grumbling Alistair. "Don't tell me you—"

"Oh, yeah." Valerie nodded. "I think everybody does. I just . . . well, I had my own reasons. I was a different person then. At least, I hope I was."

Val never talked much about her life before she joined the coven. She didn't talk about her family at all. The people who came to her baby shower had all been Portsmouth friends. No parents or brothers and sisters—or any relations, actually—had turned up either at the party or at the house to offer to help. Or at least, if they had, Valerie hadn't said anything about it.

The kettle whistle cut off any further conversation for the moment. I put my cat down and went to fill the pot and bring it to the table.

"So, are you going to tell me what happened?" asked Val, as soon as all the teacups had been distributed and everybody had helped herself to a muffin. Alistair had finally got the hint and had curled up on my lap instead of on the table.

Of course, that was when the doorbell rang.

❧ 9 ❧

🐾 "SORRY," I SAID to the room in general. Alistair grumbled and thumped to the floor as I got up to go answer the door.

It was Sean McNally.

"I heard," Sean said by way of greeting and explanation. "I was on my way in for my shift, and I wanted to stop by and make sure you were okay." He raised the cardboard tray he held. "I brought coffee."

"Young" Sean McNally is one of the bartenders down at the Pale Ale, the tavern and restaurant where my friend Martine Devereaux works as executive chef. He's a wiry man, about five years younger and ten inches taller than me with sandy hair and a neatly trimmed beard and a smile that's pretty much guaranteed to charm the socks off the susceptible. I am, of course, not one of those.

"Thanks, Sean," I said. "But I'm fine, really. Do you want to come in?"

"Thanks." Sean ducked automatically as he came through the door, like tall guys tend to do. He also took off the very snazzy two-tone fedora he was wearing.

Grandma looked up as we came into the kitchen. Alistair was sitting on the table getting his ears scritched and washing what might just have been muffin crumbs off his whiskers.

"Sean!" announced Val. "What a surprise!"

Sean had been the subject of a lot of (pointless and unnecessary) speculation since I got to Portsmouth. Some of my friends seemed to think there was something special in the way he looked at me and in how he brought me coffee when he found out I was having a bad day, and how he and his dad, Old Sean, came around to fix the loose boards on my porch without being asked and without accepting payment. Some entirely misguided people might have even believed this was all a sign that he would like to take me out.

I didn't believe this. Even if I did, I wouldn't actually consider it. Yes, Sean is very nice, and I will admit (in a completely objective way), he's cute, and a snappy dresser and fun to be around, and a good listener. But since a little incident involving my last boyfriend and a nineteen-year-old blond from Vegas who showed up at our door at three in the morning, I'd sworn off dating for good. Val knew that. I'd certainly told her often enough.

"Hi, Val." Sean set the tray of coffee down next to the muffin plate and held out his hand to my grandmother. "And you must be Grandma B.B."

"And you have to be Sean McNally." Grandma B.B. clasped his hand in both of hers. "You look exactly like your father, although I will say, I knew him when he was somewhat younger."

"Apparently Grandma babysat half of Portsmouth," I told Sean. "So, if you want the good dirt on any old kids' stuff, I'd be very nice to her."

"*Anna.* You know I do not indulge in gossip."

I looked at Sean and Val. Sean and Val looked at me. We all nodded gravely and did not smile.

"Apple muffin?" I pushed the plate toward Sean. "Roger's finest."

"If I'm not butting in . . ."

"I'm sure you're not," said Grandma promptly. "Anna

was just about to tell us what happened to her this morning. Please sit down." To emphasize this, Val scooted over on the bench to make room.

"If it's okay?" said Sean to me.

"Sure, but only because you brought coffee." I tried to smile to let him know I was joking and that, yes, I really was okay with his being here. The only problem was, I didn't entirely mean it. I couldn't tell, though, if that was because I didn't actually want to talk about this morning or because of all the amused and meaningful glances Grandma and Val kept shooting at each other.

Sean, though, decided to take me at my word and settled onto the empty space Valerie made on the bench. Alistair curled around Sean's ankles a couple of times before jumping back up onto my lap.

Sean took a muffin, and I opened a coffee. I may have felt some petty satisfaction in the way Valerie inhaled the forbidden aroma of perfectly roasted beans.

"So, Anna," said Val pointedly over the rim of her teacup. "You were going to tell us what happened?"

I was. And I did. If I did it while awkwardly breaking my muffin into pieces, I think that's understandable.

I will say that muffin was delicious and perfectly baked, with cinnamon streusel on top, because Roger McDermott is that kind of guy.

I told them about Jake's certainty that the old drugstore was haunted. I glossed over the part my Vibe played because Sean was here. But when I got to the part about the steel door at the end of the tunnel, and the body in the dirt pile right beside it, a very uncomfortable look crossed Sean's face.

"Did . . . How long did it look like he—it—had been there?"

I shook my head. "Pete Simmons said it was probably a week. Why?"

"Something my father said." In addition to being a handyman and a bartender the senior McNally was Irish down to his little toenail, which meant he had the gift of the blarney and the love of a fine story, to be sure. "I actually had been kind of wondering—"

"Don't tell me you came here with ulterior motives?" I raised both eyebrows at him.

"No. Well. Kinda. Maybe. Do you mind?" Sean pulled out his phone. We all nodded for him to go ahead, so he hit a speed-dial button and waited while it rang.

"Yeah, hi, Dad," said Sean when the voice on the other end of the line answered. "No, everything's fine. I just had a question. That guy from the hotel you said walked off the job about a week ago? Did anybody ever hear what happened to him?" He listened. "Yeah, okay, thanks." Sean hung up.

"A guy from the hotel?" I prompted. Alistair's purring had stopped, and he oozed out of my lap, in that spineless way cats have, to sit bolt upright on the windowsill. "As in the Harbor's Rest?"

"Yeah," said Sean, turning his coffee cup around a few times on the tabletop. "Dad does a little bartending there and helps with the drinks ordering. They like him because he can track down some unusual spirits that their guests enjoy. Anyway, Dad told me there was a huge stink maybe a week ago when this guy, Jimmy Upton, didn't show for work. He was the sous chef in the hotel kitchen, and one night he just ups and vanishes after his shift and doesn't come back. Not even on payday."

Val whistled.

"Well, we shouldn't jump to conclusions," said Grandma, but it was too late. Everybody at that table, except Alistair, had worked an odd job or three. We all knew nobody would leave that last paycheck hanging if they could possibly help it.

"Jake thought the tunnel ended at the hotel," I said. "So did Pete Simmons."

"But Dale said he didn't know anything about the tunnel," said Grandma. "My goodness, he looks exactly like Gretchen."

"You're on a first-name basis with Old Mrs. Hilde?" said Sean. "Wow."

"Don't tell me you babysat her, too?" I put in.

"Babysat Gretchen Hilde? Oh, good heavens, no. We graduated the same year from high school and we always spent the summers together when we were all home from college. Although, for a while, she thought . . . Well, that's neither here nor there. The point is, how could this Jimmy Upton find a hidden tunnel that Dale Hilde, whose family has owned the hotel since it opened, didn't know about?" Unless they were all lying.

"That's a good question," said Valerie. "You don't suppose—"

Her cell phone buzzed, cutting off her question. Val sighed and pulled the phone out to check the caller ID.

"Roger," she said, to the phone and to us, as she hit the Accept button. "Yes, darling, I'm still here. Yes, everything is just fine. And everybody loves the muffins." She looked toward us and we all nodded in confirmation. "Yes, I will be completely fine while you go talk to Archie Walsh about catering the dinner." "Baby Fund," she mouthed at us. "Yes, I promise. Yes. Yes . . . you are and I love you anyway." She hung up and sighed. "I need to get back and mind the store." She rubbed her tummy. "Come on, baby girl."

Sean got to his feet and picked up his hat. "I've got to get going, too, or I'll be late for my shift at the Pale Ale. Walk you out, Val?"

"No, that's okay, I'm going out the back. But you can help me up." She held out her hand so Sean could pull her to her feet. "See you tomorrow night, Anna?"

I had a magic lesson scheduled tomorrow, and Julia always insisted on at least one other coven member being there to help cast the ritual circle and enforce the wards. Usually, that person was Val.

I agreed she'd see me and Val left by the kitchen door and headed across the garden to the back gate at a healthy clip. Alistair, apparently having picked up some of Roger's nervousness, ducked under the table. In the next eyeblink, he was outside, trotting along behind Val like a furry gray shadow.

"I'll walk you out," I said to Sean, partly to distract him

from Alistair's Cheshire cat imitation. "Back in a sec, Grandma."

When we got to the front door, though, Sean paused and turned his fedora over in his hands a few times. "Are you sure you're all right, Anna?"

"Yes, I'm sure," I told him. "Thanks for coming by, though, and bringing the coffee."

"You'll call if you need anything?"

"I will. I promise."

Sean settled his hat back on his head, snapped the brim down like Marlon Brando in *Guys and Dolls* and flashed me a smile just before he walked away. I won't say anything melted inside, although maybe there was a slight softening around certain emotional edges. Not that it was at all significant. There was absolutely no need for Alistair to make an appearance at that moment.

"Merow?" my cat inquired.

"Don't you start in on me, too," I snapped. I also turned on my heel and headed into the kitchen without looking back.

❧ 10 ❧

❧ IT WAS A long night.

Alistair curled up on my chest and let me scratch his ears as I lay awake in bed staring at the ceiling. I kept telling myself that whatever had happened to the man—who was probably Jimmy Upton—down in that tunnel must have been some kind of tragic accident. That roof was not stable. It had collapsed. It was sad, and of course I was upset, but when it came down to it, the whole thing was now in the hands of the police, which was where it belonged. The corpse, and its history, was not my problem. My problem was my mentor was mad at me. Well, that was one of my problems. Another problem was that the coffee shop where I was supposed to paint the murals, which were supposed to bring in the money I needed to start paying rent so I could keep living in this house I had fallen in love with, was now classified as a crime scene. Yes, I had other possibilities out there, including a chance at one of those adult coloring books that had gotten so popular, but I had no idea when, or if, any of them were going to come through. My only solid offer at the moment had been from Jake and Miranda.

I rolled over on my side and tried staring at the wall. Alistair obligingly curled up in the hollow by my tummy. I did not want to be awake. I wanted to be asleep. If I was asleep, I could stop thinking about how I was in the middle of yet another mystery and it was all because of my magic. Again.

"Maybe we'd be better off trying somewhere else," I murmured to Alistair. "Someplace quiet, or maybe noisier, but definitely with fewer witches and stuff."

Alistair uncurled himself and pressed his head under my chin.

"Merow," he informed me. He also jumped over onto the pillow.

"I know, I know." I sighed. Portsmouth had become comfortable in a lot of ways. I had made so many good friends. I wanted to be here when Val's baby was born. I wanted to decorate the cottage for Halloween. I wanted to invite my family up for Christmas and be there when Martine threw her New Year's party. Those were always an event and a half.

But the life I was leading here came with a lot of strings, and upsets, and people I really was not sure about. Did I want to stay in the middle of it all?

I didn't know, but there was one thing I was absolutely sure about.

"I'd take you with me, big guy," I said as I rolled over onto my back again. "No matter what."

Alistair licked my cheek and snuggled into the hollow above my shoulder so he was purring right into my ear.

That, weirdly, was when I was finally able to go to sleep.

WHEN I WOKE up the next morning, the sun was shining in through the window, the birds were singing in the trees and my left ear was numb from having a cat purr in it all night. But not so numb that I couldn't hear the sound of dishes and glasses clinking down below.

Grandma B.B. was already up and about. I showered and pulled on my jeans and my favorite sweatshirt, which was

covered with colorful squiggles and the words LIFE'S TOO
SHORT TO COLOR INSIDE THE LINES, and headed downstairs
to the kitchen.

"Good morning, dear!" said Grandma. "I've been rum-
maging. I hope you don't mind."

"Of course not." The coffeemaker was going, and the
carton of orange juice was on the table alongside a plate of
toast and the remaining apple muffins. Alistair was eating
something from his bowl by the back door that looked suspiciously like tuna.

Grandma saw my frown. "Yes, I know, dear, he should
be having cat food, but I thought, as a special treat, just this
once."

"I'm going to have to get that cat a gym membership." I
poured us both mugs of coffee.

"Have you got plans for today, Anna?" she asked me.

I sighed. I also looked over at the calendar I'd hung on
the wall by the old landline phone. I'd bought it specifically
so I could circle the twenty-third in red and write *LEASE
UP* in the middle of the day's square.

That red-letter day was arriving in less than two weeks,
and my only current clients had just found a dead body
practically under their floor, and my grandmother and my
magical mentor had had a shouting match instead of the
touching reunion I'd been hoping for.

"Is this what it's going to be like if I stay?" I murmured,
but not softly enough, because Grandma glanced at me
sharply.

"Well, I don't exactly know what you mean by 'this,'
dear," she said. "But it's never going to be entirely easy.
When you care for others, it never is."

I hung my head. "Maybe I don't want to care so much."

"I think you'd find not caring much more difficult, not to
mention much lonelier."

"Do you ever regret leaving Portsmouth, Grandma?"

Grandma B.B. was silent for a long time. "That's a complicated question. I have had such a good life. My time with
your grandfather, my children and grandchildren and now

the next generation coming along . . . How could I possibly regret any of that? I've seen so much, and there's so much more . . . But I do very much regret how I left."

I stared out the window like I was looking for answers in the autumn-faded flower beds.

"Would you like to go outside?" Grandma B.B. said. "You did promise to show me the garden."

"Sounds great," I told her, grateful for a chance to put off answering her question about my plans. She probably knew that, too. It's the sort of thing grandmothers pick up on.

I swapped my slippers for the old pair of Keds I keep by the kitchen door. I carried the plate of muffins and toast out, and Grandma followed with the coffee cups into the crisp morning.

The garden was sheltered by stout privacy fences and thick beds of flowers and herbs. Purple and gold asters stood out defiantly above the rest of the spiky brown stems. The two apple trees stood guard by the back gate that led to Val and Roger's bed-and-breakfast. Their leaves had already started to turn gold, even though there was still a pretty healthy crop of red fruit on the branches—and on the ground. The real showpiece, though, was the spiral walkway. It wound through the center of the lawn and was lined with curving flower beds. At the very center, where another garden might have had a statue or a fishpond, mine had a covered fire pit.

Closer to the house, there was a little flagstone terrace with a suite of white wicker furniture. I set the muffins on the table and settled myself into one of the chairs. I breathed in the scents of fall and mint and sun-warmed apples and instantly felt better. Alistair prowled the perimeter, looking for threats, stray birds or escaped K.T. Nibbles.

"So, Anna." Grandma handed me a coffee mug. "You were going to tell me about your plans for today."

I should have known the subject was not going to stay dropped. I sighed, drank some coffee and took a bite of muffin. What I really needed to do was get out here with shears and a trowel and probably some burlap or something.

At the very least, I needed to go to the library and find some gardening books, so I'd know how to put the place to bed for the winter.

"Anna?" prompted Grandma. "You were saying?"

No, I wasn't, but I also wasn't getting out of it. "Well, I should probably check in on Jake and Miranda. They were pretty upset about what happened yesterday."

"And who can blame them?"

Not me, that was for sure. I took another sip of coffee. "This is not exactly the homecoming I planned on for you, Grandma."

"Oh, don't worry about me, dear. I'll be fine."

"But you and Julia—"

"*That* is between me and Julia," she said firmly. "Did I ever tell you about the time your grandfather and I were in Manila?"

"Which time?"

"This would have been, oh, let me see"—Grandma's nails clinked as she drummed them against her mug—"seventy-nine, I think. Well, we were staying in a marvelous little hotel, but your grandfather got the idea that we should see more of the actual country, and, he decided, the way to do that was by bicycle.

"Well, I thought he was crazy, but once Charlie got an idea stuck in his head, there was no getting it out. He went out the next morning and came back with two of the most battered bikes you have ever seen. But he borrowed some tools from somewhere and got them fixed up, and we loaded what we had into the baskets and off we went! My!" She shook her head, her eyes distant with memory and emotion. "There we were, a couple of sunburned strangers, bumping along over these narrow dirt roads; we must have been an *incredible* sight. Word went ahead, and we'd come to these little villages, just clusters of houses, and people started to come out and wave at the Cycling Americans! Little children ran beside us and laughed and cheered and people started just *giving* us food and water. It was the most wonderful thing. And then the *rain*! Oh, my word! You've never seen anything like it. The only way not to be damp for a week was to strip everything off and stash it in the rucksacks until the storm passed, and then—"

"Grandma?"

"Yes, dear?"

"You can stop now." Because no one wants to picture their grandmother and grandfather sitting in the altogether in a tropical rainstorm.

She beamed at me. "The *point*, dear, is I have been in far less comfortable circumstances than this and survived."

"I know, Gran, I know. I just . . ." I swirled my coffee and watched the waves rise and fall. "I thought it would all look better in the morning. But here it is morning, and it all still looks like too much."

"Eat some breakfast, Anna. You'll sort the rest of it out. You always do."

It was pure Grandma-style reassurance, and I couldn't help smiling at it. We sat in silence, nibbling toast and drinking coffee and following our own thoughts in comfortable silence. Unfortunately, my thoughts refused to stay in the strictly comfortable places.

"Grandma?"

"Yes, dear?"

"Why'd you really know who Dale Hilde was? I can't believe he looked that much like your old high school gal pal."

Grandma blushed. I waited. Alistair apparently decided the garden was free of outside menaces and birds, and that rabbit that would not take the hint and leave the parsley alone. He jumped back up on the table and sat bolt upright with his tail curled around his feet. This time I did not tell him to get down.

"Oh, dear." Grandma sighed. "Old habits do die hard, don't they? Well. I think I told you, back when you first called to tell me you'd . . . discovered about the family and the true craft, that when we Blessingsounds practice magic, we tend to become seers."

Seers are, literally, witches who have a magical talent for

seeing things beyond the everyday. There are a lot of variations on this. I could see via my Vibe, of course, but I also apparently had a facility for a form of clairvoyance called automatic writing. Grandma had her own specialties.

"You told me you read palms," I reminded her.

"Yes. Well, as you know by now, the true craft is seldom anything like the popular imagination. 'Reading' palms"— she paused and made the air quotes—"has very little to do with interpreting the lines on the hand, although it *can*, of course, but that's a very imprecise, and a rather showy—"

"Grandma?"

"Yes, dear?"

"What did you do yesterday to Dale Hilde?" And to Miranda, and, just maybe, to me.

"I didn't do anything *to* him, dear. I just did something . . . near him."

"Grandma . . ."

She sighed. "Really, Anna. I'm *trying* to explain. My talent is very close to yours, only instead of gaining impressions from places, I get mine from people. It takes time and concentration to do anything *properly*, of course, and I only had an instant, but I did pick up some little scraps of intuition. Of course, I did know Gretchen Hilde back in the day. So, when I saw a man with a hotel jacket *and* heard that detective call him Mr. Hilde, *and* remembered hearing that Gretchen had children." She paused. "She also had a lot of trouble with their father, I understand . . ."

"Grandma," I said firmly. She blinked. So did Alistair. It was kind of spooky.

"I'm sorry, dear. I'm rambling. *Anyway.* Since I knew all that, I sort of had a running jump. I was able to pick up on a few very brief impressions. Dale was very worried about what his mother was going to say about this whole mess. Also, his brother. His sister was not going to be too pleased either." Grandma paused. "Anna?"

"Yeah, Grandma?"

"Close your mouth, dear. You'll catch flies."

I closed my mouth, but not for very long.

"That's what you did to Miranda, too, wasn't it? You did a reading on her?"

"I probably shouldn't have, but she was so very upset that I wanted to find out if I might be able to help." She gave me a meaningful look. "The need to help is a very powerful instinct, isn't it?"

"Yeah, I guess it is." I swirled my coffee again. Before I could ask my next question, though, Alistair surged to his feet, all his attention pointed toward the side gate.

"Merow!" he announced.

A second later, the gate rattled.

"Hello?" called a man's voice. A heartbeat later, the top of his head and a pair of bright blue eyes peered over the gate. "Anna? You home?"

It was Frank Hawthorne—editor, publisher and lead journalist for the *Seacoast News*.

He also happened to be my landlord.

11

🐾 "TO TELL YOU the truth, I thought you'd be here earlier," I told Frank as I opened the gate.

"Needed to check in at the office first." He held up a white
paper bag. "I brought doughnuts."

Word of my inability and/or unwillingness to cook had
quickly spread through my Portsmouth friends, and they
had rallied to the cause. Alistair wasn't the only one who
was going to need a gym membership real soon.

"Thank you." I took the bag. "Come join the party."

"Party?" Frank said as he followed me around the corner
of the cottage to the patio. He saw Grandma B.B. and pulled
up short.

"Frank, this is my grandmother Annabelle. Grandma
B.B., this is Frank Hawthorne."

"Oh, of course, Dorothy's nephew!" cried Grandma.
"How wonderful to meet you at last!" She shook his hand
with both of hers and I had to look away. I didn't feel any
telltale prickling, though.

Alistair head butted my shins as if to remind me of my
manners.

"Would you like to sit down?" I said to Frank. "There's coffee."

"Looks like I'm late with breakfast."

"Val was by yesterday." In fact, I was a little surprised she hadn't checked in over the fence this morning. It was still early for the leaf-peeping crowds, so the B and B wasn't very full. Val and I usually shared a cup of something in the morning. I found myself wondering if she'd gone into labor overnight and thinking maybe I should check in.

"Merow!" Alistair butted my shins again, reminding me that I had company and that Val would not appreciate it if it turned out I'd contracted Roger's hovering. Probably he was out delivering pastries to a business breakfast and she had to keep an eye on the B and B for the morning.

"I'll go get the coffee," said Grandma, and she headed into the kitchen.

"I take it you heard what happened at the new space for Northeast Java yesterday?" I said to Frank as we started setting the cake doughnuts out on the plate next to the muffins. They were still warm.

"'Fraid so. I really wanted to make sure you were all right, but, well . . ."

I didn't make him finish. "You're a journalist. I figured you'd want the story."

"Sorry. But, I didn't expect something for nothing. I thought you might want to know, they have positively identified the body you found."

"Jimmy Upton?" I said.

Frank froze with a doughnut halfway to the plate. "I thought you told Pete you didn't recognize the deceased."

"I didn't. Sean McNally's dad told him that Upton went missing from the hotel about a week ago."

"Oh, that's right. I'd forgotten Old Sean was working at Harbor's Rest." Frank set the last doughnut down on the little stack and pulled out his notebook. Frank took notes the way I doodled, constantly and on any available surface.

Grandma B.B. came back out with the coffeepot and an

extra mug, and I started to give Frank the details while he drank coffee and made notes. I could tell by the shift in his gaze that he knew I was leaving some stuff out. But Frank was a witch's nephew, and he'd seen my Vibe in action. I could trust him not to pry too far into those particular corners, at least not in his professional capacity.

"Do they know how the poor man died yet?" asked Grandma as she refilled Frank's cup. Frank is one of the world's more impressive coffee drinkers. He takes his black and hot and can polish off a whole mug in less time than it takes your average person to stir in the cream.

Frank shook his head. "If they do, they're not telling me. No comments on an ongoing investigation." He looked at me. "I don't suppose you saw anything obvious?"

"Don't be a ghoul."

He shrugged. "Occupational hazard." He also waited. I sighed.

"I didn't see much of anything. I mean, he was buried under a bunch of dirt and loose rock. I thought he must have gotten stuck in the tunnel when the roof caved in. Maybe he even loosened the beams when he was pounding on the door trying to call for help . . ." I shuddered. "Jake and Miranda said they'd been hearing banging noises."

"So awful," murmured Grandma.

"Yeah, it is," agreed Frank. "Jake and Miranda are good people. This is going to be hard on them."

"Do you know anything about Jimmy Upton, Frank?" I split a fresh doughnut in half and pretended to myself that I really would eat only the half I kept.

"Well, we did a write-up about him in the *Seacoast News* last year when we did our piece on the hotel's hundred and twenty-fifth anniversary. He was barely out of culinary school yet and he was already generating a ton of buzz."

Alistair rubbed his face against the back of my hand. I started scratching his ears distractedly. "Did he have any family?"

Frank shook his head. "There is a sister, somewhere, but

I couldn't find her. Jimmy kind of blew into town out of
nowhere. When I did the interview, he gave us a story about
how he'd been backpacking around Europe and working in
any kitchen where they'd be willing to teach him. Which
was great, and we printed it, but there wasn't anything in it
we could really verify. The few restaurants he actually
named mostly seemed to be closed."

"Did he say why he decided to come to Portsmouth?"
asked Grandma B.B. "For an ambitious young man, I would
have thought Boston or New York would be a more obvious
destination."

"I'd have to look it up to remember what he said exactly,
but it was something about wanting to be in a place that
wasn't overcrowded, where he'd have room to perfect his
craft."

"Sean's dad said the guy had attitude."

"Yes, he did." Frank reached for the pot and refilled his
mug. "And a boatload of charm to go with it."

"Dangerous combination," I said.

"Especially if someone's not afraid to use it," murmured
Grandma B.B.

We all thought about that. Judging from their expressions, Grandma and Frank didn't like their thoughts any
more than I liked mine. I looked at the plate. The half
doughnut I'd left there looked back at me. Okay, not really,
but it felt like it.

"Mm-mrp," snickered my cat. I ignored him and the
doughnut.

"What I want to know is what's on the other side of that
other door," I said. "If Jake and Miranda were hearing banging noises, somebody had to have heard them on the other
end, too."

"I can't say for sure yet, but from what I've picked up so
far, Jake was probably right. That other door pretty much
has to lead into the basement in the Harbor's Rest," said
Frank.

"That makes sense," I said. "Jake said something about

the tunnel probably being used by smugglers. I did some reading last night." It hadn't been all curling up in bed with the cat and trying to sleep. Some of it was curling up in bed with the cat and the laptop. "The building Jake and Miranda bought used to be a drugstore. During Prohibition, a lot of drugstores were fronts for selling alcohol."

"And since we're a harbor town, there was a whole lot of bootlegged liquor washing up in Portsmouth during that time," said Frank.

"Well, if the hotel and the drugstore were both open, it would make sense that the tunnel was used to move booze between them. Maybe it came off the boats in the marina and went to the hotel, and from there to the drugstore?"

"Or it could have flowed the other way," said Grandma B.B. thoughtfully. "There used to be a much bigger series of docks on the river, right along where Ceres Street is."

"It doesn't really matter," I said. "What matters is that Jimmy could have found the tunnel and gotten curious—and gotten stuck." Which would make it all an accident. A horrible, tragic accident, but that would still be much, much better than the alternative. I picked up the half doughnut, broke it in two and put half back.

"Anna, what is it? You've thought of something. It's written all over your face."

I wiped at my face. I couldn't help it. "Just remembering I didn't pick up more cat food," I mumbled as I popped the piece of doughnut in my mouth. Alistair raised his head immediately. "Sorry, big guy. Do you want a muffin, Frank? Roger made them." I pushed the plate toward him.

Frank probably had something to say, and not about the muffins. Fortunately for me, his phone buzzed in his jacket pocket. He looked apologetically at Grandma and pulled it out to answer.

"What'cha got?" he asked whoever was on the other end. There was a pause. "Yeah, yeah, okay."

He hung up and got to his feet. "Sorry. I've got to go. Mrs. Britton . . ."

"Grandma B.B.," she told him.

"Okay, Grandma B.B. Nice to finally meet you. Anna, we can talk later?"

I agreed we could. Grandma shook Frank's hands, and he showed himself out the gate. After all, it was his house.

"Now," said Grandma firmly. "What is it you thought of that you so very clearly did not want that nice young man to know?"

"That nice young man is my landlord and a journalist and already knows too much about . . . things."

"You're not answering my question."

Alistair circled my ankles a few times. "Merow," he informed me.

"Yeah, yeah," I muttered. "It's my Vibe, Grandma," I said slowly.

"What about it, dear?"

Yes, I really was having this conversation. With my grandmother. How long was it going to take to get used to this? "Julia . . ." Grandma's mouth tightened up immediately. I sighed. I also gave in and picked up the remaining piece of doughnut. "Anyway. It looks like when I get a Vibe from a building, what I'm doing is picking up the psychic echo of the strongest emotion trapped inside a place."

"That's close enough to begin with," Grandma admitted with frigid grace.

Darn it. Julia and Grandma B.B.'s relationship was clearly going to be a much bigger problem than I'd hoped. "Well, the last time I . . . got near someplace where somebody died, what I picked up on was their last emotions." That it had been in the cottage's basement was not something I felt like reminding either of us about. I was swearing off basements for the foreseeable future. "Anger and sadness, and all the rest of it."

"Yes, that would make sense. A person's last emotions would be very powerful."

"But I didn't feel anything like that in the tunnel," I said. "I didn't even know Jimmy Upton was there until I literally fell over him. All I had was this powerful impression of a secret, something that needed to be kept. There was nothing . . . nothing like a death."

"Which means Mr. Upton might have already been dead when someone put his body in that tunnel."

"When someone tried to bury his body in that tunnel," I corrected her. "Yeah."

"Oh, Anna. That's a *dreadful* idea."

I had to agree.

❧ 12 ❧

🐾 GRANDMA AND I were still contemplating the possibility of Jimmy Upton's being dead before someone stashed his body in the tunnel when the phone rang, but at a distance. This wasn't my cell, for a change, but the landline back in the kitchen. I started to my feet, surprised for a second. Then I hurried in to answer it, with Grandma B.B. right behind me.

This was not a surprise.

Alistair snaked nervously around my ankles as I picked up the receiver. "Hello?"

"Anna?" whispered the woman's voice on the end.

"Kenisha," I whispered back. "What's going on?"

"Frank Hawthorne was hanging around the station asking questions last night—"

"That's his job."

"Yeah, thank you, I know that, and I haven't got much time, so listen up, Anna. I'm assuming he told you it was Jimmy Upton you found in the tunnel?"

"Yeah, he did. What—?"

"Did he tell you Pete Simmons has started asking questions about you and Jake and Miranda?"

"No. He didn't get that far." Something I was going to have to take up with Frank later. Grandma was hovering next to me. I smiled at her with as much reassurance as I could muster. I don't think she believed me. I know Alistair didn't.

"Merow?" he told Grandma as he sat on my sneaker toes. "Merp."

"Yes, dear," murmured Grandma. "She always does."

I tried to ignore them.

"Pete's not happy you had holes in your story, Anna," Kenisha was saying. "You've got no good explanation why you were down in that tunnel or how you knew there was even a tunnel to be in."

"Uh-oh."

"Yeah, uh-oh," Kenisha agreed. "He's not really happy about Jake and Miranda either."

"But he must have seen how upset they were."

"Yeah, he saw it and he was not impressed."

I swallowed. "Detective Simmons is a good guy," I said, mostly because I needed to reassure myself. "He won't jump to conclusions."

"He might not," said Kenisha darkly. "But he's not in charge of this one anymore."

"What? Who is?"

"Lieutenant Blanchard."

I felt the blood drain out of my face. Alistair rubbed himself reassuringly against my shins.

"Maow," he told Grandma.

"Oh, dear," she murmured back.

I really was not going to think about this Grandma-to-feline conversation. I had other things to worry about. Kenisha did not talk about her lieutenant much, but when she did, it was with the kind of enthusiasm people normally reserved for tetanus shots or the stomach flu.

Kenisha's voice dropped to a whisper. "He is personally very interested in this case."

"Why?"

"Because he is," she said flatly. "That's why I'm calling." Her voice lifted to more normal tones. "I'm sorry to have to tell you, but this is official business. We'd like you to come down to the station to answer some questions about the incident."

"When?"

"As soon as possible."

"That means now, doesn't it?"

"Yes, it does," agreed Kenisha.

"All right. I'm on my way. Bye." I hung up the phone.

"What's the matter, Anna?" asked Grandma.

"The cat didn't tell you?" I was staring at the phone.

"I'm not quite that fluent, dear."

"Merow," agreed Alistair.

I pinched the bridge of my nose and tried to stay focused on the important things. "I've been asked to come down to the police station."

"Well, that's not surprising. We knew that nice detective was going to have some more questions."

Except this isn't the nice detective. I didn't say that. I just bit my lip, picked up the receiver and dialed another number.

BEFORE I WALKED into the station, I made extra sure my mental shields were up and as bright and solid as I could make them. If there was a place where I was going to be picking up stray Vibes, it was going to be in police headquarters.

Kenisha was in the lobby to meet us when Frank and I walked in.

"You brought the media?" said Kenisha.

"I wanted to bring Enoch Gravesend, but Frank will come for free." Enoch's my lawyer. Actually, he probably would have come for free, too, but Frank was working on the story, and I could tell myself that being my moral support and my witness would help him out. That made this an even exchange instead of freeloading.

Kenisha looked like she wanted to argue my decision but couldn't quite find the right angle. What I didn't say was that Grandma B.B. had wanted to come, too.

"No, Grandma," I'd told her firmly. "I can't show up at the police station with my white-haired grandmother in tow."

"I'll wear a hat," she'd said. "Then no one will see the white hair."

"*No*, Grandma."

"Well, whatever you think best, Anna." She'd sighed. "Besides, I have *plenty* to do with my morning."

As if I didn't already have enough to worry about.

Kenisha opened the door and led us through the interior of the station, past the desks with their computers and their busy occupants. From the looks on the faces, everybody seemed to know where we were headed and why. Everybody in uniform anyway.

"Just remember, you're not under arrest," Frank murmured to me as Kenisha punched the entry code on another door. "You don't have to answer anything you don't want to. If you do answer, answer only what you're actually being asked. Don't volunteer anything extra."

"I don't want to look hostile," I said as we followed Kenisha down a bland, scuffed hallway.

"Trust me, Anna, Blanchard already thinks you look hostile."

This did not make me feel any better.

Kenisha opened a door and stood aside to let us walk in. As I passed, she squeezed my hand, very briefly.

It was an interrogation room. It looked a lot like the ones on the cop shows on TV, only it was a lot smaller. It was painted the same dismal shade of oatmeal off-white as the hallway and smelled of old coffee. A big man sat on the far side of a metal table with a series of manila folders lined up in front of him. There was only one plastic chair on the other side.

My first impression of Lieutenant Blanchard was that this was a man who had not only bought his gym membership but used it religiously. His arms and shoulders strained the seams of his immaculate white dress shirt. His neck was thick and his eyes were dark and round and set deep in his square face. His graying hair was cut short and bristly.

He did not offer to shake my hand, and to tell you the truth, I was kind of glad. He also wasn't paying a lot of attention to me. He had zeroed in on Frank.

"What's the media doing here, Freeman?" Lieutenant Blanchard demanded. His voice was thick with authority and contempt.

"Miss Britton asked me to accompany her," Frank answered before Kenisha had to. "And of course, readers of the *Seacoast News* and its associated Web sites will be interested to hear how thoroughly and professionally the Portsmouth police are conducting their investigation of this tragedy. We had a call from the *Boston Globe* just this morning," he added.

"You didn't tell me that," I said. "Congratulations."

"Thanks," Frank answered. "We're pretty excited."

"You're also finished here," snapped Blanchard. "No media during an ongoing investigation. You can wait in the lobby." Blanchard jerked his head toward the door.

"You can't . . ." Frank began, but Blanchard just folded those bulging arms so his elbows rested on the table.

"Yeah, I kinda can. This is an interrogation, not a tea party." He looked right at me to see what effect that word, "interrogation," had. I made myself look back steadily and not shrink away or show how badly I wished I had my cat or my grandmother to hang on to. I had my wand to help keep my focus, but digging around nervously in my purse in front of Lieutenant Blanchard did not seem like a great idea. "Officer Freeman, you will show Mr. Hawthorne to the lobby and the coffee machine. Now."

"Yes, sir." Kenisha opened the door back up. I got ready to protest, but Frank gave me a small shake of his head and followed her out.

Lieutenant Blanchard made sure the door was shut behind them. I didn't see him do it, but I was pretty sure I heard the sound of a lock snapping closed.

"Sit down." He pointed to the chair.

I sat. He sat on the other side of the table and dragged the first folder in his tidy lineup toward him.

"You are Annabelle Amelia Blessingsound Britton," he informed me as he pulled a pen out of his shirt pocket and opened the folder.

I nodded my agreement, suppressing the urge to "yes, sir" him. Not many people can loom while sitting down. That takes special talent.

Lieutenant Blanchard asked my address. He confirmed that the house was owned by Frank Hawthorne. He glanced toward the door with a little smile.

"Now, Miss Britton." Lieutenant Blanchard squared off the file in front of him. He also leveled his glare at me. "Just what in the hell were you doing down in the basement with the coffee hippies?"

I hadn't liked Lieutenant Blanchard before. I definitely did not like him now. I reminded myself that he was the police (and Kenisha's boss), and I was in a police station and talking back was not going to do anybody any good, starting with me.

It sort of worked.

"Jake and Miranda wanted me to paint some murals for them in their new space." I tried very hard to meet Lieutenant Blanchard's glower and just about managed it. "They were showing me around so I could work up an initial design for the project."

"You were going to paint the kitchen? Maybe a couple of bedrooms and throw in the doghouse for free?"

I didn't answer that. I did press my own hands flat against my purse. I really, really wished I could reach for my wand. Not that I actually wanted to work any unauthorized magic. I just wanted the help to stay focused. Being in a police interrogation room, with this man across from me, was really messing up my concentration. If my mental shields went down and I started picking up on the Vibes in the station around me, I had no idea what I'd do or say. I could, however, safely bet that it would not look good. At all.

"You know, I've heard a lot about you, Miss Britton," Lieutenant Blanchard was saying. "And what I've heard tells me you got a serious case of Nosey Parker syndrome. In fact," Blanchard went on, turning another page, "you've hooked up with Julia Parris and her whole Nosey Parker gang."

"Is it tough to be a cop in a town where the worst gang is the Nosey Parkers?" I muttered.

To my surprise, that actually made him snicker. The sound was about as pleasant as his smile. "Nice one, Miss Britton. Yeah, I admit, I got worse problems. They come up from Boston and they come over from Vermont and down from Canada, but those problems"—he waved one meaty hand—"they come, and they go. What really gets under my skin are problems that are determined to stick around. So when I see a Nosey Parker teaming up with a couple of hippie types with FBI files that could choke a horse—"

"The FBI kept files on everybody in the sixties. My *grandmother* has an FBI file." I bit my tongue. Lieutenant Blanchard made a note.

"And when this newest Nosey Parker just happens to be there when they just happen to stumble across a dead body and a wad of cash—"

Wait. Stop. *What?*

"Cash?"

"Oh, yeah." Blanchard looked up from under his eyebrows. Eyebrow, actually. He only had the one, and it stretched straight across the flattened bridge of his nose. Somebody at some point had landed a serious punch in the center of Blanchard's square face. "The late Mr. Upton had five thousand dollars on him when he was killed. Didn't you know?" Blanchard asked with exaggerated innocence.

"No." How did a guy who worked in a kitchen get that kind of money? Unless they were celebrity chefs with endorsement deals or TV shows, most cooks didn't actually make that much. Back in the day, Martine and I had pinched pennies and clipped coupons together.

It also hit me that Blanchard didn't say "when he died." He said "when he was killed."

Whatever discomfort Blanchard was reading in my expression, he was enjoying it. His shark's grin spread from ear to ear. "Now, Miss Britton, I'm guessing you also did not know that before they became respectable businesspersons, Jake and Miranda Luce were busted for selling pot?"

"No."

He nodded. "No, of course you didn't. But I did." He pressed the tip of his index finger down in the file. "So, you gotta see this from my perspective. Here I got a couple of ex-cons, who have recently purchased a building that just happens to have a hidden tunnel, where there just happens to be a dead guy with a wad of cash. Now, just what am I supposed to make out of that?"

It took a minute, but all of this reassembled itself in my bewildered mind. "You think Jimmy Upton was killed in a drug deal?"

You think Jake and Miranda are dealing drugs. My hands went ice-cold and the back of my neck prickled with goose bumps.

Blanchard's mocking grin vanished, and somehow that made everything worse. "I could not say, at this time. But you see how it is? I've got to ask myself, Is coffee the only business opportunity these two upstanding citizens are taking advantage of? Now." Blanchard leaned forward a little further. "*Miss* Britton, do you want to tell me just what you were doing down there with the two of them?"

I might not have brought my lawyer with me, but I had given him a quick call before I came in. Enoch and Frank were in close agreement on two important points of interrogation-room etiquette:

1) Only answer the questions asked.

2) Confirm one vital fact.

"Am I under arrest?" I asked.

"Not yet," Lieutenant Blanchard admitted. Which was only a little reassuring, especially since the words "that could change" were so clearly shining behind his little round eyes. "But you have hitched yourself to the Luce gravy train, or so you said?"

"I'm painting some murals!" And I couldn't even be sure that was still happening.

"Because you need the money, don't you? Being an artsy type is not exactly a secure or stable lifestyle choice." I wouldn't have thought it possible for the man's voice to become any more oily. "So, Miss Britton." Blanchard leaned back in his chair, which creaked ominously, and he folded those bulging arms. "How about you walk me through it? When did you meet the Luces and what happened afterward? Take your time," he added generously. "Any detail could be significant."

What happened next was not my best moment ever. I stammered and I stumbled. I tried my best to gloss over the holes where the ghosts and magic and Vibes figured in events, but they were there all the same, and Lieutenant Blanchard was busy noting down every one of them. His favorite phrase suddenly seemed to be, "So, let's go over that again."

He was also suddenly very, very patient. I could feel the time crawling past on the back of my neck, and I was clutching my purse like a life preserver. There was no clock in the room, and I couldn't check my phone, but I felt sure I had been in here at least two hours.

"Let's go over that again . . ."

"Let's go over that again . . ."

When somebody knocked on the door, I almost let out a cry of relief. Or maybe a whimper.

Blanchard tossed his pencil down and got up to open the door. He was shorter than I thought he was going to be. This time I did see him work the lock.

"Lieutenant Blanchard?" Kenisha was standing on the other side of the threshold. "Telephone for you. It's the medical examiner."

The lieutenant smiled. "Well, that's all right. I think we're done here. We've got all your contact information, don't we, Miss Britton? It's highly likely we'll be wanting to talk with you some more."

"I'll be sure not to leave town," I muttered as I got to my feet.

Blanchard nodded like he thought this was a very good idea. "Officer Freeman, you can escort Miss Britton out?"

"Yes, sir."

Kenisha stood back and let me walk out of the room in front of her, but as soon as we were in the hall, she came right up to my side, like she was shielding me from something nasty that might be approaching from the back. Maybe she was.

"I owe you an apology, Kenisha," I whispered.

"What for?"

"I didn't believe you when you told me how bad he—"

She held up her hand. "Don't. Not 'til we're outside."

Outside had never felt so good. It was a warm autumn day, with plenty of sunshine and the scent of leaves and the fresh breeze off the river. I inhaled and rubbed my arms. The goose bumps had nothing to do with the temperature of the air.

"Where's Frank?" I asked.

"Emergency at the office," Kenisha answered. "I promised him I'd make sure you were okay. You are okay, right?"

"Yeah, I think so, mostly. Jeez, that . . ." I gestured toward the station doors. "Was it just me, or has Lieutenant Blanchard got it in for Jake and Miranda?"

Kenisha glanced around to make sure nobody was in earshot. "He's got it in for all kinds of people. Lieutenant Blanchard has very . . . specific ideas about what kind of a town Portsmouth ought to be."

There was a whole world of meaning waiting under those words, but I could also tell this was not something she could go into right now.

"Listen, Anna," breathed Kenisha. "I should not be telling you this, but the ME is a friend and he told me—"

"Jimmy Upton was murdered, wasn't he?"

"Yeah. We were pretty sure about that from the beginning." So was I; I just hadn't wanted to admit it. "The real question was how."

"Do they know?"

Kenisha nodded. "The medical examiner says he drowned."

"Drowned?" I thought about the Piscataqua River, so conveniently located right outside the door of Northeast Java. And the Harbor's Rest hotel, with its marina, and the little cut-in for the tugboats down Ceres Street, and . . .

But Kenisha was shaking her head again. "I know what you're thinking, but Upton wasn't drowned in the river. When they analyzed the water in his lungs, they found traces of fluoride and commercial cleaner."

"Oh," I said.

"And they found a lot of postmortem bruising, but there were some other bruises from when he was still alive, and those were on his face and skull and neck and across his chest."

"Oh. Does that mean—"

Kenisha was already nodding. "It means Jimmy Upton was in a fight, and then somebody held him facedown in a sink until he died."

❧ 13 ❧

🐾 AS SOON AS Kenisha headed back into the station, I pulled out my phone. I'd shut it off for the interview, and as a result, I'd missed the fifteen calls from Grandma B.B.

The city bus stop in front of the police station had a bench. I sat down and hit Grandma's number. She picked up before the first ring finished.

"Anna! Are you all right, dear? Do I need to come bail you out? What's that lawyer's name?"

"I'm fine, Grandma, I'm fine!"

"Why didn't you call? I've been frantic! If it wasn't for Alistair, I think I would have lost my mind!"

I heard a faint meow in the background, and I suddenly pictured Alistair sprawled on the couch, doing something reassuring like grooming or begging for extra nibbles. My familiar would know instinctively that I wasn't in real danger. I felt a surge of gratitude that he was there to help look after Grandma.

"I'm sorry, Grandma," I told her. "But I couldn't exactly be taking calls in the middle of questioning."

"Questioning! What kind of questioning?"

"It wasn't that big a deal." Except if it wasn't that big a deal, why were my knees still shaky? Suddenly, I was very glad we were having this conversation over the phone. I was pretty sure I didn't want Grandma to see the way I was huddling in on myself. "The police just wanted some more details about how we found the body; that's all."

"Oh." Grandma sounded a little disappointed—and a little suspicious. "If that's *all*."

"That's it, Grandma, really." Almost. Mostly. "They have to be thorough."

"Merow!" announced Alistair in the distance.

"You're not telling us something, Annabelle Amelia," said Grandma. "We can hear it."

"It's *nothing*," I told them both. "I promise."

"It is not nothing, and if you hang up this phone, I will call you back, a lot, and I'll make sure all your new friends know you left your *grandmother* worrying at home while you went *sleuthing* all over town."

She'd do it, too. Grandma B.B. had never been above playing the sympathy card.

"I'm not sleuthing," I told her. "And I don't think that's a real word anyway."

"Annabelle."

"All right, all right, Grandma. I just . . ." I sighed and glanced around. The sidewalk was deserted. A police cruiser was pulling into the parking lot, and another was pulling out. "I swear, I'm not in trouble, but I think Jake and Miranda might be. Lieutenant Blanchard doesn't like them very much."

"He thinks that they had something to do with that poor man being in the tunnel?"

"Yeah. The problem is my friend Kenisha—you remember her—"

"That nice officer who's in the coven? Yes, of course."

"Well, she said that"—I swallowed—"that we were right. Jimmy Upton was murdered. Somebody drowned him, probably in a sink someplace."

"Well, surely that means the Luces couldn't have done it. There's no sink in their new building."

"Except there is. There's a utility tub in their basement. I saw it when we went down there."

"Oh. Dear."

"Yeah," I agreed. "Listen, Grandma, I want to go check in on Jake and Miranda and make sure they're okay."

"Yes, yes, of course. I think that's a very good idea."

"Are you going to be okay, Grandma?"

"Perfectly, dear. Now that I know you're all right, I'll find plenty to keep me busy."

I GOT OFF the bus in Market Square and trotted down the steps to Ceres Street and Northeast Java. There, I was confronted by the inconceivable. A hand-lettered sign in the window read: CLOSED.

My coffee-loving soul cried out in very selfish alarm. I was about to turn around, wondering who I knew who might have Jake and Miranda's home phone number or address, when the door opened behind me. Jake, looking tired and more disheveled than usual, leaned out and beckoned me inside.

He locked the door immediately.

"Hi, Jake. I wanted to come by and see how you were doing." But I could already see for myself that the answer was going to be some version of "not great."

"It's the first weekday we've closed in . . . maybe seven years?" he told me. "Last time was Miranda's dad's funeral. But we just got rid of the last of the cameras and stuff and . . . well, I admit it, Miranda's taking this whole thing pretty hard."

"You don't look so good yourself." There were dark circles under his eyes, and his cheeks were stubbled above his beard. He slumped, too, like he'd aged ten extra years overnight.

"Yeah, well, it's all kind of heavy, you know?" Jake gestured me toward one of the battered tables. I couldn't remember ever having been in the shop when it was empty. The smell of coffee lingered, but the unnatural hush raised a distinct restlessness deep underneath my skin. "Here I am worrying about ghosts when it might have been somebody who really needed help and I just didn't—"

Miranda appeared out of the shop's tiny kitchen. "You couldn't have known, old man," she said, coming over to plant a kiss on Jake's cheek. "Neither of us could."

"Well, for what it's worth, whatever you've been hearing, it couldn't have been him," I said. "Kenisha told me he was dead before his body was put in the tunnel."

I know I did not imagine the relief on Miranda's face. I couldn't blame her. Who wanted to think they'd been hearing a call for help and hadn't recognized it? But there was something else as well. I could see it in the way Miranda was watching Jake. Jake wasn't looking back at her, though. He was staring out the windows into the street and across the river.

"How did he die, Anna?" asked Jake quietly.

"He was drowned in a sink."

Miranda went ghost white. "Oh, no."

"And if Blanchard hasn't noticed that old tub down in the basement, he's going to hear about it really soon." Jake laid a hand on her shoulder. "Man."

Miranda reached up and covered his hand. "You don't believe we had anything to do with this, do you, Anna?"

"Of course not!" Jake and Miranda were eccentric, sure, but they were not capable of such a thing. Even if I hadn't believed that, I'd been in the basement with my defenses down and my inner eyes wide open. If there'd been a death in there recently, especially if it was murder, I would have picked up something.

Wherever Jimmy Upton was killed, it was not in the old drugstore's basement.

I took a deep breath. "Listen, you guys should probably know I just got out from talking to Lieutenant Blanchard."

"Oh, Anna, I'm so sorry you had to get mixed up in this," said Miranda. "If we'd known—"

"It is *not* your fault," I told her and Jake. "I guess he'd already talked to you?"

"Oh, yeah, the big fuzz wanted to rap a whole lot." Jake folded his arms. "Until, like, midnight."

"Jake," said Miranda.

Jake took off his glasses and rubbed his eyes. "Sorry. Being in that station makes me forget what decade it is. Yeah, we got brought in. And, yeah, Blanchard was all over how we got caught with, like, three marijuana plants and a grow light in the attic forty years ago. And, yeah, maybe we lit up a few and talked revolution with some friends. We did the community service and we haven't sold a joint since, and I haven't been talkin' 'bout a revolution since the Carter administration."

"We don't even know who we found down there," added Miranda.

"Blanchard didn't tell you?"

Jake shrugged. "Not so's you'd notice. It was all 'the victim' this and 'the victim' that. He wanted to see if we'd spill the beans ourselves, I guess."

"Do you know who he was, Anna?" Miranda asked.

"His name was Jimmy Upton."

"Upton?" repeated Jake. I had the feeling that if he hadn't been sitting down, he would have staggered.

"Did you know him?" I asked.

"Um, no. Not really," said Miranda. "We met a couple of times after he came to town. It was his sister we knew."

"His sister?"

Miranda nodded. "She worked for us, it must have been three months ago?"

"Four," said Jake.

"Right, four. It was only for a couple of weeks, and then she split. No forwarding address." Miranda frowned. "You remembered to tell Blanchard about that, didn't you, Jake?"

"Yeah. He was real interested, too."

We all let all this settle in, and none of us liked it.

"Wow. Man. Jimmy Upton." Jake took off his bandana

and rubbed it across his face. "Poor guy. Are you sure he couldn't be our ghost?"

"Honestly, I don't know," I told him. "I don't even know if there is a ghost."

"Could you find out?"

I admit that I'd been hoping Jake would bring this up. On the way over from the station, an idea had occurred to me. I might not believe in ghosts, but I definitely believed in my Vibe. Now that we knew more about what had happened, and what kind of trouble we were looking at, I stood a better chance of being able to understand what that Vibe was trying to tell me. There was only one problem. I couldn't do this alone. I'd promised.

"I think for this one, you should call in an expert," I told them.

"I'm not bringing in any bunch of ghost hunters," said Miranda immediately. "We've already had enough cameras blocking our door. We don't need some reality TV freak show messing up the scene."

"No, no, nothing like that." I didn't think so, anyway. "I just think you need somebody with more experience than I've got, like Julia Parris."

"Julia?" said Miranda.

"You know her, right?"

"Everybody knows Julia," put in Jake. "And I mean, I knew she was into alternate religions, but I didn't know she was all that serious."

"I did," said Miranda. "She's got an aura you could see from the International Space Station."

"And a stick you can't," Jake muttered.

"Jake!" Miranda swatted him between the shoulder blades.

"Sorry. Sorry, Anna."

"It's okay," I told them. I thought about mentioning the rumors that Julia had a nightclub in her past but decided against it.

"Do you think Julia would help us?" he asked.

"Yes, I do." I might still be a little miffed at Julia for her attitude toward Grandma and for forbidding me from working magic on my own while only an apprentice, but I knew she took her role as a guardian very seriously. She would not turn down a request for help. Impulsively, I seized Miranda's hand. "Ghost or no ghost, we are going to find out who did this. I promise you." I had no idea how, but I was not going to leave these two to the mercy of Lieutenant Blanchard and his nasty grin and well-filled manila folders.

Miranda didn't say anything. She just pulled her hand out of mine and walked back behind the counter and stared up at the chalkboard menu and the battered sign, BETTER KARMA THROUGH BETTER COFFEE. I wondered if she'd painted it herself. I pictured the two of them hanging it up above the menu—laughing and optimistic.

"Starbabe?" said Jake gently.

"No," Miranda said.

Jake blinked. "No what?"

Miranda turned around and faced us both. Determination radiated from every pore. "No ghost hunting. No poking the hotel hornet's nest while Blanchard is drooling over the idea of finally catching us at . . . something. Old man, we need to let this one go."

"But we can't, Starbabe. It's on us now. We're part of it whether we like it or not."

"No, we're really not," she answered flatly. "I mean, this is not anything we did. We just found him. That's all. I feel bad for him, and for his . . . family. But if we keep asking questions about this, Lieutenant Blanchard is going to wonder why." For the first time, a hint of fear crept into Miranda's voice.

"Miranda, come on." Jake got up and leaned across the counter to take both her hands. "We can't let the cops scare us. We've got to do what's right. If we're not part of the solution, we're part of the problem, right?"

She looked up at him miserably. "We've got a good thing, Jake; we don't need to be looking for extra trouble."

"We've already found trouble." He squeezed her hands. "Now we got to deal with it."

"And whatever you've been hearing, or whatever's been happening, it might not have anything to do with Jimmy Upton," I reminded her. "From what you said, the noises started long before he . . . died. We'd just be seeing if there's anything else behind the noises and the impressions I was getting." Because the whole building had been filled with secrets, not just the basement.

A dozen expressions chased one another across Miranda's face, none of them happy, but in the end she just sighed. "Okay, if it's just checking out any energies the place might have, I guess that'd be all right."

"That's my lady." Jake gave her hands an extra squeeze. "*Everything's* gonna be all right. Every. Little. Thing."

Miranda's answering smile was weak, but it was genuine. "Do you promise, old man?"

"I promise." He stretched across the counter to kiss her.

The view out the tiny windows suddenly became very interesting. There was the river sparkling in the autumn sunshine, and a barge sailing past, and if you stood at just the right angle, you could see the Memorial Bridge and . . .

"Okay, Anna, show's over." Jake laughed.

"Just giving you two the moment," I said loftily.

"And we appreciate that." Miranda was smiling and her voice was much lighter. "So, here's the thing: Despite how it sounds, we are glad you stopped by. We wanted to let you know that we'd definitely like you to do the murals for the new shop. If you're still interested, that is," she added.

"I am interested," I told them. "But you haven't even seen any concepts yet."

Miranda waved this away. "We've seen the work on your Web site and how much you loved the space. I'm sure you'll come up with something perfect. It's going to be a while until they let us back in, but we can give you a down payment today if that's cool."

"That is cool," I said, visions of rent checks dancing in my head. "Thank you."

"Oh, I'm so glad," said Miranda. "After the night we had, we figured everybody could use some good news. How about we celebrate? Can we get you something, Anna?" said Miranda. "Latte?"

"Definitely."

❧ 14 ❧

🐾 WE TOASTED OUR new partnership with caffeine and cinnamon and a radically failed attempt on my part to draw a leaf pattern in coffee foam. Jake and Miranda insisted on writing me out the deposit check, and I tucked it into my purse. But when I left the shop, I did not turn left to head for my bank. Instead, I turned to the right. I also pulled out my phone and called Julia.

"Anna?" my mentor said as soon as she answered. "Are you all right?"

I was starting to understand how Val felt. "I'm fine." I was walking down Ceres toward the far end and the other set of stairs that led to Market Street. "I've just been to see Jake and Miranda."

"Yes, I've been hearing something about it . . . Thank you. Have a great day." I remembered Julia would be working right now. I heard her call her assistant over to the counter before she spoke into the phone again. "How are they?"

"Not great," I admitted. "Kenisha's lieutenant has been questioning them."

"And you?" she put in, because Julia is not slow.

"And me," I admitted. "Did Kenisha tell you what they've found out so far?"

"Yes, she did."

I took a deep breath. "Julia, I know since I'm still an apprentice, I'm not supposed to use my Vibe without supervision, but I was thinking now that we know . . . what we know, maybe if I went back into the building, I could get some more hints about what actually happened."

Julia was silent for a long time. "It's possible," she said finally. "We'd need Jake and Miranda's permission, of course."

"We have it. Kind of," I added, for the sake of full disclosure. "Jake still thinks the building might be haunted, and he wants us to try to find the ghost."

"Well, of course we will do what we can," said Julia immediately. "But I don't . . ." She paused. "Anna, you did not suggest to them that their ghost might be able to help discover who murdered Jimmy Upton?"

"No. Of course not. Because there's no such thing as ghosts." *Right? Right. Please say right.*

"Well, that would depend on what you mean by ghosts," said Julia. This was so very much not what I wanted to hear. The bright fall day suddenly seemed a bit too chilly.

Julia heard my silence and made that particular sigh that people give you when they want you to know they are being very patient. "Anna, you know that a death can leave behind a psychic echo. If that echo is strong enough, even people who are not otherwise magically sensitive or trained can be affected by it. They can even think they've seen something or heard something. Actual spirits—entities that are trapped or in transition between one form of existence and another—those are exceptionally rare, but they are not unheard of."

"So . . . you're saying Jimmy Upton might really be haunting the place?" I told myself to pull it together. I told myself that this was no weirder than working magic, or a cat who could vanish and reappear whenever the mood struck him. Myself was not listening. At all.

"I'm saying it's possible someone or something is, and if it will set Jake's and Miranda's minds at rest, of course we should try to find out." Julia paused, and I pictured her brow furrowing in thought. "It has been a long time since I was confronted with the possibility of a lost spirit. I'll need to do some research, but I'm positive we can at least reassure Jake and Miranda that their building is free of negative energies."

"Thanks, Julia," I said, and I meant it. Lieutenant Blanchard's accusations had me worried about Jake and Miranda. I might not have been crazy about the idea about meeting an actual ghost, but I couldn't help hoping that my Vibe might turn up something to help with the investigation. It wouldn't be anything we could take to court, but it still might point somebody in the right direction.

Julia promised she would call soon, and we said good-bye and hung up. I climbed the steps back to Market Street. I stood staring at the old drugstore that was supposed to become the new coffee shop. The door was sealed off with crime scene tape, and there were a couple of orange-and-white sawhorses in front of it, but there weren't any cars that I could see. The few pedestrians passing by turned to look, but nobody stopped.

Show's over. Nothing to see here. Move along.

Which was good advice, I told myself. I needed to get home. I'd left Grandma B.B. on her own for long enough. There was something in the way she'd assured me she'd find plenty to keep her busy that made me nervous. I wanted to give her the benefit of the doubt. If I'd been having a bad few days, things must have been even worse for her. I'd at least had some time to adjust to Portsmouth and all that came with it. Grandma had been thrown in at the deep end. Plus I was hungry and thirsty, and I needed to check my Web site to see if I had any more e-mails from possible clients, and . . .

And what I did was stand right where I was and keep on staring. Down the sloped street, where the river curved, I could see the grand white expanse and sparkling windows of the Harbor's Rest hotel. Flags fluttered from the gabled roof and seagulls hovered hopefully in the blue sky.

I wondered what was going on over there. Had the police found the other end of the tunnel yet? Had they found Jimmy Upton's sister? It occurred to me that Old Sean might be tending bar at the hotel today. It was almost four o'clock. I could stroll in, have a drink, ask a couple of questions . . .

I rubbed my forehead. *Anna Britton, what the heck are you thinking?* Helping Jake and Miranda find out if their new building was haunted was one thing. But was I really going to try to play Nancy Drew with Lieutenant Blanchard breathing down my neck? Miranda was right about one thing. If I started asking questions about Jimmy Upton or his murder, Blanchard was going to notice, and he was going to want to know why, and he probably was not going to like the answer.

But Jake and Miranda needed more than just an assurance that their new building was free of negative energies. They were confused and they were hurt, and it was really clear that Lieutenant Blanchard wanted to make trouble for them. They deserved definite answers.

My phone rang. I pulled it out and checked the number.

"Hi, Martine!" I said as I hit the Accept button.

"And exactly when were you going to tell me you found a dead body under Market Street?" she answered.

Martine Devereux is the chef at the Pale Ale, a historic Portsmouth tavern. She has also been my best friend since forever and is a big part of the reason I came to Portsmouth at all.

I winced. "I guess Kenisha called you." Kenisha had been busy on the phone this morning.

"Kenisha shouldn't have had to call me," snapped Martine. "I'm your best friend, Anna. You are supposed to have me on speed dial for this stuff."

"I was going to call you, but I didn't—"

"Britton, if you say you didn't want to bother me, I am hanging up this phone because we are through."

Don't you hate it when your best friend has a good point? "I'm sorry, Martine. You're right. I should have called. It's just . . ." I heard her drawing in a very deep breath. "I am not saying I didn't want to bother you! But everything's happened so fast, and I didn't know how bad it was going to get until this morning."

"Just how bad did it get?"

"Bad," I admitted. "Getting called down to the police station by Kenisha's lieutenant bad."

Martine was quiet, and when she did start talking again, her voice was low and serious. "Anna, I may not be one of your witches, but I've known you longer than anybody you're not related to. Do not push me away from this."

Now it was my turn to be quiet. The hurt in Martine's voice was real, which was bad enough. What was worse, though, was that she was right. Again. Lately, I had been preoccupied with my new friends in the coven. They were all entirely welcoming of Martine, but although she believed in the magic, she was emphatically not interested in taking up the practice herself. It did create a gap. I'd been letting myself drift to one side of it, and away from her.

"I'm sorry," I said. "The worst part is, I could really use your help."

"Say, 'Please, Chef.'"

I felt myself smile. "Please, Chef. Pretty please, with locally sourced, organic and sustainably harvested sugar on top."

I heard her try to smother a laugh and I grinned. "And exactly what is it you need my help with this time?"

"That dead body? It was a chef, a man named Jimmy Upton."

"Upton?" Martine let out a long, low whistle. "You're telling me somebody killed Jimmy Upton? Dang. I wonder what took them so long?"

I THINK I set a land-speed record getting to the Pale Ale. I paused just long enough to call Grandma B.B. She didn't pick up, but I left a message telling her where I was going and that I'd be back home in another couple of hours. Probably.

I didn't need to bother with the bus this time. Portsmouth

was founded long before cars were ever dreamed of, so the oldest buildings in downtown are within fairly easy walking distance of one another. In next to no time, I was sitting with Martine in her cramped office in the back of the kitchen.

Martine Devereaux is an African American woman with dark brown skin and a build like a professional athlete. She runs her kitchens with the efficiency of a Swiss watch, or would have if Swiss watches were filled with knives, fire and organic kale.

It was Monday, so even though it was going on five, the restaurant was closed and the kitchen was as empty as it ever got. That is to say, the crew had gone home while Martine got to stay and wrestle with the invoices, orders, time cards and schedules piled up on her desk in stacks of multicolored paper. Such is the glamorous life of the executive chef.

Because it was Martine, there were also cups of butternut squash soup and slices of the amazing sourdough rye bread that her in-house baker produces, because she had rightly guessed that being at the police station had caused me to miss at least one meal. We ate, and I filled her in on what had been happening, all of it, including the stuff about the Vibe and the (possible) ghost in the old drugstore.

"Well, if anybody was going to keep hanging around and being a jerk instead of heading off into the afterlife, it'd be Jimmy." Martine had taken all the weirdness of my current life absolutely in stride. It was helped by the fact that her grandparents came from Haiti. She didn't talk about it too much, but I had a distinct feeling her grandmother had a few extra abilities of her own.

"Sounds like he was . . . special," I said. I also spooned up the last of the delicately spiced soup from my mug. No matter what the circumstances, I did not let Martine's food go to waste.

"In a whole lotta ways," agreed Martine sourly. She bit off a piece of sourdough crust. "I actually met him last year at the Taste of Portsmouth festival," she told me around her mouthful. "I was still being considered for this job, and I

was . . . call it 'auditioning' for the owners. They wanted to
know if I could look good for the press and the public, as
well as cook."

"Have you got a face Food TV would love?" I suggested.

She nodded. "So, they let me pull together a recipe for
the festival's media night, and there I was, public face on,
handing out the food. It was a potato soup with sorrel and
watercress and Gruyère cheese. Simple, warming, not too
heavy. We used vegetable stock instead of cream—"

"And Jimmy was there?" I interrupted before she could
really get going. I love her, but when Martine starts talking
food, it is a long time before she stops.

"This kid comes up to the table and he takes a cup of
soup and he starts . . . needling me is the only word for it.
He smells it, tastes it, starts asking all about the cooking
techniques and the ingredients and where'd it all come from
and where'd I get the recipe and on and on forever." Her jaw
hardened. "And I've got a line of people behind him, and
I'm smiling and I'm trying to be polite, because my potential
new bosses are there, along with every food critic and blog-
ger on the seacoast, and finally this kid turns to the woman
he's with and he just shrugs. 'Whatever. It's boring, it's bland
and it's the product of a very ordinary mind,' he says, and
pitches the cup into the garbage."

"He did that?" I clutched at my own soup cup as if it might
suddenly be snatched away from me.

"Oh, yeah, and then he walks off with his privileged little
nose in the air. It wouldn't have been such a big deal, except
for who he was with."

"Who was that?"

"Gretchen Hilde."

I'd already heard that name today. "She's the head of the
family that owns the Harbor's Rest."

"That's her." Martine gestured toward me with her soup
mug. "I was sure I'd just been sunk. I thought maybe it was
a race thing going on, or a woman thing. You get that in
some kitchens. But it turns out it was just a Jimmy thing.

Upton got off on confrontation. Whenever he saw anybody who might become the competition, he attacked them first."

"Did he want the Pale Ale job?"

"No. He was already Mrs. Hilde's golden boy. He just wanted to make sure she knew she'd made the right choice. His way to do that was to demolish everybody else." She shook her head. "I didn't like him, but I will say this—Jimmy had the kind of touch that only comes along once in a blue moon. He really could have been great." Martine loves the art of cooking. When she sees a talent, she acknowledges it generously, no matter whom it's attached to.

Martine tipped her mug this way and that, watching the last drops of soup dribble across the bottom. "Anna, are you really going to do the Nancy Drew thing again?"

"No," I said immediately, but that only made Martine look down her nose at me. "Well. Maybe. But just to help Jake and Miranda. Lieutenant Blanchard is looking cross-eyed at them, and I feel responsible."

Martine made the kind of face she normally reserved for sour milk and split sauces. "In what way are you responsible for Upton finally making somebody so angry that they got drastic on his lily-whites?"

"I found the tunnel. If I'd just left things alone, Jake and Miranda wouldn't be in this mess."

"Maybe not right away, but this is the kind of thing that comes back to haunt you, whether there's a real ghost or not."

"All the more reason we should try to help." The words were out of my mouth before I had a chance to think about them. But this was the truth. It might not have been smart, but I couldn't stand by, not knowing what I knew.

Not being who I was.

"Did you ever meet Jimmy's sister?" I asked her.

"He had a sister?"

I took that as a no. "Jake and Miranda said she worked in the coffee shop for a while, but she split . . . erm . . . left, and they don't know where." Come to that, Frank had said Jimmy didn't have any family in the area.

"News to me. But it sure doesn't sound good." Martine picked up her remaining bread and tore it in two. She looked at the crumbs for a while, making up her mind how much more to say.

"And you think it's not the only thing that doesn't sound good?" I prompted.

"No." She sighed. "Listen, Anna, what do you know about kitchen organization?"

I shrugged. "Only what you've told me."

"Okay. Upton was the sous chef at Harbor's Rest. In a traditional French-style kitchen, the sous chef is responsible for making the sauces, and that is a very serious, very high-level job. The sous is also the head chef's right hand and gets to be large and in charge.

"Jimmy got this job by climbing over a bunch of people who had been there longer."

"Sounds like the kind of situation that could generate a lot of resentment," I said slowly.

Martine's nod was also slow. "If Jimmy Upton was murdered, you are going to have a whole long list of suspects to choose from, even without any missing sister. And it's going to include pretty much the entire Harbor's Rest kitchen staff."

❧ 15 ❧

❧ MARTINE HAD TO get back to work. Staffing schedules waited for no chef. She did have one other piece of
advice for me.

"If you want to find out what was going on with the service
staff at the hotel, you should talk to Kelly Pierce. She's their
food and beverages manager, and she's new," she added. "She
was brought in to help turn things around, and she's not a
Hilde, so there's no family stuff going on with her."

"Thanks," I said. "You are the best, and I'm coming by
next Monday. This time I promise it's strictly the girl's day.
No magic or corpses."

"I'm holding you to that, Britton," she told me. "Oh, and
pro tip: If you do go talk to Kelly, take coffee."

I walked out into the fall evening. I wasn't thinking of
much; I just started strolling toward Market Square.

What was I doing? Did I really think I could help Jake
and Miranda? Yes, I'd been able to help out before, but that
was when I'd just been caught up in the situation. Not to
mention the fact that I'd been a suspect then and needed to
try to clear my own name. This was different.

I sat on one of the benches in front of the North Church. I wished I had my cat with me. I wished I knew what I ought to do.

What I did do was get out my phone and dial Grandma B.B.

"Hello, Anna!" she said. "Where are you, dear? Are you all right?"

"I'm *fine*, Grandma. I was just wondering if you were home."

"Oh, well, no, not right now. I thought since you were *busy*, I'd catch up with some old friends. Maybe we should meet somewhere?"

"I don't want to interrupt the reunion," I told her. "If you're near downtown, we can meet at the River House for dinner. You'd love the fried clams." Thanks to the soup and bread with Martine, I wasn't actually hungry anymore, but after the day I'd been having, I desperately wanted a moment of normality.

"Sounds perfect, dear. How about . . ." She paused, probably to check her watch. "Seven o'clock?"

"Great. You'll be able to find it all right?"

"Of *course* I will. What a question."

We said good-bye and hung up. I looked around at the passing crowds of tourists. According to the church clock, it was just five thirty. I'd meant to get to the library and do a quick little bit of research for the murals, but they'd be closing up now. I could spend the time walking along the river and getting my head together after my eventful day. I could do something entirely mundane like heading over to the Circle K to pick up some cat food.

I could do all kinds of good, sensible things.

What I did instead was turn down Market Street and head straight for the Harbor's Rest.

I'D BEEN IN the Harbor's Rest exactly once, and that was for a celebratory dinner after I'd been initiated into the coven. The food was great; the wine was great; the dining room was elegant and old-school. I'd promised myself I'd come back. I just never imagined it would be under these circumstances.

The hotel's entrance had kept all its Gilded Age splendor. There was a fancy plasterwork ceiling, polished wood and marble-tiled floors. All the art on the walls had heavy gilt frames and looked like it had been commissioned especially for the hotel, especially the oil painting that showed a cluster of cats sitting in what was clearly this very lobby.

That bar was the most famous part of the hotel, at least locally. Its bay windows provided a beautiful view of the marina and the river. There were plaques and framed newspaper clippings on the walls telling how Babe Ruth had gotten into a fight in there with some Red Sox fans who took exception to his move to the Yankees. There were photos of the gangsters and silent movie starlets who drank bootlegged champagne there. Dashiell Hammett and Lillian Hellman had drunk and fought and written masterpieces here. Various Roosevelts and Kennedys had wined and dined constituents, donors and other connections here.

It was the right time for the predinner rush, but the bar was only about a quarter full when I walked in. Men in Lands' End khakis and women carrying designer purses sat at little round tables with beers or delicately colored cocktails in front of them. Martinis seemed to be a favorite, and when I saw who was behind the bar adding a spiral of lemon peel to the glass in front of him, I was not at all surprised.

"Young Sean!"

"Anna!" Sean flashed me a smile and a wave with his free hand, while he set a drink on a server's tray for her to take over to the waiting customer. "Pull up a stool."

"Does Martine know you're moonlighting?" I asked as I climbed up on a seat on the short side of the bar by the door. I'd met Sean because he was the head bartender at the Pale Ale.

He laughed. "Like I could do anything behind Chef's back. I'm helping Dad out today. He had an errand to run. Can I get you something?" He gestured toward the shelves of empty glasses and full bottles.

"What have you got?" I am not much of a drinker, but Sean's mixtures were like Martine's food, something not to be passed up lightly.

He studied me for a minute and then touched his fedora brim like a salute. "I know just the thing."

I watched as Sean went to work with his bottles and his shaker. As usual, he was sharply dressed. Today, in addition to the fedora, he wore a bright blue shirt, black-on-black patterned vest and black tie. The effect was cheerful, stylish and ever so slightly vintage.

"How are Jake and Miranda doing?" Sean asked as he carefully poured out the cocktail into a wide-mouthed glass.

"They're trying to be okay, but it's hard."

He nodded as he set the drink in front of me. "Pear martini," he said. "You will notice is it shaken, not stirred, which means it's milder. There's a reason James Bond drank these on the job."

I smiled and I sipped. The martini was just sweet enough and lovely and cool, and as he'd promised, fairly mild. "Thanks, Sean."

"Maybe I should ask if you're doing okay?"

"Bartender sense tingling again?"

He shrugged. "It's a gift."

"I don't suppose anybody's been talking about . . . things here?"

"Was that supposed to be a subtle reference to Jimmy Upton's murder?"

"It's a work in progress."

Sean chuckled. "As a matter of fact, Dad told me that yesterday the food and beverages manager—"

"Kelly Pierce?" I put in.

"You're fast. Yeah. Kelly got all the staff together and gave them the warning from on high that they were absolutely not to be talking to any press or police about Jimmy Upton without approval from Mrs. Hilde herself. So, somebody's worried about what Jimmy's death means for the hotel. And we've already had to chase Frank Hawthorne out."

"Why doesn't that surprise me?" I took another sip of martini.

"Because we both know Frank," said Sean. He glanced toward the door behind the bar. "Now, here comes the man you should really talk to."

The swinging door was pushed open from the other side and a gray-haired man in a battered shovel cap with his sleeves rolled up above his elbows backed in, carrying a wooden crate. It rattled.

"There's himself," said Sean, suddenly sounding very Irish.

"Himself, indeed." "Old" Sean McNally hefted the crate up onto the bar with a grunt. It rattled again.

The senior Sean McNally is a wiry, weather-beaten man with iron gray hair and calloused hands. He always shakes mine delicately, like he's afraid he's going to break something. Just then, his eyes twinkled at me and his son, in a way that threatened to make me blush. Sean, I noticed, was not looking at me.

"Well, hello, Anna. What brings you in here this fine day?" Old Sean peered skeptically at my glass. "And what's this concoction my son's talked you into?"

"It's a pear martini."

"*Pear* martini," Mr. McNally sneered in mock horror. "Corrupting good liquor, that's what the boy does with his syrups and his fruit and heaven knows what else."

Sean rolled his eyes toward the ceiling, looking for patience. "*So.* How'd it go, Dad?"

Mr. McNally laid his broad hand reverently on the crate. "What we've got here, my boy, is a dozen bottles of the finest moonshine from the White Mountains. Still can't get used to being able to bring it in the front door."

The distilling laws had recently been changed to make small-batch moonshine legal in both New Hampshire and Vermont. Now, apparently, the craft liquor industry was booming in both states. The Sean McNallys, Young and Old, had certainly been over the moon (so to speak) about the change.

A server came up with another order. Sean got to work,

pulling a couple of bottles of beer from the fridge under the
bar and then some more bottles of liquor off of the shelf. "Anna
was there when they found Upton, Dad," Sean said as he started
mixing spirits and bitters with practiced efficiency.

"Were you, now?" Mr. McNally raised his shaggy gray
eyebrows at me. "God almighty, what a thing. Not that I'm
entirely surprised, mind you."

"I've heard he wasn't very well liked," I remarked.

"Well now, that would depend on who you asked, wouldn't
it?" said Old Sean. I took another sip of martini. I knew Old
Sean well enough to know he wouldn't appreciate it if I tried
to rush a good story. Yes, I'd just heard that the hotel bar staff
had been told not to talk to anybody. But when has a warning
like that ever actually stopped an Irishman?

"I suppose you could say he was a problem child," said Sean.
"Not that you could have told Mrs. Hilde herself that, but—"

But that was as far as he got.

"Good afternoon, Mr. McNally." A woman's voice cut
across whatever he'd been about to add.

We all turned. A petite, strongly curved woman who
wore the hotel's red blazer over a black turtleneck and black
pencil skirt walked up. Her attitude and her blazer had
"management" written all over them. I picked up my drink
and tried to make myself look casual and not at all like I
might be wasting staff time with unauthorized gossip.

"Is that our moonshine?" the woman asked as she reached
the bar.

"It is indeed." Old Sean extracted a clear bottle from the
case. GRANITE SHINE was written in flowing script above
the outline of a twisted apple tree clinging to the edge of a
rugged cliff.

"And may I take it you've sampled the batch?" The woman
asked as she turned the bottle in her hands.

"Ah, well now, I couldn't risk bringing an inferior product
here, could I?" said Mr. McNally with a wink and a distinct
thickening of his Irish brogue. "I can promise you it is as
smooth as silk and twice as strong."

"Excellent. I've got a conference representative coming

in this afternoon to look us over. I'll just keep this as a sweetener. Enjoy your stay," she added to me before she walked out with the bottle.

"Your boss?" I asked.

Sean shook his head. "That was none other than Kelly Pierce, the food and beverages manager for this grand hotel."

That meant she oversaw not only the bar, but the kitchen and the coffee shop and things like the complimentary fruit baskets and the pillow mints. "She's the one who told the staff not to talk to anybody?"

"Just delivering orders from the family," said Mr. McNally. "She's not a bad sort. Too much on her shoulders, to be sure. Jimmy going missing didn't make things any easier."

"Did you know him at all?"

Mr. McNally took his time answering that. "I talked with him a few times. He was a smart fellow. Interested in the local brewers and distillers. Thought we should be suggesting pairings on the menu, like they all do nowadays."

"I'd've thought that the chef or the manager would handle that sort of detail."

"Yes, you would, now, wouldn't you?" said Mr. McNally. "Jimmy, though, he knew best, and he wasn't shy about letting other people know it, either."

"That must have caused some trouble."

"Some, yes, but not as much as you'd think. Like I said, he was one smart fellow, and he knew which side his bread was buttered on." Sean Senior got that conspiratorial look in his twinkling eyes that belongs to the best storytellers. I leaned closer. Old Sean leaned closer. He touched the side of his nose, signaling that what he had to say was dark, difficult, dangerous and very, very interesting.

"Ix-nay, ad-day," said Young Sean quietly.

We all turned and I about choked on my swallow of pear martini.

Grandma B.B. was walking into the bar, and she wasn't alone.

ᦠ 16 ᦕ

🐾 "GRANDMA B.B.!"

"Anna!" Grandma B.B. bustled up to the three of us. The woman with her most definitely did not bustle. She walked with a smooth, confident air, like she owned the place. Which she just might have. She wasn't wearing the red blazer, but the McNallys, Junior and Senior, straightened up in that abrupt way people do when the person who cuts the checks walks into the room.

"I didn't expect to see you here, dear." Grandma hugged me. "And, oh, my goodness, Sean? Is that you?"

"Annie-Bell Blessingsound!" Old Sean laughed and they hugged. "My boy told me you were back! It's wonderful to see you again!"

"Gretchen." Grandma turned to the other woman when she and Old Sean pulled apart. "Have you met my grand-daughter Anna Britton?"

"No, we haven't had the opportunity. Gretchen Hilde." She held out her hand and we shook. Mrs. Hilde was a slender woman about my grandmother's age. But where Grandma was wearing a royal purple tunic over her gray jeans, Mrs. Hilde dressed in an immaculate brown pants suit with a rust orange blouse. Her hair had been dyed a muted copper color and pulled back into a tidy knot at the nape of her neck. She wore a heavy gold necklace and a small pin on her lapel that looked like it was a miniature version of the hotel crest.

"Well, Mr. McNally." She smiled. "Was your quest successful?"

"It was indeed." Old Sean pulled a bottle of the moonshine out of the case and handed it to her. Mrs. Hilde examined it briefly. Old Sean grinned over her head at Grandma, who beamed right back.

"Excellent job." Mrs. Hilde passed the bottle to Sean Junior. "If this sells, I'm sure Ms. Pierce will want us to place a standing order. Sean, I know we can count on you for some of your original creations featuring our new acquisition?"

Sean tipped his fedora. "Already in the works, Mrs. Hilde."

"Good." She turned to Grandma. "Now, Annabelle, what would you like to drink? Or do you two have some more catching up to do?" Under this casual question, there was a very strong reminder that somebody in this group was on the clock.

Old Sean was not slow on the uptake. "I'll just get these put away. Annie-Bell and I will have plenty of time for talk later." He hefted the moonshine crate off the bar and started stashing the bottles underneath.

"Can I get you that drink, Mrs. Britton?" asked Young Sean, all brisk business.

Grandma B.B. looked wistful, and I knew she was considering ordering her own favorite beverage, which happened to be rum and ginger. "Just some iced tea, thank you."

"Two, please, Sean," said Mrs. Hilde. "You should join us, Anna." This was supposed to be a kind invitation, but, honestly, it sounded like an order.

"I don't want to intrude," I said, but only because it was polite.

"You wouldn't be, dear. Gretchen and I were just having

a little catch-up." Grandma was giving me a look like Alistair when he got into the half-and-half. I was starting to think that Grandma might be a little better at the Nancy Drew thing than I was. It was not a comfortable idea.

I picked up my pear martini. Grandma smiled and Mrs. Hilde smiled and I smiled, and we all threaded between the small tables and clusters of comfortable chairs.

"When Grandma said she was meeting old friends, I didn't realize who she meant," I said as we settled in the alcove made by one of the hotel's bay windows. We had a perfect view of the sloping lawn and the marina in the deepening twilight. "I think she said you two were in high school together?"

Mrs. Hilde nodded. "I always knew Annabelle would be back sooner or later. I'm a little surprised it took so long."

"Well, there were some extenuating circumstances."

"There usually were around you, Annabelle."

"Oh, really?" I drawled. Was Grandma B.B. actually blushing? Yes, she was. How very interesting.

"What?" said Gretchen in mock surprise. "You never told your grandchildren about the great feud of 'sixty-six?"

I about choked on my sip of martini. Was Mrs. Hilde another witch? But from the way Grandma was suddenly looking around the room for a way to change the subject, I knew this was something else altogether.

"Grandma?" I said significantly. "What feud is this?"

"It was all such a long time ago," said Grandma quickly. "Really. It was nothing."

But Mrs. Hilde was not ready to let the subject go so easily. She leaned over to me and said in a stage whisper, "Your grandmother stole my boyfriend."

Now, of course, I knew Grandma B.B. had a life before she became, well, my grandmother. And technically, I knew that meant she'd been a teenager and a young bride and all kinds of other things. But this was still something of a shock. "What? Mrs. Hilde, you dated Grandpa C.?"

Gretchen nodded solemnly. "But not for long once Annabelle finally made up her mind. She was quite the heartbreaker back in the day. In high school we used to call her Anna Fatale."

I felt a smile spreading. "You know, somehow, she never mentioned that at Christmas dinner."

Grandma was definitely blushing now, and I admit I was enjoying this a little more than I should have. Sean came over with the two iced teas and a quizzical look. I just shook my head. *Later.* He nodded and made a professionally quiet departure.

Grandma laughed, but the sound was forced. "Oh, it was nothing so dramatic as all that, Gretchen."

"No. I suppose not. We were still just girls, really."

They were nice words, but at the same time, I thought I heard an edge under them. I wondered if Gretchen was really over this little personal altercation. Especially since she also seemed to be enjoying Grandma's discomfort a little too much.

Mrs. Hilde took a long drink of her iced tea.

"I'm glad you're here, Anna," she said to me. "I wanted to come talk to you, but I admit, I didn't quite know how to introduce myself under the circumstances. I wanted . . ." For the first time Mrs. Hilde's polished confidence wavered. "Annabelle told me you were there when they found Jimmy."

"I was. I'm sorry for your loss." I hoped that was the right thing to say.

"Thank you," Gretchen whispered. "It's such a shock. I keep expecting him to walk through the door."

"I understand he was a very *talented* young man," said Grandma. "Did you know him well before he came to work for you?"

"No, actually, it was only an accident we hired him at all."

"Really?" Grandma arched her brows at me.

Gretchen nodded. Her long face had gone wistful and more than a little bit sad. "Would you believe I met him in a dark alley?" she told us.

"Gretchen! No!" exclaimed Grandma B.B.

"Oh, yes." She took another long drink of her tea. "You're

not the only one who gets to have her adventures, Annabelle."

I suddenly sat up straighter.

"Anna?" said Grandma.

"Oh, ah, nothing." Except that I could feel a cat rubbing
around my ankles. *Alistair,* I thought. *If you picked now to
show up . . .*

"Oh, Bootsie!" cried Mrs. Hilde. "You know you're not
supposed to be in here!"

All at once, Gretchen Hilde vanished. It took me a second
to realize she'd just ducked underneath the table. When she
reappeared, she had a delicate orange-and-white cat in her
arms.

"This is our cat, Miss Boots." Gretchen lifted the cat's paw
and wiggled it, as if Miss Boots was waving at me. Miss Boots
tolerated this with an expression of long and patient suffering
on her whiskered face. "She's the seventh generation of her
family to live here at Harbor's Rest." I remembered the painting of the cats in the lobby and I smiled. It's hard not to feel
warm and fuzzy about a place with generational cats. "And
she knows better than to be in the bar or the restaurant."
Gretchen held the cat up so they were eye to eye and gave her
a gentle shake. "Don't you, Bootsie-Wootsie?"

Miss Boots looked at me as if to disclaim all knowledge
of this woman, her family and anybody who might possibly
be named Bootsie-Wootsie.

"Don't worry." Grandma rubbed the cat's ears. "We won't
tell the health department on you, will we, Anna?"

"Of course not." I reached across the table as Gretchen
settled the cat onto her lap, and scratched Miss Boots behind
the ears. In response she lapped my knuckles once.

"There, now you're a friend of the family," said Gretchen.
"Miss Boots can always tell who the real cat lovers are. Not
that I'm surprised, since your grandmother says Alistair's
adopted you." My cat has a bit of a reputation around town.

"Did Miss Boots like Jimmy?" asked Grandma.

"Oh. Yes." Gretchen petted Miss Boots, a long, slow,
thoughtful motion. "She loved him from the first. We all did."

That, of course, was not what I'd heard, but I decided not to bring it up. "Did you really meet him in a dark alley?"

Gretchen smiled, an expression that was part amusement, part embarrassment. "Well, not an alley, exactly, but it was the service bay behind the kitchens. I've given most of the management of the hotel over to my children, but I do still live here, and I still do a walk-through most nights. Not as often as I used to, I admit, but I like to keep my hand in.

"Well, I was down in the kitchen, and I heard this banging noise from outside. I went to look—"

"Gretchen!" cried Grandma, loud enough that Miss Boots lifted her head and looked distinctly miffed.

"Yes, yes, I know." Gretchen rubbed the cat's head until she settled down again. "But I assumed it was a raccoon or a stray . . . something like that. What I found instead was a young man going through the Dumpsters. He saw the light come on, and he saw me, but instead of running away, he stood right up and asked if I was aware how much food the hotel kitchen was wasting."

Martine was right. The kid had some kind of chutzpah.

"Well, I could tell he was hungry, so I invited him in for a decent meal."

"Oh, Gretchen! That was kind of you," said Grandma. "But weren't you a little . . . concerned?"

"If it had been anybody else, I probably would have been. But Jimmy had what I can only call an air about him. I know that's an old-fashioned phrase, but it's the only description I've got. Even though he had clearly been on the streets for a while, he was still so confident, so sure of himself."

I remembered what Old Sean had said about Jimmy Upton's charm. Come to that, Frank and Martine had both said something similar.

"Well, we sat in the kitchen and talked," Gretchen was saying. "Jimmy told me how he'd been fired from his last job in Boston. The chef there wanted to hire his nephew, and Jimmy had said some things he maybe shouldn't have. Unfortunately, the chef there was very well connected, and suddenly Jimmy found he couldn't get work at all."

"How *awful*!" said Grandma.

"He was very impulsive," Gretchen was saying, "and proud, and his temper could get the better of him."

Now, that sounded a lot more like the man Martine had described. The problem was that this story didn't match with the one Jimmy had told Frank about backpacking around Europe to get trained, and coming to Portsmouth to "perfect his craft." He hadn't said anything about being fired in Boston during that interview. You'd think a guy who was always willing to go on the attack would be happy for a chance to do it in print.

Miss Boots seemed to decide she'd had enough of her owner's lap and jumped down to settle herself in the sunny spot on the windowsill. She rolled over onto her back, getting comfortable. I watched her, thinking about how Alistair seemed to be on a first-name basis with every sunbeam in Portsmouth. I was also thinking how it sounded like there were multiple versions of Jimmy Upton out there. Which one, I wondered, was real?

It seemed like Grandma B.B. was wondering something similar.

"But, Gretchen." Grandma leaned forward. "I can't believe you just hired a stranger on the strength of a sad story. Not as a chef, certainly."

"Well, I may be a sentimental old woman, but I'm not *that* sentimental. No. I asked him to make me an omelet."

Grandma glanced at me and I nodded. I'd heard about that trick from Martine. As part of a job interview, a new cook in a kitchen might be asked to make an omelet or roast a chicken. Those are very simple dishes, but very hard to make perfect because there's nowhere to hide any mistakes.

"I take it he did," I said.

Gretchen smiled fondly. "It was the best-tasting, loveliest, fluffiest omelet I ever had. *That* was when I hired him," she concluded, triumphantly enough that Miss Boots lifted her head in indignation at the noise.

"Wow. He must have been grateful."

That made Gretchen laugh. "Not in the least. He said he'd consider it and get back to me."

Now, that was some Grade A chutzpah. "You must really have seen something in him to put up with that."

"It's not an attitude that would work well for a manager, I admit, or necessarily in any other department in the hotel," said Gretchen. "But the kitchen is different. These days, people like a chef to be a showman. I still can't believe . . ." She touched the corner of her eye.

"You must have been terribly worried when he disappeared," murmured Grandma. "Was there even anybody for you to call?"

Gretchen's perfectly made-up mouth twisted up tight. "There was a sister, somewhere, but Jimmy said he hadn't been in touch with her in years."

I covered my surprise with a sip of martini. Jimmy's sister had been in town, working for Jake and Miranda, but he hadn't told his boss? I wondered where the sister was now and if we could find her. Then I reminded myself the police would be handling that. Then, much to my chagrin, I found myself wondering if Kenisha had a name and phone number for Jimmy's sister, and if it would be worth it to talk to her.

"I tried to find out more, of course; family is important." Mrs. Hilde said this like it was something engraved in stone. "But Jimmy just wouldn't open up."

"How sad," murmured Grandma B.B. "I can't imagine what you thought when he vanished like he did.

It was a long time before Mrs. Hilde answered. "Considering how he came in the door, I assumed he'd just decided to up and leave. It was the sort of thing he'd do. I just didn't think he'd do it to me," she added softly.

I lifted my martini glass. "If somebody'd done that to me, I'd be furious," I said over the rim.

Gretchen's face twisted up so tightly, I wasn't sure whether she was trying to hold back tears or screams. "I'd invested in Jimmy's future. For him to just abandon me and Harbor's Rest was an insult. I believe if I'd found him, I would have . . . Well, I don't know what I would have done . . . Oh, Lord, that sounds so awful."

Grandma laid a hand on Gretchen's arm. "No, it doesn't. It sounds like you cared a great deal about him."

"I did," she whispered. "When Dale told me they'd found him, I couldn't believe it . . . I . . ." She looked at us both. "It's so strange. I'm not even sure I care about who killed him. I just want to know why."

Grandma looked at me sharply. I cleared my throat. "I'm sure the police will find out soon."

"Yes." Mrs. Hilde sucked in a long, steadying breath. "Lieutenant Blanchard is very efficient. Unlike some members of the force." She glowered out the windows. "Mind you, I've had my suspicions about Jake and Miranda Luce for a very long time."

Despite the warmth of the sun shining through the window, a chill crept over me.

Grandma shot me a warning glance. "Well, I know they were radicals once upon a time, but we were all young and silly once, weren't we?"

"I suppose," Mrs. Hilde said reluctantly. "But I think this goes beyond poaching a boyfriend, don't you, Annabelle? It's just all unbelievably coincidental, them buying the building and then Jimmy being found dead underneath it."

I thought about pointing out that Jimmy had been found a lot closer to Harbor's Rest than he had to the old drugstore, but Gretchen had already leaned forward. "You were with them, Anna. Now that we know . . . what we know . . . can you think of anything you saw that might have been suspicious?"

"No. Nothing," I told her.

"Did you show Jimmy the tunnel, Gretchen?" asked Grandma.

Mrs. Hilde had been relaxing a minute earlier. Now she pulled herself up straight. "I didn't even know it was there. How could I?" she demanded. "If it did have an entrance into the basement, it must have been bricked over decades ago." She took a quick swallow of tea, as if she was trying to wash a bad taste out of her mouth. "Even the police haven't been able to find where it opens, but it was easy enough to find that trapdoor on the Luces' end."

Which was an awfully strong reaction to have over something you didn't know about.

Grandma B.B. turned to me. "Anna, when you uncovered the door on your end, Jake wanted to find out what was down in the tunnel, didn't he?" she prompted. "That's hardly the reaction of a guilty man."

I didn't answer. Of course, Grandma was right, but there was something else that was making me even colder. Because she was right: Jake had wanted to see what was down the tunnel.

Miranda, though, most emphatically had not.

❧ 17 ❧

❧ GRANDMA WAS GIVING me a very strange look. She'd realized I'd thought of something and that it was probably unpleasant. She had no idea.

Fortunately, I didn't have to scramble for a covering remark. Mrs. Hilde's attention was diverted by a man in a red blazer and Clark Kent glasses walking into the bar with a stack of folders in his hands.

I recognized Dale Hilde at about the same moment he recognized me. To say that he was not happy to see me or, rather, us there was something of an understatement. The look he gave my grandmother was something special, but it was nothing at all compared to the look he reserved for Mrs. Hilde.

"Here you are, Mother. I've been looking for you," he said as he reached the table.

Gretchen Hilde returned her son's unambiguous glower calmly. "Annabelle, this is my son Dale," she said to Grandma B.B. "He's our chief financial officer at the Harbor's Rest. Dale, this is an old friend of mine, Annabelle Britton, and her granddaughter Anna."

"Yes, we've met," Dale muttered. "Briefly."

He did not offer to shake hands. Miss Boots meowed from out of her patch of sunlight, a little disappointed at his manners, I thought. Or maybe I'd just been hanging around Alistair too long.

The sight of the cat only sharpened Dale's glower.

"Mother!" he snapped. "The health inspectors—"

"Are not here, Dale." Despite this, Mrs. Hilde scooped Miss Boots up off the sill. Affronted, the cat jumped out of her arms and threaded her way out of the bar, nose and tail in the air.

"There." Gretchen folded her hands on the tabletop. "Health code violation removed. Annabelle, you didn't say you'd met my son."

"They were standing outside with the Luces when the body was discovered," Dale told her, shuffling the folders back into a tidier pile. "With the police." He made it sound like a social disease.

Gretchen's mouth tightened into a straight line, and I got the feeling she didn't exactly disagree with Dale's sentiments, but she was too polite to remark on it. "Yes. Well. We all have our bad days. Did you have something for me?"

"It's just about the spring tour packages that Christine is putting together."

"Oh, for heaven's sake." Gretchen's sighed. "What is it now?"

"Well, there are several issues . . ." Dale flipped open the folder he was carrying and began rifling through the pages. He stopped and looked at us all from over the rims of his Clark Kent glasses. "But I don't want to interrupt."

Except, of course, he did. What I couldn't tell was whether whatever was in those folders was really a vital concern, or he just didn't like the company his mother was keeping.

"I'm afraid we're the ones who are interrupting," said Grandma pleasantly. "I know you have work to do, Gretchen. Where you find the energy, I can't imagine."

"Well, it's never been easy." Gretchen sighed and got to her feet. "Please let's have a real catch-up soon, Annabelle."

"Of course we will," said Grandma.

"You're both of course welcome to stay and enjoy our view," she said, and it seemed to me that was as much for her son's sake as for ours. "All right, Dale." She sighed. "Show me what problem Christine's created this time."

Grandma and I both smiled, and we kept right on smiling until the Hildes were out of earshot. Then I leaned across the table and whispered at my grandmother in my most pleasant and reasonable tones.

"What are you *doing* here?"

"Visiting an old friend," replied Grandma calmly. "What are you doing here?"

There are few things as frustrating as someone giving you a flimsy excuse for what she's doing while at the same time exposing the fact that you have no excuse at all.

"At least I have a reason to be asking questions."

"So do I."

"I'm a guardian of Portsmouth, Grandma," I whispered. "I'm supposed to be helping."

Grandma leaned forward, and I can only hope when I reach her age I'll still be able to put as much steel in my gaze and my voice. "And my granddaughter is in trouble," she said. "I'm not going to just sit on the sidelines."

"I'm not in trouble." At least I didn't think I was. I certainly hoped I wasn't. But then I remembered Lieutenant Blanchard's bright little eyes, and I wasn't so sure.

"Good. You're not in trouble. All I'm doing is making sure you stay that way," Grandma said firmly. "That Lieutenant Blanchard seems to have gotten hold of the wrong end of the stick. We can't be sure what else might pop into his head." She paused. "I wonder if he's related to Mousey Mickey Blanchard? I never did like that boy's attitude—"

"Grandma B.B.," I said urgently, and softly, hoping this might encourage Grandma to keep her voice down. "You have got to stay out of this."

"Too late, dear. I'm already in it."

"No, you're not."

"Yes, I am, as long as you are."

I closed my mouth. There was absolutely no way I was

going to be able to argue her out of this. I slumped back in my chair, but Grandma looked down her nose at me and I automatically sat up straight. And then I rolled my eyes, because I really couldn't believe any of this. Not only was I dealing with a dead body and a (possibly) real ghost; I had my grandmother riding shotgun.

Well, if life gives you grandmothers, really, all you can do is make the best of it.

"Lieutenant Blanchard isn't the only one who has problems with Jake and Miranda," I said. "Your friend Gretchen seemed pretty ready to believe they were up to something illegal."

Grandma contemplated her half-empty glass of tea. "Well, you have to understand, Anna, Gretchen grew up working. This is a grand hotel, but the profits were always very slim, and her whole family had to pitch in to keep the place running. Other people might've spent their summers hitchhiking around the country and talking about flower power and so on, but to someone like Gretchen, that doesn't look like finding yourself; it looks like laziness. For a family like the Hildes, sloth is the deadliest of all the sins."

"I wish you'd found a different expression," I muttered.

"Oh, I'm *sorry*. That was insensitive of me, wasn't it?" She patted my hand. "Well, never mind, dear. Tell me how you've been spending your day, now that you're sprung."

"Nobody says 'sprung' anymore, Grandma." At least, I didn't think they did. I was a little outside my linguistic comfort zone here. "Anyway, I wasn't arrested. It was just some questions."

Grandma waved this away. "Anna, I do know something about how the world works. If this Lieutenant Blanchard is looking at Jake and Miranda, he's looking at you as well."

This was the problem with having a well-traveled grandmother. She'd seen a whole lot. But she was always so sunny and cheerful, I could forget that as quickly as anybody else.

We sat in silence for a minute. The room moved around us. The servers came and went with practiced efficiency, but there weren't enough customers to fill up the hush. Sean's dad came out of the back and the pair of them slapped each other on the arms in a kind of father-and-son tag-team gesture, and Sean left and Mr. McNally tossed a bar towel over his shoulder and got busy setting out fresh glasses and wiping down the counters. He gave Grandma a cheerful salute and she raised her glass back to him. What guests there were finished their drinks and left and a few new guests came in. Mostly, they were middle-class and above, well dressed and relaxed. They talked and they laughed and they pointed out the lights of the boats passing on the river.

While I stared out the darkening window and tried to sort out my ideas and my feelings, I saw Miss Boots in all her sleek orange-and-white splendor come strolling across the green grass. And she wasn't alone. A much rounder, much more smug, smoke gray cat galumphed after her.

Alistair?

My familiar glanced toward the window, blinked once, and proceeded to plump himself down next to Miss Boots and start grooming his hind leg.

Seriously, big guy?

Well, what did I know? Maybe girl cats liked that sort of thing. But at the moment, Miss Boots seemed more interested in nosing around in the neatly trimmed grass.

I turned my attention back to the room. Yes, it suddenly felt like I was spying on somebody else's date. No, I didn't really want to think about that too much.

"Well, I don't know about you, but I'm *starving*," said Grandma. "You said something about fried clams?"

I had, and I was glad the subject had come back up. We said good-bye to Old Sean and headed back up toward the square and the River House.

Grandma and I both agreed that we needed a break from murder and suspicion, so as we squeezed lemon over fried seafood and drank Perrier, we'd engaged in some aggressively normal conversation about the rest of the family. We'd talked about my father, Robert, who was probably going to move in permanently with my brother Bob, his wife, Ginger, and their son, Bobby III. We shook our heads over my sister,

Hope, who was out in California and planning on joining a bar band, last we heard anyway. We wondered when or if my other brother, Ted, was going to propose to his current girlfriend.

It was great. It was comfortable and entirely normal, and there was no way it could last.

"Grandma," I said slowly. "I've got an unfair question to ask."

"I thought you might, dear," she replied with a satisfied smile. I resisted the urge to make a face.

"Do you think that story Gretchen told about meeting Jimmy Upton in a dark alley was true?"

"I think it very likely was, but I don't think it was the whole truth." She paused, and her eyes went distant, turning over recent conversations and old memories to see what lay beneath. "Poor Gretchen."

"Why 'poor Gretchen'?"

"Well, surely you noticed, dear, she had very strong feelings for the young man."

It would have been hard not to. "Could Upton have been using her?" What we'd heard about the man so far was not good. Everybody agreed he could cook like a Food TV star. But other than that, he seemed to have been a pretty comprehensive jerk. Maybe that was why his sister had stopped talking to him.

"I think it's possible someone was being used, but you shouldn't underestimate Gretchen, dear."

I laid my hand over my heart. "Now, would I do that?"

Grandma huffed. "Anna, I know we look like a passel of sweet little old ladies now, but you will *please* do me the favor of remembering we were your age once. Gretchen took full control of the hotel at a time when the only reason girls from families like hers were supposed to go to college was to find a good husband. Of course, I wasn't here for it, but I can promise you, she had to fight tooth and nail for everything she has."

"But you said she always worked . . ."

"Yes, she worked. She clerked and typed and hostessed.

Most of it without being paid, and it was to help the family out. That was expected. It was also considered entirely different from actually daring to think she could run the business."

"Different world."

"In so many ways," agreed Grandma.

"And I imagine she'd get a little upset if she thought any of that had been threatened."

"I imagine she would, yes," agreed Grandma. "And I admit I've been thinking about that. Rather a lot."

⚘ 18 ⚘

🐾 I AM VERY glad to report that Julia did not insist that our ghost hunting at the old drugstore had to be done after dark.

"If there is a soul lost inside the building, they are there in the daylight as well as in the dark," she said.

"I thought the vibrations from the sunlight could interfere with spectral activity and stuff like that." At least, that's what the Internet thought. I'd been doing a little light reading on ghost hunting along with the history of Portsmouth and its long list of smugglers, pirates and bootleggers.

"What the vibrations from sunlight mostly interfere with is people's imaginations," she answered tartly.

It was three days before the crime scene tape was taken down off the old drugstore. I threw myself into trying to find some hint as to the location of the tunnel where Jimmy had been found. I spent most of them in the Portsmouth Historical Society's library, poring over old photographs, newspaper pages and plans from its digital archives. I saw the blueprints for Harbor's Rest in the 1980s and the 1950s, and a very bad photocopy of a photocopy of the original plans from 1892. I made notes of other sources to chase down in other places. I made more sketches and printed copies and spent a couple of nights going over them with, I kid you not, a magnifying glass.

And at the end of it all, I got nothing except a headache and a stiff neck. Okay, that's not entirely true. I also got short-tempered from having to keep lifting Alistair off the pages. Being a cat, he felt it was his duty to sit in the middle of any pile of paper that happened to be on the dining room table. Or the coffee table. Or the breakfast table. He particularly liked the books I checked out of the library and seemed to prefer *Portsmouth: Evolution of a Riverside Town.* But then it was an oversized volume.

I found exactly nothing about the tunnel, rumored or otherwise.

Trying to keep a good thought, I also made notes on material that would be useful for the new murals for Northeast Java. I spent mornings before the society and the library opened working on some watercolors and pencil sketches so I could show them to Jake and Miranda for their approval before I started in on the main work.

In the end, there were three of us in Grandma B.B.'s Galaxie, driving out to meet Julia and the dachshunds in front of the old drugstore. Val left the bed-and-breakfast in the care of Marisol, their new assistant manager, while Roger was meeting with the tourist board about McDermott's placement in the information packages for people looking for places to stay on their leaf-peeping and winter vacation trips.

"He's really serious about jump-starting the baby girl's college fund," I remarked.

"I don't know when I've seen him so busy," she said. "But it means I'm guaranteed at least an hour without a phone call."

Midnight Reads was being minded by Julia's assistants, Marie and Oscar. We had hoped Kenisha would be able to meet us, but she had called to beg off. The investigation had taken a turn, she said, but that was all she said.

Grandma and I helped get Val and her bulging tote bag out of the Galaxie.

"Hey, wow, welcome, good morning!" called Jake. He was jogging up the street, the ends of his bandana flapping in the breeze. "Sorry. Got my wires crossed. Wasn't expecting you yet."

"Do you need us to come back later?" said Julia. Max and Leo were snuffling around the threshold, wagging their tails (actually their whole behinds) excitedly.

Jake scratched his chin and glanced back down the street toward the square. "Uh, nah, it's cool. I think it'd be better we get this, you know, cleared up."

"Very well," said Julia. Did she hear how nervous Jake sounded? Well, put it down to finding out if there was a real ghost in here. I sure wasn't feeling my normal calm and collected self.

"Anna, do you need a moment?" Julia asked me as we got up to the door.

Actually, I did. I closed my eyes and deepened my focus to make sure that this time my mental shields were firmly in place. I did not want the old drugstore's Vibe sneaking up on me while we were trying to raise a ghost. Or anything else that might be lurking in there.

When I opened my eyes, Grandma B.B. gave me a very prominent wink. Julia frowned. I tried to ignore them both.

The inside of the old drugstore looked just the same. The antique oak bar gleamed in the dim light that filtered through the paper on the plate glass windows. The dachshunds instantly began scampering around the entire room, shoving their noses into every crack and corner and filling the place with the sound of doggy toenails clicking and scratching against the floorboards. To me, the air still smelled of plaster and dust. Val sneezed and fished in her purse for a Kleenex, but Julia had one out first and gave it to her.

Julia put her bag down on the bar. "Valerie, Anna, would you set up the altar, please?"

"On it," said Val.

"Do you guys need me to leave?" asked Jake.

"You can stay if you want," said Julia. "There's nothing secret happening. I will have to ask you to be quiet while we work."

"Cool, great, okay." He took himself over to the stairs and sat down with his arms folded on his knees. "So what happens?" Jake asked. "You sit around the table and join hands?"

"Certainly not as a first step. First, we consult the experts."

"Cool." Jake rubbed his hands together. I felt a pricking in the back of my mind that had nothing to do with magic.

According to Julia, an altar, though, would help establish our magical presence and attune the space to any workings we did have to accomplish. We laid a blue cloth over one of the scarred tables and set out a pair of candles. I filled a glass dish with salt while Val poured water into an antique silver cup and set a box of dried herbs. These symbolized the magical elements; earth, water, fire and air. We set each of these on its appropriate direction on the circle.

I laid my wand down in the center, just in case.

As I did, I felt sure someone was laughing at me. I shook myself and tried to pull my focus down more tightly around me.

"Are you all right, dear?" Grandma B.B. asked.

"I'm fine." I was, mostly. I could feel the Vibe out beyond the edge of my mental shields. The back of my neck was already prickling. So were my fingertips and the backs of my hands. Worse, my curiosity itched, creating a dull, nagging sensation in my mind. I tried to ignore it, but it was not easy.

"We won't be casting a formal circle unless we find a spirit, but we should take our places at the cardinal points," said Julia. Grandma rolled her eyes. Julia ignored this. "Anna, by the windows there. Valerie, by the door. Annabelle, by the basement stairs, please."

We all moved to our designated spots, while Julia stepped to the center of the room.

"Max, Leo. Here, boys."

The dachshunds immediately halted their explorations and scrambled up to her, wagging, panting and yipping, clearly delighted with everything they'd seen so far. Leaning heavily on her walking stick, Julia bent down slowly and ruffled their floppy ears and whispered to them something so low I couldn't hear. Then, she straightened up, and stood with her eyes closed and her hand resting lightly on her cane. A deep quiet radiated out from her to spread like a blanket over the room. My skin prickled, but I wasn't afraid. I felt very aware and very awake.

Julia thumped her walking stick once. "Maximilian. Leopold," she called, her voice low and clear. *"Inveniet!"*

My art school Latin came to my rescue. The command was "find."

It is difficult to take a miniature dachshund seriously. I mean, they are just about the cutest dogs on the planet. But when Julia gave the command, Max and Leo stopped all their snuffling, wagging and yipping. Their ears and tails came up, instantly alert. Leo dropped his nose to the floor and began casting about in a very deliberate circle, while Max showed every sign of being on watch.

My shields bent and shifted. I swallowed hard and clenched my hands. Grandma glanced worriedly at me. I nodded and gave her and Val a thumbs-up. I was okay. Really. But I couldn't relax. The restless prickling in my skin was getting worse. So was the feeling of being watched. Movement caught my eye, and I looked out the window. There was Alistair on the sill, pawing at the latch. I shook my head at him, and he shrugged and vanished. That was when I saw something else. The windowsill, right by the latch, was freshly splintered, like it had been gouged by a sharp tool.

My brother Ted installs burglar alarms and home security systems, which is both appropriate and ironic since he taught me everything I know about breaking and entering when I was still a teenager. While I am certainly not advocating this as a lifestyle choice, Ted told me that if you ever do really want or need to break into a house, windows are a great bet. People will spend all kinds of money on door locks, but they'll forget all about the window latches.

I looked to Jake sitting on the stairs, rubbing his long hands together. I looked to the splintered wood.

Leo's circles were widening. He was almost at the stairs leading up to the second floor. Jake was watching. He shifted his weight uneasily. I put my hand on the latch. Yeah, it was, in fact, just a little loose. I also looked out the window, and I saw a battered tan car pulling up out back. Two men climbed out and slammed the doors.

Leo stopped in his tracks, his ears up, quivering from nose to tail.

"Yip!" Max trotted up beside his brother.

"There," breathed Julia. "Someone is there."

"Julia . . ." I began.

She raised her hand. "Welcome, spirit."

Something rippled across the back of my neck. It was that feeling of being laughed at. We weren't alone. I couldn't see anything, but inside my head, my shields wobbled and strained, and I gulped down a spark of fear.

Footsteps thudded above us. I jerked my head up and my shields shifted again. Leo darted over to stand beside Julia, head down and hackles raised.

"Oh, no," said Julia. "You'll have to do better than that. Will you share your name with us?"

"Oh, I think we all know each other all right."

A cop walked into a barroom. Unfortunately, it wasn't the opening line for a joke. But it was Lieutenant Blanchard.

❧ 19 ❧

❧ THE ATMOSPHERE SNAPPED. I felt the jarring like I'd just broken a board over my knee. Julia staggered. Jake jumped to his feet and Grandma and I rushed forward, while Val grabbed a chair and pushed it toward her. Both dachshunds yipped and scampered back to her side, whining anxiously. With all this going on, I almost didn't notice that Pete Simmons walked in behind Blanchard.

Somebody laughed. Even Jake heard it. He actually spun in a circle, his face as white, as if, well, as if he'd seen a ghost.

"Well, well," said Blanchard. "The gang's all here."

"You okay, Jake?" asked Pete. "Miss Parris?"

"Yes, fine," Julia said, but she still collapsed into the chair.

"Is something wrong, Lieutenant?" I asked, putting myself between the policemen and my mentor. Val pulled a baggie of homemade granola bars and a bottle of water out of her tote bag. Grandma uncapped the bottle and Julia accepted it gratefully.

"Got the munchies, Miss Parris?" inquired Lieutenant Blanchard.

The sneer seemed to snap Jake's focus back to the present.

"Hello, Lieutenant. Hello, Pete." Jake moved to stand beside me. "If you're looking for a cuppa joe, you should go down to Ceres Street. Miranda'll be glad to fix you up. We're not exactly open here yet."

"We got a call about some suspicious activity, Jake," said Pete.

"Looks like they were right." Blanchard fingered the altar cloth. Val glowered and took a step forward, but Leo darted in front of her and nosed her ankles. She took the hint and stayed where she was.

"Nothing suspicious here, Officers," Jake said. "This is my place and these ladies are my guests."

Blanchard watched, grinning while Julia swallowed her granola and chased it down with about half of the bottle of water. Max pawed and wagged and whined.

"Yes, yes," she told her familiars. "I'm fine. I am." She blinked, hard, and now her eyes, and her mind, really focused on her immediate surroundings.

"Since nothing's wrong, you won't mind letting us look around?" Blanchard folded his arms. "You know, just to be sure?"

Jake's normally mild expression hardened. I knew there was about to be a perfectly reasonable question raised about a warrant, but apparently Grandma B.B. had decided this was all quite enough, thank you.

"You're Lieutenant Blanchard, aren't you?" Grandma stepped around the chair where Julia was sitting. Max tried to intercept her, but she stepped around him, too. "The one who's been harassing my granddaughter?"

Oh. No. I was reaching out, like I thought I might have to drag her back by force. But she was already standing right in front of the lieutenant, looking him up and down. "I would have expected something better from Mickey Blanchard's son."

"Do I know you?" Blanchard asked, his voice full of cold and warning.

"No, but I'm sure Mickey remembers me." Grandma had said something about a Mousey Mickey Blanchard. "Did he ever tell you about the time he snuck out after eleven when

I was babysitting and tried to smuggle himself to Boston in the back of Avery Pope's El Camino . . ."

Blanchard's little eyes just about popped out of his head. "You . . . you're Annie-Bell? Holy . . . He told me about you. He . . ." He pointed his finger at Grandma B.B. and then at me. "Wait. You're her *grandmother*?"

"I'm older than I look, dear," she said pleasantly. "How is Mickey doing? It's been forever. Does he still put pickles on his peanut butter sandwiches?"

"Every time. Man, would you believe . . ." Blanchard stopped and stared, like he couldn't believe he'd actually said something vaguely pleasant.

Grandma laughed and patted his arm. "Oh, don't worry, dear. There's nothing here to cause any fuss for the police. Unless . . ." She paused significantly. "You want to help us catch the ghost?"

"Ghost?" repeated Blanchard.

"Ghost?" said Pete to me. I smiled and nodded, vigorously. Pete covered what may have been an entirely unprofessional smile.

"Why, yes." Julia gestured toward the table with its candles, cup and wand. "We were about to conduct a séance to attempt to contact the poor, restless spirit haunting this place. All true believers are of course welcome to join us."

"Are you a true believer, Lieutenant?" asked Jake pleasantly.

"Oh, for the . . ." Blanchard strangled on his own words. "That's what this is about?"

We all nodded, including the dachshunds. They also wagged their tails.

"I should have known it'd be something like that," the lieutenant muttered. "Christ. Okay." He waved his hand, dismissing us all. "You got one hour," he said. "We'll be watching, just in case something . . . happens. This is a crime scene, after all."

"Was," said Jake. "Was a crime scene."

"I'll be sure to take that into account when I am contacting the spirits," said Julia distantly. "I'm sure such a presence as yours will serve to create a positive and receptive atmosphere."

"Um. Yeah. Right," muttered Blanchard.

"And please tell Mickey I said hello," said Grandma cheerfully. "Perhaps I'll stop by while I'm in town."

"Um, yeah, sure." But he was already backing away.

Jake flashed him the peace sign. Blanchard looked ready to spit on the floor, and all the muscles in his forearms tensed.

Grandma and Julia both stepped right between the two of them. So did Max and Leo.

Blanchard straightened his shirt cuffs, and he left. Pete gave us all a backward glance, and I'm not entirely sure he liked what he was seeing. The bell jangled as the door closed, and Max and Leo scampered over, nosing around the threshold to make sure the bad man was really gone.

"Thank you," said Jake to Grandma.

"Oh, it was nothing, dear," Grandma patted her hand.

"Well, it may have been nothing," said Julia. "But it was also very well done, Annabelle." She sounded a little surprised, which was not a reaction Grandma was going to appreciate.

"Oh, well, thank you so much, Julia," she said pointedly.

Julia stiffened, and the dachshunds closed doggy ranks.

Time to interrupt. For better or worse.

"Hey, Jake. Um, I've got a question."

"Sure. What's up?"

I didn't really want to do this. I didn't want to be thinking the things I was, or worrying about what it all meant, but keeping quiet was not going to help.

"Who jimmied the window?"

Jake stiffened. "What?"

"Anna, what are you talking about?" demanded Val.

"Somebody got in here through the window, or at least they tried to." I was still looking at Jake while I said it. "Maybe even while this building was still a sealed crime scene."

Jake didn't answer; he just worked his jaw back and forth.

"Is Anna right, Jake?" asked Julia. "Is something going on? You have to tell us, or we won't be able to help you."

But she wasn't the one who answered us.

"It's okay, Jake," said somebody from upstairs. "It's done anyhow."

We all whirled around to see a wiry young man with dark hair and a sparkling stud in one ear clump down the stairs. Max and Leo yapped in surprise.

If my jaw dropped, I feel that is a perfectly understandable reaction. Chuck, aka the Rhinestone Barista, came slowly down the stairs.

Chuck's gaze flickered from Jake to the rest of us, and I wasn't sure if he was going to bolt or just be sick on the spot. I couldn't help noticing he had his sleeves rolled up and a pair of bright yellow latex gloves on his hands.

"Oof!" Val covered her nose. "What is that smell? Is that bleach?"

"Did you get it all?" asked Jake quietly.

"Yeah, pretty sure."

"Good." He turned to us and sighed. "There. That's who was upstairs."

"What was it you were cleaning up?" I said before anybody else could speak.

"Just get on out of here, Chuck." Jake patted the kid's shoulder. "You can go tell Miranda everything's cool here. She might have seen the cops coming out."

But Chuck didn't move. "No way. I'm not going anywhere, not if they think you've done something."

"Except you have, haven't you?" I said to Jake.

Jake shoved his fingers under his wire-rimmed glasses and rubbed his eyes. "Well, that depends who you ask. Look, we might as well go upstairs. That's going to be the community meeting space, and this looks like it's going to be one heck of a meeting."

❧ 20 ❧

🐾 UPSTAIRS, WE UNFOLDED some of the gray, rust-spotted chairs. Julia sat with the dachshunds in her lap and her walking stick laid beside her. Val took the chair next to her. She also checked her phone in its hip pouch. Satisfied with whatever she saw on the screen, she tucked it away again. Grandma passed Julia a fresh granola bar. She'd brought Val's tote bag upstairs with us, because while she might not cook, she never let anybody go hungry.

Chuck did not sit. He just went over to the windows and looked out into the street while he stripped off his gloves. The sky was gray and a couple of raindrops spattered against the glass.

Jake didn't sit either. He pulled the stepladder away from the wall, climbed up and pressed his hand against the ceiling panels. Unlike downstairs, the original ceiling up here had been replaced with cheap white acoustic tile, which was a crime against architecture, if you asked me.

"Um, you need some help with that?" I asked.

"Nope. Got it." Jake grunted, and a section of the dimpled white tile shifted and came away in his hands. "See, the reason I was so surprised to see that trapdoor downstairs was I thought we'd already found the secret panel in here."

Jake climbed back down the steps and of course we all crowded around and looked up. Now that the cracked plaster ceiling was exposed, we could see the rectangular outlines of a door to the attic, the kind that you pulled down to get to a folding ladder.

"You remember we told you about that security camera?" Jake said as he climbed back down. "It showed us somebody coming in and out of here after dark, and so we took a look and we found—"

"Don't tell me." In my head, Blanchard's questions at the station bumped up against his crack about Julia having the munchies. "Four marijuana plants and a grow light?"

"Well, maybe more like two dozen," he said. "And a whole modern hydroponic rig-out. But, yeah, there were grow lights."

"Chuck?" I asked.

"It wasn't much," said Chuck. "I mean, not really." He wasn't looking at any of us. He pressed his fingertips against the window, lining them up with the raindrops. "You know, just a little on the side to some friends. I was going to quit it before this, swear I was. Jake and Miranda . . . they talked to me about how it was going to come back on me, but then—" He stopped. "My girlfriend's pregnant."

Val laid her hands on her belly.

"Oh. Dear," murmured Grandma B.B.

"We're both trying to get our degrees, and we got loans, and all I've got is the barista gig. She wants to keep the baby, and I—I want to be a dad, you know? I have to come up with some money for us."

"I understand, Chuck," Val told him with a small smile. "It's crazy expensive, isn't it?"

He nodded.

"We told you we'd find you something," said Jake. "The word's out. It'll be all right."

"So that's it," I said. "That's the reason for all the secrecy. Because if Blanchard found out there was pot growing in the attic here, with Jake and Miranda's record, and you working for them, he'd connect the obvious dots."

"I tossed most of the stuff, like, weeks ago," said Chuck miserably. "But then Upton turns up dead with all that cash on him and it all hit the fan. I was up there today, trying to scrub the place out." He waved his hand toward the jug of bleach. "What's going to happen? I just—I can't go to jail." He twisted his fingers together. "Cherie's counting on me, and the baby and . . . crap." His knees buckled and he slid down until he was crouching against the wall, both hands knotted in his hair.

"Nothing is going to happen to you," said Jake as he knelt beside the younger man. "No one here is going to turn you in for a mistake."

Chuck didn't seem to have heard him. "I have effed this all up so bad. I didn't mean to. But we needed so much stuff and a bigger place, and Cherie's fighting with her folks . . . and I promised I'd be there, and now it's all gonna go straight down the toilet."

The dachshunds trotted over and nosed Chuck's knees, but he didn't respond. I wracked my brains for something to say. His distress was real. He was tired and afraid and still not much more than a kid. There had to be something we could do.

"Annabelle," said Julia quietly to Grandma B.B. "Do you think you might be able to help here?"

Grandma flushed. "Well. It has been a long time. But I'll do my best." Grandma walked over and sat down cross-legged on the bare floor in front of him. I could only hope I was still that limber at her age. "Give me your hands, Charles."

"What?" Chuck lifted his head. His cheeks were wet.

"You want to know what's going to happen, don't you?" Grandma said. "To you, and to Cherie and your baby? If you give me your hands, I might be able to show you."

She was telling the truth. I can't explain how I knew. It was just there, like the sound of the rain against the glass.

Chuck felt it, too. He swallowed nervously, but he also laid both palms against Grandma's, and she closed her fingers around his wrists.

The air around us stirred. No one was laughing now. The dachshunds were sitting on their haunches beside Julia, ears alert, but still. Even Alistair, who had climbed up the stairs from . . . somewhere, had tucked his legs under him and was watching us without twitching even the tip of his tail.

Grandma B.B. closed her eyes.

I felt the prickling begin, starting at my fingertips and traveling up my arms. There was no mistaking it. Grandma B.B.'s mouth moved in a silent whisper, invoking her personal energies and asking assistance from the elements and the spirits. Chuck's eyes darted this way and that. Even he could feel something was happening.

"Charles Dwyer," murmured Grandma. "So very worried. So very afraid." She paused, and her eyes snapped open. "She loves you," she said firmly. "Loves you, is sorry, wonders if she's doing the right thing, wishes you would talk to her . . ."

"We've been telling the kid that," muttered Jake.

"Strong," said Grandma. "Heart is strong; head is catching up. You will . . ." She let go of one of his hands, and covered the other with hers. "Work will out; heart will out. There's news coming. An answer. Movement. Change. Good health and hope to you. All of you. You can do this. You have the heart to do this thing. A reunion." She turned his hand over. Her fingers traced one line of his palm, but whatever Grandma was looking at, it wasn't in this room with us. "A reunion will bring the answers."

Grandma blinked heavily and slowly lifted her hands away from Chuck's. He was breathing like he'd just run the four-minute mile. So was Grandma B.B., and the prickle of the magic faded slowly away.

"That's all," she said. "That's what I have for you."

"Wow," said Chuck. "That was . . . intense, you know what I mean?"

"Yes, dear, I certainly do." She patted his hand.

"I'll second that wow, Grandma," I said. "You could take it on the road."

"Oh, no, dear. It doesn't always work so well. Charles is a very good subject." She beamed at him and Chuck ducked his head bashfully. It was good to see, because it meant that crushing worry had eased up some.

Jake cleared his throat. "It's not that I don't respect your practices, and I'm sure Chuck—"

"No, it's okay, boss," Chuck told him. "I . . . I called my brother out in San Francisco a couple weeks ago. He's working with a tech start-up. They might be interested in my online coffee connection idea." He stopped and swallowed. "I haven't seen him in, like, five years. So, you know, a reunion really might bring the answers."

Jake let out a long breath. "Far out," he whispered.

"Merow," agreed Alistair, who was sitting at the top of the stairs, casually licking his paw.

"Um, Anna," said Jake. "How'd your cat get in here?"

"Don't ask," I told him. "You'll be happier that way."

"Anna, dear," said Grandma B.B. "I think I may need some help getting up."

That got us all into motion. Jake unfolded a chair and Chuck helped pull Grandma B.B. to her feet and walk her over to it. Valerie dug another bottle of Vitaminwater out of her bag. I opened the cap and put the bottle and the last granola bar in Grandma's hands.

"I'm going to have to start packing more snacks." Valerie laughed. "Roger will be so pleased."

"So what are you going to do now?" asked Jake.

That was a really good question. I ran both my hands through my hair like that would help me smooth out my thoughts. Everything had been flipped around and I was having trouble getting my bearings again.

Except. Maybe. I felt my gaze swiveling to Chuck.

"Chuck?" I said.

"Yeah?"

"I hate to do this, but I've got to ask—"

"Oh, no, Anna," Grandma waved the granola bar. "After everything this poor boy's been through, you are not going to ask if he murdered Jimmy Upton. Don't you think I would have noticed that at once?"

"I, um, don't know?" I answered. "But that's not what I was going to ask. I was just going to ask if you ever pulled some shifts with Jimmy Upton's sister when she was working at Northeast Java."

"Mow-aow," grumbled Alistair, who had moved on to washing his right paw. I knew that tone. It meant *finally*.

"Do you mean Michele?" Chuck's eyebrows went up. "The chick who went AWOL? You know her name's not Upton, right? It's Kinsdale."

Well. That was news.

"Kinsdale?" said Jake. "When did she tell you that?"

"When she came back."

"Back?" There were three or four of us humans joining together on that particular exclamation, and at least one dachshund.

"Yeah, she showed up again, yesterday, no wait, the day before. She was all decked out in a suit and heels and everything."

Jake frowned. "You never said."

"Yeah, well." Even though he was sitting down, Chuck shuffled his feet. "This was after we found out about Jimmy, and the way things were going, I figured you might not want to hear it."

Jake looked uneasy at this. "It's not the crime; it's the cover-up," he muttered. "Man, after Nixon, you'd think I'd've learned."

"So what happened?" I prompted Chuck.

"Michele who the heck ever says she knows I'm looking for a better job," he said. "She tells me she's opening up some kind of a new property in town, and I can come talk to her, anytime."

"What new property?" I demanded at the same time Valerie asked, "Where?"

"Don't know," Chuck told us. "I mean, after you found

her brother all dead in that tunnel? I told her thanks but no thanks. I didn't want anything to do with it, or her."

"Wait." I made the time-out sign. "She was back *after* Jimmy was murdered?"

"Yeah. I figured she was talking to the police or identifying the body or something."

"Do you know where she is now?" We needed to talk to her. Of course Pete and Kenisha would have interviewed her as soon as they found her, if they'd found her that is. But Blanchard's appearance here said the police were still watching Jake and Miranda closely. If we were going to help find out who'd really killed Jimmy, we were going to have to keep digging on our own.

"No idea."

I said several things then, and earned a hard frown from my grandmother. I'd apologize later.

"Sorry," said Chuck.

"Not your fault," said Jake.

"Yeah, I just—" Chuck stopped, and he swore. Now Grandma B.B. was frowning at him. "The fishbowl!"

"Fishbowl?" said Julia.

"Yeah, the fishbowl." Chuck gestured, like he was trying to conjure the shape of what he was talking about out of thin air. "For, like, the, like, cards, like, you know . . ."

We were all staring at one another, trying to translate this.

"We keep a fishbowl on the counter," said Jake. "People drop a card or a note or something in there and we do a drawing for free coffee."

Val grabbed one of Chuck's flailing hands. "Michele dropped a card in the fishbowl?"

"No. I did. After she gave it to me."

"Karma!" Jake shouted. "Beauty!" He strode down the stairs and out the door, which we knew because the bell rang sharply.

"Right," Val heaved herself to her feet. "To the Batcave, everybody?"

"Yip," agreed Max.

*   *   *

WHEN WE GOT to Northeast Java, the crowd was at low ebb. Miranda was behind the counter. Chuck charged up and grabbed the fishbowl. Now I remembered I'd put a card in myself once or twice, to try to win a free beverage.

"Chuck, what the heck?" Miranda demanded as the barista dumped a snowdrift of business cards out onto the counter. "Jake?"

"It's cool, Miranda." Jake slid behind the counter to stand beside her. "Chuck might have found a clue."

She raised her eyebrows. "Sweet. I guess."

"Got it!" Chuck yanked a small paper rectangle out of the pile and passed it to me. Julia, Grandma and Val all crowded around and we all read:

SHELLY KINSDALE
VP of Properties
Dreame Royale Group

There was a red logo of a pillow with a crown floating over it. At least, I think that's what it was supposed to be. It was so stylized, it was hard to tell.

"What's the Dreame Royale Group?" asked Grandma B.B.

Valerie made a face. "They're one of the biggest hospitality chains in the country. They specialize in the high-end and exclusive, boutique and luxury properties, all that . . . stuff."

"So, what does it mean?" asked Miranda. "Was she in town to talk to her brother?"

"But then why would she bother getting a job with us?" asked Jake. "I mean, why hide at all?"

"I don't know, but I know who we better call." And it definitely wasn't Ghostbusters. We'd had enough of that for one day.

I pulled out my phone and hit Kenisha's cell number.

"Britton," she answered. "What's going on?"

"We found Jimmy Upton's sister." I admit there may have been a teensy ring of pride in my voice.

The silence on the other end was very long and very patient.

"So?" said Kenisha at last.

My pride did this little thing where it kind of just . . . evaporated. "I thought maybe you'd want to talk to her."

"We have talked to her," said Kenisha. "And before you say it, yes, we found her first. We're the police, Anna. It is what we do."

I glanced at my friends and family, who were all looking back expectantly. "Um, right. Of course. I just . . . I thought if you had, you . . ."

"You are not going to ask what we found out, right? Because you know better than to ask me that, especially when I'm on duty."

"Um, right. Of course," I said again. "Sorry. We'll talk later?"

"Yeah, we will," agreed Kenisha, and she hung up and I hung up.

"Something tells me that did not go well," said Miranda.

"Anna?" said Grandma B.B. "What happened?"

My Nancy Drew pride just took a hit, and the most obvious way to find out what Michele-slash-Shelly Upton-slash-Kinsdale was doing in town had gotten a big roadblock put up in front of it. I turned the card over in my fingers.

But maybe there was another way.

"Hang on, just one more second." This time, I hit Frank's number.

"Anna? What are you doing?" asked Grandma B.B.

I didn't answer, because just then Frank picked up on his end. "Hey, Anna? What's up?"

"Hi, Frank," I said as I flipped the business card over in my fingers. "I need you to arrange an interview."

"With who?"

"Jimmy Upton's sister," I told him.

"You found her? I can't get Blanchard or Pete to even admit she exists."

I smiled at my friends and family. "We found her and she's been back in town, really recently."

"Back? She was here before?"

"Looks that way. Now it turns out she works for a big hospitality chain, and I thought maybe she'd like to talk to the local paper about what her company's future plans are in Portsmouth."

I could picture the flash in Frank's blue eyes. "She just might, and I know the paper would love to talk to her."

❧ 21 ❧

❧ PEOPLE WILL ALWAYS tell a stranger more than you might think, and when that stranger is a journalist, they'll make space in their schedules for the chance. So, it didn't surprise me when Frank called back saying he'd gotten an appointment to talk with Shelly Kinsdale at five o'clock the next day.

What did surprise me was when he told me where it was.

"She's staying at the Portsmouth Inn."

"She's here? Right here? In town?"

"Apparently."

"The police must need more information from her."

"Maybe," said Frank. "But she was really interested in talking about Dreame Royale's plans in Portsmouth and didn't mention Jimmy once. Usually when you tell people you're from the paper and they've had a murder in the family they kind of assume that's what you want to talk about. She didn't even mention it."

"Wow. That's . . . that's . . ."

"Cold?" said Frank. "Seems to run in the family. See you there."

* * *

ONCE UPON A time, the Portsmouth Inn had been a Victorian mansion. It was nowhere near as big or as grand as Harbor's Rest, but it was a long way from the Quality 6 out by the highway.

Shelly Kinsdale, aka Michele Upton, opened the door right away when Frank knocked. She was a striking woman with dark, waving hair and dark eyes set in a thin face with high cheekbones. Her shoulders were wide, her chin was sharp and her smile was open and brilliant.

"Mr. Hawthone?" she held out her hand. "Shelly Kinsdale. Delighted to meet you. And you, Miss . . . ?"

"Nancy Parker," I said. Frank and I had agreed on a cover story on the way over, just in case she'd heard someone mention my name in connection with the Luces. We might not know for sure if the police had talked with her, but if she really did have something to do with Harbor's Rest, the Hildes might have.

"Won't you come in?" Shelly stood back and we thanked her and did just that.

The room had been freshly made up and all signs of personal belongings tidied away, except for a gleaming black laptop on the desk. Oh, and the fruit basket, which had two bottles standing beside it. The first was some high-end burgundy wine. The second had an apple tree and a cursive script label.

My mind's eye flashed on the bar at the Harbor's Rest, and Kelly Pierce holding a bottle just like that and saying she was going to take it as a "sweetener."

I was really glad Frank was doing the talking right then.

"Miss Parker's doing a trial period at the paper," Frank told Shelly as she gestured us to the sofa while she took the desk chair. "I hope you don't mind I brought her along?"

"Oh, no, not at all. But, as I told you on the phone, I've got another appointment in thirty minutes, so I'm afraid I can't give you as much time as I'd like."

"I understand, Ms. Kinsdale." Frank pulled out his digital

recorder and his notebook. "I appreciate you making the time."

Frank started by asking some fairly innocuous questions about how long Shelly Kinsdale had worked for the Dreame Royale chain (five years); was the chain feeling the economic recovery (delighted to say that hotels are almost all filled to over eighty percent capacity, a tribute to the high standards of excellence found at all Dreame Royale properties). I sat beside him with a notebook and pen in my hands and occasionally checked the pocket recorder on the coffee table to make sure it was still running. But mostly, I watched the woman in front of me.

She certainly didn't act like someone whose brother had just gotten murdered. She was smooth, poised and elegant, clearly comfortable with herself and her surroundings. Upbeat corporate jargon flowed easily from her and her answers were heavily laced with projections and market shares and exciting opportunities for the future.

"So, since you're here, can we assume Dreame Royale is looking to expand in the Portsmouth area?" asked Frank.

Ms. Kinsdale smiled. "Dreame Royale is always keeping an eye out for new opportunities to serve the community," she said breezily. "We know that Portsmouth is a sought-after destination for recreational and business travelers, so we know that Dreame Royale has a place here."

"And does Dreame Royale have an eye on any property in particular?" I asked.

Ms. Kinsdale waved this away. "I'm afraid I can't discuss any deals that may or may not still be in negotiation."

"No, of course not," said Frank. "It's just that there's a rumor floating around that someone is in talks with the owners of one of Portsmouth's more established hotels."

"The Harbor's Rest," I added, for clarity's sake.

Shelly Kinsdale paused and frowned. "Can I ask where you heard this rumor?"

"That would be a confidential source," said Frank immediately.

"Of course." For the first time, I heard the tension under

Shelly's corporate happy-talk. "Well. I suppose I can say that we were at one time interested in the Harbor's Rest, but unfortunately we were not able to come to an understanding with the whole family. It was a disappointment, of course, but unfortunately, not everyone was able to see the advantages of becoming part of the Dreame Royale suite of properties."

"But some could?" I prompted.

"Some, yes." She smiled in that way people do when they want to make it really clear they're done talking now.

Frank and I exchanged glances and I knew he was asking the same question I was. Which Hilde had wanted to sell out?

"So," Frank was saying. "There's nothing we can tell our readers about Dreame Royale's plans for the seacoast?" Frank had an amazing ability to sound gently disappointed.

"We-e-e-elllll . . ." Ms. Kinsdale clasped her hands around her knee and leaned in. "How about this? You can say we are actively pursuing an exciting new opportunity, partnering with local entrepreneurs. This will be a unique, luxury boutique hotel, with all the same standards of excellence our guests expect from the Dreame Royale brand." She beamed, but she also glanced at the clock. "I'm afraid I have a dinner meeting, so we'll have to wrap this up fairly soon. Were there any other questions?"

"Yes," I said. "Just one."

Shelly raised her immaculately plucked eyebrows at me. Frank cleared his throat; he also nudged my foot. I ignored him. There was no way to tell if or when we'd get another chance to talk to this woman. The time for subtly was over.

"Why'd you spend two weeks working for Jake and Miranda Luce?"

Whatever reaction I'd expected from Shelly, I don't think it was a small squirm indicating mild embarrassment. Not that this was her only reaction. She also reached out and snapped the Off button on the recorder.

"So," she said. "You found out about that?"

"Yes," I agreed. "We found out about that."

"Well, I knew it would go public sooner or later." She sighed. "I was just hoping later."

"That was kind of wishful thinking, considering they've been implicated in your brother's murder."

The word "murder" dropped heavily between us, but Shelly didn't even blink. "Jimmy's death has nothing at all to do with my coming to Portsmouth."

Frank reached for the recorder.

"Turn that back on and I'm not saying another word," snapped Shelly. Frank lifted his hand away and held it up, fingers splayed, showing her it was completely empty.

Her eyes narrowed. "I'm assuming that's why you're really here, isn't it? To talk about Jimmy?"

"It's on the list," I said. "So, why the Luces?"

"I needed some cover while I came to Portsmouth to assess the market. If people get word that a major developer is coming in, suddenly everything is spruced up and the red carpet is rolled out, and all kinds of cracks are painted over. It's very hard to get an accurate picture of the local situation."

"But your deciding to come to Portsmouth had nothing to do with your brother being in town?" An online search for Jimmy's name had turned up the article the *Seacoast Times* had run on Jimmy and his prospects as a star chef. I know because I checked.

Shelly's jaw shifted back and forth a couple of times. "Now you're thinking, wow, she's cold, aren't you, Miss . . . whoever you are? Well, how's this for cold? My brother ran out on his family. My father had to go on disability when I was sixteen, and his insurance covered exactly squat. I worked all the way through high school just to help cover the rent. But what does Jimmy do, right when he's getting old enough to really help out? He decides to hit the road and leave me and Dad to sink or swim. Ten years, and the only time we hear from him is when he's trying to weasel some money out of us or, I should say, out of Dad, because he knew I was on to him."

If I hadn't liked Ms. Upton before, I most definitely did not like her now. "So, you took advantage of a couple of nice people so you could scope the place out and maybe find a way to put one over on your brother?"

She shrugged. "Nobody got hurt. They even got two weeks' worth of free labor. I figured it was a fair trade."

"Nobody got hurt? They might be accused of murder!"

"I've told the police what I know. If they have their reasons for suspecting the coffee hippies, it's got nothing to do with me."

I sat back. My stomach was churning. I could not believe Shelly could sit there talking about her brother's death so calmly, especially to a reporter and, well, me.

"And what was the money for?" asked Frank. "Jimmy had five thousand dollars on him when he died."

That actually made her blink. "Oh? Did he? I had no idea."

"You're sure?" I asked.

"Very sure. I had no idea Jimmy even had that kind of money. He never did before. My brother got fired from every job he ever had. He couldn't stand anybody being the boss of him. He'd last two months, maybe three, and then he'd start picking stupid, petty fights, and when he got fired, he'd blame everybody else for it."

I remembered the story about the Boston chef. I remembered all those restaurants he'd named for Frank, all of which were conveniently closed down so there was no way to follow up on how he'd come to work there and, more important, how he'd left.

"Ms. Upton . . ." began Frank.

"Kinsdale." She held up her left hand and waggled her fingers, making the gold and diamond band sparkle in the gray light filtering through the arched windows.

"Ms. Kinsdale," Frank corrected himself. "Did you meet with your brother before he died?"

"Yes. I met with him on that very sofa!" She gestured dramatically. "I listened to him whine for as long as I could stand it. Jimmy had found out I was back in town to discuss a deal on a new luxury hotel, one specifically designed for the twenty-first century, and so he came around begging me to leave Portsmouth and the Harbor's Rest alone. He told a lovely story all about this nice little old lady who runs it with her kids and how that's all they have. Please, pretty please, sis, don't do it." She batted her eyelashes and for a minute I saw a flash of the family charm.

But it did not last. The flinty attitude was back before anyone could finish another breath. "So, you see, I had no reason to kill him. I was going to ruin him." She spread her hands. "Perfectly legal, and a whole lot more satisfying."

I thought about Chuck, risking his neck because he was trying to find a way to provide for his baby. I thought about the difference between making a lousy choice for a lousy reason and doing it for revenge.

I thought about what I would have felt like if one of my siblings had run out when Mom got her cancer. Even Hope had come home and done the best she could.

I suddenly wanted to call up every member of my family just to tell them how very, very much I loved them.

Shelly looked at her watch again. "Now, I have a real appointment, so we are done with this conversation. However, here's one last thought for you both." She raised her index finger. "What if Jimmy had that money in his pocket because he was planning to skip town? It was much more his style than trying to help out his employers."

As much as I hated to admit it, that was definitely something to think about. In fact, I'd already started.

Shelly stood, and we stood.

"Thank you, Ms. Kinsdale," said Frank. "You've been very helpful."

"I'm so glad, Mr. Hawthorne. Dreame Royale is always glad to speak with the media." She actually shook his hand. Her smile did not once waver. "If, however, you try to print anything that jeopardizes my employment or could be considered detrimental to my employers, not only will I deny it, but I will slap your little tiny paper with the biggest libel suit in New England history. Are we clear?"

"Oh, yes," agreed Frank. "Very clear."

We all said good-bye very pleasantly, and Frank and I took ourselves out onto the inn's beautiful wraparound porch.

"Well," said Frank.

"Well," I agreed. "Do you believe she really didn't know Jimmy had that money on him?"

Frank shook his head. "Nope. Ms. Upton Kinsdale is definitely shading the truth there."

"And maybe elsewhere," I said. "Did you see the moonshine she had? I saw Kelly Pierce at the Harbor's Rest take a bottle of that brand. She said she was going to use it as a sweetener for a conference planner."

"Really?" Frank pulled out his notebook and scribbled something down. "Now, that's very interesting."

"Frank? Do you know if the cops still think Jimmy died in some kind of drug deal?"

"I know they do," he said as he snapped his book shut.

"Why? I mean with all that stuff she told us about development deals and everything. That'd be a lot to ignore."

"Yeah." Frank sighed. "That makes for two possibilities. Either Blanchard has decided to ignore the entire business angle. Or Shelly Upton Kinsdale, who is already shading the truth, has told the police something different than she told us."

❧ 22 ❧

❧ "ANNA, YOU ARE not concentrating." Julia punctuated this pronouncement with a thump of her walking stick.

Four of us, plus dachshunds, had gathered in the cottage's deeply shadowed attic. Julia had seen no reason why our ghost hunting this week should cancel out my regularly scheduled magic lesson.

"At the drugstore, you observed, Anna. You did not practice," she said firmly. "And considering how eventful things are becoming, we cannot waste this chance. You need your training."

I really hadn't been able to work up any kind of good argument against that.

My attic room (mine for now, anyway) was right under the cottage gables, which meant the roof beams sloped overhead, and it had a low nook in each of the four directions. Each nook had a multipaned window to let in the sun during the day and the moon after dark.

When this attic had been Dorothy's, it had been mostly bare wood. I was starting to experiment with colors. According to Julia, and the reading I'd been doing about ritual magic, certain colors represented specific aspects of the elemental and spiritual energies. East is air, so in that nook I had propped up some abstract canvases done in swirls of white and yellow. South is fire, and its colors were orange and crimson. West is associated with water, so the colors there were blues and turquoises and silver. North is earth and blacks and browns, streaked and studded with gold.

I had kept the rest of the space lightly furnished, except for the bookcase. That was filled to overflowing with the Books of Shadow, magical journals I'd inherited from Dorothy Hawthorne. The entire combination made for a place that was lush and mysterious and comfortable all at the same time. It was, quite literally, where the magic happened. At least, sometimes.

"I am concentrating, Julia," I protested. Julia declared that after everything that had happened, we could all use a little spiritual housekeeping, so the plan had been to conduct a cleansing ritual. I was to practice raising and holding positive energies so they could fill the space and "gently redirect" any negative energies that had crept into my spirit and my space.

I wondered if Lieutenant Blanchard counted as a negative energy. I wondered the same thing about Shelly Kinsdale, with all her anger toward her murdered brother.

"Of course you're concentrating, dear," said Grandma B.B. from her place on the attic's north side.

For the ritual, Julia, Val, Grandma B.B. and the dachshunds marked out a protective circle around my altar. As a concession to her pregnancy and aching feet, we'd moved a chair to the east side of the attic so Val could sit during the ceremony. The circle would provide a shield against any malign influences that might be attracted by our magic. It also—and Julia was very firm as she reminded me about it tonight—would prevent any harmful or just plain misguided reactions from my working from getting loose.

Like Val and Grandma, Julia and I wore our ceremonial

robes. Julia's was deep blue spangled with white stars. Mine was a simple green, a sign of my apprentice status. Grandma B.B. didn't have any of her own ceremonial clothing anymore, but Valerie had brought along an extra black and silver robe. So now my grandmother looked sweet and smiling and witchy all at once.

"You have to clear your mind of extraneous concerns, Anna," Julia was telling me. "You cannot hold the energies if your thoughts are scattered."

I wanted to ask how I was supposed to clear my mind with Julia and Grandma B.B. giving each other the mutual stink eye, but in a rare moment of good sense, I kept my mouth shut. Unfortunately, Grandma didn't.

"She *is* doing her best, Julia," said Grandma.

"This is hardly Anna's best," replied Julia. "As *I* have reason to know."

Val glanced at me. I did my best not to wince. *No, please,* I begged silently to whoever might be listening. *Do not let them start this up again.* I'd really hoped the events at the old drugstore were the beginning of a genuine reconciliation.

"Yip," Max shoved his nose against my ankle.

"Yap," pointed out Leo.

Great. Not only were Grandma and Julia still butting heads, but I was failing Witching 101 and being critiqued by dachshunds. This was so not my night.

"Merow," added Alistair, who had not been there a moment before. He sauntered forward and gave Max a head butt, clearly indicating that my ankles were his personal property.

"Yip!" warned Leo, but Julia picked him up before anything more could happen.

"Thanks loads, cat," I muttered to Alistair. "Where were you earlier when I needed the magic help?"

My familiar blinked and yawned, closing his mouth with a click of cat teeth, indicating his deep concern for my human problems.

"All right." Julia sighed heavily. Leo whined and wriggled

in her arms and she set him down next to his brother. "I can see cleansing is not happening this evening."

"I'm sorry," I said. I also stood up. I hadn't been to yoga class in a while and kneeling was not as easy as it should have been. "It's just that I'm so worried about Jake and Miranda."

"I'm sure it'll be okay," said Val. "We know Pete and Kenisha have spoken with Shelly Kinsdale. They must know about the new development." Before we started the lesson, I'd told everyone about the interview over a dinner of Chinese takeout.

"Has Kenisha said anything new?" I asked.

Julia shook her head before I could get any further. "Kenisha has plenty to do without risking a reprimand for trying to pass us extra information."

"I know. I just . . ." I waved my hand vaguely toward the outside. Alistair circled my ankles and I picked him up.

"I'm worried," I said. "From what Frank said, Lieutenant Blanchard really wants to make the case that Jake killed Jimmy over some kind of drug deal. If he finds out about Chuck and the marijuana, it's just going to feed into that theory." I snuggled my cat close and he graciously permitted it.

"You're right," said Val slowly. "It's only a matter of time. We have to have the truth before then."

"But what can we do?" Grandma asked. She was, I noticed, looking very pointedly at Julia. "We have to proceed so *very* cautiously."

Max looked pleadingly up at Julia, wagging his tail so hard his entire hindquarters wiggled. Val had also turned toward Julia with a surprisingly similar expression, but no wagging.

"Anna could try her automatic writing," Val suggested.

I'd been debating whether to try to bring this up. Automatic writing, or drawing, was a type of clairvoyance, a way to see something hidden by time or distance, and it turned out I was kind of good at it. Unfortunately, this particular talent had a few little drawbacks.

"You do remember that last time, Anna passed out for over eight hours?" remarked Julia acidly.

"Anna!" cried Grandma B.B. "You never told me!"

At this, much to my surprise, Leo's hackles came up. He growled right at Grandma, low and hard. His brother yapped in warning.

"Leo, Max," murmured Julia. "Quiet."

The dogs obeyed, but reluctantly. But Grandma was staring at Julia now; so were the rest of us.

"That other time wasn't anybody's fault," said Val quickly. "Anna just wasn't ready for it."

"Exactly," said Julia without taking her eyes off Grandma B.B. "Unready and on her own."

"How careless," said Grandma. "Especially when there are so many established methods for testing the strength of the talents of a witch of the bloodline."

"Yes," said Julia. "Someone was very careless."

"Merow!" Alistair stretched, extending all his claws. He also stalked across the circle to Grandma B.B. and hunkered down on her toes, putting his whole self between her and Julia and the dachshunds.

"Well, I wouldn't pass out this time, would I?" I said. Grandma was already drawing herself up, and I could tell from her expression that whatever she was about to say was not going to help defuse the situation. "I mean, this time you're all here. I'd be grounded."

"And shielded," added Val. "There wouldn't be any risk of her overstretching her powers."

"There's always risk with someone who has not been properly trained," said Julia directly to Grandma. Grandma's mouth hardened to a thin line, and I felt how very hard she was holding herself back. Something in her attitude and expression must have finally gotten through to Julia, because she rubbed her eyes. "However, under the circumstances, it might be worth a try. But only if you're sure, Anna?"

I admit, I hesitated. That whole blacking-out-and-falling-over thing was exactly as much fun as it sounded. Besides, even if I could get this to work, it wasn't going to produce anything anybody could use as actual evidence in an official investigation. But maybe, if we were lucky, it could point us in the right direction.

"Okay," I said. "I'll try."

"Annabelle?" Julia faced Grandma B.B.

"Oh, of course," said Grandma coolly. "I'll go along with whatever you think best, Julia. As you have pointed out, you are her mentor."

Julia ignored this, mostly. "Very well. We'll close off the circle and cast a fresh one," said Julia.

"I think I'd better be on my feet for this." Val heaved herself out of the chair. She also pulled out one of the drawing pads I'd started keeping in the attic bookcase and handed it to me along with a fresh pencil from the box on top.

Grandma didn't say anything.

I sat cross-legged in front of my altar with the pad on my knees. Witches' altars come in all shapes and sizes. Mine was a low table covered by a length of green velvet decorated with gold pentagrams. It had all the magical elements represented on it—with wine in a cup symbolizing water, salt in a silver dish for earth, a lit white candle for fire and a brass dish of dried aromatic herbs and flowers from the garden for air. My wand lay at the center on a white cloth, waiting for me.

I tried to ignore the fact that Grandma B.B. was watching me, and not in a happy/proud grandma kind of way. There was something sad and a little deflated in her attitude that I didn't entirely understand. I just focused on the candle flame and breathed deeply in and deeply out. I pictured a blanket of light spreading across the floor. The others, including Max and Leo, moved around me, clockwise, then counterclockwise, releasing the energies and reshaping them into a fresh, and stronger, circle of protection. I kept breathing and kept focusing. This was important. This was what I wanted to be doing. If I could keep my magical stuff together, I'd be helping Jake and Miranda.

I just wished I could stop wondering how we were going to finally put things back together between Julia and Grandma B.B.

"Merow." Alistair climbed into my lap, shoving his way under the drawing pad. I sighed. Cats. I decided to bow to the inevitable and put the pad on the floor and my free hand on his back.

Julia took up her position at the southeast. "We invite to this circle the spirits of protection, wisdom, healing and clarity. We ask that the truth be shown and nothing be hidden. In need we call, in hope we ask, an' it harm none, so mote it be."

"So mote it be," answered Val and Grandma.

"Merow," agreed Alistair.

I waited. I breathed. I stared at the candle flame. I did my best to clear my mind and focus entirely on Jimmy Upton, on who he had been, on what had happened. I tried to open my mind to the truth, whatever that truth turned out to be. We needed to know what had happened to Jimmy Upton, the good, the bad and the ugly.

So mote it be.

Julia repeated the chant, and the others took it up, turning it into a steady cadence. The room filled with the scent of warm wax and herbs. The shadows cast by the tree branches outside shifted in the autumn wind. Alistair purred, and we all waited and waited.

I tried to stay focused on Jimmy and the murder, I really did, but the truth is, I was starting to get bored. The other women's chanting droned heavily around my head. I wanted to stretch. I wanted to move. I had places to be. Things to do. People to meet. This was the time. Finally. The stars were all aligned, and this time I wasn't going to let anything mess it up.

My hand was moving, the pencil was scratching against the paper, but the movement of my hand seemed entirely divorced from the thoughts filling my head. My motions were quick, practiced, broad. My thoughts, though, were tiny, hard things, dropping like pebbles from an open hand.

Screw this. I should just go now.

Not this time. Chance like this won't come again.

Need to try.

Better get out now.

My hand moved faster. Impressions tumbled through my mind, crowding together, practically fighting to be poured out onto the page. I felt love and hate and desperation. I felt steam heat and greasy paper rolled against my palm. I felt triumph, and the furtive hope that came from clutching secrets too close for too long.

I was sure I could do this, but at the same time, I was terrified it would all fall apart again.

Stay. Go. Stay.

I was so sure.

I was so scared.

I was . . .

I was . . .

❧ 23 ☙

🐾 SOMETHING STRONG AND soft banged against my hand. My pencil skittered from my fingers.

Someone was saying my name, a long way off.

"Annabelle Amelia Blessingsound Britton. Your sisters call. Come back to us. Come back to yourself, Annabelle."

I blinked heavily. I was right where I had been, in my attic, in front of my altar. Julia was still here, and Val, and Grandma B.B. And Alistair, of course. Alistair was kneading my stomach with his paws and mewing with concern. He must have knocked the pencil out of my fingers. Slowly, the pain of the writer's cramp filtered into my fuzzy brain. Normally, my hand felt like this only after hours of frantic sketching.

"Merow?" said Alistair. "Merp?"

"I'm okay," I said or, rather, croaked. My throat felt like I'd been swallowing sandpaper.

"Annabelle," said Julia to Grandma B.B. "We need to open the circle."

"Yes, of course," said Grandma B.B., and this time there was no hidden sarcasm under the statement.

They walked the edges of the circle, opening the spell the same way they'd closed it. I sat in the middle with my cat on my lap and tried not to shake.

I swear I felt the energies flowing out like the whole house had been holding its breath.

"Here, Anna, drink this." Val shoved a cup into my free hand and I took a long swallow of lukewarm peppermint tea. It was a good thing it was lukewarm, too, because suddenly I was gulping it down like there was no tomorrow.

"Are you all right, dear?" Grandma crouched down next to me.

"Merow!" said Alistair, which I took to mean, *I'd have told you if she wasn't.*

"I will be; just give me a second." I had to use my hands to push myself up off the floor. I glanced at my watch. It had been less than an hour since we started. It felt like a month. "I . . . did we get anything?"

"Did we ever." Val held out the sketch pad.

I took it from her, and I stared. It had been a fresh pad when I started. Now the first three pages were covered with drawings. They weren't consistent. There were some rapid, sloppy sketches and some more detailed drawings. And I didn't remember making a single one of them. I just remembered the feelings, and I shivered, because those feelings hadn't been mine.

"I think I need to sit down," I said.

"We should go downstairs," said Val. "What you really need is something to eat."

The only surprise there was that she said it before Grandma B.B. could.

JULIA TOOK CHARGE of the sketch pad. She informed us that we would be able to look at the results once I had been taken care of. Nobody was willing to argue with her, not even Grandma B.B.

In short order, we were all gathered in the kitchen. Valerie and Grandma, after making disparaging remarks about

the lack of actual food in my refrigerator, fixed up a plate
of sandwiches and leftover muffins. Julia brewed more tea,
while Alistair and the dachshunds alternated between supervising the humans and stalking around the house in case of
unauthorized entry or stray negative energies.

I downed most of a ham-and-cheese sandwich and a glass
of orange juice and felt a lot better.

Apparently satisfied, Julia set the sketch pad down in the
middle of the table. Alistair jumped up on the table and took
a personal cat-moment to look smugly down at the wiener
dogs whining and wagging below.

I set my tea mug down, held my breath and flipped back
the cover on my sketch pad.

The first page showed a drawing of a young man wearing
a chef's jacket.

"Jimmy Upton?" said Julia.

"Jimmy Upton," I agreed. It looked a lot like the photo
that had run with the *Seacoast Times* article and the resemblance to his sister was striking. I'd spent a lot of time on
the portrait. All the aspects were clear and distinct. His dark
hair was slicked back under a bandana, and his wiry arms
were folded over his chest. His face was detailed enough to
catch his movie-star looks and the way he looked out of the
page like he owned the place and didn't think much of the
rest of us cluttering it up.

"And this is?" Grandma B.B. laid a finger on the paper
and we all craned our necks, including Alistair. His whiskers
tickled my cheek.

Jimmy held center stage on the paper, but around him was
a smaller drawing. It showed a man—Jimmy, I thought—
standing between two women; they were standing hand to
hand, facing straight out, like a line of old-fashioned paper
dolls. Something was passing from the left-hand woman to
Jimmy and from Jimmy to the right-hand woman.

The problem was that this drawing had been made a lot
more quickly than the portrait, and the figures were little
more than outlines. Both women were curvy; one was short;
one was tall, with straight hair down to her shoulders. It was

hard to tell anything more—hair color, ethnicity—since neither was much more than an outline.

"Anna?" said Julia, but I shook my head. Once I've woken up from the trance state, the vision's specifics fade pretty quickly, like a dream, and I'm left with only a bundle of feelings. And like a dream, it can be difficult to explain in a way that makes any kind of sense.

"There was anticipation," I said slowly. "And . . . closure. It was like . . . a problem was going to be fixed. Someone, I guess it was Jimmy, was really looking forward to whatever it was being solved. By this." I touched the square that was passing from the left-hand woman to Jimmy. Alistair, helpfully, pawed at the same spot. "Whatever it is."

"Money?" suggested Val.

"Papers?" suggested Grandma.

"A ledger?" murmured Julia.

Better not. Better just pay and go. The words popped into my mind.

"Money," I said, and as soon as I did, it felt exactly right. "It's that five thousand dollars. He, Jimmy, was meeting her," I pointed to the right-hand woman again. "To pay her off. One of these has to be his sister," I said. "Doesn't it?"

"One of them could be Gretchen," added Grandma. "Or what about her daughter, Christine? She's the hotel marketing director."

"And then there's Kelly Pierce," added Val. We let this fall into the silence, because none of us wanted to say the other name.

Miranda.

"But whoever he was meeting, the deal must not have gone through," said Val. "Jimmy still had the money on him when they found him. Shelly Kinsdale denied that Jimmy offered her a bribe at all."

"Merow," Alistair put his nose to the page.

"Off, cat." I lifted him onto my lap. He humped resentfully and slid down under the table.

Grandma B.B. adjusted her glasses. "Could it have been the other way around?" she said. "Maybe we're reading it backward. Maybe this woman was meeting Jimmy to pay him off."

"Or maybe it was a setup," suggested Val. "Somebody said they'd take a bribe, or a payment or something, to lure him to . . . wherever he died?"

"It's possible." Julia cocked her head toward the sketches, considering the whole page carefully. "Unfortunately, what we can see here doesn't give us much clue as to where that might be."

"We know where it was," said Grandma. "It was in the Harbor's Rest, probably wherever that tunnel comes out."

"The police must have found it by now," I added exasperatedly. "I mean, that is one honkin' big door."

"Anna, have you ever seen the basement of a major hotel?" asked Val. "It's a maze. There's going to be a laundry, a dozen different storage rooms, a whole section of walk-in freezers, and that's just to start with. There's also going to be the power plant, furnaces, employee locker rooms, and . . . What?" she said, because now we were all staring at her. "I didn't just up and decide to open a B and B because I was bored one day, you know. I worked a lot of hotel jobs back in the day."

"It sounds like a great place to murder someone," I said, but Val shook her head.

"A hotel basement might be huge, but it'll be full of staff, pretty much around the clock—housekeeping, maintenance, maybe even the laundry, and the kitchen and at least some wait- and bell staff. There might be a little window around three in the morning, but the fresh shift will be in by five at the latest. If I was going to kill somebody, I'd want someplace a lot quieter."

Like the basement of a building undergoing renovations, which just happened to have the utility tub all hooked up and ready to go. I really wished I did not have to think about that. I slumped back but straightened up again because Grandma was watching.

"We'll worry about that later," said Julia. "At least now we know Jimmy Upton was meeting someone. We know he wanted the meeting and that he thought it was going to solve a problem for him. That is more than we did have."

"What's on the next page?" asked Val.

I turned the page over. Alistair, sufficiently recovered from his huff, jumped back up on the table, right in the middle of the pad.

"Off, cat." I put him back on my lap.

Max sneezed, and I swear it sounded like a laugh.

This page was crammed with drawings, one after the other, like panels on a cartoon page. This time, the faces were recognizable; at least some of them were. Here was Mrs. Hilde, her face furious and her mouth open, shouting at Dale. Here was Dale, shouting at another man, who was shouting right back.

"That's Rich Hilde," said Val. "He's Gretchen's youngest son, and this next one, that's Christine."

Christine Hilde wore a trim skirt suit, and she had her hands thrown up in the air as she shouted at Dale and the man Valerie said was Rich.

"Oh, my," murmured Grandma as she touched the final drawing on the page. That was Mrs. Hilde sitting across from her daughter at a hastily sketched table. I'd actually drawn in a little line of knives going from one intense face to the other. Glaring daggers at each other. My magic had a weird sense of humor.

"I'm almost afraid to turn the page," I whispered.

So Julia did it for me.

"Oh, no," breathed Val.

My mouth went dry. My hand shook where it rested on the table. Grandma covered it. "Breathe, dear; it's all right."

There were three drawings on this page. The largest was fast and sloppy, with lots of quick shading, but it was very clear. It showed two men. One had a gun in his hand. The other was falling backward, clutching his middle. The back of my neck prickled hard and I was having trouble catching my breath.

"It's all right, Anna," said Julia. "You're safe."

"I know. I know." But something deep in my guts did not believe it.

Below the shooting was another sketch, all curved lines and sloppy, quick lines to indicate shadows.

"What is this?" said Grandma.

"It's the tunnel," I said. I could recognize the curving walls, the propped-up ceilings and the dirt floor. "And . . ." I touched the page.

"A hat?" said Val.

"A fedora," said Grandma B.B.

She was right. A man's hat, like the kind they all wore in 1930s gangster movies, sat squarely in the middle of the sketch.

"What's that got to do with anything?" said Val. "Is it a clue? Did Jimmy Upton wear a hat?"

Julia shook her head. "At this point there's no way to tell, unless Anna remembers something?"

I tried. I frowned at it. I even furrowed my forehead at it. But nothing came, except a vague prickling on the back of my neck, and the very strange, very uncomfortable feeling I was being laughed at. Again.

But who in this room would be laughing at me? Even the dogs had gotten suddenly serious. In fact, Leo had drawn back his mouth to expose one very white, very sharp tooth, and he and his brother skittered across the floor, all the way to the front door.

Julia looked after them but did not call them back.

"Nothing," I murmured. Except that wasn't quite true. I knew I did not like that drawing. It wasn't quite as bad as the visceral reaction I got to the shooting above it, but it reminded me of something, and I couldn't quite put my finger on what.

"So what do we do?" asked Val. "Do we try again?"

"Not tonight," said Julia firmly. "Anna needs to rest and recover." For once, I did not feel like arguing with her. I was suddenly, deeply, severely tired. What I wanted most was to head upstairs and crawl into bed.

"What about this?" Val touched the last sketch. This was

the outline of a telephone. "Did you get any impressions about this?

It was nothing much, just a quick doodle of an old-fashioned desk phone. It had a rotary dial and motion lines around the receiver, like the phone was ringing.

"I . . ."

I didn't get any further, because right then, the phone on the wall did ring, and we all jumped. Grandma touched my hand, in concern or maybe reassurance, as I edged past her to go answer it. Alistair bounded over ahead of me and plunked himself down by the wall.

"Hello?" I said as I picked up the receiver.

"Anna?" Frank's voice answered. "Sorry if I woke you."

His voice was tense and he sounded out of breath. I felt my stomach sink down to my shoes. "You didn't," I told him. "What's happened?"

"I'm on my way to the police station; I thought you'd want to know. They've just brought Jake Luce in, and they're charging him with the murder of Jimmy Upton."

❧ 24 ❧

❀ "AND IF IT isn't Miss Britton," drawled Lieutenant Blanchard, as Frank and I barged into the police station. "How nice of you to save us all the trouble and come in voluntarily."

Grandma B.B. had the keys for the Galaxie out almost before I'd hung up the phone, and all of us, dogs included, had piled in. Only Alistair stayed behind, pacing anxiously across the front porch. I assumed he'd show up under his own steam if he felt the need.

My grandmother broke at least half a dozen traffic laws racing through the (mostly) empty streets and nearly clipped a mailbox turning the corner onto Market Street.

"You haven't changed, Annabelle!" shouted Julia, who was clutching the dashboard and the dachshunds.

"Just hang on!" Grandma shouted back, and I swear it sounded like she was having the time of her life. I'm not sure if that was from the speed or getting to watch Julia turn green as we swooped down the hills.

All this questionable speed meant we got to the station just as Frank was climbing the steps.

We'd agreed that I'd be dropped off here, while the others drove to Miranda's. At least they would as soon as Val had finished calming down Roger and assuring him that she was still fine, there were no contractions, and she'd be home as quickly as she could. I assumed no one was going to mention Grandma B.B.'s driving habits to Roger.

"Lieutenant Blanchard," I said as I struggled to get my thoughts and my attitude together. The station lobby (waiting room? entrance room? I needed to look up the proper term), with its plastic chairs and tables and community bulletin boards, was empty, but Lieutenant Blanchard stood at the desk behind the reception window, next to a very unhappy-looking uniformed officer. One of the industrial fluorescent lights overhead buzzed like a bored housefly. "I was hoping—"

"I'm sure you were." Blanchard cut me off and his square face sagged into a mock-serious expression.

The door to the interior of the station opened, and Kenisha walked through, with Pete Simmons right behind her. I glanced urgently at Kenisha, but her only response was to set her jaw. Pete, though, tucked his hand in his pocket and jingled his keys once. His droopy eyes traveled slowly from me and Frank to Lieutenant Blanchard, and back again.

"Anna," Pete said. "Hi, Frank. A little late, isn't it?"

"Too late, you mean, Detective Simmons." Blanchard gave us all a big, crooked grin to make sure we appreciated the fact that he was joking. I noticed his teeth were square and white and perfectly even. *Camera ready,* I thought. "Miss Britton, I'm afraid your boss has already been booked."

"He's not my boss," I said, more or less reflexively.

"Oh, right." Blanchard nodded. "My mistake. That check he wrote you does not make him your boss."

For a second I felt dizzy. How did he know about that? Then I realized, if there was an arrest, there was a warrant, which probably gave them permission to check Jake and Miranda's bank records.

I was about to point out (again) that the payment was for the murals I was being commissioned to paint, but I gritted my teeth around the words. Partly that was because Frank stepped on my foot. Probably he just meant to remind me that anything I said to Lieutenant Blanchard at this point would be used as evidence against, well, everybody.

Now that he'd delivered his not-so-subtle reminder, Frank had strolled up to the reception window. He'd also pulled out his notebook and pencil. "Just what are the charges against Jake Luce, Lieutenant Blanchard?" he asked.

Blanchard shook his head heavily. "Sorry, Hawthorne. You can wait for the press conference with everybody else."

"I see." Frank made a note about this. "Then can I assume you have no comment regarding the accusations that Jake Luce is being targeted by the department as a favor to a rival developer over the property at 943 Market Street?"

Well. Clearly, Frank had been doing more digging about Shelly Kinsdale and Dreame Royale properties. Were they targeting the site of Jake and Miranda's new coffee shop for their "luxury boutique hotel"?

Kenisha was staring at Frank and at me. Pete Simmons started jingling his keys in a slow, steady rhythm.

"Now, why would I have any reason to comment on something you made up on the spot, Hawthorne?" Blanchard's face remained bland, and he folded his beefy arms across his barrel chest. The desk sergeant turned to his computer and began resolutely tapping away. I sympathized. I didn't like the way that low flush was spreading up from under the lieutenant's collar either.

"So, no comment." Frank made another note. "And what about . . ."

"What about you get out of my station?" Blanchard said softly. "Before you, your bleeding heart and that little notebook all get locked up with your drug-dealing hippie pal?"

I looked to Kenisha. She didn't say anything, but she did flick her hard, direct eyes toward the door. This I interpreted to mean I should go ahead and get out of here, so she could meet me outside and we could actually talk.

I nodded once. *Gotcha.* "Um, Frank, maybe we'd better go," I said. He turned toward me, one eyebrow raised in a silent inquiry.

I caught and held his gaze.

Listen, I said to him with my eyes. *Kenisha and Pete want us gone. We are making their lives harder standing here, and Kenisha wants us to know she can meet us outside and give us an update, which might have some actual information we can use, okay?*

This is a lot to try to crowd into a look, but Frank must have picked up on at least some of it. Or maybe it was my expression of precisely mixed anger and panic that got to him. Either way, he nodded and stashed his book in his pocket.

"I'll be back," he said to Blanchard. "For the press conference," he added, just in case anybody thought he was quoting a certain ex–California governor. "Thank you as ever for your cooperation, Lieutenant."

Blanchard politely informed Frank where he should not let the door hit him on the way out, and we left.

"Did you find something about Jimmy's sister and Dreame Royale?" I demanded as soon as we reached the sidewalk.

"Nothing definite," Frank said. "But, yeah, there was some talk at the city zoning board about the old drugstore. That was before Jake and Miranda bought it, though."

"That's still awfully interesting."

"Isn't it?"

I shivered. It was probably around midnight. When I'd run out of the house with the others, I'd grabbed my purse but not my jacket. I'd be in for a grandma scolding later.

Grandma. What were she and the others doing now? Had they made it to the Luces' yet? Was Miranda okay? I rubbed my arms, trying to smooth out the goose bumps. Frank saw and slipped out of his sports jacket. "Here." He held the jacket out to me.

I shook my head. "I'm fine." I shivered again.

Frank snorted, and before I could step out of range, he draped the jacket over my shoulders. It was warm, and it smelled faintly of Old Spice, because Frank was a guy who appreciated the classics.

"Thanks."

I waited for the teasing reply, but there wasn't one. There was just a softening of his expression. He lifted his hand, but before he could finish the gesture, whatever it was going to be, my phone rang.

I smiled apologetically and turned away, uncertain whether to be relieved or annoyed. I fished the phone out of my purse and hit the button with one hand, because I was clutching Frank's jacket around my shoulders with the other.

It was Kenisha and she was not in the mood for chitchat. "The Friendly Toast," she told me. "Now."

And she hung up.

Frank looked at me expectantly.

"The Friendly Toast," I told him. "Now."

THE FRIENDLY TOAST was a diner down near Market Square. It was decked out with vintage Formica-and-chrome tables with lots of kitschy knickknacks, toys and posters hanging on the walls. It also happened to be my favorite place for breakfast in Portsmouth. I'd never pictured it as Pete's kind of place, but then, it did have great pancakes, which should make it just about everybody's kind of place.

It was also open until two a.m., and since the dining room was longer than it was wide, there were plenty of tables in the back where we would not be seen by anyone passing on the street. Not to mention a back door that would let us in discreetly from the parking lot. And yet, because we were in a public diner, nobody could easily accuse us of clandestine meetings if we were seen.

Kenisha and Frank explained most of this to me later.

Frank and I took advantage of that discreet back door and came in from the parking lot. The diner was mostly empty. A bunch of loud, burly kids I took to be fraternity brothers filled up one long central table. Past them, up toward the front, on the far side, a couple of middle-aged women in skirt suits sat in a booth by the wall, drinking coffee and examining papers over half-eaten omelets and hash browns.

I recognized one of them, and I missed a step. So did Frank.

What is Kelly Pierce doing here at one in the morning? And who is that she's with?

We both looked to the women at their crowded little table, and we looked at each other. By mutual, silent consent, we casually but quickly slid into the old-fashioned high-backed booth with Kenisha and Pete.

"Frank, Anna," said Pete. "Thanks for coming out so late."

"Hello, Anna," said Kenisha. "Frank."

"Hi, Kenisha," I said, trying not to let my gaze wander toward Kelly Pierce and her friend up front. I wasn't sure if I believed that thing about how if you stare at someone, they will eventually feel it, but now was not the time to experiment. "Thanks for the call."

Kenisha shrugged but didn't add anything. All kinds of uneasy feelings spread through me.

Our waitress was a college-aged girl with red-and-white-streaked hair and a gold ring in her nose. She brought us menus, which we ignored, and coffee, which we did not.

"What happened, Kenisha?" I asked as soon as the waitress was back behind the counter and hunched over a battered copy of *Anna Karenina*. "Why did they arrest Jake?"

"Lieutenant Blanchard put together Jake's past record with the cash that was found on Jimmy Upton's body and that trapdoor in their new building," she said. "It gave him enough to make an arrest." My heart thumped once, hard, but Kenisha didn't add anything about Chuck or the hidden attic of the old drugstore.

"Will the charges stick?" asked Frank.

"Depends." Kenisha shrugged and added a second pack of sugar to her coffee. She had exchanged her uniform for jeans, a black T-shirt and a bright pink hoodie, which meant she was off duty. Pete still wore his rumpled sports coat and checked shirt. I had never seen him in anything substantially different, but then, Pete was one of those men who never really went off duty.

Kenisha stirred her coffee, sipped and reached for more sugar. "Probably, he's going to get out on bail. But if we can't come up with a better story than the one Blanchard's got, who knows what'll happen after that?"

Except we all did know. Jake would be tried for murder. Of course he'd be found innocent, because he didn't do it. I repeated this thought to myself a few extra times. Firmly.

"You have talked to Shelly Kinsdale, right?" I said.

"We have," agreed Pete. "I take it you have, too?"

I looked to Frank. Frank just took a long swallow of coffee.

Kenisha sighed. "The press is avoiding us, Pete."

"Frank, it's late." Pete slumped even further over the table. "I would like to be home with my wife, but I'm not. I'm here, because somebody's got to try to keep the lieutenant from running away with this. So, help out here. Did you talk to Shelly Kinsdale?"

It took a lot of strength to hold out against Pete, especially when he started looking tired, because Pete was an okay guy, and you realized that as soon as you looked at him. It might have all been an act, but it was a very good act.

Frank actually managed to hesitate a whole three seconds before he said, "She had a lot to say about some plans for a new hotel." Frank took a long swallow of coffee and raised his mug to signal the waitress he needed a warm-up. "Are you sure there couldn't be a connection with the new development and Jimmy's death? Especially since he had a lot of money on him. It could have been a bribe. Or a payoff."

"It could have," said Kenisha. "But it also could have been drug money, and we've got no proof either way. Unless you know something more?"

Frank swirled his coffee and said nothing.

"What have you got, Frank?" asked Kenisha. "Come on, nobody wants to see the Luces railroaded."

"I know you don't," Pete put in. "You've known Jake and Miranda even longer than I have."

"I thought you didn't approve of civilian interference, Pete."

"I don't," agreed Pete. "Dangerous for everybody. But this isn't interference, right? This is cooperation."

"And right now we're going to need all of it we can get," added Kenisha.

I had never actually seen a good cop–good cop strategy. Like Pete's okay-guy attitude, it was surprisingly effective.

Frank took another long drink of coffee. His gaze strayed around the diner as if he was looking for clues as to how he should answer, or maybe he just wanted to check and see if anyone was paying attention to us. They weren't. A burst of laughter exploded from the frat-boy table, accompanied by a whole lot of high fives and fist bumps. Kelly Pierce and her business/midnight-breakfast partner exchanged another set of pages over their omelets.

Frank set his mug down. "I am hearing rumors, but they're contradictory. On the one hand, I've got people saying the hotel is looking at expansion."

"It's already huge," I said.

"But it's vintage huge," said Frank. "Which is attractive in its own way, but might not necessarily suit the needs of the—and I have the quote marks written in here—'modern luxury traveler.' My sources say the Hildes are pricing out what it would take to turn Harbor's Rest into a full-fledged exclusive resort."

I wondered who those sources were, and if their names were Hilde, Kinsdale or maybe even McNally. "What would that have to do with Jake and Miranda?"

"Have you got an hour?" said Kenisha. "You're about to be treated to a trip through the wide, wonderful world of zoning ordinances."

"Well, it's really not that complicated," drawled Pete. "Jake and Miranda are community activists. They—along with plenty of our fellow seacoast citizens—think enough of the riverfront has been fenced in and what's left should be saved for parks, public recreation and nature preserves, that kind of thing. If the Harbor's Rest expands, so will the amount of riverfront that's closed off. The more exclusive they want the place to be, the tighter the enclosure. You can bet that Jake and Miranda and their group will be showing up at every planning commission and city council meeting to try to keep that from happening."

"And the city council are on Jake and Miranda's side, for the moment, anyway," said Frank.

Which would go a long way toward explaining the mutual bad attitude between the Luces and the Hildes.

"So that's one kind of rumor," said Kenisha. "What's the other?"

Frank set his empty mug down. "The other rumor is that the hotel is on shaky ground and if it can't turn things around in a hurry, they're going to close."

❧ 25 ❧

❧ "I DON'T SUPPOSE . . ." began Pete, but Frank was already shaking his head. Kenisha glanced at me, and I shook my head, too.

"Which rumor do you believe?" Kenisha asked Frank very quietly. "Build or bust?"

"I'm not sure yet." Frank raised his mug to signal the waitress one more time. "It might be half and half. The Hildes might be gambling on an expansion and renovation to bring in new business to keep them from having to shut down."

"But if Jake and Miranda's protests to the city council were making that expansion difficult, the Hildes would have reason to be angry at them."

"And the Hildes are not known for playing particularly nice," said Frank. "And Mrs. Hilde is a friend of Lieutenant Blanchard."

The frat boys were laughing again. This time, Kelly Pierce and her partner looked up in irritation, or maybe it was surprise. Frank scrunched sideways and I ducked my head. The cops sitting on the other side from us exchanged knowing glances. The two women up front didn't seem to notice any of this. They just started gathering up their papers. Kelly signaled to the waitress for the check while the other woman pulled out a smartphone and tapped at the screen.

"I wonder which rumor Jimmy Upton believed." I said. Some previous customer, or waitress, had left a Bic ballpoint on the table. I pulled off the cap and began doodling on my place mat.

"Now, that's an interesting question." Pete drained his cup just as the waitress arrived. Accurately assessing the situation, she just put the full pot down on the table and walked away.

Frank poured himself some more coffee, and then some for Pete and Kenisha. I was falling behind. Could you drink somebody under the table when what you were drinking was coffee?

Out of the corner of my eye, I saw Ms. Pierce and partner walk out the front door without looking back. I let out a long sigh of relief.

"And you're thinking . . . what, Anna?" prompted Pete.

"She's thinking how money we found with Upton's body is related to Frank's rumors," said Kenisha, as she watched my blue ink lines turn into the Harbor's Rest, and the old drugstore, with a rope tying them together.

"Actually, I'm trying to figure out how Blanchard can make any kind of case for Jake and Miranda being able to hide a body down in that tunnel," I asked out loud. "The trapdoor in the Luces' basement wasn't exactly out in the open. I had to move about a dozen bricks to even see it, and Jake and Miranda had to take the hinges off to even get it open."

"And if this goes any further, I'm sure we're all going to want to talk to you about that," said Pete. "But, Anna, you are going to have to consider the fact that since you've taken a payment from the Luces, you are not exactly an objective witness."

"You're kidding me," I breathed. "It was for some artwork. I know Blanchard doesn't believe me, but, Pete . . ."

Pete cut me off. "Sure, sure, sure. I know you, but you need to see this from the outside. I know it's not fair, but it would really help us out if you could show us the contract to prove you were being considered for the job before this mess blew up."

"Why do I have to prove anything?" I snapped, because I was getting scared again, and being scared makes me cranky, especially at one in the morning. "I'm not a suspect . . ." But the rest of my protest died in my throat, because the reply was already forming in the air between us.

No, I wasn't a suspect. Yet.

I stared at the rest of the diner, at the frat boys and their heaps of pancakes and the waitress leaning against the counter with her tattered paperback. I felt a little amazed that the rest of the world could be going on as normal. At least, I assumed this was normal. Usually I was sound asleep by this time. But usually, I was not being told in so many words I was about to be accused of being an accessory to murder.

"Did you find where the tunnel came out in the hotel?" I asked. "I mean, that big door would be a lot harder to hide than the trapdoor in the Luces' basement, and we're talking about a building that's been owned by the same family for generations. *Somebody* there has to know about the tunnel."

Pete and Kenisha exchanged a long look. The tension thickened between them and my hands clenched around my cooling coffee mug.

"We can't find the door," Kenisha said.

"What?" said Frank.

"We can't find the door, Frank," said Pete, slowly and carefully, in case Frank was going to have trouble spelling anything. "We measured the tunnel and got an estimate of where it should run up against the basement of the hotel, but there's nothing there on the hotel side except a solid concrete foundation wall."

"But . . . you did try to get it open from the tunnel?"

If my question irritated Pete, he didn't show it. "Yes, Anna, we did. We tried wrenches and we tried screwdrivers and we tried bolt cutters, but to get that particular door open from the side we have access to is going to take a welding torch. Now, I don't know about you, but I'm not crazy about sending one of my guys down into an unstable tunnel to try to cut it open, especially when I already know what I'm going to find on the other side is concrete."

"Plus," said Kenisha, "everybody we've questioned so far, including all the Hildes, deny knowing anything definite about any door out of the basement. And, yes," she said as Frank opened his mouth. "We've had a look at the building plans on file with the city clerk and the historical society. There's still no door, and no place to put one."

"But, I mean, there must be a way to take measurements," I said. "Or infrared scans or X-rays or something . . ."

Pete smiled sadly. "If this were Boston or New York, maybe. Or if I had the budget of a TV cop . . ."

"Or a boss that was interested in actually solving this," muttered Kenisha.

"But, unfortunately, it isn't and I don't," Pete went on as if Kenisha hadn't said a word.

"But it had to have been opened recently," I said. "The air in the tunnel was good, and there was a draft." Jake or Miranda or I had remarked on it, hadn't we? I rubbed my head, willing my Vibe-clouded memory to clear itself up. It wasn't listening. Not that it mattered. Because the fresh air could just have meant that somebody had opened the drugstore trapdoor before I'd stumbled over it.

Pete smiled gently. "What we have got is a door that *can* be opened at the Luces' end, and a door that *can't* be opened at the Harbor's Rest end, and a body in the middle. That creates a major problem for Jake and Miranda. And, I'm sorry to say, you, too, Anna." Pete leaned across the table. "Now, I know you want to help, but you've got to do it the right way. If there's something you've seen, or even suspected, you need to tell us, right now."

That was when the important realization crept into my

thoughts. Slowly. Because even after all my dealings with the police, including Lieutenant Blanchard, I remain slow. And entirely taken in by Pete's tired good-guy act.

I was under suspicion. I was talking to a couple of cops. That meant I was being set up to spill the beans. The worst part was, I did have beans to spill.

There are not a lot of feelings less comfortable than suddenly wondering whether you can trust the friend sitting across from you.

I told myself Kenisha was not breaking anybody's trust, especially not mine. She wanted what we all wanted—to find out who really killed Jimmy Upton. But Kenisha was in a bad position. She was not in charge of this case. She had to do her job. It wasn't her I had to worry about. It was Blanchard. And this conversation changed nothing. Telling her and Pete about Chuck before we had the full story would only feed Blanchard's version of events.

I put my pen down.

"I've told you everything I know," I spoke the lie slowly and carefully. Alistair would have been very proud of the way I managed not to blink. "But I do want to help. Really. Maybe we could—"

Before I could get any further, Pete shook his head. "Look, Anna, if you really have told us everything, then you need to just go home and stay there. Do not go around asking more questions. Jake should be out again by tomorrow afternoon, *if* no one gives Blanchard, or the judge, any excuses to hold him." He said this last bit to Frank as much as to me.

Frank's jaw tightened, and that distinct, professionally stubborn gleam lit his blue eyes. "Freedom of the press. I get to hang around everyplace and ask all the questions I want."

"Yeah, until Blanchard has me arrest you for trespassing," said Kenisha. "Which I really do not want to have to do."

Frank looked at the bottom of his mug, and then he looked in the bottom of the pot. He sighed and pushed them both away. "I am not letting this drop."

"Nobody is," said Kenisha to me.

I didn't answer her. The coffee I'd drunk was at war with the exhaustion I felt, which just left me caught in the middle with a bad case of the jitters.

Frank signaled for the waitress and we all paid our share and got to our feet.

"I'll be right with you," said Frank, and he headed toward the men's room.

The rest of us walked out the back door into the darkness and the white glow of the parking lot's lights. The Friendly Toast was the only place I could see with the interior lights still on. Portsmouth had shut itself down for the night. I wished I could do the same.

I'd given Frank back his jacket, so I wrapped my arms around myself to try to hold in a little personal warmth. It didn't work.

Pete looked at me and Kenisha. "I'll be waiting in the car, Freeman," he said to her and me.

"Kenisha," I whispered as soon as Pete was out of ear-shot. "Was coming out here Blanchard's idea? Were you—"

She didn't let me get any further. "This was Pete's idea, but, yes, we were trying to get you to talk, or at least Pete was. And don't look at me like that." Kenisha stabbed the air with one finger. "Not when you're holding out on me."

I bit my lip. What could I say to that?

"I know you were all in the old drugstore with Jake," Kenisha said. "And I know you saw something you don't want to tell me. It's been in the back of your eyes all night." When you're a witch cop, your sixth sense has a hair trigger.

Kenisha touched my shoulder. "Anna, I need you to listen to me, not just as a cop but as your coven sister. I cannot tell you everything I know, but as much as I hate to admit it, Blanchard's building a decent case. We have to look at Jake and Miranda clearly."

"I can't believe you just said that!"

"Then tell me I'm wrong," she shot back. "Tell me what you found in that building so Pete and I can put this thing together the right way."

"I can't," I whispered. "Not yet."

"Then that's your choice," she said, and her expression was as flat and hard as her words. "And we're all going to have to live with it."

"Kenisha . . ."

But she just turned and walked down to join Pete beside the battered Toyota Corolla without once looking back.

❧ 26 ❦

❧ "HOW ARE YOU holding up?" Frank asked as he came up beside me.

"I'm not," I confessed. "The only reason I'm not collapsing into a quivering heap is generations of Blessingsound Britton pride."

"I hear that."

A number of ideas that really should have shown up earlier suddenly assembled themselves inside my tired mind. "I didn't stop to think. This must be so hard for you, after your aunt."

"Actually, it's not as bad as I thought it would be. Maybe it's karma; I don't know." Frank shrugged. "I mean, somebody helped me find out what really happened to Aunt Dorothy, and maybe kept me from going to jail. Now I get to turn around and help somebody else."

Almost the first thing I learned about magic was the threefold law. What you send out into the world comes back to you, tripled. This has a lot of implications.

"I just wish my karma was to find all my lost socks," I muttered.

"Yeah. That, too." Frank chuckled.

"So what did you really go back for?" I asked. I mean, it's conceivable he really did need to wash his hands, but I doubted it.

Turns out I was right. "You saw those two women sitting up front when we came in? The ones with all the papers piled on the table?" he asked. I nodded. "One of them was Christine Hilde, Gretchen's daughter, and, incidentally, the marketing director for Harbor's Rest."

I let that little fact settle into place. I hadn't recognized her from my drawings, but now a fresh puzzle piece slid into place in my mind. "If you noticed that, then you must have noticed that the other woman was Kelly Pierce, the hotel's food and beverages manager."

"No," said Frank slowly. "She's not somebody I know on sight."

"Well, doing marketing for a big hotel is not exactly a nine-to-five kind of job," I said slowly. "There could be lots of reasons they'd be meeting away from the office at one in the morning."

"Sure," agreed Frank. "All kinds of reasons."

"I take it that's why you stayed behind when I left with Pete and Kenisha? To try to find out exactly which reason it was?"

He smiled, just a little. "You begin to understand my methods, Watson. Ashley, our waitress, is friends with one of my interns. I asked her if she maybe happened to notice what all those papers they were passing back and forth were about."

"Any luck?"

"Unfortunately, between Russian Literature 210 and a table full of attention-hungry frat boys, all Ashley noticed was that the pair of them were very, very happy."

"Happy like maybe they were about to score a big deal with a major hospitality chain?" We had known Shelly Kinsdale was talking to at least one Hilde. Maybe now we knew which one. "But . . . if the deal for selling Harbor's Rest fell through, what would they be happy about?" I asked. But as soon as the question was out of my mouth, I knew. "They're going to set up a new place with Dreame Royale backing."

"And it's probably that luxury boutique hotel Shelly was telling us about," agreed Frank. "The question I've got is are they going to build somewhere new, or are they planning on taking over the Harbor's Rest when it goes bankrupt?"

I grimaced. "Either one would make for a few awkward Sunday dinners."

"Awkward enough that Christine might be trying to keep the plans a secret."

"Awkward enough that Kelly Pierce might be paying Jimmy Upton off to keep his mouth shut?" I suggested.

"That, too," agreed Frank. "Something to sleep on. Come on, let's get you home."

We climbed into Frank's very used Honda Civic. He started it up on the third try and got it to reverse on the second. I huddled in the passenger seat and tried to find some neutral topic of conversation to hold us for the drive. I failed.

"Frank, we haven't had a chance to talk about the lease," I said as he pulled out of the parking lot and signaled a right turn.

"You're not going to let that go, are you?" Frank stopped to let a cluster of young men blunder across the street. They might have been the frat boys from the diner. "Look, Anna, I'm glad to let you live in the cottage. I don't want to sell it, and I've got another ten months on my apartment lease. It's better to have somebody taking care of the place than just letting it sit empty. Okay?"

"No, it's not okay."

"Why not?"

I did not have a good answer. I looked out at the passing buildings, all closed down for the night. "Karma," I said finally. "And neither one of us knows what's going to happen tomorrow. Maybe you get hit by the crosstown bus and the cottage gets inherited by your greedy second cousin Arthur who turns around and sells it to a developer and me and

Alistair are thrown out onto the sidewalk in the middle of the New England winter."

Frank laughed. "I'd say don't be ridiculous, except for two things."

"Which are?"

"One is everything I've seen happen to you since you got to Portsmouth."

"What's the other?"

"I really do have a second cousin named Arthur."

I'd think about that later. "So, you'll give me a lease? A real grown-up legal lease with rent and tenant obligations and landlord obligations and everything?"

"With all the bells and whistles. I'm sure your lawyer can even tie it up in red ribbon if you want."

I did want, as a matter of fact. "Frank, it's not that I don't think you're being generous . . ." Really generous. Even if you factored in what amounted to caretaker duties, it was much too generous for me to accept under any circumstances, especially when those circumstances involved Frank lending me his jacket and helping me with the police and everything.

"It's okay, Anna. I get it. You don't want to feel like you owe anybody."

"Karma," I said again.

"Karma," he agreed.

We'd left the downtown, and instead of historic houses and brick storefronts and converted warehouses, we passed individual homes sheltered by the grand old trees that were part of what I loved about this town. In the daylight, the summer green would be fading to reveal the red and gold fall splendor. Now, though, they were just all the different shades of gray and ashy white.

"Penny for your thoughts?" said Frank.

"Not worth it." I looked out at the street and the pools of light and the surrounding darkness. The truth is, right then I was thinking about that Hopper painting *Nighthawks*, the one of the people at the lunch counter after dark. Except in my mind, that lunch counter was populated with Hildes: Christine and Gretchen and both sons, with Kelly Pierce bringing in cups of coffee. I thought about all those different arguments I had drawn up in my attic. But I also thought about Chuck and Jake and how they cleaned out their attic before we could go in and make sure the place was ghost-free, maybe even before it stopped being a crime scene. I thought about Kenisha and Pete and how they were both very smart and very sure there was more going on with Jake and Miranda than met the eye.

The Galaxie was parked in the cottage driveway. The lights were on inside the house. Grandma B.B. was home in there, and probably waiting up for me, most likely with Alistair curled up on her lap.

Frank pulled us up to the curb and shut off the engine. He also dug into his pocket. I thought he was going for his notebook again, but instead he held out a penny in two fingers. He dropped it, and I caught it automatically.

"Spill," Frank said.

I shot him an irritated glance, but it didn't last. "I don't know." I turned the penny over in my own fingers a few times before I tucked it into my purse. "I don't want to . . ."

"I like Jake and Miranda, too," he said softly. Neither one of us was making any move to get out of the car. "But that doesn't mean they haven't maybe made some . . . mistakes."

"Like selling marijuana out the back door forty years ago?"

"I was thinking there might be something more recent. Something you've decided you can't tell Pete and Kenisha, at least not yet."

I didn't look at him. I couldn't. Thank goodness we were sitting in the dark and he couldn't see how my cheeks were burning.

"Anna, you know, whatever it is, you can trust me."

I wanted to. Frank was a friend, and I liked him. But he was also a journalist, and whichever way it went, this was a huge story. I did not want to hurt Jake and Miranda. I wanted to keep seeing them as nice people who just wanted to help the community and the people who worked for them. There was one problem.

"Is there any way to find out how Jake and Miranda bought that building?" I asked. "I mean, that's a pretty amazing piece of real estate. I know one of their baristas got a social media campaign going . . ."

"Oh, yeah. That'd be Chuck. I saw some of that. Very smart."

Chuck. I stared out at my lovely, peaceful cottage. Chuck had developed an online coffee connector. Except, what if . . . what if it wasn't just coffee that he was connecting people to? And what if Jimmy had found out? I closed my eyes. What if Blanchard had been right all along? What if this wasn't about real estate or riverfront development or family business? What if it was exactly what it looked like?

"Anna, you've got something. What is it?"

"I don't know," I said slowly. "I mean, I know that thanks to Chuck, Jake and Miranda have been doing really well lately, but buying and renovating a historic building takes a major outlay."

Yes, I said it, but I didn't like hearing it.

Frank let out a long breath. "Okay. Okay. But, remember, you're the one who said Jake had no problem going down in that tunnel. If he and Miranda were involved with Jimmy's death, why would they take you down there?"

I nodded, but I didn't feel any better. "Frank, I'm going to tell you something, but you have to swear you'll keep it out of the paper until we've had a chance to check it out."

I was doing this. I was hiding crucial evidence. I was lying to the police and my coven sister. But I was also trying to keep a kid who said he just wanted to marry his girlfriend and provide for his new baby from getting his name smeared.

"Okay, I swear," said Frank.

I told him about the ghost-hunting expedition and about Chuck and what Chuck had told us. "But now that we've seen Kelly Pierce and Christine Hilde, it changes things," I said. "Because if there's something bigger going on, it might not be Jake and Miranda who are in it with Chuck. It might be Christine and Kelly." Because funding a new hotel, even with Dreame Royale backing, was going to take cash, and lots of it.

Frank let out a long breath. "That's a lot to conclude from one meeting in a diner."

"But it's not just one meeting." It's a vision of a payoff, with Jimmy in the middle between two women.

"Anna," said Frank. "This thing with Chuck. You really should tell the police."

"Not yet," I said. "Please. You promised. We just need a little more time."

"You know I respect you and what you can do, Anna, but this is too much."

"I'm sorry you feel that way." I moved to get out of the car.

Frank groaned. "Anna, stop. Wait. Think this through. This changes the whole picture."

"Maybe," I said. "But maybe not. The Hildes are still in trouble and their family home and business are still on the line. We can be pretty sure Shelly Kinsdale is making plans with Kelly and Christine, and whatever they are, it's going to spell bad news for the hotel." I was talking too loud and too fast. "All we need are a couple of days to find out if Jimmy was involved with that bad news and if what he knew was worth killing for."

"And if we find out what he was involved in really was a drug deal?" he snapped. "Here's another combination for you. Maybe Chuck and Jimmy were working together. Maybe they were taking Jake and Miranda for a ride."

I opened my mouth. I closed it again. I hadn't even thought of that. Was it possible Chuck had been trying to sell us a sob story? No. It couldn't have been. Grandma B.B. would have been able to tell when she did her reading on him. I mean, sure, she hadn't practiced in a while, but she'd jumped back in with both feet. She'd know if he was telling that much of a lie. Even if he was only working with Jimmy to get the money to support his girlfriend and the baby, she'd get a feeling about that.

Wouldn't she?

"Just a couple of days," I said again. "If we don't turn up another story, I promise, we go to the police."

"You better get out of the car, then," said Frank. "Because you've got a lot of work to do.

❧ 27 ❧

🐾 "MEROW?"

Alistair's soft call came out of the living room; so did the sound of somebody snoring.

I snapped off the porch light, dropped my purse on the table by the door and tiptoed in.

Grandma B.B. was stretched out under the rainbow-striped afghan I'd picked up at a rummage sale. She had her glasses perched on her forehead and she was snoring, gently but persistently. Alistair had curled up on her stomach like a furry gray pillow.

"Thanks, big guy," I whispered and rubbed his ears. I knew Grandma B.B. was perfectly capable of looking after herself, but somehow I felt better knowing that my familiar was on duty.

"Merowp," he mumbled as he rearranged himself and tucked his face under his tail.

I wandered into the dining room and stared at the piles of books and paper that was the sum total of my research into the Harbor's Rest hotel and historic Portsmouth.

I was tired. I was more than a little bewildered. What

had I been thinking? I should call Kenisha right now. Tell her everything I knew. Maybe Chuck and Jimmy had been in business together after all. Maybe they were using Jake and Miranda as cover, and maybe scapegoats.

But then I pictured the toothy smile spreading across Lieutenant Blanchard's face. If I helped stitch up his case against Jake and Miranda because I revealed that there really was a drug connection, I'd never forgive myself.

Then there were the sketches that had come from my automatic drawing session. They had all been of the Hildes and Jimmy. Chuck was nowhere to be seen. I stopped. Unless. The drawing pad was lying on the table with the other research papers. I flipped it open to the last page and stared at the sketch of the two men in the middle of a murder. Neither figure was very distinct, but that could be Chuck getting shot, or maybe holding the gun.

"Merow?" said Alistair from down beside my ankles. He jumped up onto the chair and the table and promptly sat down on the nearest book.

"We need to think, Alistair," I whispered to him. Grandma B.B.'s snoring hitched, but she settled down. "What do we actually know?"

"Merow." His tail lashed back and forth.

"We know Jimmy Upton was drowned in a sink and put in the tunnel. We know he had a wad of cash on him." I stopped. "Why would the murderer leave the money?"

"Maow." Alistair jumped off the book into the middle of the table, scattering papers everywhere.

"Shhh! Come on, cat," I hissed as I started gathering the papers up. "I've got a system going here."

"Merow," said Alistair doubtfully.

I automatically shuffled the papers into a neater pile. "You know, if the murderer knows Lieutenant Blanchard doesn't like the Luces, maybe they deliberately left the money on Jimmy when they dumped the body, so he would think about their past record and get all kinds of very wrong ideas." I stopped. "Which means whoever did this knew about that relationship and knew enough about Blanchard to know how he'd react. *And* it means they wanted to make trouble for Jake and Miranda. If Jimmy and Chuck were using Jake and Miranda for cover, why would they deliberately want to draw attention to them?"

Alistair started nosing around the table, probably looking for crumbs.

"The problem with all this," I said, "is there's still no way to prove Jimmy was killed in the hotel or dumped from there, unless we know where the tunnel is."

There was a rustling from the living room as Grandma B.B. shifted on the couch. I should go up to bed. I didn't want to wake her. She had to be at least as tired as I was. "But we've got to find that tunnel entrance," I told my cat. "Blanchard is building his story around that one fact—there is a way into the tunnel from the old drugstore and there isn't one from the hotel."

"Merow!" Alistair jumped up on the table and plunked himself down, right on top of his favorite sitting book, *Portsmouth: Evolution of a Riverside Town*, which happened to be lying open.

"Jeez, Alistair," I whispered sharply. I also picked him up and put him on a chair. "You'll wrinkle the pages."

"Merow!" he shot back.

"And wake Grandma." Alistair huffed at me and flowed down to the floor.

The book was open to one of the best pictures I'd found so far. It was from the Roaring Twenties and showed a ballroom packed to the walls with women in gowns covered in sequins and fringe alongside men in white ties and tails. The photographer must have stood on a ladder to get that panorama. Every last person in that crowded room was raising a china teacup and smiling for the camera. My plan was to reproduce the scene as a long border running along the top of the walls of the coffee shop, with all those teacups transformed into coffee mugs.

The irony here was that the ballroom was the one in the Harbor's Rest. The caption dated it from 1921. I paused. There had been something about that photo. I remembered thinking I ought to go back and check it, but then everything had hit the fan.

"Merow!" Alistair jumped back up on the table and onto the book.

"Come on, cat," I muttered and shooed him off again. I smoothed the page down and reached for a piece of paper I could use as a bookmark. And stopped.

I squinted at the caption underneath the photo again, right where it read: *Prohibition "tea" at the Harbor's Rest.* Because after that it read: *Courtesy of Harbor's Rest private archive.*

"Archive!" I shouted.

Grandma B.B.'s snore turned into a cough and she started awake.

"Oh, goodness, Anna!" Grandma pushed herself upright. The motion dropped her glasses onto her nose. "You're home!"

"The hotel has a private archive!" I answered. "Why didn't anybody tell me?"

"I imagine because we've all been a little busy." She climbed out from under the afghan. "And perhaps because none of us could possibly know something like that."

I winced. "Right. Yes. Sorry. How's Miranda? Is she okay?"

Grandma started folding the afghan up. "I'm afraid not. She was in tears when we got there. She said she'd called their lawyer, and he was apparently very reassuring, but . . ." Grandma shook her head. "The poor dear. She's afraid Jake's arrest is because of something she did. She's positively terrified she betrayed him. As if she could when she loves him so deeply . . ."

"Grandma B.B.! Did you . . . you know . . ." I made a vaguely witchy gesture.

"With Julia sitting right there the whole time?" Grandma looked at me over the rims of her glasses. "Honestly, Annabelle Amelia, what do you take me for?"

"A witch, a grandmother and Miranda's former baby-sitter."

Grandma lifted her chin. "Well, I suppose you do have a point, dear. But, no. I just held her while she cried a little."

"Did she tell you what happened when the police arrested Jake?"

"No. She couldn't. She wasn't there. She only found out when Jake called her from the station."

"She wasn't there? Where was she?" I asked, but Grandma shook her head.

"I told you, a meeting of some sort."

"A meeting?" I repeated, and the goose bumps were back, running straight up my arms. Because Shelly Kinsdale had been on her way to a dinner meeting when she'd kicked me and Frank out. Which was surely just a coincidence. Right? Right.

But I couldn't help wondering exactly when Jake had been arrested. I mean, it might have taken Frank a few hours to get the news.

"It was one of her committees," Grandma was saying. "Riverfront preservation, I think. I didn't want to push her on the subject. Even Julia felt it would be better if we just got her to bed."

"I just wish she didn't have to be alone."

"She's not. Julia stayed with her when I drove Valerie back home."

I pinched the bridge of my nose. Every time we turned around, it seemed like things were just getting worse for Jake and Miranda. This needed to stop. Now. I'd promised to help them. I'd also promised that in a couple of days I'd tell Kenisha about Chuck. That didn't leave a whole lot of time.

I petted Alistair again and turned over the bits and pieces in my mind. I thought about Frank and his two rumors about the state of the Harbor's Rest. I thought about Shelly Upton Kinsdale and Dreame Royal. Then I thought about Christina Hilde and Kelly Pierce hunched over their omelets and their papers at the diner. I thought about new hotels and old hotels and the need for concrete proof.

We needed to find that tunnel. It was the simplest,

quickest way to get the police looking toward the Hildes. The drawings I'd done pointed to them. Now I knew that Harbor's Rest had it's own private archive. The history of the hotel was stored in the building itself. It would have clippings and pictures like this one and maybe guest registers. Correspondence. Account books. Blueprints.

"Maow," agreed Alistair.

I took a deep breath. "Grandma, I need your help."

"What can I do, dear?" She leaned forward, and Alistair looked up at me expectantly.

"Could you talk to Gretchen again? The hotel has its own archives and I want to look inside. They might just have some old blueprints that didn't get copied into the historical society's files. You can say it's research for the murals for the new coffee shop. See if you can get her to tell you if they've got any plans for development that maybe have been running into trouble? Especially if Jake and Miranda have maybe been protesting or showing up at zoning board meetings? I mean, I hate to ask," I added. "But we don't have much time."

"Because Lieutenant Blanchard may be a close-minded officious so-and-so, but he's not stupid and he's going to find out what Chuck's been doing," she said. "Yes, I've been thinking about that, too. Don't worry, dear. I'll talk to Gretchen, and she'll talk to me." Grandma's eyes gleamed behind her glasses. "I'll get you in. You just watch me."

☙ 28 ❧

♣ EVEN THOUGH I was yawning my head off when I finally climbed into bed, I was still surprised at how quickly I fell asleep. There were so many thoughts and worries surfing the remains of all the coffee I'd drunk, I felt sure I was in for a good hour of staring at the ceiling and listening to Alistair purr.

Instead, it felt like I'd barely blinked before I woke up to a room full of morning sunshine and a pillow full of highly entitled cat nuzzling my ear. There was also a mouth full of that metallic taste that says you forgot to brush your teeth the night (or very early morning) before. The display on my ancient clock radio read 9:30, which for a morning person like me practically counted as sleeping the whole day away.

"Grandma B.B. up yet, big guy?" I asked or, rather, yawned as I scratched Alistair's ears.

"Merow!" Alistair answered. He sounded distinctly miffed, and worry bubbled up in the back of my brain.

I shrugged into my old pink terry-cloth bathrobe and padded downstairs. The kitchen was empty, except for the smell of fresh coffee, and my phone, which was lying face-down next to a note on the breakfast table.

Dear Anna,

Valerie came by and we decided not to wake you. She's gone to see Miranda and says you should meet her there. I'm on our secret mission. Will update you soonest.

Grandma B.B.

"Secret mission," I muttered as Alistair jumped up on the breakfast table and shoved his nose at the note. "Good grief, Alistair, what have I let loose on Portsmouth?"

"Merow," he answered, which was no reassurance at all.

JAKE AND MIRANDA lived in a little bungalow over on Burkitt Street. The place was painted a bright orange and yellow with a big sunburst pattern right over the doorway where a fanlight might have gone on a bigger house. The small front yard was a tangle of wildflowers, or at least it would have been in summer; right now it was mostly stems, rosemary shrubs and purple asters. A maple tree shed scarlet leaves onto the front walk.

If I'd had any visions of Miranda sitting huddled on a couch with an empty coffee cup in her hand, they vanished the second I pulled my Jeep up in front of her bungalow. A half dozen kids played tag on the lawn and the sidewalk, and to my surprise, Val was sitting in a rocking chair on the front porch, crocheting the lavender baby blanket she'd been working on for the past three months. She waved when she saw me and pushed herself to her feet.

"You must have Roger on oxygen by now," I said as I hugged her.

"We've had a little family meeting," Val answered, and I saw the gleam in her eye. "He understands that even when

in the closest relationship we all need some individual space.
I left him making cinnamon buns for the Library Associa-
tion meeting."

"Is Julia here?" I asked.

"She had to get over and open the shop. She'll be back
later."

I lowered my voice. "What about Chuck? Does Miranda
know . . . ?"

Val glanced over my shoulder and then she nodded. "He
came over last night, shortly after we all got here. He said
he was going to turn himself in."

I bit my lip. Why did that scare me? It was good news. It
had to mean that Chuck really wasn't using Jake and
Miranda as cover, right? "Did he do it?"

"No. We talked him out of it."

"Who's 'we'?"

Valerie frowned, but she did answer. "Miranda mostly.
She said if he went to the police now, Blanchard would just
make it look like Chuck was working for Jake and Jimmy'd
found out and they killed Jimmy to keep him quiet."

This was the exact reason I had come up with for not
telling Pete and Kenisha. In the background I could hear
the kids laughing. The sun was shining and everything was
beautiful, but I was as cold as if it were the middle of Decem-
ber. Why did it unnerve me to hear Miranda and I had
reached the same conclusion?

"Anna?" Val touched my hand.

I shook myself. "It's nothing."

"Uh-huh," said Val. "Well, you'd better come on inside,
because that nothing has turned you white as a sheet."

The living room of the bright yellow bungalow was full
of men and women of all ages, most of them in jeans and
homemade tie-dye. The people who weren't on their phones
were busy assembling poster-board signs with hand-painted
slogans like FREE JAKE and COFFEE IS NOT A CRIME.

I don't know what that one was supposed to mean either,
but I could appreciate the spirit.

Miranda was on her cell phone, but she beckoned for me

to come in. "No, no, Brad. Yes. No. I appreciate your efforts, but chaining yourself to the station door is not the best action at this time. The protest is at five, unless Jake's sprung before then . . ."

I guess people did still say "sprung." I was going to have to apologize to Grandma B.B.

"No, I'm not expecting tear gas. Yes, bring an extra bandana just in case. Yes. Moonchild's organizing the petition drive. And, yes, definitely, spread the word. Thank you so much for the support. Peace." She hung up and came over to me, stepping carefully around the signs and their painters. "Oh, Anna, thanks for coming."

"I just wanted to make sure you weren't alone," I said as I hugged her. "Guess I shouldn't have worried."

"Everybody's been just so cool." Tears glittered in the corners of Miranda's eyes. "I can't believe it."

"As if we'd leave Miranda on her own," said a statuesque woman whose T-shirt read FREE TIBET. There was a chorus of agreements, including from Val, and a thumbs-up from Chuck, who was back in the corner painting a sign. I swallowed and looked away.

"I brought bagels," I said, holding up the bulging paper bag I'd brought from Market Basket. Yes, this was a distraction for myself, and Val, who was looking at me a little too closely.

"Thank you," said Miranda. "That's so sweet. You can put them in the dining room."

I could if I could find room. The table was already covered with dishes. There were quinoa salads, homemade granola bars, tofu wraps, deviled eggs, muffins, cookies, fruit salads, and cartons of yogurt, all with their ingredients handwritten on index cards taped to each dish, with the common allergens underlined in different colors.

"How's Jake holding up?" I asked as I retrieved a (one hundred percent recycled materials) paper plate from the stack on the end of the table so Val and I could start piling bagels on it.

"I'm just waiting on the call now," Miranda said softly.

"Don't tell anybody else this, but our lawyer says Jake should be out by noon. Everybody wanted to help, though, so this is kind of keeping us all busy until . . . well, until it's finished." She smiled weakly.

"Miranda . . ." I began. She looked at me expectantly. I opened my mouth. I closed it again. How in the heck do you ask a friend where she was at the time of her husband's arrest?

Before I could get the words together, the doorbell rang.

"Miranda?" called a man's voice. "Okay if I come in?"

Miranda's eyes widened, and she brushed past me and Val to head into the foyer. Val arched her brows at me and we both abandoned the bagels and headed for the foyer.

A stocky man was just closing the front door. He looked to be about Miranda's age, but otherwise he bore absolutely no relation to the rest of the tie-dyed, bandana-wearing gathering. This man was tanned, clean-shaven and dressed in an immaculate black sports coat over a forest green button-down shirt. He had the look of an athlete combined with a bit of an aging Matt Damon around the cheekbones.

I recognized him. I'd seen him in my drawings, in a shouting match with Gretchen and Christine.

"Rich." Miranda took both the man's hands in hers. "I didn't expect to see you here."

"Hello, Miranda." The man kissed her cheek.

I looked at Valerie, and she mouthed, "Rich Hilde." I widened my eyes to show I was surprised.

Which I was.

Very.

Because what the heck was a Hilde doing here and now? And why was Miranda glad to see him?

"I hope I'm not intruding," Rich Hilde said. "I just wanted to stop by and make sure you're doing all right."

"Oh, yes." Miranda smiled, but the expression was tired. "Everything's fine."

A bearded man in a Harley-Davidson jacket thudded down the stairs. "Hey, Miranda, is this guy hassling you?"

"No, no, Kenny." Miranda said quickly. "It's cool."

"If you say so." The bungalow's foyer was small enough that Kenny had to turn sideways to edge past us all, but that didn't stop him from giving Rich an openly suspicious once-over as he did.

"Maybe I should go," said Rich to Miranda. "Don't want anybody to think you're fraternizing with the enemy. Ha-ha." He eyed us all to make sure we appreciated the joke. Val frowned and folded her arms over her belly.

"So, Rich," Val said. "Does your mother know you're here?"

Rich sighed and shrugged. "My mother and I agreed to treat each other like adults thirty years ago, Mrs. McDermott. I don't ask her where she goes and she extends the same courtesy to me."

"Really? You can't tell by looking."

Okay, clearly there was some background here, and whatever it was, the exchange between Rich Hilde and my normally sweet neighbor had Miranda looking more than a little desperate. I decided it was time for an intervention.

"Hi. Anna Britton." I held out my hand to Rich. I may also have gently kicked Val's ankle as I reached past her. She did not so much as flinch. "I guess you must be Dale and Christine's brother?"

"That's me. Good to meet you." Rich flashed me a big, toothy smile, the kind you learn in management courses and includes looking the other person right in the eye so you can put that person at ease and demonstrate that you are actively listening.

I do not like people who look like they want me to be sure I know I'm being listened to. But I smiled, because right then I had no reason not to, and the management course might not have been Richard's idea.

Rich held out his left hand to take mine and we did that awkward hand-switch thing, complete with the polite little laugh. "Sorry." He held up his right hand to display the bandages across the knuckles on four fingers. "I was working on the house, planing down some doors, and slipped. It was a mess. Three stitches on each finger and a tetanus shot."

"Ouch." I winced.

"That pretty much sums it up, yes. Now, am I right—you're the Anna Britton whose grandmother was friends with my mom back in the day?"

"That's me."

"Back in the family homestead." Rich beamed. "That's just great. And you're an artist, I think I heard?"

I wondered if one of the Hildes had been talking about me, or if he'd been actively asking around. I mean, he had the McNallys right there in the hotel. I found I did not like this idea, especially with Val still giving Rich that distinctly knife-edged glare.

"Anna's going to paint some murals for us," Miranda told him. "At least . . . she is when we get things back on track."

"Don't worry, Miranda," Rich said firmly. "With the defense committee you've got set up in there, I'm sure you guys will have Jake out in no time and everything will be right back to normal."

He spoke these last words firmly, like he was trying to reassure somebody. Except I couldn't tell if it was Miranda, or us, or himself. I looked to Val for a hint, but she was too busy making sure Rich didn't make any sudden moves.

"I'm sorry about all this, Miranda." Rich shook his head. "I really am. You shouldn't have to be in trouble because Jimmy . . . well, was what he was. You'll let Jake know I stopped by, all right? I don't want him to think there's still bad blood between us."

"There isn't any bad blood between us, Rich." Miranda squeezed his good hand gently.

There sure was something unsaid between the two of them, though. I could feel it pressing against me as strongly as I'd felt any Vibe in my life. But there was absolutely no way I could ask about it. Heck, I couldn't even ask any of the questions I'd come here with, like what meeting had Miranda been at when Jake got arrested and why was she afraid she'd betrayed him?

"Well, we need to pull together, right?" Rich said earnestly. "This isn't just about us. This is about the community."

"Exactly. And don't worry, I know . . ."

Whatever Miranda was about to say was cut off by her cell ringing. She yanked the phone out of her back pocket and hit the button.

"Enoch? Is there news? Oh, fantastic! Everyone!" Miranda brandished the cell toward the living room. "The judge has set bail! Jake's getting out!"

Cheers and applause went up from the crowd of activists. Miranda was immediately surrounded by people asking questions and getting ready to pass the hat to raise the bail money.

"Well, that's great," said Rich. "Maybe now they'll finally figure out who really is responsible for this mess."

"Let's hope so," I said. "But somehow I don't think Blanchard's going to give up so easily."

"Him? Give up?" Rich snorted. "Not gonna happen. Especially not when . . ."

Val pounced. "When what, Rich? Something we should know about? Maybe when your mother's been talking to her friends on the city council again?"

Rich's response was to check his watch. "Oops. Wow. It's late and I've got to get back to work. Very nice to meet you, Miss Britton. I'm sure I'll see you around. Mrs. McDermott." He nodded stiffly toward Val and trotted down the porch steps to the black Mercedes that was parked across the sidewalk.

Val watched his retreat the way a German shepherd watches the mailman.

"Val?" I shook her shoulder. "Ground control to Valerie? What the heck was that all about?"

"Rich Hilde's a hypocrite; that's what it was about," she snapped. "Every time his family does something or wants something, he's always the one coming around smiling and charming and making it all okay, no matter what they've done or who they've done in."

"And you know this because . . . ?" I prompted.

"When I got set to open the B and B, there was all kinds of delays getting the permits, especially the liquor license.

I almost had to give up. Then I found out from a friend of mine at the clerk's office that Gretchen Hilde was leaning on them to hold things up. Not that I'd suspected anything, because Rich was always around, smiling and asking how things were going, offering helpful suggestions, and being charming." She bit the word off. "I only found out later that his mother and sister were working the whole time to try to kill a little bit of competition. As if one more bed-and-breakfast in this town would mean anything to a monster like the Harbor's Rest."

Except, according to what Frank said, Gretchen and the Harbor's Rest might have a whole lot of reasons to care about competition.

She had to fight tooth and nail for everything she has. Grandma's words trickled back into my mind. If we were right, Kelly and Christine weren't planning just a little bit of competition with Dreame Royale. They were setting up a major challenge. If Mrs. Hilde was willing to lean on the city clerk over a B and B, what would she be willing to do about a new hotel?

"Why didn't you say something before?" I asked.

"I didn't realize the Hildes were actively sticking their fingers into the works. But if Rich is out with the charm offensive, that changes everything."

❧ 29 ❧

♣ THERE WASN'T MUCH chance to talk after that. The gathering started planning how to change the scheduled protest into a welcome-home party. Then Roger showed up with a tray of hummus and gluten-free pita bread and took Val away for some baby-related shopping. I stayed and chatted and ate and tried to maneuver myself through the crowd so I could actually talk to Chuck.

Sometime between spreading hummus on pita and explaining to a tiny woman in a flowing yellow dress how I knew Jake and Miranda, Chuck quietly disappeared. I tried to make myself believe it was nothing personal, but I had a tough time believing myself.

I finally made my own excuses and my own exit. I climbed into the Jeep and pulled out my phone to check my messages. There weren't any. I tried calling Grandma B.B., but she didn't pick up. I tried calling Frank, and the result was the same. I rubbed my forehead and thought about how it was only noon and there was a whole day ahead where I needed to be out and doing. Talking to people. Researching. Sleuthing.

Making sure it wasn't my friends who were guilty of murder. Proving to myself that I wasn't making a huge mistake in trusting the Luces and that there were lots of reasons Miranda could be talking to Rich Hilde and that it was perfectly reasonable for her not to want Chuck to talk to the police. I'd come to that exact same conclusion, hadn't I?

With all this ringing around my head, I did what anybody would do. I put the Jeep in gear and started driving, right out of town to Hampton Beach.

THIS LATE IN the year, the beach was fairly deserted. Nobody was out on the water except one very determined guy on his boogie board. The sands were almost as empty. There was just me, a family flying a rainbow-striped kite, and a couple out walking their golden Lab. I sat down and wrapped my arms around my knees. The fierce wind whipped around my head, and I breathed the salty air deeply as I stared at the gray breakers. I willed all that fresh, cold air to clear the clutter out of my brain and my conscience. I wished I had someone to talk to. I wished there was somebody I *could* talk to. But everybody I could say anything too was either busy or mad at me or missing in action.

Well, almost.

"Meow?" Alistair, who hadn't been there before, was rubbing against my elbow. I took this to be the feline equivalent of *penny for your thoughts*.

"What have I done, Alistair?" I said. The wind whipped a few locks of hair in front of my eyes. "Frank's mad at me. Kenisha thinks I'm hiding things from the police. Which would be really unfair, except I am hiding things from the police. I can't concentrate on making a living because I'm trying to solve a murder, and I may be trusting all the wrong people."

"Meow!"

"Of course I don't mean you. But I don't know if I can handle this, Alistair." I folded my arms on my knees and rested my chin on them. "Maybe I have just gone too far."

Footsteps thudded against the hard-packed sand. A lean man in black running shorts and a bright green T-shirt thudded past. He stopped short, turned and doubled back.

That's when I saw it was the younger Sean McNally.

"Anna! Thought that was you." Sean crouched down so we were more or less eye level. He was breathing hard, and despite how chilly it was, there was a sheen of perspiration on his forehead.

"Sean! What are you doing out here?"

"Day off," he told me. "The weather was so great, I thought I'd get a run in. Mind if I sit down?"

"It's a free beach." I gestured to the sand.

Sean folded his long legs and settled next to me. "Hello, big guy." He scratched Alistair's ears, completely unfazed by seeing the cat with me. Alistair graciously permitted this familiarity.

"Everything okay?" he asked.

"That's what I'm trying to figure out."

Sean nodded, but he didn't push further. There are people who have a restful presence. Sean McNally was like that. He just sat beside me, looking out at the waves and catching his breath. I guess being a professional bartender, he'd learned when to talk and when to just keep quiet and leave someone to her own thoughts.

The problem was I didn't much like my own thoughts right now.

"They arrested Jake," I told him.

"I know," he said. "I heard he made bail, though, so that's something."

When it came to the speed of spreading news, the Internet had nothing on the small-town grapevine. "He didn't do it."

"I know that, too. Jake's old-school. Believes in nonviolent resistance. If he really had a problem with Jimmy, he'd just sit on his doorstep, probably with six or eight friends."

"And sing 'Kumbaya.'"

"Oh, he'd definitely sing 'Kumbaya.' I've heard him do it. It's better when he's had a couple beers. Miranda plays a mean banjo accompaniment."

I completely believed that. "Why am I doing this, Sean?"

"What?" he asked. "Sitting on a beach with a bartender and a cat?"

"Merow," muttered Alistair.

My mouth twitched. Not that I was close to smiling. Now was definitely not a smiling time. "Getting involved in other people's problems again. My grandmother's stuck in it, too, and all my friends. And it's all my fault."

Sean scratched his bearded chin thoughtfully. "Let's try that last part again. How did it get to be your fault?"

"Because I'm the one who could have walked away and didn't. I'm the one who . . . decided to maybe not say something I should have. So I'm dragging them all in with me."

"Wow. That's one heck of a superpower you've got there, Anna. I had no idea."

I glowered at him. "That's sarcasm, isn't it? You're being sarcastic at me."

"Nah. Just a small splash of irony." He smiled. "Listen, I don't know your grandmother that well yet, but I know Val and I know Julia. If they're in this thing, whatever it is, it's because it's where they've decided they want to be." He cocked his head toward me. "Maybe you need to decide that, too."

"Maybe I do. Maybe I have. Maybe I'm just . . . scared."

"That's normal. Change is scary. So is getting involved. Involved means attached and attached means if it doesn't work, more people than you get hurt."

"So, what do I do?"

"Either don't get involved or make sure when you do, it does work."

"Wow. Words of wisdom. You'd make a great bartender."

"Nah. I'm allergic to corn nuts."

"Seriously?"

"Seriously. It's something in the seasoning. I swell up like a balloon."

"Well, I promise never to feed you corn nuts."

"Thank you."

There was a pause. We both watched the waves for a while. The wind whipped my hair in front of my eyes again. I pushed it down.

"My friends think you want to take me out."

Sean nodded, clearly giving this statement some careful consideration. "What do you think?"

"I don't know."

He smiled. "Fair enough."

"What do you think?"

Sean watched the ocean for a while. The guy on the boogie board wiped out and surfaced a moment later, shaking water out of his hair. "I think I'm going to plead the Fifth," said Sean. "For now."

"It's not nice to keep someone in suspense."

His smile turned positively mischievous. I had the sudden, terrible urge to stick my tongue out at him. Not that what I did was a whole lot better.

"Why me?" I asked.

He shrugged. "Not sure yet, but I'm pretty confident we'll figure it out." Good grief, it was like he could make his eyes twinkle on command.

"I've always had terrible luck with guys," I tried.

"Bet none of the others were charming Irish bartenders."

He had me there. "My life's a little messed up right now, and it's looking like if I stay in town, that's going to become a permanent condition."

"You're helping friends," he said. "Sounds like the good kind of messed up to me."

"You're not going to be talked out of this, are you?"

He shook his head slowly.

"I'm not saying yes," I warned him.

"Are you saying no?"

I sucked in a deep breath. "No. I'm not. It's just . . . things really are complicated."

"Well then." He got up, dusted himself off, and held out his hand. I took it and let him pull me up. "We'll just have to see if we can make them simpler. Hey, I hear there's this swell party happening over at Northeast Java this evening. I was going to head over and drop off a bottle of that new moonshine Dad found. Would you like to come?"

"I would, but I promised . . ." I stopped. I stared. Not at Sean, exactly, but at the idea that was blossoming inside me. "Sean, is your dad working at the hotel today?"

"I think so. Why?"

"Because I need him to get me in to talk to Kelly Pierce." Yes, Grandma was talking to Gretchen, and hopefully that would land me an invitation to the archives, but I still needed to talk to the food and beverages manager who liked her midnight omelet with extra cheese, and it might be better if her employers didn't know. It would have been best if I could have arranged something away from the hotel, but I'd wasted enough time this day. The clock was very much ticking.

Sean cocked his head at me. "Should I ask why you need to talk to Kelly?"

"Ummm . . . no."

"Okay," he said. "But there is one thing I am going to ask."

I felt the blood drain from my cheeks. "What's that?"

"Where'd your cat go?"

❧ 30 ❧

♣ TO SAY OLD Sean was pleased to see me and his son walking into the Harbor Rest's bar together was something of an understatement. I swear he was ready to break out the champagne and toast the happy couple right there. And this wasn't just me. My Sean saw his dad's grin and turned a truly remarkable shade of red.

No, I did not actually call the younger Mr. McNally "my" Sean. That far gone I am not. Especially not after I saw the broad grin and the broader wink his dad gave him when Sean said he was going to go home to shower and change and he'd meet me at Jake's party.

Despite the fact that Old Sean clearly regarded my request that he take me to Kelly Pierce by the route least likely to be seen by any Hildes as a feeble ruse to hide the depth of my feelings for his son, he did agree. I followed him carefully, carrying two very full take-out cups down into the hotel basement.

I'm used to basements being cold, but as soon as Old Sean pushed open the door at the bottom of the service stairs, it felt like I was walking into a steam tunnel. A very noisy steam tunnel painted the color of cold oatmeal and full of men and women in gray-and-white uniforms who barely glanced at either of us as we edged past them.

Next to the locker rooms waited an open door (also oatmeal colored) with MANAGER painted in black on it. Inside, Kelly Pierce sat at a battered metal desk that was as piled with paper as Martine's. She was typing madly at a laptop keyboard while talking on the phone jammed between her shoulder and her ear.

"*Please*, Luis. We're in a bind. Yes . . . yes . . . you're my hero. We'll see you in an hour."

Old Sean knocked on the doorframe. Kelly glanced up and waved us in.

"Miss Pierce, this is a friend of my son's, Anna Britton," Old Sean told her.

"I don't suppose you have any experience waiting tables?" she asked me.

"Not since art school."

"Damn. I'm three servers down for dinner rush and my substitute chef has just informed me that we only got half the steaks we ordered today, and we might be about to run out of our most popular vodka, and the soda dispenser in the coffee shop's on the fritz," she announced. "*What* can I do for you?"

"I, um, got your name from Martine Devereaux." I held up one of the paper take-out cups. "I brought coffee?"

She glared at me, and then at Old Sean, and then at the coffee. We all waited. I might have held my breath.

Kelly gestured with two fingers. "Give it here."

I did. Sean winked and beat a hasty retreat while Kelly pulled off the to-go cup lid and downed a healthy swallow. "Ah," she sighed. "Thanks. I needed that." She took another long swallow. Wow. She could give Frank a run for his money. "All right, you can stay, and you got five minutes. What do you want?"

"I was hoping I could talk to you about Jimmy Upton."

Kelly grimaced. "What do you want to know about the little grunge-meister?"

"Umm . . . that may have done it right there."

She shook her head. She also took another gulp of coffee. "I'm new in town," she said. "I only took this job six months ago. If I'd known what I was walking into . . ." Something came up on her screen. She swore and started typing faster one-handed than I can with both. "No, no, no! We need thirty-six cases, you . . ." There followed some more drastic language and some more frantic key clicking.

"There have been problems?" I asked.

"There are always problems with a restaurant, and it's worse in a hotel, because you're dealing with room service and catering for major events and maybe a coffee shop and all that."

"I'm guessing Jimmy didn't make things any easier?"

She made a face like she was drinking pure lemon juice. "Jimmy was a hotshot, and he was a hustler. That's okay; you get 'em in a kitchen. A good executive chef can usually put them in their place. But Jimmy was in a league of his own."

"I heard he was good."

"That's part of the problem. He really was. His food was amazing. He probably could have been great." She eyed what coffee remained in her cup. "And he wasn't a complete jerk. I saw him down by the service drive a few times. We get some homeless down there. Jimmy was passing out sandwiches and cards for the shelter. He said he'd been on the streets and nobody ought to be that hungry."

This was something no one had mentioned yet. "Does anybody know how he wound up on the streets?"

She shrugged. "I never asked and he never offered. But my guess is his temper and his ego got in the way of him working real steady." She took another sip of coffee, and this time she eyed me over the rim with the kind of thoughtfulness that made me distinctly uncomfortable. "Who did you say you were with, Miss Britton? Aside from the McNallys?"

I'd been expecting this question, or something like it, and I'd even gotten an answer ready. "I'm not really with anybody," I admitted. "But, well, my family is friends with the Hildes, and, you know, I heard things are tough right now and I . . . I don't know. I thought maybe I could help, or something." I smiled at her. Innocent. Sunny. As harmless as Grandma B.B. with a lollipop.

Yeah, right. Kelly wasn't buying it either. At least, not entirely. She set the coffee cup down and she sighed.

"Listen, you want to help? Tell whichever of them you're friends with that they need to get their collective act together. Have a family meeting, hug it out, spank their inner child, what-the-heck-ever. But unless and until the Hildes get it together, this place is going to collapse." She said it fast, like she was trying to get all the words out before common sense caught up with her.

"Was that what you were telling Christine Hilde at the Friendly Toast last night?"

She tried hard to cover the shock of being seen by taking another long swallow of coffee, but it was too late. "Who told you about that?"

"Nobody. I love pancakes at one a.m."

Another thing I'd learned from hanging out with Martine is that people in the service industries all have insane schedules. The idea of somebody out getting breakfast in the small hours of the morning did not seem at all strange to Kelly.

I made myself smile the smile I reserve for potential clients. "Or maybe it wasn't about the family? Maybe you were talking about the new hotel Dreame Royale is going to be opening?"

Kelly groaned. "I am going to murder that . . . She promised she would keep the whole thing under wraps until Christine had a chance to present our final proposal."

"Secrets this big are hard to keep," I said. "I imagine a lot of Hildes would get upset if they found out you two were talking to Shelly Kinsdale."

Kelly set her coffee cup down and leaned across the desk. "What do you want, Miss Britton?"

"I want to know if you are helping Christine open a new place, or if you're planning on taking over Harbor's Rest," I said bluntly. "And whichever it was, did Jimmy Upton know?"

Kelly's jaw dropped. Literally. Unfortunately, before she could collect herself, the door flew open and Dale Hilde strode in, his face as red as his blazer and his hair all but standing on end.

"Ms. Pierce! What is going on here!"

Kelly was on her feet before I could even move. "Mr. Hilde. What's happened?"

"What's happened is you're sitting here gossiping with your girlfriend while you're on the clock."

Kelly drew herself up and her eyes flashed, but Dale wasn't paying attention. Instead he rounded on me. "Unless maybe you've come to apologize, Miss Britton?"

"Apologize? What . . . ?" I stammered.

"Mr. Hilde," tried Kelly grimly. Oh no. I'd gone to far. She was going to tell him. I'd blown it.

But right then Kelly's laptop beeped. So did the phone.

"You'd better take care of those, Ms. Pierce," said Dale coolly. "Ms. Britton, you'll come with me?"

I guessed I would. I picked up my purse and my cup of mostly untouched coffee and followed Dale out the door as Kelly hit the button on her phone.

"Yeah? Go. *What?* No, you . . . Who told you that?"

The door swung shut behind me, and I suppressed a sigh.

DALE'S OFFICE ON the first floor was the polar opposite of Kelly Pierce's loud, hot, crowded space down below. This was a deeply old-fashioned and serious place. The lamps were polished brass; the fireplace was actual wood burning, no gas logs here. The multipaned windows had been pushed open to let in the cool river breeze. The desk was the oldest piece of furniture in the room, plain and scarred and turned dark by long years of use.

As soon as I got inside, Dale shut the door. He also ran a shaking hand through his thick, dark hair.

"You've got a lot of nerve, Ms. Britton."

"I'm sorry, but . . ."

He cut me off. "Thanks to you and your grandmother,

my mother is sitting in her room sobbing into a handker-chief!"

"*What?*"

"I haven't seen her cry since our father walked out. What kind of—"

"Hang on!" I help up both hands. "Look, Mr. Hilde, I'm really sorry your mother's upset, but I've got no idea what the problem is." Well, except for maybe that thing with Grandpa Charlie, but that was fifty years ago. It couldn't possibly be that. Or Grandma asking if I could see the hotel archives. I mean, why would that be a big deal? Except, it wouldn't take a lot to guess that I might just be looking for the tunnel entrance. But Gretchen Hilde was a tough busi-nesswoman. Nothing like that could make her cry.

Could it?

Dale and I stared at each other, with contempt on his side and confused near panic on mine. Near panic lasted longer. Dale Hilde slowly crumbled and at last sat in the leather wing-backed chair.

"This office was my great-grandfather's," he said as his gaze wandered about the room. "My mother gave it to me when I took over as financial manager. Rich had wanted it, but she gave it to me." The ring of pride in his voice was painfully audible. "She said since I was the one keeping the hotel on an even keel, I deserved the captain's cabin."

"You two must be close."

I meant it as a compliment, but Dale looked at me like I'd criticized the color of his great-grandfather's drapes (green plaid, in case you're wondering).

"You're going to do it, too, are you?" he said.

"I don't—"

"People make a lot of assumptions when they find out a man my age is working for his mother. If it's his father, nobody's got a problem. But if it's his mother, they start looking at him cross-eyed, like she's got to be a dragon and he's got to be a wimp or terribly, terribly resentful because she's in charge and I'm not."

"Erm . . ."

"Look, Miss Britton." Dale Hilde planted both hands on that acre of antique mahogany. "My mother held this place together single-handed after my father left. She fought because it is our home and because she loves it. I'm proud of my whole family and I'm proud of what we've built. That's why I'm still fighting to keep us going."

"So, you wouldn't be in favor of selling the hotel if an offer got made?"

Dale's reached up and very carefully shoved his glasses back into place on his nose. "Who told you there'd been an offer on the hotel?"

I just looked at him. He sighed. "That would be Frank Hawthorne, of course. Publisher of the local fish wrapper." He slicked back his hair nervously. "All right, yes, I admit it. We had an offer. We get them. We are an extremely valuable and lucrative property."

"I'd heard the hotel was actually in a little trouble," I said. "I mean, everybody's still climbing out of the recession and all . . ."

"Oh, well, of course I'm just going to tell you all our business. I know I can trust you because you're with the Luces and we can always trust them, especially when it comes to sabotaging our plans with the zoning board. And of course, you're also friends with Frank Hawthorne and everybody knows we can trust him to be fair and impartial when it comes to business development in Portsmouth." He waited for me to make some kind of protest, but not for very long. "I think you'd better go, Ms. Britton, and I really do not want to see you around here again."

I got to my feet. I'm sure I meant to make some devastating parting comment, but I didn't get the chance, because somebody knocked on the office door, loud and fast.

"Excuse me," said Dale without taking his eyes off me. "This could be *important*."

He didn't wait for an answer; he just opened the door. Rich Hilde stood on the other side.

"Dale," he said, a little breathlessly. His hair was tousled, too. Had he been running? "Mom said you were"—Rich spotted me right then, and he drew up short—"in here. And, oh, ah, yes. You're busy."

Dale sighed and stepped back so Rich could come inside. "Miss Britton, you've met my brother, Richard?"

"Yes, of course we met." Rich said before I could. He also tried to give me his manager's grin, but this time he couldn't quite pull it off. "She and her grandmother have been making themselves right at home."

"Well, not anymore," said Dale firmly. "Rich, did you actually need something?"

"Well, yes, actually, just . . . Anna, could you excuse us?"

"Sure. Of course."

Of course I walked out into the hallway and looked behind me with longing. Unfortunately, it was a busy hall. A hotel is a people-intensive operation. Men and women in uniform jackets were already passing by, wondering what I was doing there.

But there was that open window. So perfect for a little autumn eavesdropping. Which was very rude, of course, and kind of risky, because I had no cover story for why I should be hanging around outside office windows after I'd been told to get the heck off the grounds. But if this was the last time I got to set foot in the hotel, I was going to have to get as much information as I could, right?

Right.

The Harbor's Rest has two long wings. They curve around the marina like the building is embracing the river. There were also approximately a hundred windows that faced the water, so that as many guests as possible could enjoy the scenic view. Two or three dozen of them were on the ground floor, and a lot of them were open. If anything interesting was being said in that office, the conversation was going to be long over by the time I figured out which one I needed.

"Merow?" Alistair strolled past me. "Merp?"

"Good kitty," I said, purely to the boats in their slips, of course. "Can you find me a window?"

That was when I noticed Alistair was not alone. Miss Boots was also trotting alongside. Alistair looked at her.

"Merow?" he inquired.

"Merow," she agreed, and bounded off ahead.

Alistair looked over his shoulder and, I swear, gave me a wink.

I wasn't going to argue about any of this. I just followed the cats. Trying to be nonchalant yet hurry at the same time is harder than it sounds.

Finally, Miss Boots charged ahead and leapt up on a sill.

"Ahg!" shouted a familiar voice.

"Easy, bro." Rich laughed. "It's just Bootsie."

"That cat is a menace, popping in and out everywhere. It's going to give somebody a heart attack!"

You have no idea. I settled myself onto the sloping grass underneath and tried to look like I was watching the boats on the river. Alistair curled up beside me. I scritched his ears. I was going to have to pick up a fresh bag of K.T. Nibbles for this, and possibly some more tuna. And that kitty gym membership.

". . . and just what was I supposed to do?" Rich was saying over my head.

"You were *supposed* to do your job and manage the day shift and leave the whole thing alone!"

"Dale, this was not some stranger they're accusing. You've known Jake as long as I have!"

"Yes, and I'm shocked. I hope it wasn't him. I hope he's cleared in a New York minute, but we have to let the law do its job. This is not our business!"

"Jimmy was our employee. We owe him—"

"What? Exactly what do we owe that arrogant little troublemaker?"

"I didn't mean we owe Jimmy. I meant we owe Jake."

Jake? Rich thought they owed Jake something? I looked at Alistair. He blinked up at me. Rich thought they owed Jake something. And Rich was going out of his way to make sure Miranda knew they were still friends.

And Rich was the one who spearheaded the family's charm offensives.

Alistair's whiskers twitched. *Oh, yeah,* I thought toward my familiar. *Something definitely smells fishy here.*

"Look, Rich," Dale was saying. "I know you want to help. I know you want to be the good guy, but there are times when that's not one of the options."

"I know, I know, I just—"

"I wish it was different, too. Seriously. But that ship's sailed. We've got to be smart, okay?"

"Yeah, yeah, okay. I'm good, I'm good."

"Okay. Now, go see if you can calm Mom down, and I'd better go warn Christine about . . . all this."

"Yeah. Right. Thanks, bro. I don't know what any of us would do without you."

"Neither do I."

There was the sound of a door closing. I waited, and then, carefully keeping out of sight, I got up and stretched and strolled away. I glanced at my watch. It was going on five. Jake's party would have started by now. I should go. I'd said I'd meet Sean there after all. And I might just run into Frank, which would be good, because I had a few things I needed to tell him.

❧ 31 ❧

🐾 I'D TURNED OFF my phone when I went into the hotel to try to talk with Kelly Pierce. When I got back to the parking lot and climbed into my Jeep, I turned it back on and checked my messages. There were three, and they were all from Grandma B.B.

Alistair appeared in the passenger seat as I played back the first message and listened to Grandma saying there might be a tiny complication with her mission.

In the second, she said I shouldn't worry and she'd meet me at home.

In the third she said I shouldn't worry, but she was turning her phone off for a bit.

"Mer-owp," said Alistair.

"Yeah," I agreed as I hit Grandma's number. The phone rang ten times, but all I got was her voice mail.

"This is a message from Annabelle Blessingsound Britton. Of *course* I want to talk to you, so *please* leave a message at the tone . . ."

"Grandma B.B., if you don't call me back this second I'm going to hold my breath until I turn blue."

I hung up and stared at the phone. Then I hit her number again.

"This is a message from Annabelle Blessingsound Britton . . ."

"I didn't mean that, Grandma, but when you tell me not to worry, I worry. Call me back."

"Merp," said Alistair.

"Yeah." I hung up again and shoved my phone into my purse. I drummed my fingers on the steering wheel. Maybe I should just go straight home. With what Dale told me, something had clearly gone wrong between her and Gretchen. But I needed to talk to Frank. And Miranda. And Chuck. And the day was almost over.

"Go look after her, Alistair," I said. "I need to know she's got a friend there."

"Merow!" He swished his tail determinedly, and he vanished.

I threw the Jeep into gear.

ORDINARILY, I WOULD have walked the short distance between the hotel and Northeast Java, but since Dale Hilde had thrown me out, I thought it would be a bad move to leave my Jeep in their lot. So instead I parked in the public lot off the square. I could already hear the music rising from down by the river as I slotted my card into the automatic payment machine.

Jake's welcome-home party spilled out of Northeast Java into Ceres Street and effectively blocked the foot traffic for three hours. There was a river of coffee, an ocean of congratulations, a banjo, and a bongo, and, yes, people did hold hands and sing "Kumbaya," as well as "If I Had a Hammer."

Sean was right. It was definitely a happening.

I squeezed into the crowd, saying hi to people I knew (more than I would have thought) and getting introduced to new and enthusiastic friends of Jake and Miranda (a lot more). I craned my neck, looking for Sean, but didn't see any sign of him or Chuck, or Miranda or Jake for that matter. I did find Frank, though. He stood beside the coffee shop door, notebook in hand, talking to a plump woman with a toddler on her hip and another by the hand. I could see his lips move, and her answer, but I couldn't hear a darn thing but the blur of voices and bongos.

I took a deep breath and eased my way forward. Frank glanced up, but his face remained professionally bland. He raised one finger to signal me to wait. I did.

"Did you want something?" he asked.

"I've got some news."

"Oh?"

"I talked to Kelly Pierce this afternoon. She pretty much confirmed that she and Christine are doing some kind of deal with Shelly Kinsdale."

Frank looked at me very steadily for a long moment. "Did she have details?"

"We got interrupted. But I also talked to Dale Hilde, who said there'd been an offer for the hotel, but it was turned down."

Frank sighed. "Okay. Right." He glanced at his watch. "Was that it?"

"Look, Frank, I know this is a big mess. All I can say is I really am trying to help."

Frank turned his notebook over in his hands a couple of times. "We all are."

"What happened at the press conference?

He shrugged. "Just the expected. A whole lot of 'We cannot comment on the ongoing investigation,' laced with 'The department and the district attorney are confident that we will be able to make our case and the murderer of Jimmy Upton will shortly be brought to trial.'"

"So, Blanchard still thinks it's Jake."

"Yep. This is just a reprieve, and, according to my sources, everybody's pushing for a speedy trial date."

"Shoot," I muttered and Frank nodded in sincere agreement.

I leaned closer. I was planning on telling him about my conversation with Dale, but fresh movement beyond the edge of the crowd caught my attention. A familiar, tall, bearded figure in a pinstripe waistcoat and gray felt hat trotted down the steps from the square.

"There you are, Anna!" Sean called, as he shouldered his way through the crowd. "Thought I'd missed you. Had to go back and get that bottle." He lifted the gift bag he was carrying. "Figured when the roar dies down Jake might need something a little stronger than coffee," he said to Frank. "Have you seen where they're at?" he asked me.

"No," I said. "As a matter of fact, I was just going to look for them. Maybe in back?" I suggested.

"You guys go," Frank said. "I'm on the job here. I've got to get some quotes from the community." He looked around at the laughing, arguing, banjo-playing crowd. "I don't think this is going to be one of my harder assignments."

Frank pulled out his notebook and headed over to a cluster of men and women by the guardrail between the curb and the river.

"I wasn't interrupting something there, was I?" asked Sean.

"No. Nothing."

If he sounded a little tense, it was probably just all the noise. And those bongos. I couldn't hear anything clearly because of the bongos. I certainly couldn't have heard Sean whisper, "Too bad."

I shouldered my way deeper into the coffee shop, with Sean behind me, holding up the bottle in its bag and tipping his hat to the people who called out to him or lifted coffee cups as we edged past.

I ducked around the counter. All the baristas were on duty, but they all were too busy handing out coffee and exchanging congratulations to notice us coming through. Except Chuck. Chuck looked up from the steamed milk he was pouring and saw me and turned a very nasty shade of gray.

We stood and stared at each other. I watched his Adam's apple bob. He broke the stare down first, turning all his attention back to the espresso in front of him.

He wasn't the only one having a less than swell time,

either. When we got to the kitchen door, Sean and I both stopped in our tracks.

Jake and Miranda stood nose to nose in the tiny kitchen. Miranda had her hands on her hips and was staring up at Jake, anger plain in every line of her body. Jake was looking down at her, slumped and pleading. While we watched, Jake slowly spread his arms toward his wife. Miranda's jaw worked back and forth for a minute, but then she all but fell into his arms. They hugged each other tightly, and Jake rested his chin on top of her head. Even from where I stood, I could see the tears gleaming in his eyes.

I glanced at Sean and he jerked his chin back over his shoulder, indicating we should leave. I nodded. Together, we started to ease backward, but some coffee purveyor's instinct made Miranda look up just then.

"Oh, hey, Sean, hey, Anna." She backed out of Jake's arms and wiped at her face. "Thanks for coming."

"Um, yeah, sure," I said. "Just wanted to make sure you're doing okay."

"Oh, yeah. Everything's cool," said Jake, but he also pulled his glasses off so he could knuckle his eyes. "It's just been kind of intense."

"This might help." Sean handed the gift bag with the bottle to Miranda.

Miranda peeked inside at the moonshine. "Thanks, Sean." She tried to smile and almost made it. "Hey, Jake, honey, why don't you stash that? I'll take care of things out front."

"Sure thing." Jake was trying to smile, too, but he didn't move.

I looked at Miranda. I looked at Jake standing beside her. I examined my conscience and did not like the way it was looking back at me, so I ignored it.

"Miranda, have you got a second? I was hoping we could . . . talk?"

She straightened her shoulders. "Anything you've got to ask me, you can ask it right here. We'll never hear anything out there anyhow."

"You sure?"

Miranda took Jake's hand. "I'm sure."

I felt Sean looking down at me, uncertain where any of this was going and whether he should stick around for it. I swallowed. Well, he wanted to get to know me better. Here was his chance.

"Where were you when Jake got arrested?"

"Meetings," she said. "Believe me, I've been kicking myself—"

"Was it with Rich Hilde?" I said it fast, like I was afraid I'd lose my nerve in the middle. Which I might have.

Miranda's face flushed, but her husband gave her hand a little shake. "Go on, Miranda. No secrets."

"No secrets," she breathed. "All right. Yes. I was meeting with Rich. I . . ." She stopped and swallowed. "He told me Harbor's Rest is looking for a new coffee supplier. Our renovations for the new place were costing more than we expected, and I thought, well, maybe if Rich and I could come together, we could find a way to talk with Gretchen and maybe make some peace. Find some common ground, and maybe Northeast Java could get the contract to supply the hotel with their coffee . . ." She stopped. "And that's where I was when Blanchard came to take Jake away."

Jake squeezed her hand. "You were trying to make peace. It's a good thing."

Miranda cleared her throat. "We're not really set up for that kind of volume, but I thought, maybe, we could talk about some specialty batches to sell in the hotel store, but, well, I was worried Jake might not—"

"She was afraid I'd accuse her of selling out to the capitalist establishment," Jake finished. "And maybe I would have, because I am not always as cool as I should be."

"So I decided not to tell him before I had more details, and some kind of plan, and could run some numbers to see . . ." She shook her head. "Well, if it would be worth it."

"Would it be?" asked Sean. The sound of his voice startled me more than it should have. I'm embarrassed to admit it but, he'd been so quiet, I'd kind of forgotten he was there.

Miranda shook her head. "I don't think so, no."

"Because you're not set up for it?" I said.

"Because things are too crazy over there," she said. "Rich talks a good game, but I don't think his mom would actually go for it."

"Thanks, Miranda" I said. "I appreciate the honesty."

"I know, but don't go poking Chuck," said Miranda. "He's upset enough as it is. Okay?"

"Okay," I agreed. "I'll let you get back to your party."

I turned and edged past Sean, heading back out into the crowd and the music and trying not to feel like I was slinking away.

Sean followed me out into the open air, until we got to the railing that separated Ceres Street from the river.

"And there it is," I said to Sean, folding my arm on the railing and staring out at the river. "That's me in a nutshell."

Sean glanced over his shoulder. "Am I supposed to be scared?"

I smiled weakly. "Scared? No. Mildly appalled, maybe."

"Sorry. Can't oblige. Unfortunately, I also can't stay. Virginia called in sick, and I've got to go cover her shift at the Pale Ale. You going to be all right?"

"Fine. I've got to get going, too." Specifically, I needed to find Grandma B.B. and hear what had happened between her and Gretchen Hilde.

Sean said something and touched my shoulder. I reminded myself that it would totally break up this beautiful, peaceful happening if I pitched the bongo player into the river.

"What?" I shouted.

Sean laughed. "I was *saying*, if you need help, or anything, all you have to do is whistle." He adjusted his fedora. "You do know how to whistle, don't you?"

I did. I also knew how to blush, and I was doing it now. But it only lasted a minute, because as I grinned up at Sean, another memory was surging up from the back of my brain.

"What?" He touched my shoulder. "Are you okay?"

"Oh, ah, um, yeah. I just remembered I forgot to buy cat food. Alistair's going to shred all the sofa cushions."

Sean laughed. "Circle K is open twenty-four-seven. You'll be fine."

"Sure I will. You'd better get going, or Martine will shred more than the sofa cushions."

Sean winced. "You got that right. Talk to you soon."

I agreed he would. I also stared after him as he walked away, adjusting the brim of his hat so the wind wouldn't blow it off his head. I was thinking about how he sometimes worked at the hotel, filling in behind their bar. I was also thinking about the drawing I'd made the other day, the one of the fedora lying lost and lonely in the tunnel between the hotel and the old drugstore, the place where we'd already found one corpse.

Suddenly there wasn't enough coffee in the whole world to make things okay.

🐾 32 🐾

🐾 WHEN I GOT home, I just about melted with relief. The Galaxie was in the driveway and Grandma B.B. was in the dining room with Alistair supervising as she pulled carryout containers out of three separate bags from Raja Rani, my favorite Indian restaurant.

Under the circumstances, I think I can be forgiven if I eyed the fragrant array of containers a tiny bit skeptically.

"So, Grandma B.B.," I said. "How'd it go with Gretchen?"

Grandma sighed and reached for another container. This one released the scent of warm spices and chicken tikka masala. "Well, let's say it was not *quite* all I hoped for."

"How bad is 'not quite'?" I asked.

Grandma opened the last container, displaying a golden rice and lamb biryani. "Well, Gretchen said she had tried to be polite, because we had been friends once and because she was willing to let bygones be bygones. But as things went on, she rather firmly stated that she had absolutely no reason to help any of my family after the way I treated her in college. She further suggested that instead of nagging her about local gossip, I should be talking to you about the reputation you're getting as a busybody and troublemaker."

"Oh."

"I may have made a few indiscreet remarks after that."

"Oh."

"I should have known better," she murmured. "After all this time, I didn't think she'd still . . . Well, Gretchen always could carry a grudge."

I couldn't help noticing both the uncharacteristic puckering of Grandma B.B.'s normally cheerful face and her even more uncharacteristic long stretch of silence. Clearly, her argument with Gretchen had gotten to her. But there was something else as well.

"I think I got too much food."

"Good," I said. "We'll have leftovers."

I helped Grandma set out the plates and silverware. We'd eat first; then we'd tackle the hard subjects. Like how I was going to get myself into the hotel archive.

Later, Britton. I sat down and spooned biryani onto my plate. Alistair took this as his signal to jump back up on the table and hunker down, practically daring me to try to move him. We eyed each other for a minute. Then I spooned a couple of pieces of chicken tikka onto a plate and set it down on the floor. Alistair eyed me sourly. He also jumped down and started eating.

"You get a stomachache and it'll serve us both right," I muttered. My familiar ignored me and kept right on lapping at the spicy, buttery sauce.

I dug into my biryani. It was warm and rich and entirely satisfying. Grandma, who had been to India at least three times, ignored her fork altogether and just scooped up her tikka with the bread.

"So, did you do it?" I asked.

"Did I what, dear?"

"Steal Grandpa Charlie from Gretchen Hilde?"

"No," she said firmly, but then she added, "Not really. We were still girls. Or near as. We were home from college, and, well, maybe I flirted a little more than I should have back then, and Charlie—your grandfather—he was such a dish. He could dance like a dream. He brought flowers. He . . . Well, he could sweep a girl off her feet with a wink and a smile."

It's not easy to think of your grandfather as a Casanova. I mean, I'd seen the photos of them as a young couple, and I was mature enough to admit the man had been, to use Grandma's words, a dish. But still, he was my grandfather. I'd ridden on his shoulders when I was little, and he'd come to my doll tea parties. It was hard to make the switch.

"Is that what he did to you?" I asked. "Swept you off your feet?

"Exactly the opposite, I'm afraid. I thought he was too smooth for his own good, and he didn't have much time for anyone who wasn't bowled over by all that charm."

"What changed?"

Grandma blushed. It was a really amazing shade of pink, too. "Perhaps I'll tell you one day, but for now, suffice it to say, we had a lot of arguments and then your grandfather did something rather unkind."

"To you?"

"And Gretchen. He started dating Gretchen to . . . well, to show me that he could."

"Oh."

"It was while he was dating her that the feud between the old families reached its height, and I was a bit of a wreck, I will admit. Charlie saw how badly I needed to get away, and he proposed."

"So, one second Gretchen's dating this fantastic guy, and the next . . ."

"He's more or less eloped with somebody else. So, if she has hard feelings, they're not *entirely* unjustified."

I pushed a few grains of rice around with my fork and studied the effect. I added a lamb cube and some peas.

"You came back to a lot," I said.

"The consequences of an eventful life, I suppose." Grandma tore off another piece of bread and swirled it through the tikka sauce.

"Could have been worse. You could have been bored."

She smiled. "With you as a granddaughter? Impossible."

I smiled back, but only for a minute. "I shouldn't have asked you to do this, Grandma. You just got to town, and after all this time and . . . well, things. I should have let you sort your own stuff out first."

"No, I wanted to do it. I . . ." She set her bread down on the edge of the plate. "What I did not expect was how coming home would wake up all the old instincts. How very much I'd want to help, especially when I saw you . . . involved with the true craft."

"And in trouble with the police?"

"Yes, that as well. And now, here I had a chance to do something for you, and Jake and Miranda, and I can't, because of those silly mistakes I made so long ago."

"You are helping, Grandma. But . . . maybe you should just take it easy for a couple of days? This is supposed to be a vacation. Have you called Bob and Ginger yet?"

"Annabelle Amelia." Grandma eyed me over the rims of her glasses. "Are you telling me to stick to my knitting?"

"Would I ever do that?"

"Meow," said Alistair as he started to wash his whiskers. "Mer-om."

"Yes, and she always does," agreed Grandma.

I was outnumbered. "Look, Grandma, I just think if you're having trouble because of things that happened back in the day, maybe you should take the time to mend a few fences. You could start with you and Julia."

Grandma's mouth puckered up stubbornly at this idea, but before either one of us could say anything more, the muffled ringing of my cell phone rose from the depths of my purse. Grandma waved her slice of naan at me.

"Go ahead, dear."

"Thanks. Sorry." I grabbed the phone. I didn't recognize the number, but it was local. I hit the Accept button. "Hello?"

"Hello? Miss Britton?" said a man's voice. "I hope I'm not interrupting your dinner. Rich Hilde."

"No, that's okay, Mr. Hilde," I said. Grandma's head shot up. So did Alistair's. "What can I do for you?"

"Well, this is a little awkward, but I was sort of calling by way of apology."

"Apology?" I said. "What for?"

"For my mother, actually," he said. "She's very upset about the argument with your grandmother today."

"Dale?" mouthed Grandma.

"Richard," I mouthed back. "Thank you, but it's really okay," I told him. "No harm done." Except I couldn't help wondering if his mother was so upset, why was Rich calling me? Shouldn't Gretchen be calling Grandma B.B. instead?

"Well, maybe. I just wanted to make sure you both know that Mother really is sorry about the argument. Strictly between us, she's just too proud to say it. So I was thinking you and I might be able to do a little something to smooth things over."

*Every time his family does something or wants something, he's always the one coming around smiling and charming and making it all ok*ay . . . Val's words echoed back to me.

The fixer, I thought. *There's one in every family.* Except during the conversation I'd heard through the window. There, it sure sounded like Dale was the one making everything okay.

I wondered if Dale knew Rich was making this phone call.

"What kind of thing were you thinking?" I asked him. I glanced at Grandma, too. She had her gaze pointed at her plate and was tracing patterns in the curry sauce with the last of the bread, but she was listening so hard, I could practically see her ears quiver. Alistair wasn't bothering to hide his interest. He was all but sitting on the toes of my Keds while he blinked up at me.

"We-e-elll," drawled Rich. "Harbor's Rest is in the middle of an expansion and renovation, and as part of that we're looking at tightening the hotel's connection to the community. Some new art by a local artist would be just the thing for us."

I drummed my fingers softly on the table. Alistair seemed to take this as his signal to jump up onto the table and shove his nose under my hand so I'd switch from drumming to head scratching.

"I . . . well, obviously I'd love to talk with you about it. But are you sure? I wouldn't want there to be a problem because of . . ." I let that trail off, mostly to see how he'd finish the sentence.

"No, no, no. There won't be any problem. I've already okayed it with the whole team here."

"Does the whole team include Mrs. Hilde? And Dale?"

Rich chuckled, a smooth, warm sound.

"I can understand the hesitation," said Rich. "Especially after what Dale said to you. But that's all taken care of. Shall we say nine o'clock? I hope that's not too early. You'll be talking with my sister Christine. She's our marketing director, and it's the only time she has free during the next few days."

I pictured Kelly Pierce and Christine Hilde in the dim diner with their papers. Rich could have said this meeting was going to be at 2 a.m. and I would have given him the same answer. "I'll be there."

We said our good-byes and hung up.

"What was that all about?" demanded Grandma B.B.

"That was Rich Hilde." I stared at my phone. "And I think he just offered me a bribe."

"A *bribe*?" exclaimed Grandma. "What on *earth* would Richard Hilde be trying to bribe you for?"

"That's a really good question. Did I tell you Dale threw me out of there today?"

"What? Why?"

I told her about my conversation with Kelly, and with Dale, and then I told her what I'd overheard outside the window. If I glossed over my interlude with Sean on the beach, well, I could always tell her about that later.

"And now, here's Rich, talking about the hotel maybe commissioning some original artwork and . . . What?"

Grandma's face was all scrunched up, like she was trying to hold something back, and it wasn't a pleasant something.

At all. "Well," she said. "That's wonderful, dear. I admit, I was a little worried about how we were going to get you in after I . . . well, fell short."

"You didn't fall short, Grandma."

She smiled. She also changed the subject. "I never can remember, dear, do you like rice pudding? I hope so, because I got enough for two." Alistair looked up at her as pitifully as if he'd been an orphan kitten in the pouring rain. "Well, yes, of course, Alistair, I meant enough for three."

I sighed and wondered out loud if Portsmouth even had a kitty-cat gym, or if we were going to have to start commuting to Boston for that.

❦ 33 ❧

🐾 I REALLY DID not mean to let rice pudding and Grandma's sweet little old lady act distract me. But the truth was, after an eventful day and a heavy dinner, it wasn't long before I was nodding off where I sat. I told myself that Grandma and I could continue our conversation in the morning. By then, I'd have my brain back in working order and we could make plans. We could call Bob and Ginger, maybe, and she could spend a few nights in Boston spoiling her great-grandson. Maybe this meeting with Christine would allow me to put together the final puzzle pieces about what had really happened to Jimmy Upton. Maybe by then we would have things sorted out here. Maybe I'd be able to sit down with her and Julia and finally sort out what was happening between them.

I told myself nothing was going to happen overnight. I kept telling myself this while I tried to stay awake long enough to brush my teeth and climb into my pajamas and into my bed. Despite all my worries for Sean, Jake and Miranda, and Grandma—and, I admit it, for me, too—I proceeded to sleep like the dead.

At least I did until something very cold and wet pressed up against my face.

"Gah!" My eyes snapped open and I shoved myself backward.

"Merow!" Alistair jumped in the opposite direction, landed on my feet, stumbled sideways and caught himself just before he toppled off the edge of the bed.

"Wh . . . a-a-at?" I said, remembering to drop my voice just in time. I didn't want Grandma B.B. running in here. She could sleep through anything, except one of her grandkids sounding distressed. It was still dark, and my beside clock blinked over from 2:30 to 2:31.

"Mow-erp." Alistair jumped off the bed and started pacing in front of the door. "Meow!"

I stared at him, trying to figure out if this was a real emergency or just that I'd forgotten to fill up his dry food bowl. Then I felt that slow, steady prickling running up my arms. My eyes widened.

"Merow," agreed Alistair, and he vanished.

I kicked back the covers, grabbed my robe and tiptoed into the hall. Alistair was at the top of the stairs, his tail lashing back and forth. I followed him downstairs and into the kitchen.

Golden light flickered through the windows. I leaned over the sink and pushed back the curtains.

Somebody was using the fire pit at the center of the garden's spiraling path. I could see the flames flickering up along with a swirl of smoke and sparks. Somebody stood with her back to the window and her arms stretched up to the sky.

Grandma B.B.

"What's she doing?" I whispered.

Alistair shrugged, a long ripple of gray fur.

"Do you think we should go out there?"

Alistair hunkered down on the counter, with all four feet tucked under him in what I think of as the "cat-loaf" position.

"You're right," I said. "Let her have some space. But maybe . . ."

I didn't finish that thought. Alistair was on his feet, ears and whiskers quivering. "Merow!" he announced, and vanished.

"What the heck?"

"Merow!" said Alistair again, and this time the sound came from the direction of my foyer. So did the distinct *ching-ching* of a bike bell.

By the time I got to him, Alistair was pawing impatiently at the door. I undid the dead bolt and pulled it open. Jake Luce stood on the porch, bike helmet in one hand and his finger poised to ring the bell.

"Oh, ah, hey, Anna," he said, lowering his hand. "I guess you were awake after all."

"One of those nights," I said. "Come on in. What's happened?"

"Nothing, really. Nothing new anyway."

"Well, come on in. Can I get you some tea?" I led him into the living room and gestured that he should sit in the wing-backed chair. I sat on the curving window seat. Alistair, of course, came with us. Instead of jumping up onto my lap, he circled a few times around Jake's ankles.

The offer of tea was reflexive and I tried to keep smiling. I didn't really want Jake following me into the kitchen, where he could see Grandma at her meditations, or whatever it was she was doing, through the window. With her being so disappointed about not being able to help before, and now Jake showing up out of the blue, I suspected that there might have been more than a personal calming and cleansing ritual going on out there.

"I'm good, thanks." Jake set his helmet down on the floor beside him. He also scritched Alistair behind the ears. "I just, I needed to get some air after the cell, and I saw the light on, and I wanted to thank you for everything you're trying to do."

"Thanks," I told him. "I was worried after this afternoon, well, maybe I overstepped."

Jake waved this away. "No. It's just been hard on everybody."

"How's Chuck holding up?"

"Not good," he admitted. "He's blaming himself for Blanchard keeping the screws on. I wish . . ." He sighed. "Well, I just wish there was some way to get this cleared up, for the kid's sake if nothing else."

"You should try not to worry, Jake," I said softly. "I'm sure everything's going to work out."

"I wish I was." Jake was hunched over, his long hands dangling between his knobby knees. "I'm trying to put on the brave face for Miranda, but, man, she's not buying it." He took off his glasses and stared at the round lenses. "We've been together almost fifty years now. I have never once been able to put anything over on her. And this time, we both know the trouble's real."

I bit my lip. It was impossible not to hear how Jake was cracking apart inside from doubt and worry. I wanted to hug him, hard. I wanted to promise him I'd use every means, magical and non-, to find out what was really happening, so he and Miranda could get back to normal and not have to worry about anything except making sure their coffee beans were certified organic and fairly traded. Unfortunately I couldn't do any of that, at least not right away. Alistair mewed and jumped up onto the window seat. He shoved his way onto my lap and under my hands so I had no choice but to pet him.

"Listen, Jake," I said slowly. "I want to help; you know I do."

"There's a 'but' coming, isn't there?" said Jake.

I nodded. "But I've got to ask a really awful question. I mean another one, and I need you to be completely straight with me."

Jake rubbed his hands back and forth on his knees. "Okay. Go for it."

"Did . . . is it possible Chuck was using you guys as cover of some kind for his pot operation?"

"*What?* No. Look, Anna, it's been a while, but I've done some living on the road. You learn fast to tell the difference between the dumb kids and the hard cases. Chuck is a kid and he's in over his head. And he never once tried to lean on us, if that's what you're really asking."

"Then is it possible Jimmy tried to lean on him? Maybe Jimmy found out about the attic and demanded a cut, or something like that?"

Jake pulled back. He rubbed his chin and his neck. He took off his bandana and ran his hand across his scalp and put the bandana back on.

"No," he said. "Or at least, if he did, I haven't seen any sign of it, and we've been rapping a whole lot, me and Chuck."

I nodded. I believed in Jake as a judge of character. But I also believed a kid who had been blackmailed by a man who turned up dead would find all kinds of reasons to keep quiet.

"Okay. One more. Did you and Miranda buy the old drugstore to keep the property from being redeveloped? I know you've clashed with some of the business community over riverfront development."

"Riverfront enclosure, you mean," he growled. "Riverfront pollution. Do you know how much oil and diesel and garbage from the boats in that marina ends up in the Piscataqua? Do you know how Gretchen Hilde got together with the rest of her fat-cat . . ."

"Merow!" Alistair glared at him, but Jake was too worked up to notice.

". . . buddies and blocked the city passing a living-wage ordinance?" Jake went on. "Not to mention the law on zero tolerance for river dumping and . . ." He clenched both hands. In my mind's eye I saw Miranda again, smiling up at Rich Hilde and saying there was no bad blood between them. I clamped my mouth shut hard while Jake took a deep breath. I was able to count to five before he let it out, slowly. "I'm sorry, Anna. I'm not being cool."

"You just got out of jail," I reminded him. "You get to be stressed."

Jake shrugged. "This isn't about jail. The cops were actually pretty polite, except maybe for Blanchard." He shook his head. "Seriously, compared to what we got put through after some of the student protests and stuff, it was a walk in the park. I'd just be shrugging it all off if I wasn't so worried about what's coming next." He flexed his hands, as if he was trying to grapple with something only he could see. "But the answer to your question is, yeah, part of the reason we decided on that location was to stop additional . . ." He froze. "You're not saying *that's* what this is about? You think the Hildes are trying to frame us?"

Actually, I was thinking that this was a lot to have going on between the hotel and the people Rich was trying to get to be their new coffee supplier. I believed Miranda when she said she was trying to make peace with the Hildes. But what was Rich trying to do?

I suddenly wondered if Rich was trying to bribe Miranda or distract her. Maybe he thought if he had her concentrating on trying to smooth things over, she wouldn't see what was really happening. Just like he'd done with Val when his family was trying to deny her opening permits for the B and B.

"I don't know anything for sure," I said out loud. "But if the Hildes were trying to frame you, it might explain why Jimmy's body had been left in the tunnel with so much money on it."

"Oh, son of a . . ." groaned Jake. "I mean, I knew they played hardball, but I never imagined anything like this."

"We've got no proof," I reminded him. "And there're other possibilities."

"Like what?"

"Like Jimmy might have found out that Christine Hilde and Kelly Pierce were planning on selling out to Dreame Royale. I mean, his sister is working for them."

"Yeah, but Chuck said those two were totally on the outs."

"Still. Maybe Jimmy went to talk to Shelly and saw her with Kelly and Christine or something, and then Christine had to bribe Jimmy to keep him quiet."

"Because there's no way Mama Hilde would sit still for any of her kids setting up a rival operation." Jake sighed. "Man, what some people choose to do with their lives."

I nodded.

"Oh! Jake! Is everything all right?"

Grandma B.B. stood in the doorway. Her hair was tousled from the wind and the smell of wood smoke swirled around her. She looked a little flushed. She'd been working magic all right. I could feel the prickle in my fingertips, and I saw the way Alistair's whiskers quivered.

"Hey, Annie-Bell." Jake climbed to his feet. "Yeah, everything's fine. At least I hope it will be." Grandma really wanted him to clarify that, but he'd already picked up his bike helmet. "I better be getting back."

"I'll call you as soon as I've got anything more definite," I told him.

"Thanks," he said, and we all said good-bye.

"What happened, Anna?" said Grandma B.B. as soon as I shut the door behind him. "What did Jake want to talk to you about at this hour? You should have come to get me." This last she said to Alistair. My familiar put his nose in the air. He also vanished.

"Jake's just worried about . . . stuff."

"And of course you told him we're doing everything possible to help."

"Of course! But . . ." I stopped. I was having a hard time finishing sentences all of a sudden. "Grandma, you didn't have anything to do with Jake coming here, did you?"

"Why should I?"

"I saw you out back, at the fire circle. You were . . . doing something. Was it a summoning?"

Grandma B.B. drew herself up, and just like that, my sweet, comforting grandmother was gone, and in her place was the stern-faced woman who could face down hurricanes and hooligans and send them both home to their mothers. "Annabelle Amelia, I am getting very tired of your questioning my judgment."

"I'm not, well, okay, I am, but . . ."

"Merow," interrupted Alistair, pacing back and forth. But Grandma didn't let either of us get any further.

"I am not irresponsible and I know the laws of the true craft. I came here to help you understand your heritage, and now every time I turn around you are accusing me of interfering with people!"

"I'm not . . ." Except, of course, I was.

"Maow!" Alistair jumped up on the window seat. We both ignored him.

"I am aware I have made a mistake," Grandma said. "I have apologized, and I have paid for it in more ways than you know. I am *endeavoring* to make amends. If I had known *you* would stop trusting me . . ." Her chin quivered.

"I do trust you, Grandma. I just—"

But she wasn't listening. "Maybe I really should have left you to Julia."

That was when the doorbell rang.

🐾 "WHAT THE . . . ?" I stammered. "What now?"

"Meow!" announced Alistair.

"Yes, I know, you did try to tell us," said Grandma to the cat, although she kept her gaze on me. "For your information, Anna, I expect *that* is Julia."

"Why would it be Julia?"

"Because your grandmother cast such a summoning I'm surprised she didn't wake the whole neighborhood."

That wasn't Julia. That was Valerie. My neighbor waddled in from the kitchen. She was wearing a powder blue sweat suit with a lavender terry-cloth bathrobe tied over her baby bulge. One of us, clearly, had forgotten to lock the back door. "So," she said around an enormous yawn. "What's going on?"

"Annabelle? Are you all right?" Now, that was Julia, and the dachshunds scampered in from the foyer, yipping and nosing and wagging everywhere. Alistair began washing his paws at them.

"You know, some people use the phone," I muttered to Grandma.

"Yes, but magic doesn't go to voice mail," she replied. "And it was time for me to talk with Julia. *That's* what I was doing in the backyard." For the first time she did look a little sheepish. "I didn't think it would wake everyone up, though. It's been so long . . . I guess I don't know my own strength anymore."

Julia, leaning heavily on her walking stick and carrying a bright orange tote bag with a publisher's logo on the front, came in from the foyer. One of us had forgotten to lock the front door, too. It was a good thing the place was magically warded.

She stopped in front of Grandma B.B. "In that case, I may take it you and Anna are all right?"

"Yes," Grandma answered. "I'm sorry to have woken you, Julia. But I am glad you came."

Julia blinked and I watched her bite back whatever her initial reply had been. Instead, she turned and set the bag in the one clear space left on my dining room table. "I thought I should bring some breakfast."

"It's four in the morning," I stammered.

"Which means we need our stamina," my mentor replied calmly. "And we can't leave it all to Roger. How is Roger, Valerie?"

"Asleep, thankfully." Valerie eased herself down onto the living room sofa. "But I have to be getting back soon or he's going to wake up and freak out. So, will somebody please tell me what we are all doing here?"

"Well," began Grandma B.B., but right then, my phone rang. I yanked it out of my purse, checked the number, and hit the Accept button.

"Hi, Kenisha."

"What is going *on* over there?"

I pushed my hair back from my forehead. "Um, Grandma B.B. called a meeting. Apparently, she used a little too much oomph."

It's amazing. When you know someone well enough you can hear the aggravation even when they haven't said anything. "Some people use the phone. And wait for daylight."

"That's pretty much what I said."

"Right. Okay. So, I take it the world's not about to end?"

I eyed Julia and Grandma B.B. They were pulling containers of yogurt and homemade granola out of the tote bag. Julia being Julia had brought the healthy snacks, and bowls and spoons to go with them. "I don't think so."

"Good," Kenisha said heavily.

"Um, Kenisha?"

"Yeah?"

I took a deep breath. "You should probably know, I'm going to talk to Christine Hilde tomorrow about . . . stuff. Do you want me to tell you what I find out?"

The pause was long and it was heavy. "No," she said. "But I think maybe you'd better."

"Okay. I will, then."

"Okay," she agreed. "Now I'm going back to bed. I got this feeling I'm going to need my sleep."

Something inside me eased. I had been worried about how we left things the night before. Now, despite some perfectly justified grumbling, I knew that our friendship held.

"Night, Kenisha. We'll talk later."

"Darn straight." She hung up and I hung up and put the phone back next to my purse to find myself facing Julia and a bowl of blueberry yogurt and granola.

"Thank you," I said and took it. I also sat on the window seat. Alistair, of course, immediately jumped up and began nosing the bowl.

"Down, cat," I said, which had as much effect as usual.

"Now." Julia turned to Grandma B.B., who was sitting beside Valerie and stirring her own bowl of yogurt. "I presume you had something you wanted to say to us?"

"Yes." Grandma took a deep breath. I tensed. Both dachshunds took up sentry posts in front of Julia's toes. Even Val put her bowl down on the coffee table like she thought she might need her hands free.

Grandma B.B. licked her lips. She set her bowl down and clasped her hands on her lap.

"I'm sorry," she said.

We all looked at one another. The dachshunds whined in surprise. Only Alistair seemed unfazed.

"I'm sorry, Julia, that I left you here all those years ago. I'm sorry I didn't try harder to find a way to come back. I'm sorry, Anna, that I didn't obey my better instincts and face the fact that my beautifully talented granddaughter had inherited our family magic."

My throat tightened. Julia let out a very long breath.

Grandma lifted her chin. "I imagine you have a lot of things you want to say about my behavior, so we'd better get on with it."

Julia shook her head slowly. "No," she said softly. "I cannot think of anything I need to say. Well, except perhaps one thing."

"Which is?"

Julia lifted her gaze and met Grandma's. "Welcome home, Annabelle."

I'm not sure who moved first. All I know was that in the next minute, both women were on their feet and my grandmother and her oldest friend were in the middle of my living room hugging each other like there was no tomorrow, with Julia's dachshunds barking their approval and wagging everything they had.

I found myself looking out the bow window at the dark street.

"Merow?" Alistair nudged my hand.

"Something in my eye." I sniffed. "And allergies."

"Merow," said Alistair.

"Yip," agreed Max. Leo just sniffed around my ankles in case I'd dropped anything interesting.

"See?" Valerie rubbed her belly. "I told you everything would work out, baby girl. Sometimes it just takes them a while. So," she went on as she lifted her eyes to the rest of us. "As long as we're here, why don't you catch us up with what's been happening since last night." She pointed her spoon at me. "And don't you dare even think about saying 'nothing.'"

So we ate, and Julia and Val listened while I told them

about my conversations with Kelly Pierce and Dale Hilde. I told them about the discovery that Harbor's Rest had it's own private archive, and the phone call I'd gotten from Rich, and about Miranda and her meeting. I may have left out my time with Sean on the beach, but it was already so late it was early, and that whole episode was a little beside the point.

"What about you, Annabelle?" said Julia to Grandma B.B. "This summoning didn't come about simply because you wanted to apologize."

"No, I'm afraid not. I went to talk with Gretchen and it did not go well. In fact, it got rather . . . heated."

"How surprising," remarked Julia dryly. "I imagine she's still angry about what happened with Charlie."

"Yes," admitted Grandma. "I hadn't realized how much that had hurt her."

"You and Charlie are not the ones who really hurt her," said Julia. "At least, it was not just you. Gretchen has been left by many other people since then, and it's wounded her badly."

"Oh, dear," murmured Grandma. "I mean, I knew about her husband."

"Who walked out with his administrative assistant," said Julia. "It was all horribly clichéd. In fact, it was one of the few times I wished I really could turn someone into a toad. But after that, Gretchen met another man and fell in love and it looked like they might get married. In the end, however, he couldn't cope with the responsibilities of a family and a business and an independent woman. So he walked out as well, at about the same time as her mother died. All this left Gretchen with the hotel and her fractious children and a badly broken heart."

"So that's why Gretchen's clinging so tightly to the hotel," murmured Val. "It's all she has left."

Julia nodded. "And why she's done her very best to make sure her children stay attached to it, and to her as well."

"Why didn't you tell us this before?" said Grandma.

"I might have, if you weren't so busy charging off without talking to me."

Val made a slashing gesture with her spoon. "Oh, no. We just got you two reconciled. You are *not* starting up again."

Grandma looked at Julia, and Julia looked at Grandma.

Grandma nodded first. "No, dear. Of course not. It's just that Gretchen is not the only one who finds it a little hard to let go of old grudges." She paused. "I'm talking about me, of course."

"Yes," said Julia. "But it applies to others as well." She sighed and rubbed her forehead. "Now, the question becomes, how do we help Gretchen come to terms with her past so she can find her way through her present?"

"I have an idea about that," said Grandma B.B., and I admit I tensed again. "Tomorrow, Anna's going to be sleuthing at the hotel . . ."

"Grandma . . ." I groaned. "That's not what I'm doing, and it's not a verb anyway."

"It is, you know, I looked it up."

Of course she did. I rolled my eyes. Grandma ignored me. "Julia, I think that now might be a good time for you and me to do a little intervention."

❧ 35 ❧

❀ "GOOD MORNING, ANNA." Rich strode up to me as I walked into the lobby. He paused briefly to smile at a harassed-looking young mom with a toddler braced on her hip. He enveloped one of my hands in both of his as he shook it, and the rough edges of his bandages grated against my knuckles.

"Hi, Rich. Thanks for arranging things." I tried to give him a cheerful smile, but I did not feel cheerful. I felt exhausted. After Julia and Val had left, I'd stumbled back upstairs and fell into bed. I am by nature a morning person, but this time it took the alarm three tries to drag me out of bed, and the last time worked only because Alistair came and put his cold nose on the back of my neck. The gallon of coffee and the fresh bowl of granola had barely taken the edge off my post-late-night blur.

"I'm so glad you could see your way to making time for us," Rich was saying. "Christine's in her office." He nodded toward the open doorway off the side of the registration desk. "Can I show you the way?"

"I think I can find it," I said as I extricated my hand. "I

don't want to take you away." He wore the red blazer over his white button-down shirt and was clearly on duty this morning.

"Oh, it's no problem. Now, have you talked to Jake and Miranda?" he asked softly, but anxiously. "Are they doing okay?"

"As of yesterday," I said, which was about as much answer as I was going to give him.

"That's great." Rich beamed. "I hear they had quite the celebration at the coffee shop. I wanted to come, but all things considered, I figured I better not. Don't want to rock that boat."

"Have you and Miranda been friends long?" I asked.

He smiled, but it was a little strained around the edges. "You sound surprised that we could be friends at all."

"A little." *After all, Jake was accused of killing one of your employees.* I did not say this out loud. What I did say was, "I've heard there's some . . . tension between you and the Luces."

"Between the Luces and the hotel, not me," said Rich. "I had my first cup of coffee at Northeast Java. Spoiled me for Starbucks forever. Jake and Miranda are a vanishing breed. They really believe in making the world a better place. I can't . . . I can't picture Jake doing anything cruel to another person." His voice dropped to a whisper and he looked down at his bandaged hands. "And, well, I hate to admit it, but we're not always quite as . . ."

"Zen?" I suggested.

"Zen, as we should be," Rich agreed. "But I really do want to help."

I believed him. The question was, did he really want to help Jake and Miranda, or was he just trying to help the Harbor's Rest?

"Well." I hitched my purse strap up on my shoulder. "There is something you could do that would help out, in a small way."

Rich beamed. "What's that?"

"It's not really anything to do with Jake and Miranda's

problems, but . . . you know I'm working on these murals for the new coffee shop? Well, I understand Harbor's Rest has its own archives."

That startled him. "An archive?" He frowned. "No . . . not that I know of anyway."

"Oh," I said. "My mistake, then. I've been doing a lot of research lately, and I thought for sure I found a photo that was supposed to be from the Harbor's Rest archive."

He smiled ruefully as he shook his head. "I know our great-grandfather collected clippings and so on, and there's the things hanging in the bar." He gestured behind him. "But that's all really more Christine's department than mine."

"Well, then I'll ask her." Although, it seemed really strange that one of the kids who grew up here wouldn't know about an archive. "In fact, I should get going. I don't want to be late."

"Yes, of course," he said smoothly. "But come find me afterward, okay? I want to hear how it went." But even as he said this, Rich's attention had shifted to the front desk. The clerk was beckoning to him over the head of a woman in slacks and a cashmere twin set who looked politely peeved.

"You'll have to excuse me." Rich touched my shoulder as he hurried past to the desk, the clerk and the guest. I shifted my grip on my portfolio and walked toward the hallway for the staff offices. I may have had a little trouble with my shoe. Nothing much, just enough for me to have to sit down on one of the padded benches by the wall for a second, where I just happened to be able to hear the lady in cashmere complain about the charges on her room, and Rich quickly and quite voluntarily void an entire night's stay.

I put my shoe back on and headed down the thickly carpeted corridor to the business side of the Harbor's Rest.

Christine Hilde's door was the fourth on the right, and it was open just a crack. I made sure I'd muted my phone, tucked a stray lock of hair back behind my ear, hitched my purse strap up on my shoulder, and raised my hand to knock.

"Merow?"

I jumped back, startled. Miss Boots slipped out of the office and wound around my ankles once. "Meep?"

"Hello, to you, too." I bent down to give her a quick scratch and whispered, "Listen, we need to have a talk about Alistair, okay?"

She looked at me with full-on feline skepticism.

"Come in!" called a woman. "And close that door, would you?"

I did, and I did, and it was like walking into another world.

Compared to the vintage luxury of the hotel's public spaces, this room was positively stripped down. The floor was bare except for one Persian rug. The furniture was all chrome, glass and white leather. The photos and books on the blond wood shelves were widely spaced, and the bay windows at her back were hung with neutral-colored vertical blinds rather than drapes or shades.

Her glass-topped desk was completely empty except for a pen in a crystal stand, and her Apple laptop, where she was typing away at a rapid-fire pace.

"Sit. There's coffee if you want." She waved one hand toward the brushed-steel carafe on the table between the visitors' chairs. With the other she worked her mouse. "I'll be right with you."

"Thanks." I set my portfolio and purse down and poured myself a cup.

Christine Hilde was a match for her office: modern, pristine and efficient looking. She shared her brothers' coloring and if I'd had to guess I would have said she was at least ten years older than me. She'd had help from a very good salon keeping her hair that rich chestnut color. Her makeup was likewise done with a light and professional touch. Unlike Rich and Dale, Christine did not wear the hotel's red blazer. Her gray skirt suit was perfectly tailored and her blue blouse was silk.

Christine made another few mouse clicks and then closed the computer. She also took off her half-moon glasses and stowed them in her desk's central drawer.

Then, somewhat to my surprise, she came out from behind her desk, poured herself a cup of coffee and sank into the other visitor's chair with a long sigh.

"God, what a morning!" She slurped her coffee. "Anna

Britton, right? I hope you are. I couldn't stand another screw-up before lunch."

"I'm Anna," I said, and we shook hands.

"I feel like I should say, 'So we meet at last,' Miss Britton." Christine took another slurp of coffee. "It seems like I've been hearing your name nonstop, or at least your family's name."

"Oh, erm . . . yeah, I suppose you would have. Well." I folded my hands across my portfolio. "Thank you for agreeing to look . . ."

She raised an eyebrow at me. "Do we really want to pretend this is a job interview, Miss Britton?" She gestured toward my portfolio with her mug. "We both know you agreeing to come here has nothing to do with any new artwork, or us partnering with local artists or anything of the kind. This is all about Jimmy Upton."

The words were flat, declarative and just the tiniest bit combative. Christine was throwing down the gauntlet.

I blinked. "I'm trying to work out if you're waiting for me to deny it."

"Are you going to?"

"No." I shook my head. "I'm pretty sure it wouldn't do any good anyway."

"Not a lot, no," she agreed.

"So, if you know Rich's setting us up for a job interview was a smokescreen, why did you agree to see me?" *And why did Rich think he had to try to put one over on you?* He might aspire to being smooth, but if this was a sample of his organizational skills, I could understand why he was just a manager when his siblings were in the executive offices.

Christine settled back a little farther into her chair and crossed her ankles. I got the feeling she had decided I was someone she could do business with. "I wanted to get a read on you for myself," she said. "You've gotten the whole family up in arms. My mother is furious at your grandmother. Dale thinks you're spying for Frank Hawthorne and his paper. Rich thinks you can help smooth things over with Jake and Miranda."

"What about Kelly Pierce?" I asked. "What does she think? And Shelly Kinsdale?"

Christine barely blinked. "How about if I ask you what your friends on the force think about us, especially after about three pots of coffee consumed in the wee hours of the morning."

"Oh. You saw that."

The corner of her mouth curled up. "I don't need bifocals yet, Miss Britton, and you are not that subtle. Besides, I saw Frank the second he walked in the door."

"I didn't realize you knew Frank that well."

Christine laughed. "Of course I know Frank. I'm the marketing director. He publishes the local paper and contributes material to at least three other news Web sites. And since you're his tenant and since all of a sudden I couldn't turn around without hearing your name, I asked him about you. Surprised?"

"No, not really, I guess." What I was, though, was miffed—suddenly, distinctly and sharply. Frank could have at least warned me he was talking to Christine Hilde. You could argue that he didn't know I was coming here this morning and that he was still annoyed with me about my refusal to go to the police with what I knew about Chuck. But at the moment all that felt distinctly beside the point. "Um, what did he say?"

"That you're a fine professional artist and an up-and-coming amateur busybody." She saw the expression on my face and smiled. "All right, he did not say 'busybody.' He did say that he thinks you've gotten in over your head trying to help Jake and Miranda."

That made at least two of us. "What do you think?"

Christine looked at me for a long time. I tried not to squirm or break the silence. I very much wanted to hear what she had to say. The truth was, her no-nonsense approach was refreshing. At the same time, the office was setting me on edge. I had my shields up so I wasn't getting a Vibe, exactly, but the place was jarring. It was like she'd gone out of her way to make sure everyone knew she wasn't like the rest of her family.

"I think you're sinking in this mess, just like the rest of

us." Christine's sigh was short and sharp. "Rich brought you in here because . . . well, Rich likes to be seen as the good guy. It's what he does, and it makes him a great floor manager, but it means the rest of us are the ones who have to take care of the tough stuff."

"You and Dale mostly?"

"Mostly," Christine agreed. I found myself wondering if she realized the "job" was probably a bribe. If she didn't, she was seriously underestimating her brother. It also meant her brother was trying to put one over on her.

"What about your mom?" I asked. If someone was finally willing to talk with me, I wasn't going to waste the chance.

Christine's smile was tight. "That's a toss-up. She still has a lot of her own ideas, and a controlling interest in the hotel. Rich may be her golden boy, and Dale is the wind beneath her wings, but this hotel is her life."

It's all she has left. The words from last night echoed in the back of my mind.

"And what are you?" I asked softly.

Christine's smile was rueful. "I'll have to get back to you when I actually know." She swirled her coffee. "Have you ever been part of a family business, Miss Britton?"

"No. My dad was a civil engineer. Mom was an art teacher. The rest of us, it's kind of been catch-as-catch-can."

"There is, a, I guess, a kind of legacy, though."

"Land or money?"

"History."

Christine grimaced. "Don't tell me; let me guess. This history has ruptured the family, and now you've got to decide which side you're on, and that means what you're really doing is trying to figure out if you can just walk away from the whole huge mess." She stared out the windows, toward the sloping grass lawn and the marina with its white boats on the clear water. "But let me tell you, it gets worse when the family is all tied up with land and money. I mean real money," she added, in case I thought she was talking about the kind Grandma used to keep in the old sugar canister for emergencies. "All of us grew up right here on the grounds, in the same suite the Hildes have occupied since our family built the place. We've all got kids in college, and we're all staring down the road at futures that are pinned to this land and this building."

Because Gretchen had done her best to make sure none of them would ever leave her. I looked down at my coffee cup and tried to keep my thoughts from showing. It would be so hard to be part of a family like this, with their mother unable to heal from her losses and all the kids trying to make up for things they might not even know about, and all of them fighting with one another because nobody could make it, or her, any better. I might not always get along with my siblings, and there were some screaming matches with my parents I'd really rather not have to remember, but when it came down to it, we all knew we had each other's backs. Even Hope, the family wild child.

Christine set her coffee mug down again. Then she adjusted it so that its handle was pointing at exactly the same angle as the handle for the carafe. "Miss Britton, the real reason I agreed to talk to you is that you are connected one way or another to most of the people around Jimmy Upton's death." She paused and locked her eyes on mine. "Do you know who killed him?"

I opened my mouth. I closed it again. "No," I said.

"But you must have an idea? A suspicion?" Christine uncrossed her ankles and leaned forward. "Someone must have said something."

"Why should I tell you?" I shot back.

"Because you know my family has a certain amount of influence with the town's decision makers. I could help make your friends' lives easier, because I think the police are after the wrong people. And because I'm trying to save my family, Miss Britton. But mostly because I think my mother might be responsible for Jimmy's death."

🐾 THERE ARE A limited number of reactions available when somebody tells you point-blank their mother might be involved in a murder. There's:

1) Shocked disbelief, with assorted exclamations

2) Stunned sympathy

3) Shocked disbelief with a long silence

However, given that this was me, and my life, I used a fourth option.

"Why?" I asked.

"I beg your pardon?"

"Jimmy Upton was held down in a sink until he drowned. Why do you think your mother could do that?"

"I don't. But I think she could have gotten it done."

"But why?"

"Because before Jimmy vanished, she was furious. Rich said she had a screaming fight with him. No, I don't know about what," she added before I had a chance to ask. "But when he didn't come back, she was . . . entirely calm. My mother is never calm about a personal betrayal, unless she's found a way to make the person pay for it."

She's had to fight tooth and nail for everything she has, Grandma B.B.'s words came back to me. "I'm guessing she'd see you working out a separate deal with Shelly Kinsdale and Dreame Royale as a betrayal as well."

"And we're back to that."

"You can't be surprised."

"No. Of course not. It was all going to come out soon anyway." There was a world of regret under those words. "All I ask is that you try to believe me when I say I am not doing this to break my family. I'm doing it to try to save them."

"Save them, how?" I felt my eyebrows inch up. All the Hildes kept claiming they were trying to save the hotel and the family. "By setting up some direct competition? Or are you just going to make sure that there's a deal in place for Dreame Royale to pick up the property when things finally sink?"

The words came out much harsher than I meant them to, but my jitters were getting worse, fueled by this glittering office and the feeling that I was finally getting close to the answer. The problem was, the answer might be that Christine was right. The person responsible for Jimmy Upton's murder might just be my grandmother's former classmate.

"You have to understand, Miss Britton, all I've got in this world is my family, and all my family's got is this great big godforsaken building." Christine spread her hands. "It is going to close. You have no idea what the maintenance costs are or how empty we've been the past several seasons. I'm tired to death of the fights to try to stave off the inevitable. I'm sick of playing both ends against the middle to try to get the rest of them to do anything *practical.*" The word was steeped in bitterness. "But if I can get the new property up and running in time, maybe there'll be a safety net for the family when this place finally has to close."

"And being able to show them all you were right isn't so bad either."

Christine didn't even flinch. "Maybe I could have saved Harbor's Rest, if I was given a chance. But my brothers won't let me try, and my mother"—she stabbed a finger toward the door—"stopped listening to me years ago. I'm not like Jimmy or Rich, Miss Britton. I'm not charming. I can't smile and hold her hand and flatter her about all the sacrifices she made for the rest of us. Mother can try to arm wrestle an expansion out of the zoning board, Dale can go into denial, and Rich can run all the interference and charm offensive with the opposition he wants. It's not going to do any good. I've seen the numbers. It. Is. Too. Late."

"Dale's the financial manager; is that what he thinks?"

Christine shook her head. "Dale can't separate the family from the building. To him, if we lose one, we lose the other."

Just like his mother, then. I pictured Dale in his great-grandfather's office. I heard the pride in his voice as he talked about inheriting that particular space.

"Then Dale doesn't know about you and Dreame Royale either?" I asked.

She smiled bitterly. "Not yet. If he did, I'd be the one in the tunnel. Or the police station."

Those sad, soft, angry words sank deep into me. I suddenly felt very sorry for Christine, sitting alone in here, sealed off from the building she grew up in, talking to me instead of to her family.

I think something of what I thought must have showed in my face, because Christine's granite facade began to crumble. Her face fell into its natural lines, and they were deep, worried grooves around her eyes and her brow. She looked tired. She looked old. "Do you know what it's like to think someone in your family is capable of such a thing?"

"It must be terrible."

"I can't sleep," she whispered, and a tremor crept into her voice. "I can't focus. I keep thinking, is there something I should have seen, or done? And then there are my children. She's their grandmother. I think about them coming home for Christmas and being with her while this thing is hanging over our heads and I . . . I swear it's like I'm going to pass out."

I could believe that. Just talking about it, Christine had gone very pale under her suntan.

"I want to find out who killed Jimmy Upton, whether or not the evidence will hold up in court. As long as I know"—she tapped her chest with one neatly manicured finger—"then I don't have to go on suspecting my mother. And if"—she took a deep breath—"if I've got to get ready for the worst, then I want some warning. I just want to be able to talk to her. Try to reason with her." Christine bit her lip.

"You know I'm a friend of Jake and Miranda's?" I reminded her. "Aren't you afraid I might lie to protect them?"

To my surprise, she gave me a small, tight smile. "I'm in marketing, Miss Britton. You get very good at reading other people in this business. What I've seen so far tells me you're just not that good a liar."

Well, she had me there.

"So how does Kelly Pierce fit into all this?"

If Christine was surprised, she didn't show it. "Kelly's got years of experience at hotel management, plus about a thousand connections for suppliers and staffing. She's the backbone of the entire plan and she's going to be a full partner." Christine leaned forward. "Well, Miss Britton? Will you help me?"

I swallowed. "I've got a question first."

She waved, indicating I should go ahead.

"Do you know anything about the tunnel?"

Christine rolled her eyes. "Good lord. That tunnel again. All right. No. I don't know anything about it. Have I heard it existed? Yes. When I was a little girl. Did I look for it? Yes. Again, when I was a little girl. I never found it."

And that made it unanimous. Not a single Hilde would admit to knowing about an entrance to the tunnel. They'd all grown up right here. They'd been rambunctious, curious kids, running around on these lawns, exploring these hallways, playing hide-and-seek in the basements and storerooms, and none of them had found something as cool as a secret door.

Maybe everybody else was right. Maybe it really had

been bricked, or cemented, over during one of the renovations.

I did not like that idea. Because if it was true, then the only way for Jimmy Upton's body to have gotten into the tunnel was through the old drugstore, right under Jake's and Miranda's noses. Which brought us back to Chuck and to the Luces.

"Did you ever look in the hotel archive for hints?" I tried.

Christine gave me a blank look. "Archive? What archive?" She paused. "You don't mean the file closet?"

"I don't know," I admitted. "I found a photo in a book with a caption that said it came from the Harbor's Rest private archives."

Christine laughed. "Wow. Someone was being kind. We've got a collection of old records and clippings, photos, all that, that goes back for, well, forever, but we've never had the resources to catalogue them properly."

"So you haven't looked at them? Or told the police the records exist?"

"The police didn't ask. They were all about the security camera footage and the information from the time clocks. And, no, I haven't looked myself, because frankly, between dealing with the police and the press and Shelly Kinsdale, I haven't had time or reason. You're welcome to go digging yourself if you want." She paused. If there was a clearer indication that Christine really wanted to find out what had happened to Jimmy Upton, I don't know what it would be. But she wasn't done. "This will be on the condition you promise to tell me what you find before you go to the police or Frank."

"If I can," I said.

Her perfectly made-up face twisted tight, and for a moment I saw the very strong resemblance between her and her mother. "I'll have to settle for that, then." She opened the center drawer of the desk and pulled out a set of keys. "I'll take you down there, but I really don't think you're going to find anything."

"Why not?"

"You'll understand when you see it. Come on."

I grabbed my purse and portfolio and followed her out into the hall. Instead of turning toward the lobby, she took us in the other direction. I assumed we were headed for a flight of service stairs, but before we got there, the fire door flew open in front of us and Rich Hilde, flushed and out of breath, shot out.

"Christine!" He pulled himself up short.

"Rich," replied his sister. "What's the matter this time?"

He didn't seem to notice the strained patience in her voice. "Have you seen Mother this morning?"

"Not yet, why?"

"I can't find her, and Dale . . ." His eyes skittered back to me. "Oh. Sorry. I didn't realize you were still—"

Christine cut him off with a curt gesture. "Never mind that. What's Dale done?"

"He's fired Kelly Pierce."

❧ 37 ❧

🐾 "YOU DID NOT just say that." Christine grabbed her brother's shoulders, and I swear, she actually shook him. "Dale did not just fire Kelly!"

But Rich was looking over my shoulder, and whatever he saw made his eyes pop open. Of course I looked, too, and so did Christine. We both saw Dale striding down the corridor, slicking back his hair with one hand.

"Yes, as a matter of fact, I did fire her," he said as he stopped in front of us. "And I'd fire you both if I could. But as it is, we'll have to wait until Mother gets back to tell her the whole sorry story." He glowered at me. "And you, Miss Britton, can leave, right now."

"Dale, Chrissy." Rich held up both hands. "We don't have to do this."

"No, we really do," said Dale coldly. "*Chrissy* hasn't left us any choice."

"*Not* here," announced Christine. "My office, both of you. *Now*."

That was the last I heard before I stepped through the doorway and into the lobby.

I slid sideways until I was out of the line of sight for the hallway. The lobby was empty, except for Miss Boots lounging on one of the benches. I couldn't see either of the McNallys behind the bar.

What should I do now? Head for home? Dale would never let me back in. Try to find Kelly Pierce? Who did I know who would know where she lived? I dug my hand into my purse, reflexively reaching for my wand to try to help focus my thoughts. But my wand wasn't there. I was alone.

On her bench, Miss Boots rolled over onto her back and gave me a long, unblinking look.

"Right," I whispered. Of course I wasn't alone. I was on my own for the moment, but there was a difference.

I knew what I had to do, and thanks to my previous visit, I knew how to do it.

THE STAFF LOCKER room, with its time clock, was right at the bottom of the service stairs. When I got down there, the place was deserted. All the staff was already at work, and it was hours until shift change. I walked in and looked around quickly. It took only a minute to see what I was looking for. There was a new, computerized time card on the far wall, and hanging on a hook next to it was a clipboard.

Bingo.

I slipped my portfolio into the narrow space between the bank of lockers and the wall and helped myself to the board. I fished a pen out of my purse.

I might not have worked in a hotel, but I'd done my share of service-industry jobs, and there was one thing I'd learned. No one ever asks questions of the person with the clipboard. That person is always making notes about something, and you probably do not want it to be you.

With pen in hand and my best determined look on my face, I strode out into the streaming, bustling basement of the Harbor's Rest.

Val had it one hundred percent right. The place was huge. I'd gotten only a hint of that when I'd been down here before.

It was also full to the brim with staff. The kitchen was a madhouse of shouts and activity and smells and steam. It was nearly as hot as the laundry with its racks of clothes and the monster machines you could have washed my entire wardrobe in and had room left over for all the bedsheets and towels I'd ever owned.

I didn't find any sign of the tunnel door. I didn't really expect to. I might not trust Blanchard to know his posterior from his highly muscled elbow, but Pete definitely did. If he hadn't been able to find it, I wasn't going to—at least, not this easily.

But I also didn't find that extra-special Vibe that indicates that a murder had happened here. Not that I was actively breaking my magical apprenticeship oath. I kept my mental shields in place the entire time. Pinkie-promise. But I knew from painful experience that the feeling left behind from someone being killed is especially strong, because not only is there the echo of the dying person; there's the rage and remorse and fear of the person who committed the act.

I did not have a lot of faith in my own ability to block all that out, at least not entirely. I should have felt something, somewhere. But I didn't, and that really did worry me. Because if Jimmy Upton wasn't killed down here, where there were more different sinks and washtubs than you could shake a stick at, and he wasn't killed in the old drugstore, where had he been killed?

I kept walking and I kept making fake notes and I kept looking. Nobody stopped me. Nobody asked if they could help me. I was somebody else's problem and they all had work to do. Time stretched out. I wondered where the Hildes were and if any of them was about to come down here. I wondered what they were saying to one another upstairs. Probably it was loud. I remembered the sketch of Christine shouting at both her brothers. Maybe that hadn't been the past I was drawing. Maybe that scene was happening right overhead.

I found the room full of wires and circuit breakers that must have been the power plant. I found the furnaces. I found storerooms for dirty laundry (you do not want to know about the smell), another for Dumpsters (ditto), and another full of workbenches where two guys in jeans and leather aprons were busy repairing chairs and lamps. I found the break room with the vending machines and the room for the carpet-cleaning equipment and the clean linens.

And, finally, just as I was beginning to lose hope and nerve, and, worse, realizing I'd made a full circuit and was heading back toward the locker room, I found a scuffed white door with some badly chipped black lettering:

FI ES

"Fos and fums." I breathed. I also tried the knob. Of course it was locked.

I gripped my pen. A woman with deep brown skin wearing a gray housekeeper's dress was pushing a laundry cart down the hall toward the elevators. "Excuse me," I said. "Can you open this for me?"

She gave me the once-over with her tired eyes. She saw my professional outfit and my clipboard. "Sure thing," she said in a lilting Jamaican accent.

I smiled and she pulled the key ring on its stretchy cord off her belt and unlocked the door. "There you go."

"Thank you." I made a note on my clipboard and walked inside without looking back.

The smell of dust and damp paper engulfed me. I found the switch on the wall and flipped it. The fluorescent lights buzzed as they came on and I saw Christine had not been exaggerating.

The room really was little more than a closet. It was also stuffed to the brim. There were eight full-sized filing cabinets. All of them had cardboard boxes piled on top. Above those was a battered shelf filled with yet more boxes. Not one of them was labeled that I could see.

I turned in place. The portion of me that got an A in art history cried out at the horrible state of all these precious documents. The part of me that wanted to find out who killed Jimmy just growled in the extremes of frustration. How was I supposed to go through more than a hundred years' worth of accumulated paper by myself?

Fortunately, I knew just whom to call for help.

I shut the door and twisted the knob lock. I faced the room again. I took a deep breath and tried to focus my mind. Julia was probably not going to be happy when she found out about this, but at this point I was willing to take a chance.

"Alistair," I said to the empty, dusty air. "Here, kitty, kitty."

Nothing happened.

"Come on, Alistair," I said. "Please?"

Still nothing. I sighed. We really were going to do this, weren't we?

"I'll buy more tuna," I said. "I promise."

"Merow."

I blinked. Alistair, who was now sitting on the edge of the high shelf, blinked back.

"Yes, well, thank you," I told him. But then I hesitated. I'd successfully summoned my familiar (go, Team Anna!), but now what? I wasn't even sure what I was looking for. Blueprints? Photos? News clippings? The clues I needed could be in any of those, or all of them.

"Mer-oow," grumbled Alistair. He jumped off the shelf onto one of the stacks of boxes, and from there all the long way down to the floor.

Behind him, the top box slipped and teetered. Without thinking, I dropped pen and clipboard and lunged forward. Of course I missed. Of course the box hit the floor and burst, sending a cascade of papers sliding across the floor.

I stood there, hand pressed across my mouth, waiting for the sound of shouts and running feet. But no one called out or rattled the knob, and slowly I was able to start breathing again.

"Meow?" Alistair picked his way delicately across the grimy floor. There was a distinct *what is your problem, human?* tone to his complaint.

"I wonder where Julia adopted Max and Leo from," I

muttered as I crouched down to start scooping papers up. "They don't seem to have to make a mess to find something."

Alistair glowered at me and vanished.

I sighed. "Yes, right, fine. Sorry."

I really was. But I was also scared. I needed to be out of here. I needed to know what was happening with Kelly and with Gretchen. And Jake and Miranda. I needed not to get caught by the wrong Hilde leafing as quickly as I could through the spilled papers and brittle newspaper clippings.

"Come on, come on, come on," I whispered to myself. "There's something. There must be."

But there wasn't. I had handfuls of receipts, and newspaper clippings dating from the sixties and seventies. I clenched my teeth around a whole set of curses and set the papers as carefully as I could in the remains of the box. I straightened up, looking around for someplace I could safely stash the whole mess. And I froze.

Because there, on top of the filing cabinet, where it had been hidden by the box, was a long, black cardboard tube. I set the box down on the floor, since there was nowhere else to put it, and with my heart in my mouth, I reached the tube down. It was battered and dented and the white cap on the end was held in place with ancient elastic. Somebody had written a date on the cap: *1920.*

I eased the elastic back and pulled the cap off. Inside was a roll of blue-and-white paper.

"Well, well. Hello, you beautiful little Prohibition-era blueprints," I murmured. "And just where have you been all my life?"

❧ 38 ❧

❧ "MARTINE, I NEED to borrow your bartender."

Since I had not actually been planning on stealing a large roll of documents from the hotel, I hadn't driven to the appointment this morning. Now I was jogging toward the bus stop, trying to juggle my portfolio and the tube of blueprints, while keeping the phone jammed between my shoulder and my ear.

In heels. Yes. Bad plan. I know. At least I hadn't had to try to smuggle myself and my illicit acquisition out across the lobby. On the list of things I'd found in the hotel basement was the service bay and it's lovely door open to the driveway outside.

"And just what is it you need my bartender for?" demanded Martine. I didn't blame her for being short with me. I was a little surprised she'd picked up at all. I could hear the sounds of her kitchen going full tilt in the background. "And I'm assuming you mean Sean and not Wanda."

"Yes, Sean." I wobbled to a stop at the bus stop and sat down on the bench. "I need him and maybe his dad to help me read some very old blueprints." A blueprint is not like any other kind of drawing. It's a highly technical, information-packed document with all the specifications written in a special combination of jargon and shorthand. The McNallys both did construction and repair work to supplement their bartending, and they'd have more experience with blueprints than I did. If I was really lucky, Old Sean might even have seen some prints of the same vintage I had currently tucked under my arm. There were, after all, a lot of old buildings in Portsmouth.

"And this is so urgent because . . . ?" prompted Martine.

"Because I might be able to find out where the tunnel where Jimmy Upton's body was dumped comes out at the Harbor's Rest, and if I can do that I might be able to prove who really killed him, and if I can do that—"

"You get Jake and Miranda off the hook. Got it."

"Jake and Miranda and Chuck," I said. "You told me to call you about this stuff," I reminded her.

"Yeah, but I didn't tell you to steal my staff during lunch rush." She paused. "There's something you should maybe know."

"What?" *Talk fast.* The bus was turning the corner. I stood up.

"Kelly Pierce was in here earlier, and she was meeting somebody."

I found I was not at all surprised. "Tall woman? Dark hair? Serious cheekbones?

"That's her."

"That's Shelly Kinsdale, Jimmy Upton's sister." The bus crept down the hill. "Was Christine Hilde there, too?"

"Didn't see her."

"I don't suppose you heard what they were talking about?"

"Do I have time to stand around eavesdropping on the job?" she snapped.

"No, Chef."

"Too right. But let me tell you, it's amazing what people will say in front of their servers." I heard the grin in her voice and felt an answering smile spread across my own. The bus was almost here. I grabbed my portfolio and the blueprint tube. "According to Victor, Kelly told this other woman not to worry. She said as far as she was concerned, the deal was still on. She had nothing left to lose now, and she said she was looking forward to giving the old lady a small taste of her own medicine."

"Somehow I'm guessing that's not a direct quote."

"You do not need the direct quote."

"Thank you, Martine. I owe you and your whole staff . . . something."

"Too right," she said again. "I'll let Sean know you need him."

I wanted to tell her she didn't need to put it exactly like that, but the bus pulled up and the door opened, letting off a couple with three kids of varying sizes. I hung up the phone and juggled my stuff so I could shove it back into my purse. At the same time I thought Christine must be breathing a sigh of relief. She'd told me Kelly was essential to her plans.

I wondered if those plans were why Dale had fired Kelly. I wondered if the termination had been his idea or somebody else's. I dug in my wallet for the fare so I could continue my getaway.

I also wondered where Gretchen Hilde was right now.

THAT LAST ONE, it turned out, was easy to answer. I knew something was up even before I walked in my front door or, rather, ran, because somewhere between the bus stop and the cottage, it had started to rain.

Alistair was sitting on the porch as I came running up the walk with my portfolio held over my head and the tube of blueprints clutched to my chest.

"Merow," he tried to tell me.

"Yeah, there's visitors," I said as I shouldered the door open. "Got it, big guy, thanks."

"Merp," he acknowledged, and vanished, probably headed for someplace drier.

The door was unlocked. "Grandma B.B.?" I called as I

pushed it open. The rain outside filled the room with an early autumn twilight and all the lamps were on, making the house feel snug and warm. I shook off my portfolio and the ends of my hair. "I'm home!"

"Hello, dear. We're in the living room."

"We" were Grandma B.B., Julia (with wiener-dog entourage under the wing-backed chair), and Gretchen Hilde.

I froze in place, hotel blueprints clutched in front of me.

"Erm. Hi, Julia. Hello, Mrs. Hilde." I set the blueprint tube down next to the hall table, along with my portfolio. All casual-like. I made myself smile. I made myself walk over and kiss Grandma B.B. on the cheek. "Sorry if I'm interrupting. But . . ."

"But you're just a little surprised?" suggested Grandma, leading the witness like the expert she was. "Particularly since we're sitting in your living room drinking your tea?"

"And as lovely as it's been, I was just leaving." Gretchen set her cup down on my Arts and Crafts–style coffee table. She looked very different from the immaculate and confident woman I'd seen at the Harbor's Rest. Her copper-colored hair was hanging loose around her shoulders, and instead of a pants suit, she wore a loose button-down blouse over a pair of rumpled black slacks. "Thank you for inviting me, Annabelle, Julia. It's always good to . . . talk."

"I'm sure Anna doesn't mean to chase you out, Gretchen," Julia told her.

"Yes, please, stay," I said. I shot for cheerful and missed. I did manage polite, though. "Grandma B.B.'s friends are welcome here and she knows it. It's just that if you're going to keep inviting people over, Gran, I'm going to need to dry some more mint." I tried another smile. I also settled myself on the window seat.

Gretchen looked at us, one after another.

"Just tell me one thing," she said evenly. "Would you even have invited me here if the three of you weren't still trying to clear Jake and Miranda Luce for Jimmy's murder?"

I had absolutely no answer for that. Fortunately, I didn't need one.

"Of course we would," said Grandma B.B.

"We're friends," added Julia.

"We *were* friends," Gretchen corrected her firmly. "At least I thought we were until Annabelle stole my boyfriend and you got us mixed up in that disastrous nightclub scheme . . ."

Julia turned a truly incredible shade of pink.

"Yip?" Leo scrabbled to his feet.

"Yap." Max had evidently heard it all before, and he just tucked his nose under his forepaws.

"You will recall I paid back every penny," said Julia. "With interest."

"And walked out on the deal," snapped Gretchen. "Leaving me with egg on my face."

"I'm sure—" began Grandma.

"Listen, Mrs. Hilde," I interrupted. I'd already had a long day. I could not shake the feeling that things were closing in on us all, one way or another. "I know you're tired of this, and you're worried because nobody's got any real answers about what happened to Jimmy—"

"Yes, they do," Gretchen cut me off sharply. "Lieutenant Blanchard has been very clear—"

But Grandma B.B. shook her head. "You know he's wrong, Gretchen. You have from the beginning."

"I have absolute faith that the lieutenant is on the right track."

"Because if he isn't, people might start looking at your family for who killed Jimmy." I said, even though I couldn't seem to raise my voice above a whisper. "And maybe even you."

"Anna," said Julia. "That's eno—"

"You have no idea what you're talking about," Gretchen snapped. "Any of you."

"Then tell us, Gretchen," said Grandma, quietly but firmly. "Make us understand."

For a moment, I thought Mrs. Hilde was just going to grab her purse and walk out. I could tell at least part of her wanted to, but pride won out. Whatever else had happened, she was still Gretchen Hilde, and she was not going to let anyone see her run away.

Yes, I did pick up on some of this right away. Grandma B.B. explained the rest later.

"It's bad enough that Christine was going to leave the business, and you," I said, and the ideas were falling into place almost as quickly as the words were coming out of my mouth. "The bad publicity around the family being investigated for murder would be too much. Did you use your influence with Blanchard to get him to go after Jake?"

"I have done what I had to do to keep my home and my family together," she answered, each word as hard as stone. "Nothing more and certainly nothing less. What earthly reason could I have had to kill Jimmy?"

"Only one reason," I said. "Because he was walking out on you."

Gretchen froze.

"We found Jimmy's sister," I said. "She works for Dreame Royale. She told us Jimmy came around to sweet-talk her into not opening a new hotel in Portsmouth." The Hildes were ready to fight dirty to keep out even a little bit of competition. This might not even be Gretchen's first bribe. "Did he get the five thousand from you as a bribe for her?"

Grandma B.B. reached for Gretchen's hand.

"Oh, Gretchen, you didn't—"

"I didn't do anything!" She yanked her hand away. "And if I had, I would never have tried to bribe Dreame Royale with a measly five thousand dollars! Really! I'm not that much of an old fool!"

Her anger had turned Gretchen pale, and I was sure she wished she were a thousand miles away, talking about anything but this. I could see it in her sad, tired face, just like I could see her resemblance to her daughter and her sons. What I couldn't see was any furtiveness or guilt.

"Yip," Leo agreed, and his tail went *thup-thup* against the floor.

Which settled it. Gretchen Hilde was telling the truth,

about the money at least. I'd think about how I was starting
to trust the judgment of a mini-dachshund later. Right now
I was too busy wondering about that money and about the
sketch I'd made of it changing hands.

"Jimmy might have scraped it together himself," Gretchen
told us. "He had a great deal to lose if Harbor's Rest went
under."

"And how much was a great deal?" asked Julia.

"Despite what some people seem to think, I am fully
aware that Harbor's Rest is in trouble," replied Gretchen
coolly. "Since I will not sell out, something else has to be
done. Food tourism is becoming increasingly popular. I'd
been thinking for a while that even if the hotel itself is a little
old-fashioned, we could still turn the restaurant into a destination. We could put together packages for exclusive dinners, wine tours, cooking classes, all sorts of things. Perhaps
we could even partner with one of the river-tour companies
and sponsor seacoast tasting tours. We'd fill rooms as well
as tables. But to do that we'd need a brilliant chef in charge.
A real headliner."

"Jimmy," I said.

She nodded. "I knew he had everything it would take
almost as soon as I laid eyes on him. He had skill and he had
presence, and, yes, he had enough charm to light up a room."

Gretchen squeezed her eyes shut. I grabbed a box of
Kleenex off the bookshelf and handed it to her. She stared
at it for a moment before she pulled one out and dabbed at
the corner of one eye.

"I made sure he knew that we were going to put a full
effort behind him. As soon as we had the expansion and the
loans, we'd start on the restaurant. He'd have complete
charge of the project. He'd be able to design it from the
ground up. Our success would be his.

"But in the end, it wasn't enough."

And I would bet I knew why. Shelly. He had gone to see
her, to try to convince her to keep from setting up as a
competitor, and she had laughed at him. Shelly had told us
she planned to ruin him, and I was willing to bet that during

that meeting she'd done her level best to play to his impulses and his temper.

"What some people do with their lives," I murmured.

Gretchen sniffed and began folding the tissue into a tidy rectangle. "When I found him that night, he . . . he was cleaning out his locker. He said he'd made a huge mistake. He said he had better things to do than to try to salvage a white elephant and an old . . ."

"It's all right, Gretchen," said Grandma.

"It wasn't all right!" Gretchen's fist knotted around the tissue. "I poured everything I had into him! I knew he could save us and he . . . he . . ."

He was walking out. She was being abandoned. Again. And she'd been right there when he was getting ready to leave. I swallowed hard. Was it possible Christine had been right about this woman? Could she have found a way to have Jimmy killed?

This time, when Grandma took Gretchen's hand with both of hers, Gretchen did not pull away. "I'm so sorry," Grandma whispered. "It must have been terrible for you."

"Did your children all know about your plans?" asked Julia.

"Of course they did." Gretchen sniffed again, but this time the sound was just irritated. "We had several meetings about it. Richard and Dale thought I was infatuated and that Jimmy was using me to further his career."

"What about Christine?" I asked. "What did she think?"

Gretchen's mouth twitched. "She thought I'd picked the wrong chef, and she said so. At length." She sighed. "I should just be grateful it was Richard who caught me crying. Christine probably would have just laughed at her poor old mother."

"Mrs. Hilde," I said. "Can I ask one more question?"

"I don't suppose I can stop you."

This was probably true. "Did you tell Dale to fire Kelly Pierce?"

She bowed her head. "I did."

"Was it because you found out she was working with Christine?"

She didn't answer.

"Oh, Gretchen." Grandma B.B. sighed.

"Christine's worried about you, Mrs. Hilde," I told her. "She feels like she can only save the family or the hotel, and she chose the family. That's why she's doing what she's doing. She wants there to be somewhere for you all to land if Harbor's Rest fails."

"Then she should have been working to make sure it doesn't fail!" snapped Gretchen.

"So, Christine is stupid," said Julia flatly.

"What?" Gretchen drew herself up. Max and Leo lifted their heads, their ears and tails suddenly on alert. "Are you calling my daughter stupid?"

"No." Julia rested both hands on top of her walking stick. "But you are."

"I most certainly am not! I would never call Christine stupid!"

"Then, since she is not stupid, will you admit she might be right that the hotel could fail?" Gretchen's jaw clenched. Julia inclined her head. "I see."

"She wanted me to sell my home!"

"And those are the only two options?" Julia inquired. "Sell or go down with the ship? It's not possible your daughter, who is a marketing expert, and who, as you point out, is not stupid, *and* who has the future of her own children as well as the rest of the family to look to, could find a third way?"

"She shouldn't have done *anything* without talking to me!"

"And if she had talked to you? What would you have done?"

Gretchen was silent for a long time. "I would have told her what I just told you."

Julia thumped her walking stick. "It's time to let go of that anger, Gretchen. It's not serving you anymore."

"It was Joshua and Millicent who walked out on you, not Christine," Grandma B.B. added.

Gretchen looked up, startled. "Who told you about Millicent?"

Grandma smiled sadly. "Does it matter?"

"No, I suppose not."

"Gretchen," said Julia. "Even you have to admit that so far all that not talking to your children has gotten you is drinking tea with two old prunes and being afraid for your family's future."

"I couldn't have said it better myself," said Grandma B.B. "Except for maybe the part about prunes. I've never felt less prune like in my life."

"No, being an antique suits you."

Gretchen was staring at them both. "You know, you two haven't changed a bit."

"Neither have you, Gretchen," said Julia. "You're still a terrible liar."

Gretchen laughed, a tiny little hiccup of a sound, and she covered her mouth. "Oh, goodness. It feels . . . wrong to laugh. But I'm not sorry. I just . . ." She folded her hands together. "I've made so many mistakes. You have no idea."

"Then begin again," said Julia.

"It's too late."

Julia raised one eyebrow. "Are you still breathing?"

Gretchen glared at her, but the expression slowly melted into a tired smile. "Yes, I see, then it's not too late. Perhaps. I don't know." She adjusted the cuffs of her blouse and the delicate gold watch on her wrist. "What I do know is I need to get back to the hotel. I . . . I think I need to talk to my children."

❧ 39 ❧

🐾 IN THE END, Gretchen agreed to drive back with Julia. "We'll stop at my place first," Julia told her. "You need dinner and a good stiff drink."

Gretchen did not argue with either statement. As soon as we closed the door behind them, however, I turned to Grandma.

"Well?" I said.

"Well what, dear?" asked Grandma B.B.

I rolled my eyes. "Seriously, Grandma? We're still doing this? You were trying to do a reading on Gretchen. Did she have anything to do with Jimmy's death?"

I watched Grandma B.B. get ready to be righteous at me. I just folded my arms and raised my eyebrows.

"Marow," added Alistair, which apparently was a stronger argument than any I could muster.

"I couldn't tell," Grandma admitted. "There was so much guilt and anger, I couldn't sort any of it out. She certainly *feels* responsible, but did she actually do anything? I don't know."

I'm sure I meant to make a coherent answer to this, but

much to my embarrassment, my stomach spoke first, and it growled like Alistair in a bad mood.

"Right. That's enough of that, young lady," announced Grandma. "Clearly it is time for the Blessingsound Britton gourmet specialty."

All at once, everything that had happened and was happening fell away. I was six years old again and sitting at the kitchen table, banging my heels against the chair rail.

"Grandma eggs?" I asked hopefully. "With bacon chunks right in the eggs?"

"Of course." Grandma smiled. "I even think I saw some cheese in that fridge of yours. *Really*, Anna . . ."

Still chattering, she headed for the kitchen, and I followed, perfectly ready to let all discussion of murder, bribery and the rest of it drop, for now.

But, of course, for now was not forever, or even for longer than it took to fry up the bacon bits, stir in the eggs, toast the bread, get down the plates and decide we'd both really had enough peppermint tea for one day and break out the good coffee. We cleared a couple of spots in the middle of all the books and papers and plans piled on the dining room table and set our plates down. I even decided to bow to the inevitable and put a plate of eggs and bacon on the floor for Alistair.

My cat purred and circled around my ankles, letting me know I was an acceptable human.

While we all ate, I told Grandma about everything that had happened in the hotel.

"So." Grandma picked up the coffeepot and poured me a fresh cup. "Assuming everyone is telling the truth—"

"Big assumption," I muttered around a mouthful of eggs and bacon.

"Oh, yes, I know, dear." She poured herself some coffee as well. "But at least this time it's lining up properly, which is a sign."

I agreed. "So, Jimmy goes to see Shelly to try to get her to go away, so she won't mess up Harbor Rest's plans for a comeback . . . Does he have the money with him? Was it a bribe for Shelly or was it a bribe *from* Shelly?" Shelly had flatly denied knowing about the five thousand, but that could have been a lie. Admitting to wanting to ruin her brother was one thing; admitting to bribery might have professional implications.

"But, as Gretchen pointed out, none of the Hildes would offer Shelly such a small bribe." Grandma pushed the corner of her toast through her eggs.

"I've been thinking about that." I pointed my fork at her. Grandma frowned, and I immediately lowered the offending utensil. "What if the bribe wasn't from one of the Hildes to get Shelly to leave? What if it was from one of the Hildes to try to get Jimmy to leave?"

"Now, that is an idea," murmured Grandma. She bit into her toast and chewed thoughtfully. "Christine, then? To keep the plans for a comeback from going forward?"

I set my fork down slowly. "Oh, good grief!"

"What is it, dear?"

"The sketch! Grandma, it showed Jimmy in the middle of two women. I thought the money was passing through him, but what if he was taking bribes from both sides? Gretchen was sure dangling a whole lot in front of Jimmy to get him to stay at Harbor's Rest. Maybe Christine offered him something to go away. Then, he goes to talk to Shelly. Maybe he's going to try to hustle her as well. Why leave an income stream untouched, right? But instead, He hears at least some of what she's up to and decides that Gretchen's plan isn't going to work, so he decides to skip town." I speared my last bit of bacon. "He wasn't carrying that cash because he was planning on bribing somebody. He was carrying it because he had made up his mind to skip town."

"So he goes back to the hotel to clear out his locker," said Grandma. "And he has his argument with Gretchen, and she leaves, very upset. Jimmy finishes getting his stuff together and . . ."

"Gets killed by . . ."

"Person or persons unknown." Grandma speared a bit of egg.

"Or whoever Gretchen told when she left him." Whom had she told? I furrowed my brow at my plate. Someone had said something. I knew it. I could feel it, but I couldn't remember who, or when.

It could have been any of her children. They all lived in. Maybe we could eliminate Christine, but maybe not. She might have been afraid that Jimmy spilled the beans to her mother. Christine was no lightweight. If Jimmy was drunk maybe, or she'd knocked him out first, she might have been able to do it. Kenisha had said Jimmy was bruised like he'd been in a fight. Or it could have been Kelly Pierce, for similar motives and with similar opportunities. She might have been pulling a late shift or had to come back in to address some problem.

Or it could have been Rich, with his bandaged hand. Or it could have been Dale, with his absolute loyalty to the hotel.

I pushed my plate away. It could have been way the heck too many people. How was I going to figure out exactly which one had actually committed the crime?

"You'll do it, dear," Grandma patted my shoulder. "I have every confidence."

"You reading me now, Grandma?" I muttered.

"Only because you have a dreadful poker face, dear. You always have."

I was saved from having to answer this by the doorbell ringing. I got up to answer it while Grandma started clearing the dishes away.

A pair of McNallys stood on my front porch.

"Sorry about the delay," said Old Sean as he slid out of his raincoat and hung his shovel cap on the hook by the door. "I was out on a bit of a job."

"It's okay, thanks for coming. And thanks for bringing him," I added to Young Sean.

"All part of the service," he said as he hung up his hat and coat beside his father's. He also winked. I felt my cheeks heating up. I told them to stop that.

"My boy says you've got some prints that need reading,"

said Old Sean. "I've a shift to do at the hotel, so there's not a lot of time, but I'm glad to take a look." He clapped his hands together. "What have we got?"

"Right." I grabbed up the tube and pulled out the roll of prints. Everyone helped clear space on the dining room table. It took both me and Grandma to carefully unroll the fragile plans and weight them down with extra books.

"All right, let's see what we have here." Old Sean fished his glasses out of his shirt pocket and settled them into place on his nose. "Should I ask where you got these, young woman?"

"Probably not," said his son.

"And it's all probably nothing," I said, as I watched him carefully lift away one page after another. "A smugglers' tunnel is not exactly going to be marked in red on the plans."

"No, you're right about that," agreed Old Sean. "But from what you've said, that door you found was no tiny thing. Somebody meant for it to be there and stay there. Somebody might have made notes."

The outlines of the hotel were obvious. Old Sean peeled back a page that showed vertical cross sections for what must have been a new wing, and a page that detailed the foundations and the basement.

"I've seen the original plans," I told him. "And the ones from the fifties, but these are from the twenties. There weren't any of that vintage on file with the city."

"Ah, well, the city's a bureaucracy and bureaucracies tend to lose things. Especially old plans once the fresh ones go on file." He leaned so close to the prints his nose nearly touched the page. "Now, Anna, my dear, you wouldn't happen to have a copy of those plans so we can do a little compare and contrast?"

"Um . . . yes." I even knew where they were, because Alistair was sitting on one particular stack of paper on the corner of the table. I picked up the cat and passed the pages to Old Sean. "These are from the 1950s, and these are from the eighties."

"Thank you." Mr. McNally leafed through the fresh (and much smaller) pages. Sean put out a hand to stop the shuffling, and his father, Sean, nodded. "And right you are, my boy. That could be the jackpot."

"What? Where?" Grandma B.B. and I, and of course Alistair, all crowded closer.

"Now, this here"—Mr. McNally gestured at the large rectangle on the twenties blueprints—"is the ballroom."

"Says so, right there." Sean pointed at the neat lettering in the middle. "That's some great detecting, Dad."

"Is this detecting or sleuthing?" I murmured.

"Sleuthing's for girls," Sean murmured back.

"We'll be talking about that remark later, McNally."

"Be quiet, you whippersnappers," said Old Sean. "Now, here, you see this?" He pointed to the plans I'd so recently acquired. "That's a staircase there. But it's not here." He touched the page from the 1950s. "Or here." He touched the page from the eighties. "Now, call me old-fashioned, but that seems a wee bit careless, losing a whole stairway out the back of the ballroom like that."

"The ballroom?" I straightened up. "The ballroom! Oh, good grief!"

That would explain why no one could find any opening into the basement. There wasn't one. I lunged for the end of the table. Alistair jumped down to the floor so I could grab *Evolution of a Riverside Town* and flip it open to the big photograph of the Prohibition tea.

I squinted at the picture, trying to see between the elegantly dressed people and their teacups. There was something at the back. Maybe. Possibly. There, right at the split between the pages.

"Grandma. Can you hand me that magnifying glass?"

She did and I grabbed it and held it over the photo. But I wasn't looking at the people. I was looking at the far wall. There, right next to a truly horrible cherub fountain in an alcove, was a narrow black rectangle. I held the glass over the grainy photo.

"Sean?" I handed him the magnifying glass. He rubbed his bearded chin and leaned forward over the book.

"Yeah," he said. "That's a door."

Grandma took the glass from his hand, lifted up her spectacles and peered at the page. "Yes. Well, a big room like that should have more than one . . ."

"There's only one problem," said Old Sean. "I've spent plenty of time in that ballroom. All the doors are up front, or to the east side, out onto the balcony."

"Maybe its not where anybody can see it." I took the glass back and stared at the photo again, like I thought that door might vanish if I let it out of my sight. "Maybe it was specifically built to give people a back way out of the ballroom if there was a police raid on the place during Prohibition."

My phone rang, startling me so badly, I dropped the magnifying glass, which earned a scolding from Alistair, who flowed under the table. The younger Sean reached my phone before I could and tossed it to me. I caught it and checked the number.

"Frank?" I said as I answered. "I'm so glad you called! Listen, did you know that the Harbor's Rest has its own archive? I found—"

"We found," Grandma reminded me.

"Merow," agreed Alistair from under the table.

"We found a set of blueprints from 1920 and we think—"

"Anna, stop," said Frank. "Listen to me. I'm at the hospital. They just brought in Kelly Pierce. Somebody tried to kill her."

❧ 40 ❧

❧ "WHAT HAPPENED?" I demanded as I barreled into the hospital waiting area. "Is she okay?"

I hate hospitals. Nobody likes them, but I really hate them. I don't care how modern and clean and comfortable they've been made, with carpet in the lounges and inoffensive artwork on the walls and fountains and meditation rooms. They're still hospitals and they're still full of the sad and the frightened and the grieving. There aren't strong enough shields anywhere to keep that kind of Vibe out.

Frank got to his feet. Except for him, the lounge was empty, which was probably a good thing, because I was out of breath and out of nerve, even with Grandma B.B. coming up behind me for support, and, well, for being my grandmother. The McNallys had wanted to come, too, of course, but Old Sean was supposed to be at work at the hotel, and given all the very bad possibilities swirling around regarding Jimmy's death, it would not be good for any of them to know anything was wrong. It did, however, take both me and Grandma talking at full speed to convince the McNallys of this.

"They won't tell me; I'm not a relative," Frank said, but then he glanced over his shoulder at the nurses' station. "At least they're not supposed to," he added more softly. "But one of the nurses is a friend. She said Kelly was found unconscious in her apartment. Somebody'd hit her over the head. They got her on the right temple and . . ." Frank looked down at his notebook. He was holding it in both hands like a talisman.

"And they're sure it wasn't an accident?" I asked, even though I knew I was clutching at straws.

"It wasn't," Frank said grimly. "They found a wine bottle next to her, and it had blood on it."

"Oh, no," breathed Grandma. "Oh, how *wicked*!"

"She's in a coma," he said hoarsely. "And they're not sure . . ." He didn't finish, but that was okay. He didn't have to. I gripped Grandma's hand. Somebody had tried to kill Kelly Pierce. Kelly had been the lynchpin of Christine's plan for a new hotel. Until the tension inside the Hilde family had gotten to be too much. Until Dale had fired her and maybe threatened her to try to keep her away from Christine.

Just like his mother told him to. I clapped my hand over my mouth. He'd followed his orders, but it hadn't been enough. But now? Christine had said the project needed Kelly, her experience and her connections. Harbor's Rest would be safe from the competition, for now. But not safe from its own bills and the very real danger of bankruptcy. With all the bad publicity of one murder and one attempted murder, no developer would touch the idea of a Hilde-run resort with a ten-foot pole.

In my mind, I could picture them all lined up—Christine and Kelly on one side, and both brothers and Gretchen on the other.

Which of them did this? Dale, who couldn't separate his love for his family from his love for their hotel, or Rich, who wanted everything nice and everybody happy, and who used his charm to hide and distract anybody and everybody from what was really going on? And who no one in his family trusted to be able to do anything else right. Not even his mother, who adored him. I had been ready to cross Christine off the list. Kelly was the last person she'd kill. Unless . . . unless Kelly had changed her mind. Unless she'd decided to pull out of the deal after all. There could have been an argument. There could have been an accident.

There was one problem. Christine had been willing to let me into the archives to look for the tunnel. Either she was ready to gamble with her future and her freedom, or she really didn't know where the tunnel door was.

But did the person who killed Jimmy have to be the same person who tried to kill Kelly?

I clamped my teeth shut around the scream. I had no answer. It didn't matter. There are times when all the reluctance and all the worry fall away, and you move because standing still has become impossible. Kelly Pierce was hurt, maybe dying. But maybe not. Maybe she'd wake up and be able to identify the person who'd done this. Whoever that was would hear pretty soon, and he or she might just be ready to come back to the hospital to try again.

Then there was Lieutenant Blanchard, who had probably already heard about this. He might even be on his way.

"Grandma B.B.," I said. "I need you to put on your sweetest little old lady act and get into Kelly's room somehow. You sit right there. Don't move; don't let anybody else be alone with her, especially any Hildes."

"Of course, dear," Grandma said promptly. "What are you going to do?

"I'm going to go find that tunnel before anybody else gets hurt." I was distantly amazed at how steady my voice stayed when I said it, too.

"I'll come with you," said Frank. In fact, he already had his keys in his hand.

"No," I told him. "We need you to get on the phone. You have to tell Jake and Miranda what's happening, and you have to get the media down to Northeast Java. We need lights, cameras and action there, just in case Blanchard and company decide to try to rearrest Jake. Somebody should probably call Val, too, so she can start up the coven's phone tree."

"Anna." Frank looked me right in the eye. "You're not going to Harbor's Rest alone."

Under other circumstances I might have said I could take care of myself. But I was sure Kelly and Jimmy had felt the same way. "I won't be alone," I reminded him. "It's not even nine o'clock. There should be at least one Sean McNally behind the bar."

Grandma grabbed both my hands and squeezed hard. I felt the faint prickle as the magic flowed from me to her. I didn't object, because I also saw the love and the determination in her eyes.

"Be careful anyway, dear."

I kissed her cheek. "Count on it."

Then I turned on my heel, and I ran.

I STOPPED BACK at home just long enough to grab *Evolution of a Portside Town* and my wand.

"Yes, I'll tell Julia," I said to Alistair, who sat watching me from the dining room table. "But I'm going to need all the help I can get."

"Merow," he agreed, and vanished.

"Right. Good," I said as I slung my purse over my shoulder. "Meet you there."

TURNS OUT I was right. There was a McNally behind the Harbor's Rest bar. It just happened to be Young Sean instead of Old Sean. He was wiping glasses. He'd changed into work clothes and now he wore a purple paisley vest and his two-tone fedora. He was chatting with a redheaded server who looked up at him with rapt adoration. It was true. Every girl is in fact crazy about the sharp-dressed man. But I was staring at his hat. I was also flashing back on the sketch I'd made, the one with the fedora lying in the old tunnel.

The one that gave me (for lack of a better word) the creeps every time I looked at it.

I tried to tell myself that I had no real reason to believe the sketches from my automatic-drawing session meant Sean was in danger of being shot. There were a lot of fedoras in the world. Right? Right.

But did I want to take that kind of chance?

I immediately decided the best course of action was to tuck my book firmly under my arm, sail on past the bar and lose myself in the lobby's crowd. There were two problems with this. First, there was no crowd. Second, Sean looked up as I was in midsail.

"Anna." He slung his side towel onto his shoulder and came around to the bar's entrance. "I thought we'd be seeing you here."

"Who's 'we'?" I tried. "Where's your dad?"

"I'm taking his shift," answered Sean. "He's keeping watch outside Kelly Pierce's apartment. You know, in case."

"In case what?" I tried. It was a very lame try. Sean folded his arms at me and gave me a skeptical look worthy of Alistair on a bad day. I sighed. What had I done that life should inflict me with sharp-eyed bartenders?

"Okay," I said. "Listen, you've got a phone on you? Stay here and keep an eye out for the Hildes. If anybody looks like they're heading for the ballroom, you call me, okay?"

"Or I could just come with you."

No. No. This was not happening. My hand trembled and I clutched the book harder. "You're supposed to be working. They'll know something's up if you're not in the bar."

Sean did not move.

"Sean, please don't do this," I tried. "I'll only be gone for a second. Just long enough to confirm there is a door."

I turned. I strode across the empty lobby. The desk clerk glanced up from the screen and keyboard he was typing at and gave me an odd look. I heard leather-soled shoes clacking against the marble behind me.

"That's you, Sean, isn't it?" I said without turning around.

"It is," agreed Sean. "We're headed for the ballroom, right?"

I sighed and I pinched the bridge of my nose. The clerk left the desk, heading toward the space behind the desk where the printer was whirring away.

"Right. The ballroom," I said weakly.

"Great," Sean answered. "Olivia in housekeeping's a friend of mine. She can let us in."

LIKE THE BAR downstairs, the Harbor's Rest ballroom had been allowed to keep its old-school grandeur, including the gleaming parquet floor, multipaned windows and fancy plasterwork ceiling. Alcoves were set into the walls, each decorated with a potted fichus or a large Greek urn.

Only the bank of lights nearest the door was still on. The rest of the room was dark, except near the floor-to-ceiling windows that opened onto the river. Silver and gold light spilled in from the Memorial Bridge and Kittery on the other side. Alistair was nowhere in sight.

Sean closed the door behind us and I flipped the book open to the double-page spread of the Prohibition tea party and held it up for him to see. It would have been better if I could have brought the blueprints, but they were too unwieldy.

"Okay," I muttered. "We know it's here. Where is it?"

"Let's have a proper look." Sean turned the dimmer switch nearest the door. The grand chandelier came up full and bright. I blinked hard, trying to force my eyes to adjust. I also held up the book.

"Okay, so. This photo is a broad panorama, but you can't see the windows. So, they must have been facing this way to take the picture?" I pointed to the right-hand wall.

"No, straight toward the back," said Sean. "Look. There's the cherub fountain." He pointed to the antique mounted on the wall. A chubby-cheeked angel pursed his lips at us.

I checked the picture again. "Okay, that looks right, but—"

My phone rang. I jumped. It rang again.

"You going to get that?" asked Sean.

"Yeah," I said reluctantly. I also handed him the book so I could pull my phone out of my purse and check the number. My heart froze.

It was Kenisha.

"Kenisha," I said as I hit the Accept button. "I was going to call." I was, too, really. Soon. I'd promised. "What's happened?"

"I'm at the hospital. Get on the phone to your lawyer. You're going to need him."

"What?" I croaked, painfully aware that Sean was hearing all of this. "Why?"

"They're saying Kelly Pierce might not pull through," she answered grimly. "Blanchard is on his way to arrest Jake and Miranda, and as soon as he can get the judge to finish up the paperwork, he's coming for you."

Oh.

No.

Kenisha hung up without waiting for me to say anything else, and I couldn't blame her. She was risking way more than a reprimand with this call. I was a suspect. I was wanted, along with Jake and Miranda, and pretty soon Chuck Dwyer. All for something none of us did.

I had to end this. I had to find that tunnel. Now.

"Anna," Sean laid his hand on my shoulder. "Anna? *Talk* to me, will you? What's happening?"

I bit my lip and glanced toward the doors. "Sean, I'm going to have to ask you to trust me."

"I do trust you," he said. "But you're still making me a little nervous here."

"I know, I know, and I'll explain everything." I put my hand on his. "I've just . . . I've got to do a thing first and it's going to look kind of strange. I just . . . need you to give me a second."

Sean lifted his hand away. He also closed the book, with his finger stuck inside to mark the page. "I'm not sure I got enough cryptic in that, Anna."

"I'll try harder next time. Just, if you hear somebody coming, say something, okay?"

"Only sort of."

Despite this, Sean went and stood by the main door. He folded his arms in an imitation of an old-school bouncer. "Okay, boss. Do your thing."

Yeah, Anna, do your thing. I reached into my purse and I pulled out my wand.

"'S truth," breathed Sean, channeling all his Dublin ancestry.

"Yeah," I agreed. "'S truth."

I closed my eyes. I pulled all my focus inside me.

In need I call, in hope I ask, an' it harm none, so mote it be, so mote it be . . .

Help me. Help me. Please.

I took a deep breath and I let it out slowly. At the same time, I lowered my mental shields. I gripped my wand like a lifeline. I tried to hang on to the need to discover the secret and the awareness that I must find the door that had to be here. The one I could not see.

Almost instantly, I heard somebody laugh. I felt a weight, like a palm pressing in the small of my back. A very cold, heavy hand. My heart stuttered and something inside my head was wrenched around. This wasn't my Vibe. This was something else. Something cold and familiar and very, very close.

Then, from the darkness of my own head, I heard music.

It wasn't real music, of course. It was the echo of music, the feeling of it—the happiness and celebration, the sense of motion and enjoyment. I was caught somewhere between vision and memory. Only it wasn't my memory or even the memory of the room around me. But it was there, sliding into my thoughts. I saw the ballroom was full to the brim. There was so much happiness, so much tension, so much *money.* Excitement surged through me, threatening to sweep me away on its tide.

A sharp, shrill sound cut through the whirl and enjoyment. The lights flashed.

The young man in the red blazer stood by the open door, ushering everybody out. *Quickly, quickly, everyone. This way. That's right. Nothing to worry about, just a raid.*

My feet were moving, I was running with the rest. Perfect! We'd make our getaway right under the cops' noses!

"Anna?" Sean's voice sounded a long way away.

"Merow?" Something soft and heavy butted at my shins.

I blinked, my mind half in the present, half in the past. At some point, I'd crossed the ballroom and now I was standing beside the cherub fountain.

"Anna?" said Sean again. "How'd Alistair get in here?"

I blinked again and looked down. Alistair was in fact here, circling the fichus tree in the alcove beside the fountain.

"Um, open window?" I tried. My voice sounded thick. I wanted a drink of water.

"Not even," said Sean as he strode across the ballroom. His shoes echoed loudly against the parquet floor. "We are having a little talk after this, aren't we?"

"Yeah," I agreed. "We are."

Alistair rubbed his head against the edge of the ficus's brass pot. Hard. "Merow!"

I grabbed the edges of the pot and dragged it toward me. It was heavier than it looked. Underneath, flush with the parquet, was a shiny brass circle.

"Merow!" announced Alistair triumphantly.

Sean was looking at both of us, and I couldn't tell if he was impressed or scared, maybe a little of both.

"It's going to be a very long talk," I said.

"Yeah. I'm getting that."

But for right now, I stepped on that circle.

Something went *click*. Something behind the curved alcove wall creaked. I stepped on the circle again. Something behind the wall went *twang*. I put out my hand and pushed. The alcove's back swung inward. Sean came up close enough behind me that I could feel his breath against my ear.

I blinked into the dark until I could see the dust-covered stairway that ran sharply down to the right. As my eyes adjusted again, I could make out the riveted steel door down at the bottom of the stairway. I could also see how the dust had been cleared away from the middle of the treads.

Somebody had been down these stairs, and very recently.

Sean pulled out his own phone and shone its light down onto the steps. "Anna." He pointed over my shoulder at the rust-colored splotches on the splintered wood. "Is that blood?"

I opened my mouth to say something; at least, I think I did. But I'd also forgotten to get my shields up again, so there was nothing between me and the Vibe that rose from that staircase. Anger wrapped around me, and cold fear, and absolute, utter disbelief.

"How . . . ?" I stammered. "How could he . . . Oh, that *idiot . . .*"

Then the world was spiraling down into darkness and all I knew for sure was that somebody, somewhere, was laughing at me.

❧ 41 ❧

❧ MY HEAD HURT. So did my neck and my shoulders.
That was the first thing. The second was it was dark, and I
was flat on my back. Somebody was making an undignified
groaning noise. That, as it turned out, was me.

I stopped that, eventually anyway. I also opened my eyes
and struggled to sit up.

I was on the bed in a comfortable hotel room. The curtains had been drawn and I had to blink hard to adjust my
eyes to the dimness. A man got up off the desk chair and
came over to the bedside. A stray sliver of light glinted on
Clark Kent glasses.

"Didn't think you'd wake up so fast," Dale Hilde said.
"You were out pretty good."

"I . . ." I shoved myself backward. My hands were shaking and my head was spinning. "Where's Sean?"

"Rounding up the backup, I think," he said. "Grandmothers and bookstore owners and coffee hippies and probably
the police. I said I'd call the ambulance and keep an eye
on you."

"Thank you," I told him, my voice sounding shaky, hoarse

and unfamiliar. I coughed. "I'm sorry, but I think I need a glass of water."

"Oh, yeah, sure, of course." Dale went into the bathroom. I heard the water running. I could see my purse over on the desk by the window. I needed my phone and my wand. I needed somebody to know where I was. Preferably Kenisha and Pete. Now.

I swung my legs off the bed and tried to get to my feet, but my legs were shaking so badly, I dropped back down onto the rumpled spread.

Dale came out with a glass in his hand. "I really should have called an ambulance, I know."

"No, I'm fine." I gulped down the water. "At least I will be."

"I just . . ." He ran his hand over his thinning hair. "I wanted to know what was coming first. You know who did it, don't you? You know who killed Jimmy Upton."

I set the empty glass down and tried one more time to get to my feet. This time I made it. "I think it'd be a good idea to wait for the police before we talk about that," I said. "Maybe we could go down to your office?"

"Please, Miss Britton," Dale croaked. "Do you know who killed Upton? Was it Christine? My mother? I just . . . I've been fighting so long to keep us together. I just want to know."

"I'm not sure," I lied. "We should go downstairs and wait for the police."

But Dale was just shaking his head. "You have no idea what it's like. I'm not the smart one. I'm not the ambitious one. I'm just the one who counts the beans and tries to keep things together, for the family." His voice shook. "I love them, Miss Britton, even Christine, after all she's done to us. Please tell me who . . . just give me some kind of chance to get ready."

I hesitated. I shouldn't. I knew that. But I saw the desperation in his face and my common sense melted. If it was my family, I'd want to know. I'd want some way to brace myself for it.

"It was Rich," I told him. I'd suspected him, and my Vibe had confirmed it as I stood at the top of those hidden stairs.

"Your mother said Rich was the one who found her crying that night. He must have gone to try to talk Jimmy out of leaving." I'd been thinking bribery was the Hildes' way of doing business, but it was really Rich's. He was the cover-up artist. When he couldn't charm somebody, he tried to buy them off, whether it was a competitor or a disgruntled guest— or me. My first idea about the five thousand had been the right one. It was a bribe. Only it wasn't Christine paying Jimmy to leave. It was Rich was paying him to stay, and it didn't work.

Rich was also the one with the bandaged knuckles, which could have been cut trying to force open a steel door so he could dump Jimmy's body into the tunnel.

I tried to lick my lips. "I think Jimmy laughed at him, maybe took a swing at him. I'm sure his temper snapped. I'm sure it was an accident."

Rich always wanted to make everything better. I'd seen it for myself. Rich would give a client a free night for a minor mix-up. Rich would try to make up for getting Jake and Miranda implicated in the murder he committed.

Rich, who couldn't even get his family to promote him, had done this desperate, dangerous, disorganized thing because his mother was upset, and he had to make it all better.

"He wouldn't have planned it." Dale's face twisted up tightly, and I knew he was trying not to cry. "Rich . . . he's impulsive. He always has been. He's got those good looks and that smile and he's always had people to clean up after him, so he never worries about the mess." Dale shoved his fingers up under his glasses and rubbed his eyes. "You're right, you know; Jimmy laughed at him. Rich had cleaned out the register to try to buy him off. But Jimmy said the hotel was going down the drain and he wasn't going to stick around to watch. Said some things about our mother as well that wouldn't bear repeating."

I stood there, paralyzed, and I listened to how Dale Hilde had stopped talking in the abstract. He lifted his head and now I saw it was tears shining in his eyes.

"You're right, Miss Britton. Rich did it. He held Jimmy Upton facedown in a men's room sink until he died."

The men's room. I clapped my hand over my mouth before I could laugh—or swear. That was why I hadn't been able to pick up a Vibe about where Jimmy had been killed. He'd died in the one place I was not even going to think of searching.

"What you don't seem to realize, Anna, is that I saw it happen."

❧ 42 ❧

❧ THE LAST PIECE dropped into place, cold, hard and very, very bad.

The fixer. There's one in every family. I'd just been wrong about who it was for the Hildes. Rich was the one who got them into trouble, by always wanting to be the good guy. But it was Dale who got them out.

Dale smiled softly and sadly. "That blood they're going to find on the stairs to the tunnel? That's from when the body was dumped into the tunnel. The problem is, it's not Rich's." He pushed back his sleeve, showing the long, ragged scab on his forearm. "It's mine."

My knees were shaking again and the room wavered.

"You helped move the body," I said. "Whose idea was it to use the tunnel?"

Dale ran his hand over his scalp again. He looked old and deflated, and for a moment, the fear rising in me cleared enough to feel sorry for him.

"Do you know what it's like to see your brother doing something unforgiveable? Do you have any idea? He's a family man. He's got kids! He's . . . I all but worshipped him growing up, and then I come in and he's . . . he had Upton by the neck; he was holding him down . . ." He choked on the last of the words. "I stood there. It took forever, and I just stood there the whole time." He was shaking from the sheer force of the memory and the emotions.

"You must have been terrified," I whispered. It had been three in the morning. Nobody would be around. Jimmy had cleaned out his locker. Gretchen was in her room, her heart breaking all over again because somebody else she'd counted on was walking out on her. Rich found his mother crying and went looking for some way to make it better.

"You have no idea," Dale said again. "You can't even begin to imagine."

"Listen to me, Dale," I said softly. "You are not helping anybody by covering this up. You'll only make it worse for Rich and your family—"

"How?" he demanded. "How does it possibly get worse than this?"

I put a hand on his shoulder. He looked into my eyes. I reached deep. I wasn't ready. I hadn't done any kind of invocation, and my wand was over in my purse on the nightstand. But I was a sister. I had siblings and parents and a grandmother whom I'd do anything and everything for. I understood. I really did, and I let this small, frightened, confused man see all of that. At least, I tried to.

"If you come with me, Dale, we can go to Detective Simmons. He's a good man. He'll listen to whatever you have to say. It won't be easy, but it will keep anybody from getting hurt any worse."

"His kids," whispered Dale. "My nieces and nephews. Oh, God, my *mother.*"

"She suspects one of you, Dale," I said. "It's better if it's in the open. Then she won't have to hurt herself anymore trying to protect you."

He was listening. Even in the room's dim light, I could see the resistance draining away. I breathed. I focused.

There was a knock at the door. "Housekeeping," said a soft voice.

Dale answered before I could. "Come in."

My throat clamped tight around my breath because I knew who it was going to be before I saw him. But I couldn't run. There was nowhere to go. Dale was between me and the door.

The key card rattled on the other side of the door, and Richard Hilde pushed the laundry cart inside. He saw me standing there with his brother.

"Dale?" Rich breathed. "What's going on?"

"It's over, Rich." Dale stepped back. He was trembling as he turned. "She knows."

Sharp, slim hope pressed against the back of my sore throat. But then I saw the frantic look on Rich's face, and it vanished just as quickly. "If she can't tell anybody, it won't matter," he said.

"We can't do this, Rich." Dale spread both hands, pleading. I stared at the brothers, and the laundry cart, and then past them, trying desperately to measure the distance and the tiny gaps between them and me and the door. "She's not like Jimmy. She's got friends. Her grandmother . . . If she vanishes . . . we've got no explanation."

"Whatever any of them know, it's too late." Rich said. "It's all taken care of, Dale! They're going to find the stash of pot under in her back yard, and we're going to be able to point Blanchard straight at the Luces. Blanchard's going to kiss us, Dale! We're going to solve all his problems at once!"

"Right, you said you didn't want to hurt Jake," I murmured. "You said—"

"I know what I said!" Rich snapped. "I didn't want to hurt *anybody* I didn't have to. But we've got no choice; don't you see that?" He was saying this to Dale.

"We have to stop, Rich," whispered Dale. "We have to *think*."

They weren't paying attention to me. The way out was blocked by the two men and the laundry cart. But my purse and my phone (I hoped) and my wand were all behind me.

I took a step backward.

"And we will stop," Rich was saying. "This is it. I promise.

After today, all the loose ends are wrapped up." Rich grabbed both of Dale's shoulders. "I need you, little brother. I can't do this without you."

I watched Dale wavering. I held my breath. I curled my hand around the edge of the laundry cart. I couldn't help noticing there was a roll of duct tape on top of the pile of towels inside.

"Not going to help, Miss Britton." Rich turned to me. His white teeth gleamed in the room's half-light. "There's two of us and one of you. Right, Dale?"

Dale licked his lips. He looked at me and at his brother. "Right."

I shoved the cart forward, hard. Dale threw himself sideways. Hands grabbed the back of my neck.

That was the last thing I remembered for a while.

"HURRY UP!"

The words brought the world back, but that world spun and slammed against my back. I tried to scream but my mouth was sealed shut. My hands were trapped behind my back. I had just time to look up at Rich Hilde, grinning down over the edge of the laundry cart, before a soft bundle dropped on top of me.

Towels. I was covered in towels, and they'd used that duct tape on my mouth and my wrists and my ankles, too.

I was trapped in the bottom of the laundry cart. Now they were pushing me forward. I felt the cart lurch as it banged against the wall.

I squirmed; I wriggled. I tried to scream around the gag and almost ended up choking myself. I tried to ignore the tears streaming down my cheeks and think. It was stifling in here and the smell of bleach was working its way down my throat, and I had a towel draped over my head and I couldn't shake it loose.

Then I heard a familiar sound.

"Merow!"

Alistair!

"What the . . ." Dale swore. "Where'd that cat come from!"

"Ignore it! Ignore it!"

The cart jostled again.

"Aragh!" shouted Dale.

"Let's *go!*" Rich shouted back, and the cart jolted forward.

"Meeeyooowwww!" wailed Alistair. "Merrroowwww-wwww!"

I heard the sound of doors opening.

"What on earth is that caterwauling!" cried a woman.

"Oh, so sorry, ma'am. A stray cat got in through the back door. We're trying to catch him now."

"Merow!"

I wriggled. I kicked. I tried to scream. My throat burned. So did the skin around the edges of the tape.

"Here, kitty, kitty, kitty . . ." Dale's wheedling wouldn't have worked with a normal cat on a good day, never mind Alistair right now.

Doors opened. Doors closed. People were talking and offering suggestions. Someone laughed.

"Some *help* here, Dale," said Rich through clenched teeth.

"Yes, of course, just let me—"

I was shoved roughly forward and I heard the sound of a door closing. I had no idea where I'd been put, but I couldn't hear anybody else in here with me. Okay. Okay. Alistair had got them away. I strained all my stomach muscles. This time I got my knees under me. The towels slid off my head and around my shoulders as I wriggled around. I clamped my teeth down tight, and with all my strength, I threw myself sideways against the side of the cart. The wheels shifted. I did it again, and again.

And the next thing I knew I was toppling forward. I screamed around my gag as the world turned over. My chin hit concrete and I just managed to avoid biting my tongue.

The next thing I knew clearly, I was sprawled on my front on the stairway landing with the laundry cart on my back and towels scattered around me.

And my purse beside me.

My eyes widened. Someone had tossed my purse in the cart with me, probably just to get rid of the evidence. But right now, I felt like I was looking at the holy grail.

As quickly as I could, I got myself into a kneeling position. All at once, Alistair sat on the stair in front of me.

"Merow!" he said pointedly, and vanished.

The message was clear. He was keeping Dale and Richard distracted. The rest was up to me. But I was trussed up like a chicken with a gag over my mouth. How was I supposed to get out of here? I was not scooting down those stairs on my butt.

Instead, I scooted as fast as I could over to my purse and wriggled around until my fingers could fumble for a grip. I closed my eyes and I wished and I hoped. My fingers strained and scrabbled . . .

"Merowwww!" the sound vibrated through the door up above.

. . . and closed around my wand.

Sorry, Julia. It's an emergency.

I had no circle. I had no way to create any proper spell. I clutched the wand as tightly as I could and closed my eyes. I tried to picture a circle with the directions. I tried to think of the proper invocation.

I gave up and just pictured a pair of scissors. Big, sharp scissors.

In need, I call, in hope I ask, an' it harm none, an' it harm none . . .

I'm not sure how to describe what happened next. I strained my jaw and my wrists, and everything just . . . broke apart. The tape over my mouth, the tape holding my wrists. I fell over from the force of it.

When I did sit up, I was as weak as a kitten and the world spun. I grabbed the stair rail to keep from falling.

"Merow!"

Alistair was right in front of me.

"Right. Got it." I heaved myself to my feet and scooped

up an armload of towels. Then I started running—okay, staggering—down the stairs. The number 2 was painted on the wall of the next landing. Second floor. Ballroom floor.

The door banged open overhead. I toppled through the door in front of me.

"Get her!" It was Dale or Richard—it didn't matter. I tossed the towels behind me and ducked forward.

A door opened. "What . . ."

Behind me somebody shouted and tripped and hit the floor.

"Stop, thief!" shouted Rich, or maybe Dale.

"Call 911!" somebody else shouted.

Yes, please! I found my feet and ran. I couldn't see straight. My heart was hammering, my head was light, and every part of me was trying to float away. Alistair galloped down the hallway ahead of me. I was out of breath; I was panicking. All I could think was I had to get away, had to get out of here, had to hide.

Alistair raced up to the ballroom door and vanished.

I had a split second to make a decision, and I did. I followed my familiar.

I dashed, or tried to, across the ballroom. The door opened behind me.

I knocked the ficus sideways and stepped on the switch. The door opened and I staggered through into the dark.

Rich swore. I shoved the door shut. Alistair meowed. I knew where he was. Exactly. I didn't need a light. The world cleared, and even though I couldn't see my hand, I put it on the wall and started down the stairs.

The door clicked open. Light flashed behind me, filling the staircase. I kept going. The door was right in front of me, and it was open.

Rich's hand closed on my shoulder and spun me around.

"Saved me all the trouble," he breathed as he clamped his hands around my throat.

He was laughing.

No, he wasn't.

But somebody was. The loud, raucous sound echoed through the tunnel. An icy wind whirled around us. Rich let me go and we both staggered backward.

"What?" cried Rich. "What? Who . . . ?"

That ain't no way to treat a lady, pally.

That artic wind blew again and I heard Rich scream. I dropped to my knees and covered the back of my neck like I was in a tornado drill.

"Freeze!" shouted somebody.

My head snapped up. There was light all around, and somebody at the top of the stairs, and more somebodies charging up the tunnel. And just for a minute, there was a slim man in a wide-shouldered suit with a fedora on his head and a toothpick in his mouth and a blue-white glow all around him.

He touched his hat brim to me, and he vanished. Just like Alistair did.

43

❧ RICH HILDE WAS arrested for the murder of up-and-coming chef Jimmy Upton and the attempted murder of Kelly Pierce, food and beverages manager of the Harbor's Rest hotel. Dale was arrested as an accessory after the fact and for obstructing justice, as well as for assaulting a free-lance artist.

Kelly regained consciousness in forty-eight hours and the use of her voice two days after that to tell Pete Simmons that Rich had come to her house with a bottle of burgundy, which he'd used to hit her over the head.

Gretchen and Christine rallied around each other and bought the brothers the best legal counsel they could afford. It didn't do any good, and I don't think any of the family really expected it would. What I do know is that mother and daughter came out on the other side in a much tighter bond. The hotel did not get sold. Christine did not open her exclusive resort, and the restaurant did not become a destination. But the smugglers' tunnel did, especially after the historical society and the tourist board started talking it up, along with the jazz weekend and Prohibition New Year's ball.

They did also actively try to hire Sean away from the
Pale Ale to tend the new Roaring Twenties–themed cocktail bar.

I slept for twenty-four hours straight, which, Grandma
assured me, was not unusual after that level of magical exer-
tion. She brought me chicken soup from Kirkland's Deli.
And ice cream. And lots of tuna for Alistair.

Julia agreed that I had used my magic under emergency
circumstances and said it would not be held against me.

Two days later, Val gave birth to Melissa Maureen McDermott, seven pounds eight ounces, with her mother's red hair
and a strawberry birthmark on her derriere that Grandma
B.B. declared was a sign of a prosperous future. The birth
was entirely uncomplicated, except for the part where her
waters broke at midnight, and she almost didn't make it to
the hospital because their own car wouldn't start and she
nearly gave birth in the backseat of the Galaxie with her
husband holding one hand and Julia holding the other and
working birthing chants nonstop while Kenisha gave us a
police escort to the hospital. But, you know, that's compara-
tively minor. The important thing is mother and baby are
doing fine.

Kelly Pierce entered into negotiations with Jake and
Miranda to create a custom blend of Northeast Java coffee
to serve at the Harbor's Rest.

Northeast Java opened its new location to a huge crowd.
The murals were a big hit. But one corner of the café was
fenced off by old-fashioned velvet theater ropes. On the other
side stood a bentwood chair and a vintage marble-topped
table with a shot glass and a bottle of whiskey on it. Framed
articles and photos about the history of the building and its
role in Prohibition in Portsmouth hung on the wall. We'd
even found a picture of one Nate Kelly, bootlegger and ladies'
man. It hung beside a copy of the newspaper article detailing
how Nate had been shot during a raid on the Harbor's Rest
when he'd stayed behind to help his moll (who had probably
been pickpocketing the rich guests) escape. Café customers

could pour a shot for the ghost and have their picture taken in the chair, in the hopes of catching a reflection of the spirit.

So far Nate had declined an appearance, but Jake swore up and down that that whiskey glass was empty every morning, no matter what. I believed him.

And when it was all finally over, Grandma B.B. packed up her suitcase and came down into the kitchen for a farewell cup of coffee and a muffin (Roger might be a new dad, but he still found time to bake) with me and Julia and, of course, Alistair and the dachshunds.

I watched her sip tea and chat with her old friend, and a whole fresh round of feelings welled up inside me.

"Grandma?" I said.

"Yes, dear?" She smiled over the rim of her teacup.

"Don't go."

The smile faded and Grandma B.B. set the cup down. "Oh, Annabelle."

"I mean it. Don't go. Stay here. Why shouldn't you? I mean, everybody would love it if you lived closer, and now that I've got the house, I've got plenty of room."

"I couldn't, dear."

"Sure you could," I said brightly. "We'd fix up the front room, just for you."

Julia looked out the window. She swirled her tea a few times, but she didn't say anything.

"No, Anna." Grandma covered my hand with hers. "I appreciate what you're saying, and I know you mean it. But, dear, you have a full life. Having me living in your house would only get in the way of that."

"No, it wouldn't," I insisted.

"Then stay with me," said Julia.

Grandma looked startled beyond words. Julia just drew herself up a little straighter. Max left his usual spot at Julia's side and trotted over to Grandma B.B. He whined and wagged and pawed at her hem.

Alistair combed his whiskers in disbelief. Even Leo looked embarrassed. "Yip!" he announced.

Finally, Grandma B.B. found her voice. "Julia, do you mean that?"

"Would I have said it if I didn't? It's time to come home, Annabelle."

"I . . . well . . . it wouldn't be immediately, of course. There are so many *arrangements*, so *much* to pack . . ."

"But you will, won't you?" said Julia. "I have that room, and I could always use some help around the store. It's not a nightclub, but still . . ."

Grandma spread her hands and beamed at her old friend. "Oh, Julia! I don't see *how* I could possibly refuse!"

"Merow!" exclaimed Alistair.

"And I *certainly* wouldn't dream of arguing with that kind of logic!"

About the Author

Born in California and raised in Michigan, **Delia James** writes her tales of magic, cats and mystery from her hundred-year-old bungalow home in Ann Arbor. She is the author of the Witch's Cat Mysteries, which began with *A Familiar Tail*. When not writing, she hikes, swims, gardens, cooks, reads and raises her rapidly growing son.

Also from

Delia James

A Familiar Tail

A Witch's Cat Mystery

Unlucky-in-love artist Annabelle Britton decides that a visit to
the seaside town of Portsmouth, New Hampshire, is the
perfect way to get over her problems. But when she stumbles
upon a smoky gray cat named Alastair, and follows him into a
charming cottage, Annabelle finds herself in a whole
spellbook full of trouble.

Suddenly saddled with a witch's wand and a furry familiar,
Annabelle soon meets a friendly group of women who use
their spells, charms, and potions to keep the people of
Portsmouth safe. But despite their gifts, the witches can't
prevent every wicked deed in town....

Soon, the mystery surrounding Alistair's former owner, who
died under unusual circumstances, grows when another local
turns up dead. Armed with magic, friends, and the charmed
cat who adopted her more than the other way around,
Annabelle sets out to paw through the evidence and
uncover a killer.

**Available wherever books are sold or at
penguin.com**

facebook.com/TheCrimeSceneBooks